They Crossed the Quiet Meeting Room

and fumbled in the dark for the latch on the sliding glass doors.

"I've got it," Ross said, but did not move to open it. One hand was on the latch, and in the dim light from the spill of the ballroom above, he reached out to touch her face. "I've wanted to do that all evening," he confessed, and he cupped her face in both his hands as he kissed her.

Jennifer was at first startled, and then she felt her own need answer his. She put her arms around him, and as his hands dropped away from her face so that he could wrap her in his arms, she let herself enjoy the first giddy stirrings of desire. This was not like the first kiss—now his mouth was firm and insistent, and as her lips parted, his tongue probed her mouth. She had not always liked being kissed so, but now there was an awakening in her, an urgency that had not stirred in her for a long time.

"My God," Ross whispered as they broke apart at last. "I knew there was fire in you, but . . ."

Dear Reader:

We trust you will enjoy this Richard Gallen romance. We plan to bring you more of the best in both contemporary and historical romantic fiction with four exciting new titles each month.

We'd like your help.

We value your suggestions and opinions. They will help us to publish the kind of romances you want to read. Please send us your comments, or just let us know which Richard Gallen romances you have especially enjoyed. Write to the address below. We're looking forward to hearing from you!

Happy reading!

Judy Sullivan
Richard Gallen Books
8-10 West 36th St.
New York, N.Y. 10018

A Taste of Wine

VANESSA PRYOR

PUBLISHED BY RICHARD GALLEN BOOKS
Distributed by POCKET BOOKS

A RICHARD GALLEN BOOKS *Original* publication

Distributed by
POCKET BOOKS, a Simon & Schuster division of
GULF & WESTERN CORPORATION
1230 Avenue of the Americas, New York, N.Y. 10020

ISBN: 0-671-43559-0

First Pocket Books printing January, 1982

10 9 8 7 6 5 4 3 2 1

RICHARD GALLEN and colophon are trademarks
of Simon & Schuster and Richard Gallen & Co., Inc.

Printed in the U.S.A.

for
Felicia Andrews
takes one to know one

❧ February ❧

The slow-falling, sullen rain precisely fitted Jennifer Wystan's mood. As she drove along the highway toward Calistoga, her mind drifted back to the unpleasant scene in her attorney's office two hours before. Jennifer did not like arguments, and her discussion with Henry Fisher had been little better than that. She knew that he had been right, if money were the sole consideration, but that was not the case. Henry's sensible, rational comments had gone against the grain so badly that she had almost stormed out of his office, which was most unlike her. Henry had warned her months ago that the restoration of her resort hotel would be more costly than either of them had anticipated when she had begun the project, and he had turned out to be right. The rising costs of labor and supplies had eaten away at what had once seemed an overly-large reserve, until now she was dangerously near the lowest figures on her projections.

Jennifer turned up the windshield wipers to their highest setting as the rain began to fall faster. She watched the sweep of the blades snick away at the wet that cascaded over her three-year-old Datsun. She peered through the silvery sheetings for familiar landmarks, knowing that she was nearing her

turn-off. Defiantly, she shook her head, the dark hair that fell
to her shoulders swinging silkily. There was so much to do,
and very little time left to get it done if she were going to have
the resort open in April. Just thinking that made her feel
more confident, and as she slowed for the turn onto Empress
Road, she felt a bit of her old optimism return. She would not
be like so many other divorced women she had known,
turning away from a marriage that had gone bad in favor of a
job that went nowhere. She would make the White Elephant
a success!

Ahead, she made out the tall ornamental windmill that
stood at the front of the Benedetto Tasting Room and
Restaurant. She pulled to the left and signaled for her turn,
shaking her head at the remembered snobbery of the Benedetto family. She had been living next door to them for seven
months, and had yet to see one of them. She admitted to
herself that next door in this case was almost three miles, but
it didn't change how she felt about the slight. If the Benedettos were unwilling to notice her, she would not notice them.

The road climbed in gentle turns for the better part of two
miles, cutting between vineyards on the east and open, rolling
hillside on the west. Jennifer loved this section of road, and
thought of it as uniquely her own. She passed the first of three
billboards that bore the announcement of the opening of her
resort, which was set for April tenth. The date seemed to
mock her, but she refused to be overcome by the gloom she
had felt earlier. Now it was necessary to get her mind on her
work.

At the gate to her resort, she saw a heap of sodden earth on
the side of the road that had not been there the day before.
She hoped that meant they had dug out the hole for the
foundations for what she had come to think of as her mascot.
There was an excavation like a large grave by the turn to her
drive, and she smiled in satisfaction. The day after tomorrow,
a large white fiberglass elephant built over a steel frame
would stand there, guarding her entrance and advertising the
resort at the same time.

The road curved around the shoulder of the hill, and came
into a shallow, sloping valley. It was not large, hardly more
than a mile in length. At one end, backed against the hillside,
was the White Elephant. Once it had been called the Empress
Resort, but that had been long ago, when women in large
picture hats and lace dresses had played croquet on the lawns,
when families came up the Napa Valley in private railroad

cars to be met by ornate buggies drawn by matched teams of horses. The women in the picture hats were gone, the private railroad cars had disappeared shortly after, and war, Depression and war again had ended those leisurely days forever. But the Empress Resort still stood, a gorgeous, out-of-time white elephant of a building. It had four and a half stories, each one embellished with balconies and covered porches and the elaborate ornaments of Victorian carpenter gothic. Four broad, curving steps led up to the long, covered verandah that embraced half of the first level of the main floor. Beyond it was the lobby. Above the porch was the deep bow window of the ballroom, and above that, a floor of guest rooms. The whole thing was surmounted by a cupola that perched above the rest like a white silk hat. On the basement level, which was half-hidden by the rise of the hillside, were the most functional rooms—laundry, storage and kitchens. Behind the main building, there were a dozen cabins, and a sprawling building that housed the hotsprings. Between them were two huge swimming pools waiting to be filled, one with the hot water from the springs, the other with cooler water from the regular pipes.

Restoration of the main building was almost complete, and only on the back of the hotel were repairs and painting still going on. Jennifer could not help but smile at the glistening, absurd splendor of the place, and some of her pride was renewed. She pulled around the front of the building and into the overhang of the main dining room. With her usual care, she made sure her lights were off and the wipers stopped before she turned off the ignition and got out of the Datsun.

The air smelled fresh and loamy, and her breath made little puffs of fog before her face as she hurried toward the loading door, reaching out automatically for the admittance bell to the right of the steel doors. She was cold, and there was enough wind to cut through the warmth of her sensible wool suit. Jennifer rubbed her hands together briskly, and hoped she would not have to wait long.

A couple minutes later, the door opened, and the familiar figure of Drew Usher, her chef and confidant, was revealed. He was no taller than she, and a year younger. His dark hair was groomed with finicky neatness, his moustache was meticulously cut, and the rest of his face was so closely shaven that he seemed to have no beard at all. He had large, candid green eyes under well-shaped brows. Even in old blue jeans and a sweatshirt, there was no concealing his good looks, or his vanity. "Thank God you're back," he said as he stepped aside for her. "How was the drive up?"

Jennifer stepped inside and gave a restless shake to her dark hair. "Not too bad," she said, so carefully and so neutrally that he looked at her with a great deal of suspicion.

"It wasn't as bad as I was afraid it might be," she hedged.

"My, that *does* have an ominous ring," Drew said archly. His crepe-soled boots squeaked on the newly-laid tile as they stepped into the kitchen. "At least they've finished the painting in here."

"That's great," she said automatically, waving to Johnny Chang, Drew's Korean assistant, who was busy making an inventory of the crockery.

Johnny waved back, smiling at both Jennifer and Drew.

"Johnny, why don't you go down to the housekeeping office and type up as much of that list as you've got done?" Drew suggested, making no apology for his lack of tact.

"Sure. How long should I take?" Johnny said without rancor.

"At least half an hour. Make yourself a sandwich or read a novel or have a nap if you get the list done." Drew's autocratic manner was altered by kindness.

"Half an hour it is. If you need longer, just keep the door closed." He waved to Jennifer again and loped out of the room.

"Now what's this nonsense about it not being as bad as it might be?" Drew demanded with a smile.

Jennifer sighed and set her purse down on the large cutting board that stood to one side of the eight-burner stove. Seeking to evade a bit longer, she asked, "Is there any hot chocolate?"

"Okay, boss. Hot chocolate it is," Drew said. He set to work at once, getting milk from the industrial-sized refrigerator and taking down a copper saucepan.

"I talked to Henry, of course," Jennifer began.

"Of course."

"He's been a great help, you know that. All through the divorce, and settling Uncle Samuel's estate, he's been wonderful. I know that he has my best interests at heart," she said, a bit defensively.

Drew glanced at her over his shoulder. "It sounds worse and worse."

"Well, it's not as bad as that," she amended. "We're going

to be awfully near the bone on the budget, and he warned me about increased prices in supplies, but we can manage if nothing terrible happens."

"How terrible is terrible?" Drew asked, his attention on the heating milk.

"If something major goes wrong, we're in trouble. Otherwise, we should make it." She did her best to sound as optimistic as she could.

"That's just fine," said Drew with the ghost of a chuckle.

"You'll always get your salary. I made sure of that," Jennifer went on.

"I'm not worried about my damned salary," he told her with more vehemence than he usually showed. "I'm worried about this place. I'm worried about *you.*"

Some of her spirit returned. "It's not necessary. There's still enough money in the trust fund to carry us for the next eighteen months. After that, we've got to show some return, but we can still absorb a thirty-three percent loss for another year if we have to. But Henry doesn't want to transfer funds around right now with the interest rates the way they are. He's a cautious man, and I know that he's been right in the past, but he's, well, a bit dour." Henry was an old-maid pessimist, she thought to herself.

"Don't remind me, don't remind me," Drew protested. "That man looks as if he was weaned on vinegar."

Jennifer started to laugh, and then, quite unexpectedly, tears stung her eyes and she brought up her hand to dash them away. "We're going to open," she said defiantly.

"Hey . . ." Drew turned to her, filled with concern. "Jenny. . . ."

"We are going to open," she insisted, more confidently. "We are going to stay open. We're going to make this place a success. I don't care what Henry says. I don't care what George says. . . ." As soon as she said George, she felt her cheeks flush.

Drew nodded knowingly. "So you saw George after all, did you? Why?"

"He called," she said rather lamely. "Right after I checked in."

"I'm sure," Drew said, and this time his sarcasm had a nasty edge. "Never misses a trick, does old George." He turned back to the stove, and busied himself with stirring the chocolate. "Of course he called you. What did he want, as if I didn't know."

"Drew . . ." she began, and then she stopped, resigning herself to the lecture that was sure to follow. "He wanted to see me."

"He's been wanting to see you for months, but you've been able to avoid him. What was the bait this time?" Drew whisked the chocolate more vigorously than necessary.

"The restaurant's in trouble. He's been losing customers, and the banquet business has fallen off."

"Of course it's in trouble. And you knew business had slowed down. What else did George hold over your head?" He sniffed critically at the chocolate, then opened a near-by cupboard and pulled out a bottle of brandy. "I think a little of this would improve it," he said in another voice as he poured a generous tot into the steaming liquid.

"Well, for one thing, they want you back in the kitchen. George says that he hasn't found anyone to replace you." She hoped this would flatter Drew enough that he would not continue his questioning.

"They're not getting me," was Drew's comment. "When you left, Jenny, I left. If this place goes belly-up, I still wouldn't work for George. I'd rather open a fried chicken franchise than work for George."

"That's damning," she said, adding, "George suggested a limited partnership." Hearing Drew's scoff, she went on quickly. "I turned him down, don't worry. Once is enough, even for me." What was it about her ex-husband, she wondered, that always made her feel that she had done an unforgivable thing when she had gone out on her own? George had a knack for playing on her sense of loyalty, and often left her with the uneasy fear that she had betrayed him when she had decided to restore this old resort, though the restaurant they had owned and operated together were nearly three hours away by car, in South San Francisco. George would turn his beguiling, wounded eyes on her and favor her with a brave smile, and she would believe that she was a traitor. Rationally, she knew that her marriage to George Howard had not been a good one, but she was unable to resist his appeal to her for help. When he approached her with that boyish charm, she always felt the pull of the old patterns of their six-year marriage reassert themselves. Even now, she could not deny the attraction of his beautiful body, though sex with him had always been ultimately disappointing. What annoyed her the most was that George knew he had this effect on her, and used it deliberately. On the one hand, he made her feel guilty, and on the other, he roused her desires just enough to keep her off-balance. "Well, yes, we all know the restaurant's going badly," she said when she became aware that Drew was watching her.

"Let me guess. He took you out to lunch. He probably brought you flowers, too."

Jennifer blushed and nodded. "We went to that new place on Nob Hill. It's all very fancy, and the wine list is a treat."

"It would be tacky to take you to the Savoia," Drew agreed, mentioning George's restaurant with veiled contempt. "You might find out what is really wrong there."

"What do you mean?" Jennifer asked sharply.

"Maybe George is hoping that if he can get back with you, you'll take your money out of this place and put it back in the Savoia. But he's not going to let you have any control over it, of course. You remember what it was like that last year you were with him. You know how he was always giving you the runaround about costs." The chocolate was almost ready, and he lowered the flame under the saucepan.

She sagged against the cutting table. "Drew, don't make it any worse than it is. I don't think I can cope with another problem of any kind today."

Drew relented at once. "I'm sorry. That was out of line."

"Yes," she said. "But I asked for it."

"It's just that I hate to see him pull numbers on you. I know how he treated you at the Savoia, and I wanted to break his beautiful nose for it. That night you walked out on him, I cheered." He removed the saucepan from the heat and turned off the flame.

Jennifer started to protest, but could not defend George Howard. It embarrassed her to recall that night.

"Does George still want to get you back into bed?" Drew asked baldly as he reached for mugs.

"He certainly acted that way," Jennifer answered, then shrugged. "That was his answer for a lot of things." She wished now, as she did on occasion, that Drew was not so acute, or so blunt.

"And you? Did you want to go to bed with him?"

"Hell, no," she said, almost honestly, knowing that she had almost succumbed to her ex-husband's persistence. Guiltily, she turned her head away.

Drew looked over at her. "Hey, Jenny, you're not a nun,

and it's been a long time. George was probably depending on that. Who can blame him?" He began to pour out the chocolate, measuring amounts with a practiced eye.

"But he's not good for me, is that it?" She reached over for her purse and rummaged in it for a handkerchief.

"True enough. But, then, you're not good for him, either. Did you ever think of that?" Drew asked as he put the mugs onto plain white saucers.

Jennifer looked over at her friend. "Drew, can I tell you something? Something I don't think I've ever said to anyone before?"

"You can tell me anything you want to, Jenny," he said easily. "I'm not going to blab it to the world, whatever it is."

"George used to tell me, at the worst possible moments, that I was frigid. And I used to think that maybe it was true. I gave him reason to think so, anyway. But having lunch with him, listening to him and the promises he made, I thought about all those nights and the accusations and the pouting, and I couldn't bring myself to do it. I couldn't go through all that again, in spite of being half turned on by it all. It wasn't worth it anymore. Does that make sense to you?" She twisted her handkerchief in her fingers, not willing to meet Drew's inquiring gaze.

Drew abandoned the chocolate and came over to her. Gently, he put his arms around her and hugged her. "Oh, Jenny, don't tell me *that's* been hanging over you all these years? I always knew that George was a creep. If I could go for women, you can damn well bet you'd be the first one I'd come after. And you wouldn't disappoint me." He gave her a kiss on the cheek, patted her shoulder, then went back to get the two mugs of chocolate.

Jennifer finally choked back the tears that had threatened to overcome her. She chided herself for being self-indulgent. "Thanks, Drew."

"For what? For stating the obvious?" He picked up the mugs and brought them over to her. "I wouldn't recommend the terrace in this weather, but if this will do . . ."

She accepted the mug and drank gratefully. "You make great chocolate. "

"I know. My Steak Diane is terrific, too." He winked at her over the rim of the mug.

When they had finished the chocolate and washed the mugs—Drew was maniacal about used dishes—they took the stairs to the main floor. In the lobby, the restoration was nearly complete. The new carpets had not yet arrived, so the hardwood parquetry shone up at them, gleaming with new varnish and wax. A half-dozen plush-upholstered chairs and three settees were stacked against the wall, waiting to be put into place.

"Where does Fred Jenkins have his men today?" Jennifer asked, wondering how much the rain had slowed work on the building.

"They're upstairs doing the ballroom, working on the trim and the curliques. Jenkins gets a kick out of doing the fancywork, I think." Drew grinned at Jennifer. "Probably reminds him of his misspent youth."

Jennifer laughed and grinned back at Drew. As she crossed the lobby toward the hall that led to the bar—a long, L-shaped room on the north end of the building—she glanced up, as she always did, at the portrait of her uncle. Samuel Wystan had loved this resort, and knew that Jennifer shared his love, which was why he had left it to her, along with a startlingly large trust fund for restoring the building. She was like him in more than her affection for the Empress Resort. As a child, she could remember sliding down all four floors on the highly-polished brass and redwood bannister, whooping. Uncle Samuel had thought it was funny, and so had she; the rest of the family had thought it was terrible, and said so. She could still recall the twinkle in her uncle's eyes as he caught her rocketing off the end of the bannister, and her throat tightened.

Uncle Samuel's portrait, painted in 1945, showed a man in riding clothes, not too western-casual, for that had not been the style. At that time in his early fifties, Uncle Samuel had been neatly handsome, and not the seedy old gentleman he had become at the end. There was a strong family resemblance: Samuel Wystan had had dark, almost fey good looks, which in Jennifer became a long, lean coltishness. Both were tall brunettes, both had deep blue eyes of such purity and depth of color that it was jokingly said in the family that a person could drown in them. Jennifer tried to smile at the portrait, but failed.

"What's the matter?" Drew asked.

"I was just thinking of Uncle Samuel," Jennifer answered.

"Wishing that he hadn't left this place to you? A little late for that, isn't it?" He considered Samuel's portrait. "He was one good-looking man."

"Yes, he was," she said. "And, no, I wasn't wishing he hadn't left me this. In fact, I'm very glad that he did. I've never had something that was really all my own before. Now I have this."

She went to the reception desk and looked down at the leather-bound registration book. There were no names in it yet, and it was disturbingly pristine. She had decided, when work began on the White Elephant, that this area would be as it had been long ago. No computer cards would clutter up the desk, no machines would click and rattle, each guest would be met by another human being and would be dealt with by human beings. In the trapezoidal office behind the desk, a staff of three would do the job in the old way, the way the work had been done when the Empress was new.

"Do you ever wonder what Uncle Samuel would think about what you're doing with the place?" Drew asked as he came up behind her.

"Sometimes," she admitted, closing the register and running her hand over the cover. "I don't always know, but I hope he'd be pleased."

Drew shrugged. "I think he'd be proud. You've made this place alive again. From what I've heard, the Empress was half a ruin the last couple years he was alive, and only dowagers came here, when they couldn't afford to go to any other, nicer place."

"That's not quite true," Jennifer responded, coming to her late uncle's defense. "It's true that Uncle Samuel didn't do much with the Empress, but it wasn't because he couldn't. The money he left proved that. I think he believed that the last decades had passed him by, and there was no point in doing anything to this place. I don't know how he'd feel about the elephant, or the trout pond, or any of the rest of it. But he wouldn't have left this to me if he'd been afraid I'd ruin it."

"Hey, hey, I didn't mean anything against him." Drew held up his hands in mock surrender. "I take it all back, whatever I said."

This time Jennifer was able to laugh. "I didn't mean to sound like such a fishwife. I know that you feel kindly toward him."

"Sure. Without him, I wouldn't have a job." He gave the portrait a crisp salute.

Jennifer came away from the desk. "I think I'll have a look upstairs," she said, putting her reflective mood behind her.

"Oh, don't do that," Drew objected. "You know what

Jenkins is like—he hates having anyone looking over his shoulder."

She made a face. "Especially if that anyone is a woman. You're probably right, but I still think I ought to keep an eye on what's going on."

"All you'll get is an argument from him," Drew warned her.

Jennifer made a mock grimace of dismay. "You're right. That man is impossible, not to mention cantankerous and high-handed and temperamental and . . ."

"And a male chauvinist pig to boot," Drew finished for her. "But his work is magnificent—and cheap."

The two looked at each other and exchanged resigned nods.

"All right, I won't bother Fred Jenkins. What do you suggest I do instead?" Jennifer asked.

"Well, first, I think I ought to make us some lunch," Drew said, after giving the matter his due consideration.

"But it's three-thirty," she reminded him with a glance at her watch.

"Call it an early dinner, if you'd rather." Drew gave her a friendly pat on the shoulder. "Come on, boss. We've got a lot to do."

The next day was wet again, and Jennifer passed most of it working on housekeeping inventory with Johnny Chang. At the end of the evening, she was so tired that she retired to her room in the cupola early, and had read less than a chapter of the thriller she had picked up a few days before when she fell asleep.

When she awoke, she saw that the sky was clearing, and a few minutes later the radio confirmed that the rain was over for a few days. Jennifer felt her mood lightening, and made a call to the company that was contracted to pour the concrete for the elephant's foundation, and a second call to the company that had made the elephant to confirm delivery for that afternoon. She was humming by the time she headed downstairs. For one nostalgic moment, she considered sliding down the bannister.

In her jeans, heavy boots and fisherman's sweater, Jennifer Wystan did not have much of the look of a resort owner, and so the man driving the cement truck informed her.

"I got to see a J. Wystan. You send him out," he blustered as he stood by his truck.

"You're looking at J. Wystan," she answered. "And if you don't get that cement poured, I'll call Stu Gregory and tell him that you're not doing what you were contracted to do."

The truck driver faltered at the mention of his boss's name. "Now, wait a minute, ma'am."

"Are you going to pour the concrete?" Jennifer asked firmly.

Fighting a losing battle, he took his invoice from the cab of his truck. "You've got to sign this. I can't do it without a proper signature."

Jennifer strode over to him. "Fine. If you will lend me your pen?"

Hastily, he thrust an old ballpoint into her hands and defiantly showed her the invoice. "If anything goes wrong about this, it wasn't my doing," he announced to the air.

"I'll agree to that as long as the concrete gets poured," Jennifer said grimly.

The driver scrambled back into his truck and maneuvered it around to make the pour. He grumbled all the while.

Jennifer stood off to the side of the drive and watched, her hands on her hips and a tight smile on her mouth.

The driver had just finished his work and was starting to pull away when a second truck showed up. It was as large as the cement truck, but flat-bedded. In the back, laid ludicrously on its side, was a white elephant made of fiberglass. The two trucks jockeyed around one another on the narrow road, then the cement truck roared away and the men in the second truck set to work, first attaching their winches to the elephant, and then beginning the precarious job of setting the thing in place. In half an hour, the elephant swung over the deep pool of cement, the long steel supports projecting two feet beyond the legs of the figure. The foreman of the crew shouted and urged his men to be careful, as this was the most difficult part of the installation. Slowly, carefully, the elephant was lowered into position until it appeared to be standing on the patch of cement.

At once the crew got heavy-duty sawhorses and braces to keep the elephant from sinking any further into the cement. Three heavy planks were passed underneath the animal's form, supporting the bulk until the cement set.

When the foreman was satisfied, he came over to Jennifer. "Well, that's it, Mrs. Wystan. I can't say how long it will take for the cement to set up with the ground so wet, but one of us will be back tomorrow afternoon to check it out. If it's okay then, we'll take our equipment away, but it might need another day before it's safe. Now you make sure that nothing moves those braces, or it could throw the whole thing off."

"Yes," Jennifer said. "I've got flashers to put out, so it will be marked properly."

"That's good. But I don't imagine you get a lot of traffic yet, not being open and all." He was an older man and spoke with the ponderous gallantry that Jennifer had often encountered while working at the Savoia.

"That's just as well, don't you think?" she said, and shook his hand. "I appreciate how much you've done for me."

"That's real nice of you, Mrs. Wystan," the foreman said before turning to motion to his crew. "Come on, we got other work to do."

After the flat-bed truck had pulled away, Jennifer finally crossed the drive and approached the nine-foot-high bulk of the elephant. She admitted to herself that she had not thought the thing would be so large. She laid her hand gently on the curving trunk. The fiberglass was cold under her touch and unnaturally smooth, but Jennifer smiled. "Hi there, pal," she said to the white statue. "Welcome home." She looked it over closely, thinking that it had caught the true *feel* of an elephant. "If an elephant doesn't look like you do, then it ought to," she told the white figure, with a touch of the pride of ownership in her voice. She was about to turn away when she heard the sound of hooves on the gravel behind her. She looked around, and saw that there was a man astride a bay horse watching her.

"Do you always talk to elephants?" the man asked her, obviously amused.

"I don't always talk to strangers," was her response; she spoke politely, but without encouragement.

The man chuckled. "Puts me in my place." Then, as Jennifer started along the drive back toward the hotel, he called out, "Wait a minute. Don't go."

She paused and looked at the man. "I'm sorry, but I have things to do."

"So have I," he said genially enough. "But since we're neighbors, I thought I might take a little time to find out how things are coming along here."

Jennifer kept a frozen smile on her face. She knew that in this part of the valley most of her neighbors viewed her restoring of the old Empress with tolerant amusement or contempt. She decided she preferred being ignored to being laughed at. "Well, you've seen the elephant. You can tell the others what it looks like, or they can come and gawk at it for themselves."

"They probably will," the man on the horse said. "I'm gawking myself."

"I'm delighted," she said acidly.

"I can see that," he said with a solemn expression. "Are you always so friendly, or have I committed a *faux pas?*"

Jennifer flushed. "Look, I don't know why you're asking me all these questions. Have a look at the elephant. I'm glad you find it amusing. And I probably should tell you that I have no intention of taking it down."

"Why should you? It's the name of the place now, isn't it?" He nudged the horse closer to her. "We haven't met. That's largely my fault. I half-expected you'd come to see me first, but since you didn't . . ."

"Here you are," she said in a disinterested tone.

"Here I am," he said cordially.

As Jennifer looked up at him, she realized that he was younger than she had first supposed, no more than thirty-six or thirty-seven. The white streak in his tawny-brown hair had thrown her off at first. That, and the deep laugh-lines around his china-green eyes, which were deepening as he looked at her. "All right," Jennifer said, giving him a skeptical look. "I'm Jennifer Wystan."

"Old Samuel's niece," the man said. "He used to tell me about you. He said you were the only relative he had who gave a damn for the Empress."

"That's pretty much true," Jennifer agreed, not quite sure why she was still talking to her unexpected visitor.

"He's lucky you were willing to take it on. It isn't the kind of thing most women would want to do."

Jennifer bridled at that. "I'm not 'most women,' and I love it." She shaded her eyes, the better to glare at him.

"Whoa there," he protested. "I seem to be able to open my mouth just long enough to change feet. I didn't mean it that way." He swung down out of the saddle and Jennifer saw that he was a bit shorter than she had thought—about five-foot-ten, broad-shouldered and trim. Under other circumstances, she told herself inwardly, she might have found him attractive. He came toward her with his hand out. "I'm Ross Benedetto."

She stared at him. So this was the vintner, the high-handed, uncommunicative autocrat who headed up the old family business. Her tone was barely polite. "Hello, Mr. Benedetto. I've been wondering if you'd ever show up."

Ross accepted this meekly enough. "I should have come over weeks ago, but we've had something of an emergency in the business. In fact, that's one of the reasons I was hoping to meet you." He pulled the reins so that the bay followed after him. "I've got a business proposition I'd like to talk over with you."

Jennifer nodded fatalistically. "Sure. It figures." She made no excuses this time as she started along the road back toward the hotel.

"I didn't know that news traveled that fast," Ross said with some chagrin. "You must have heard it from the Hasslunds." The Hasslunds had the land across the road from the White Elephant's.

"I don't know what you're talking about," Jennifer admitted. "It's just that the only time anyone talks to me around here is about business."

"Oh." Ross seemed a bit nonplussed, then dismissed it. "I wouldn't be surprised if I were you. You've got twelve hundred acres of good land here, and land is at a premium in the valley."

"So I understand," Jennifer said quietly.

"Good. That gives us somewhere to start." He smiled, and Jennifer saw that his white teeth were slightly irregular. She liked that.

"Go on," she said, still thinking about his smile. It was always the little things, she thought inconsequently. With George it had been the way he would crinkle his eyes when he looked at her; with Ross Benedetto, it was his smile and not-quite-perfect teeth.

"That isn't very promising," he remarked, but went on. "You have just about twelve hundred acres here," he repeated. "Of that, almost five hundred of them are not being used for much of anything. You've got timber on the south ridge, but that won't be ready to take down for another five years or so. The rest is open hillside. You don't appear to be using it for the resort. . . ."

"I'm planning to, eventually," she declared. "I want to have a stable next year, which will mean riding trails. After that, it would be nice to have a garden, a big formal garden where . . ."

"But five hundred acres of garden?" he objected with another one of his fascinating smiles. "I'll accept up to fifty, but not five hundred." He waited for her to say something more, and when she didn't, he went on. "I'm interested in about half of that. Just half, nothing more. We're trying to get more acreage under cultivation—we're stepping up production, and trying some of the new hybrids that are being developed at Stanford and Davis. For that, we need more land, which we don't have."

"I see," Jennifer said stiffly. "You're in a buying mood then?"

"Buying, leasing, it doesn't matter that much to me if we can work out acceptable terms." They had come around the shoulder of the hill and the hotel was in sight. Ross stopped and stared down at it. "Goddam!" he declared, after staring for the better part of a minute.

In spite of herself, Jennifer began to feel pride in the place. "Yes?"

"That's nothing short of a miracle," he told her with frank admiration. "You've worked wonders on that old building. Look at it!"

Jennifer grinned. "I wanted to do it right," she said.

"Well, you sure did. It's amazing." He had a rich, rolling chuckle that was almost as intriguing as his smile. "Old Samuel would be in his glory if he could see that."

Torn between irritation and delight, Jennifer took refuge in her satisfaction. "Want to make any more remarks about women taking on a job like this, Mr. Benedetto?"

"Hell, no. You can serve my words up to me with a generous helping of crow." He shook his head again. "If you've done as well on the inside as the outside, it'll impress half the county."

"Only half?" she inquired with deceptive sweetness.

"Okay, two thirds. The rest of them don't know how to appreciate a place like the Empress anyway." He reached back to pat his bay's neck.

"The White Elephant," Jennifer corrected him.

"The White Elephant," he said meekly. "You can call it anything you like, after what you've done."

"Nice of you to allow me so much," Jennifer said, afraid she was being bitchy, but determined not to encourage her neighbor until she knew precisely what he wanted.

"It is, isn't it?" he asked. "Come on, Ms. Wystan, you've made your point, and I admit I was an ass. Don't you think we might be able to get back on even ground again?"

Jennifer could not help answering his smile with one of her

own. "All right, Mr. Benedetto, I'll listen to whatever you have to say to me, and I won't bristle too much."

"Sounds reasonable," he assented. He began to walk again, still leading his bay, his eyes on the building as he spoke. "I told you that we want to buy or lease some of your land. It would be as near our holdings as possible, of course. It would make things easier all around. I'd want to put in vines. I'm more than willing to pay a reasonable price either in outright sale or lease, and to provide the usual protections if for some reason the money isn't forthcoming. Does that make sense to you? Because if it doesn't, we can stop right now and forget I ever said anything."

It had been Jennifer's intention to refuse outright, but he sounded so reasonable that she sighed. "Mr. Benedetto, at the moment the only thing I've got my mind on is opening this resort in mid-April. I'm not really in any position to discuss new business until I've started getting this place filled with paying guests. Ask me in May, all right? Until then, I won't be able to pay proper attention to any deal you suggest."

"Sounds reasonable to me," Ross said. "I think we might come to terms then. In the meantime, would you mind if I arranged for some soil samples to be taken in the area I'm thinking about? Now, before you say anything, I'll give you my word that I won't send in huge machines or hundreds of people to do the job. My soil chemist and his assistant—that's a total of two, Ms. Wystan—will come on a couple of afternoons and take a few borings. There won't be any ruining of the landscape, nothing ugly to clean up after. I hope you'll agree to that. I'm willing to give you a reasonable fee for the access. Say, two hundred dollars: That's a hundred dollars per afternoon—not bad."

They had almost reached the porch of the hotel by then, and Jennifer was turning the offer over in her mind. "I tell you what, Mr. Benedetto," she said slowly. "I'll permit you to take your samplings for two afternoons in the middle of March. If it turns out that you want to continue negotiations with me, you can pay me then. If you find out that you can't use the land anyway, no charge." If he was going to be generous about the deal, so would she.

"You're more than fair, Ms. Wystan." He held out his hand to her again, and this time she shook it with some enthusiasm. "Your Uncle Samuel told me your name is Jennifer. May I call you that?"

Jennifer was taken aback. "Sure, I guess so."

"Good. I'm Ross. That was my Scottish mother's doing, by the way. She was determined to graft a bit of Caledonia onto all this Italian stock." He looked up at the covered verandah, which was freshly-painted and immaculate. "I still can't get over this. I hope you start a trend, Jennifer. I love these old places, and I can't stand to see them torn down, though it happens every year." His face clouded as he said this. "I hope you make a real go of it."

"Thank you," she said, her confusion about him increasing again. "I intend to."

"Good for you," he said with real sincerity.

They stood facing each other, both feeling suddenly awkward. It was Ross who broke the silence, his voice sounding very loud after the stillness. "Well, that's all that I came to say."

Jennifer recovered herself. "Would you like to see the inside?" she offered.

"Yes, but not today. I've got a couple calls to make that can't wait. And besides," he said as he gathered up his bay's reins and prepared to mount, "I want an excuse to come back soon. Give me a raincheck on the interior?"

"If you like," Jennifer said carefully, doubting now that his earlier enthusiasm had been entirely genuine.

"I do like." He swung into the saddle and smiled down at her. "I'm sorry I haven't been over until now. I mean that." He gave her something between a salute and a wave, then turned the bay's head back toward the shoulder of the hill.

Jennifer watched as the bay trotted off down the road, and she found she was frowning again. So that was Ross Benedetto. She could not make up her mind about him. Sternly, she told herself to put him out of her mind, but for the next hour or so, she was distracted by the memory of his smile.

Ross was equally impressed with Jennifer. As he rode back toward the main house of the Benedetto Vineyards, he considered what he had seen. That Samuel's niece had done so much for the Empress . . . the White Elephant, he amended, was nothing short of astounding. He had been prepared to be polite about anything she might have accomplished, but his admiration for her restoration of the old resort was unfeigned. He turned down the long road that led to his home, and pulled Nicodemus to a walk. Automatically, he looked over the neat rows of vines that spread over the gentle slope, and felt the familiar pleasure he always took in the sight. The Benedettos had been raising grapes here since 1839. He was the fifth Benedetto to run the family business, and that long, uninterrupted line filled him with a sense of his responsibility as well as a great deal of comfort in the stability of that part of his life. For a time, eight years earlier, he had relied on the vineyard to give meaning to his life when nothing else did, after his wife had been killed in a plane crash. He had never wanted any life but the one he led now; still, he missed Rosemary, and when he thought of her, there was always a flicker of grief in his heart.

He dismounted in front of the stable and called out for the groom, handing over the reins when old Sandy Benson came out to him. "I'm not going out again today, so see that he's rubbed down and turned out for a run. I didn't give him much of a workout."

"Sure thing, Mr. Ross," Sandy said, taking the bay in hand.

Ross went toward the house, which was of about the same vintage as the White Elephant. It, too, was in superb condition, having been lovingly kept up by five generations. Ross had his office on the second floor, and it was there he went first, pausing only long enough to ask his aunt what time dinner would be on the table.

"Seven, as usual," was the answer he got as he headed for the stairs. "We're having guests, remember," she called after him.

"Fine," he acknowledged absently. "I'll keep it in mind." And promptly forgot it.

Rosa Carlson put her hands on her hips and glared after her nephew. Then, with a shake of her head, she folded her arms. "Young man," she said to the missing Ross, "you need to be taken down a peg or two. You've let yourself get out of touch again."

Although Ross did not hear her, he had listened to her lectures on other occasions, so her observation would not have unduly surprised him. It might have startled his Aunt Rosa, however, if she had known that he agreed with her. He sat at his large desk, one hand on the receiver of his phone, staring vacantly into space. "Don't be an idiot," he said to himself a bit later, and began to dial.

Jennifer listened to Henry Fisher explain again, in his calmest, most reasonable tones, why she should consider the offer from Ross Benedetto. "It would give you a guaranteed income level, which, right now, you need. The terms he has offered are more than reasonable, and he has done business with others in the past in this way and all have been satisfied. Think about the advantages, Jennifer," Henry insisted. "You would have that money, and you need cash coming in."

"I know I do, but . . ." She could not describe to him what it was about the offer that bothered her, in part because she did not know herself. "I don't have to make up my mind right away. I told him I'd talk it over again in May. In the meantime, you can figure out what would be the best way to handle it. But, Henry, I'm not going to sell one inch of this property. If I decide to let Mr. Ross Benedetto have some of my hillside, it will be on a lease basis only. Uncle Samuel did not leave the White Elephant to me so that I could cut it up into a million little pieces."

"Of course," Henry soothed. "He turned down his share of offers in the past."

"And, Henry," Jennifer added, "I don't want this talked about, not for a while. If Mr. Benedetto calls you again, just tell him I'm considering the proposition, and will reach a decision in May."

"All right," Henry said. His voice sounded a bit unhappy. "There is one more thing. Did you really tell him that if the soil tests went badly, he would not have to pay you a fee for the use of the land?"

"Yes," Jennifer said. "Shouldn't I have?"

Henry gave an enraged sniff. "Young lady,"—Jennifer knew he was seriously annoyed; he only called her "young lady" when he was—"next time, before you make these goodwill gestures, will you please check with me first? It's customary to arrange these things more formally, and this leaves you in an awkward position if there should be other inquiries about the land. Since you've said you were willing to waive your fee for him, there are others who might expect the same from you."

"That's assuming I let them onto the land at all," Jennifer said, a bit more firmly. "The Benedetto lands are right next to mine. It's not the same as someone coming in from a distance." For an excuse made up at the spur of the moment, it wasn't bad.

"I don't know how that would stand up, but I suppose you have a point," Henry said after considering it. "But, remember, no more offers of that sort without my approval." He paused, then said, "I hope that all is going well."

"So do I," Jennifer answered. She had had a busy morning, the afternoon was already half-gone, and she had another six hours of work to do.

"How's the elephant?" Henry asked, coming as close to banter as he was able to.

"It's fine. You'll like it. I'm trying to think of a name for it, but nothing seems appropriate." She had spent the better part of an hour the previous night sitting with a notepad on her lap, trying to find that one, right name for the elephant.

"I'm sure you'll come up with something."

Jennifer sighed. "I don't know."

"Then ask someone else," Henry suggested. "You might have a contest with an appropriate prize. Perhaps a weekend, all expenses paid, in the Silverado Suite. That might stir up interest in the place and create some goodwill in the community."

"It's a thought," Jennifer said, knowing it was an excellent idea. "I might do it."

"That's the ticket," Henry said, and then, in a more serious tone, "I should tell you that George has not yet made his settlement payment for the month."

"There's nothing unusual about that," Jennifer responded. She was glad now that she had entrusted the whole of that dealing to Henry.

"He hasn't called, either, and that is a bit unusual. I'm afraid I may have to send him a letter. Do you want me to do that, or wait a few more days?"

"Try a phone call first," Jennifer said, knowing that either way, she would have an irate note from her ex-husband. "I don't want to deal with him any more, Henry. I want the thing settled. I'll be glad when the last payment is made and he can go his way." She meant this, and hoped that Henry would agree with her. Another scene with George Howard would be unwelcome.

"If that is what you want, then that's what I'll do," Henry promised.

"Thanks, Henry. If there's trouble, you'll let me know, won't you?"

"Of course," Henry said. "Good luck on the restoration. Have you fixed on an opening day yet?"

"April tenth," was her prompt answer. "You'll get an invitation."

"I'll mark it on my calendar right now. Good luck, Jennifer."

"Thank you, Henry. I'll talk to you later." She heard his dry, friendly farewell, and hung up the phone. As she sat in her office over the ballroom, she looked out over the hills, and for the first time the beautiful sight did nothing to banish the apprehension that ate away at her. If George did not make his payment, she would have no choice but to accept Ross's offer, and with unseemly haste. For some reason, she did not want to do that. She refused to be put into such a position again, where she would have to depend on the largesse and caprice of a male. She'd had enough of that with George, and had no intention of letting it happen again.

She got up from her chair and paced the length of her office. It was actually a pleasant place, but at the moment it felt like a cage. On impulse, she left the office and went downstairs.

"What brings you here?" Drew asked as Jennifer came into the kitchen.

"Nothing in particular." She looked at the four large boxes of spices, herbs and condiments that stood on the sideboard. "When did those come?"

"About an hour ago. I'm trying to inventory them and get them put away. Do you want to give me a hand?"

Jennifer laughed. "Okay, for a while. I should be phoning the papers to put in ads for staff." She went to one of the boxes and pulled out a handful of jars. "You've got some exotic goodies here, Drew."

"All of it necessary, believe me, if I'm going to live up to my reputation." He stopped scribing in a notebook long enough to look at her again. "Are you still moping?"

"A little," she admitted. "George is late with his settlement payment again."

"That's becoming quite a little ritual with him, isn't it?" He wrote a few more things in the notebook.

"Henry's going to give him a call, and if that doesn't work, one of those letters should do the trick. It always has in the past."

"If George doesn't pay you, how serious is it?"

"Pretty serious," she said, taking more cans and bottles out of the box. "Very serious, really. He's supposed to finish paying off my share of the restaurant in the next year, so the payments are pretty steep."

Drew set his work aside. "Well, look, Jenny, if it would be any help, I can go for a few weeks without pay." When she started to object, he overrode her. "No, let me finish. I know you wouldn't ask it of me, and if it were anyone but you, I wouldn't volunteer. I want to see this place open and making it, and you out from under George, once and for all."

"Oh, Drew," she said, affection for him welling up inside her. "I thank you with all my heart. Really. But I can't ask that of you. If things get so bad that I can't pay you, I'll make a deal with Benedetto and that will take care of everything."

"I don't want you to do that, either, not unless you want to," Drew said rather darkly.

"I feel the same way," Jennifer said. "But let's not worry about it yet. If it comes up, we'll deal with it then."

"Better be prepared, though," Drew warned her. "I don't want to see you get into a mess over this." He put a few more bottles away, and then said to her, "The thing is, Jenny, I like it here. I like having my own kitchen, and living in this ridiculous place. If it goes wrong for you, it goes wrong for me, too, and I don't want that, for either of us." He paused, and when he spoke again, it was more cautiously, with greater reserve than he showed most of the time. "If you have to look for an investor, and if you don't want to work out something with Benedetto, I could talk to my lover. He'd be willing to be a silent partner. He told me that months ago. I'm not making it up, or volunteering him for something he wants no part of. When I walked out of the Savoia, he offered to set me up in a restaurant of my own, but by then you had asked me to come here. I told him I'd rather work up here with you, and he told me that if things got short, I should let him know. He means it."

Jennifer listened with mixed emotions. She was deeply grateful to Drew for this, but embarrassed that the matter should have come up at all. And underneath it all, she was consumed with curiosity about Drew's lover. Who was the man? Drew would never tell her. "Thank him for me, but I don't want to try that yet, either."

"You'll keep it in mind, won't you?" Drew asked. "He's got money. He won't be hurting if he buys shares." He was quiet, then added in a rush, "He's married. I know his wife. They're both . . . wonderful. It's easier for him if I'm not around too much. If I can't be with him, Jenny, I'd rather be with you than anyone."

This burst of confidence affected Jennifer deeply. "I . . . I don't know what to say, Drew. I didn't realize that you . . ."

With a jerky smile, he made a determined attempt to lighten the mood. "God, I didn't mean to be so maudlin.

Hand me that crock of mustard, will you? The French first. After that, the German."

As Jennifer did as he requested, she found that she looked at Drew with more sympathy than she had before, and more understanding. She hoped that his lover, whoever he was, appreciated how much Drew felt for him. She could find no way to tell Drew this, and so contented herself with helping him put spices on the shelves.

By the afternoon, a new storm had blown in, and by the time it passed, so had the last two days of February.

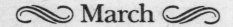

March

Wilbur Cory flipped through the typed report in his hands a third time, then looked over at Jennifer with a measuring glance. "You know that these codes are being revised, don't you, Mrs. Wystan?"

"The building inspector told me when he came out to check the light fixtures. He said that it would be at least six months before the final decisions were made, and that commercial establishments were given up to a year to comply with the requirements." She did not smile, sensing that this man would disapprove of anything that might appear to be ingratiation. "I've asked that I be kept informed of the changes, so that I'll be able to meet your requirements."

"Sensible." Wilbur nodded slowly. As president of the County Board of Supervisors, he took his responsibility seriously: unlike his fellow supervisors, he had no political ambition other than to continue in his current office. His main interest was in the county, in seeing that it was protected from the encroachments that had brought urban sprawl, pollution and fiscal irresponsibility to many other California counties. "I see that the hotsprings will be open by the middle of summer. The building is sound and the rewiring has been

25

approved. Have you got your contractor lined up for the job yet?"

"Yes," Jennifer said, and opened her purse to show him the letter of agreement.

"That's all right, little lady," Wilbur said, unbending a bit. "If you've got the rest of this in order, I figure you're set with the contractor." He read the last page again, then set the papers aside. He leaned back in his chair and gave Jennifer another careful look. "I don't mean to pry, but there are a couple questions I ought to ask you. You can refuse, but I wouldn't recommend it."

Jennifer felt apprehensive at this, but did her best to keep her features composed. "What questions, Mr. Cory?"

"Mainly about money," he said openly. "I been hearing that you're running a little low on cash. There's a rumor in town that Ross Benedetto is planning to lease some of your land. Any connection?" He folded his hands and waited for the answer.

How did these rumors get around? Jennifer wondered, fuming inwardly. Who had been talking about her financial situation? Or had her vintner neighbor announced his intentions in the hope of getting her to agree more quickly to leasing White Elephant land? She cleared her throat. "It's true that Mr. Benedetto asked about the possibility of leasing land, if his soil chemist gives him any encouragement to do so, but there won't be any decision made for at least a month, probably more. I want to have the resort open before I make any more commitments. As to the cash situation, it's true that I've got less than I'd like, but there's enough in the trust fund that Uncle Samuel left me to keep me open until the business is on its feet." There, she thought. That should do something to quiet the worst of the rumors.

"Is that what it was all about?" Wilbur asked. "I was talking to Roy . . . Roy Steadman, the soil chemist. You don't know him. He was at Helene McClennan's last night—Helene's one of our county supervisors—and he told me he'd been asked to run some tests on your land. Now, strictly speaking, it's none of my business, and there isn't much I can do one way or the other, but I got to tell you, Mrs. Wystan, that I'm not keen on giving the go-ahead to under-financed businesses. We've got to think of the employment situation here, as well as everything else. I don't want to see a lot of our local people get thrown out of needed work because you ran short of cash. And I don't want to hear about delayed paychecks, either."

This time it was more difficult for Jennifer to control her temper. "I don't want to do either of those things, Mr. Cory. When I ran a restaurant with my ex-husband, I made sure that the staff got paid even when I didn't." She caught herself playing with the catch on her purse, and set it aside so that she would not be betrayed again by the nervous gesture.

"I liked your Uncle Samuel, Mrs. Wystan. It bothered me to see the Empress get run down the way it did. Toward the end, Samuel said that it didn't matter all that much to him anymore, but I never believed that. I wouldn't want to see the old place get run into the ground."

"Why don't you come out and have a look for yourself?" Jennifer asked with asperity.

"I might do that," Wilbur said, giving her very little encouragement. "I've heard about your elephant. Half the town's talking about it. Not a bad gimmick." He rubbed the back of his neck with one enormous, hard hand. "Not everyone is happy about it, but you're going to find that resistance everywhere. A lot of folks around here are suspicious about change; they see what's going on in other places, and it worries them. It ought to."

"I'm not planning to change the county, Mr. Cory. I just want to get my resort open and paying for itself as soon as possible." Jennifer did not know if she should plead with him or try to explain. "The White Elephant is important to me. I'm gambling my future on it and if I blow it, I lose more than anyone else. You can check that out if you like, Mr. Cory." She had got to her feet, and now felt a little foolish for her outburst.

"You've got your uncle's spirit; that's something." He rose and extended his massive right hand. Years of logging had made the skin hard, and Jennifer felt that the man was like the trees he had cut. He was rough-featured and hard-weathered, but his face occasionally, as now, would crease and wrinkle into a lopsided friendliness that brought a smile to Jennifer's mouth in spite of her irritation with the man. "If you find you've got troubles, you come and talk to me about them, little lady. I don't want to find out secondhand that you're having trouble. I want to know when something goes wrong. You understand me?"

"Yes, Mr. Cory," she said, once again feeling annoyed at

him. "I've arranged for the restoration and been attending to hiring, and I've managed so far. There's no reason I shouldn't be able to continue as I've started. You don't have to be worried about me." She picked up her jacket from the back of the chair and pulled it on before Wilbur had the chance to assist her. "I hope you'll take time to come out and look at the White Elephant. You might find it a pleasant surprise."

"Having it open again will be a pleasant surprise, Mrs. Wystan. You can bet on that. Tell you what: I'll give you a call next week and we'll arrange something then. I might bring one or two others out with me, if you wouldn't mind." He gave her an expectant smile. "All right?"

"I'd be delighted," Jennifer said, with more good manners than honesty. "If you tell me a few days in advance, my chef will arrange to give you a meal."

"That's great." Wilbur escorted Jennifer to the door to his office. "We're not like some of the supervisors you find in the city, Mrs. Wystan. We care about the county and we mean to see that it gets the protection it requires. So you can be sure we're not going to tolerate anything irresponsible going on here."

"I think you've made that clear, Mr. Cory," Jennifer said in exasperation. "And I hope you understand that I'm not doing this on a lark. I've loved that hotel since I was a child, and it's the only hope I have of the independence I want. Rest assured, Mr. Cory, that I don't take any of this lightly."

"I can see that. Your Uncle Samuel would be proud of you, little lady." He held the door open for her. "So long, then, Mrs. Wystan." He nodded as Jennifer said her good-byes, gave a bit of a wave and closed the door.

Jennifer was torn between amusement and fuming anger at the man, and an hour later, when she had returned to the White Elephant, she said to Drew, "I thought that if he called me 'little lady' one more time, I would scream in his face. Little lady! I'm five-foot-seven, and twenty-eight years old! And I could tell that he was trying to be charming."

"Well, he might not know any other way. This isn't the most sophisticated part of the country, Jenny." Drew was staring around the dining room, mentally working out the waiters' stations. "I think we can get away with four waiters at first, but we'll need a fifth if the work load gets big. We've got to get the dumbwaiter fixed, too, because that's the only way we'll be able to keep up with the service. I know that Johnny and I will need at least one more hand in the kitchen, and if we have to do catering, we're going to need someone for fancy desserts. I can do them, but they aren't my strong point, you know, and I've got other things that need my attention."

"You hire whomever you need. I've still got enough to take care of that. But you haven't heard the best part about Wilbur Cory yet. He and an undisclosed number of associates are going to pay us a visit—for lunch." Jennifer took a seat at one of the tables near the tall, wide windows that overlooked a rising green hillside and a stand of scrub oak. "He'll call and let me know when. If we can give them a good lunch, but nothing too extravagant, I think he'll be more inclined to take the operation seriously. I hope we don't have to do too many freebie lunches, though. Between the price of the food, the time lost from our other work, and the waiters for a single meal, well, I'm glad I can take it off taxes."

"Oh, Johnny will wait table for you. That will save you a little. He'll get a kick out of it." Drew took the seat opposite her. "I've got to get the cellar ready, too. We need good wines. I'll work out the bar stocking with the bartender as soon as you have one hired."

"Fine. How's the old cellar that Uncle Samuel left?" She had been through the wines once and had recognized some excellent selections, but for the most part she had been willing to let Drew deal with that aspect of the business.

"Very good, but getting low. We'll need some mid-range choices and a house wine. That we'll buy in bulk, and I think I'd better make some calls about that today." He looked down at the tabletop. "What did you decide on about colors?"

This might have been incomprehensible if it had been anyone but Drew. The years that Jennifer had worked with him had made her familiar with his thought processes, and she correctly interpreted this as the color of the tablecloths to be used in the bar and the restaurant. "I thought we'd have ivory in the dining room. I don't like the way white looks with the draperies. Ivory in there and rust in here. Not red, mind you, but rust."

Drew looked around him. "That sounds good. And what about the spa?" From where he stood he could just see the edge of the building where the hotsprings were. "How's that going?"

"Interior painting starts in a week or so. After that, it'll depend in part on what I hear from the new ordinances being established by the Board of Supervisors. You can bet Wilbur

Cory will be sure that I know all about it, whether I want to or not." She sighed and said rather forlornly, "That isn't fair, is it? I *do* want to know what they're doing, and I don't want to run into any problems with them at this stage of the game. And I'm not arguing with safety regulations and careful construction except that the whole thing is such a headache that I wish it would all go away." She tried to laugh at her own outburst, and came near to doing it.

"Hey, Jenny, don't get worked up about what the guy said. Get your work done and the rest will take care of itself. You'll see." He patted her hand and smiled. "In six weeks, I'll buy you a drink, right here, like a regular customer, with the bartender and the waitresses and all the rest of it going on as if it had béen that way forever."

"Drew, you're a marvel," she said. "You're right." She got up. "Which means we both have to get back to work. Who are you going to call about the wines?"

"I thought I'd start locally—Benedetto, of course. Who knows, they might be willing to give us a price-break, seeing as how we're neighbors." He rose, too, and looked over the room critically one more time.

The impact of her memory of Ross Benedetto alarmed Jennifer. She told herself that she was being silly to feel anything more than a mild attraction for him. Those Italian dynastic families, she thought, meant he was married and had half a dozen kids all being told about wine from the time they were old enough to talk. "Tell me what he says. Use the 0445 line so I can use 0444. I've got to get the hiring in order."

"Sounds good," Drew said, and took the stairs down to the kitchen.

The younger of the two accountants Jennifer interviewed was personable enough, but she did not like his too-glib answers and his rather brash attitude toward her. She cut the interview short and watched with misgiving as the man left the hotel. If the second accountant was not prepared to do the job she needed, she would have to continue the search with very little time to do the job properly.

Muriel Wrather turned out to be a sensible woman of forty-two. "I hope you don't mind my use of initials," she said to Jennifer. "Some employers see a woman's name and think 'bookkeeper' instead of 'accountant.'"

"Lizzy Paris was the accountant at the restaurant I

was . . . a partner in," Jennifer said with a smile. "You won't get any of that from me. Come on up to my office—it's on the third floor—and we'll have a cup of coffee and you can tell me what you've done before." She was already predisposed to like this woman, and was delighted at the rapport they seemed to have established.

After an hour, Jennifer felt she was very fortunate to have found Muriel. "I can't offer you much more than what you were getting before, but at least that includes two meals a day and the use of the facilities if you want. There are tennis courts and two swimming pools, and the spa will be open in a while."

"It sounds lovely," the older woman said with a sigh. "I can't tell you how pleased I am that you're willing to take me on. I was going crazy where I was." She looked around Jennifer's office again. "When do you want me to get started?"

"Next Monday would be fine, if you can arrange to be here." It was a week sooner than she had intended, but when Muriel had asked so many intelligent questions about inventory and insurance, she thought it would help her a great deal to have the woman on the job sooner.

Muriel smiled and held out her hand. "I'll be here on Monday morning at nine, if that's satisfactory."

"Yes. I'll walk down with you. There are elevators, but I prefer to walk."

Muriel agreed, then asked, "Would it be all right if I brought a change of clothes so that I could jog on my lunch hour? I try to put in forty minutes every day, and . . . well, if it isn't out of line . . ."

Jennifer was somewhat surprised. "Jogging? Well, if you want to, go ahead. I can see that one of the dressing rooms in the spa is available for your use." Then, as another consideration struck her, she added, "In fact, some of our guests may want to jog. If you can work out some interesting runs on the old paths, I'd appreciate it. That way, when we have questions about jogging, I'll have an answer for them."

"Excellent," Muriel said. "I'm looking forward to this, Ms. Wystan."

"You might as well call me Jennifer," was her prompt response as she crossed the lobby with Muriel. "I think we don't have to be formal except when dealing with the public."

"Very good, Jennifer," Muriel said, and left the hotel.

Jennifer watched her go and felt her optimism return. If all her help turned out to be half as competent as Muriel Wrather looked to be, she would have very few difficulties.

By the end of the week, two janitors and three maids had been added to the staff, and Drew had announced he had found a bartender who was up to his standards. "The waiters are not all that good, but I'm going to run them through a quick course in proper service. I'm looking for a wine-steward, by the way, one who can act as a relief bartender. Most of the waiters are hopeless. You'd think, living here, they'd know something, but they react as if it were a question of personal loyalty rather than the merit of wines."

"Where does that leave us for the bar?" Jennifer asked. She was in the registration office behind the front desk and there were tax forms spread out around her. "I'm looking forward to turning all this over to Muriel. I can't read most of them, let alone make out proper forms for the work I need."

"I've also made calls about the wines," Drew went on after a commiserating sigh. "We're going to have a credible cellar, but nothing so great that half of San Francisco will drive up here for the treat of drinking what we've got. But the best part is," Drew added, in a tone of special delight, "we've got a chance to get Benedetto to supply our house wine. I called them yesterday and apparently their head honcho has taken a shine to you. That's a compliment. There isn't another place but their own restaurant that serves Benedetto wines as house wines."

"We're also the nearest neighbors, not that that has anything to do with it," Jennifer said with a shrug. "I can't imagine why he's willing, but as long as it works out, fine."

Drew gave her a narrow look. "Well, well! What's this? You've been working hard on cultivating a fine indifference. Is he that special?"

"He isn't special at all," Jennifer countered as her cheeks grew rosy. "He said a couple nice things about the restoration and made himself polite. With their restaurant so close, he probably doesn't want anyone else showing up his product." Jennifer knew that it would not be wise to say any more, but could not stop herself. "I don't think he means anything special by it. Really, Drew, I don't."

"Okay, I'll take your word for it. Mighty certain of yourself, aren't you?" He chuckled and added his next shock. "You're probably wrong about him, though, because he has also offered to supply the wine for the opening festivities. He said that you might as well get off on the right foot in the area."

"That's very nice of him," Jennifer said stiffly, thinking that she would have to call Ross Benedetto and thank him. How would she talk to him, and what would she say? She did not like having to be grateful. But it would be good to hear his voice again.

"It's marvelous! I'm already thinking about what we can serve with the vintages he's suggested. I want to do something elaborate with duck, and something else positively decadent with veal, if we can afford both."

"We'll talk about it later," Jennifer said. "Let's make sure we've got enough staff to handle the opening first."

"Sure, whatever you like, boss." He gave her a peck on the cheek and then left her for the lower level of the hotel.

Jennifer at last got nerve enough to pick up the phone, and after another brief hesitation, called the Benedetto Winery. "May I speak to Ross Benedetto, please?" she asked the woman who answered the phone.

"Who shall I say is calling?" was the question.

"This is Jennifer Wystan at the White Elephant," Jennifer replied, with a bit more authority than she had used at first.

"Just a moment, Ms. Wystan." Jennifer was put on hold for the better part of two minutes, and when the phone clicked into life again, an out-of-breath Ross was on the line.

"Hello, Jennifer. I'm glad you called," he said. He sounded sincere.

"I wanted to thank you for . . . the wine and the offer for the opening." She wished she didn't sound so much like a school child called upon to recite. "It was really very generous." That wasn't much better.

"You're welcome. I've been trying to think of some way to make up for that bad first impression I think I've made." He paused. "I know you have your hands full over there, but do you think you might be free one evening? I'd like to go over a few things with you—what amounts of wine you'll be needing, what your storage capabilities are, how much variety you'll need, all of those things. If you'll tell me what would be a good time, I'll come there if you like, or you can come here." He sounded very businesslike, almost terse, but there was no lack of attention.

"That might be wise," Jennifer admitted, and tried to ignore the shiver of pleasure his suggestion gave her.

"If you wouldn't object, we could talk about the lease, too." This innocent addition was a cold reminder to her that he had reasons to make himself pleasant other than a personal interest in her.

"I still don't know what my position is on that," Jennifer said cautiously, wanting to discourage him if the land were his only real interest.

"That's okay. I'd like to explain what I want to do, which might make a difference in your thoughts. Do you mind?" He paused. "I don't want to high-pressure you, so don't be put off. I tend to get pushy when I'm enthusiastic, or so my Aunt Rosa tells me."

Jennifer wanted to scream at him. Just when she had steeled herself to be coolly polite, he disarmed her with this admission and a self-effacing charm that at once attracted her and made her suspicious. "If you don't mind my holding off until I've got the White Elephant open, I won't be too annoyed if you remind me occasionally. Occasionally." She was astonished at her own bantering audacity. Ordinarily, she would have found an excuse to end the conversation, but now she seemed to be encouraging the man.

"Is once a week occasionally enough for you?" was Ross's immediate question.

"That depends on how it's done," she replied, and wished she had bit her tongue.

"I'll take that as encouragement," Ross said. "And if you don't think it's too outrageous, will you let me buy you dinner after we work out the wines? I won't take you to the winery restaurant, and I won't expect to get anything there. Let me choose a neutral place, not too far away. I know most of the local places, all right? How does Thursday suit you? I'll come by at six-thirty, and we can dine at eight." He spoke more quickly, and with a kind of eagerness that Jennifer found more flattering than she wanted to admit.

"Well, check with me in the afternoon. I still don't know how much time I have to give to work here." She wanted to be able to change her mind if she had to. "Let me call you, or you call me, about, oh, three or three-thirty."

"That's fine," Ross said. "I'm making a note to call you right now. My schedule looks pretty light that day, and if you have to rearrange your time, just tell me and we'll shift reservations. This time of year, that isn't a problem. Summer is when the traffic is the heaviest." He tried to imagine where she was, what she was doing, how she was dressed. At the same time, he wanted to convince himself this was foolish. "I'm looking forward to Thursday," he said, and began to doodle on his notepad. He noticed that the results looked something like a woman's face, and crumpled the paper at once.

"So am I," Jennifer said, not sure it was true. "A break would be nice."

"Great." He was silent again, then said, "Look, if there's something we can do for you over here, let me know, okay?"

Immediately, Jennifer felt herself grow stiff. "Certainly," she said with a return of formality. She had no intention of becoming obligated to the man in any significant way. Her previous business experience had taught her that such casually-offered favors could be called in at a high price. She recalled how often George had accepted the gesture, and then howled when confronted with the need to reciprocate.

As Ross said goodbye and hung up, he wondered what he had done wrong. He had heard the reserve in Jennifer's voice at the last, and it puzzled him. He had wanted to make her feel less ill-at-ease than she had been, and instead he had done just the opposite. He looked down at his engagement calendar and frowned. Thursday was three days away, and he had not found a reason to visit the White Elephant before then. His thoughts were interrupted by a call from San Francisco.

"How is the negotiation coming along?" asked his younger brother.

"Nothing so far." Ross had little feeling for Ian, and it always gave him a twinge of guilt to admit it. But, he said to himself, as he had since they were quite young, Ian was so different. Ian loved the bustle and glitter of running an advertising agency. While this meant the best of press for Benedetto Wines, it also disturbed Ross that his brother cared nothing for the wine except that it sell well. For Ian, it was the competition, the maneuvering, the constant battle that thrilled him; for Ross, it was the satisfaction of keeping within the long traditions of the family, of knowing that Benedetto Wines were the best in the Napa Valley.

"What kind of terms have you offered?" Ian asked.

"I haven't done that yet. I don't want to pressure her, in case that would prejudice the offer. When I have a chance, I'll sound her out a bit more. But I don't think she'd respond well to constant force. She's an independent woman and not one to be easily swayed. In fact," he added, smiling quietly to himself, "if we tried too hard to convince her that she ought to accept our offer, she'll do the opposite to show us we're wrong."

"You make the right kind of offer and that won't happen," Ian said without a trace of amusement. "This is business, Ross, or had you forgotten?"

"I know it. Probably better than you do," he added sharply. "You're the one who wants us to go into bulk wines because of high sales, but until you run the company, it won't happen. Now you're using the same approach with this woman, and I won't allow you to jeopardize my position."

"Not that old argument again." Ian sighed heavily. "One of these days the Board of Directors will come around to my point of view, Ross, and then you'll come to your senses."

"And then I'll resign," Ross corrected him, wondering what he would do without his family winery to run. Most of his life was wrapped up with the grapes he grew, and had been since he was a child. He could not imagine being away from it.

"Fat chance," Ian said amiably. "You'll go along with it because you've got too much family pride to do anything else." He seemed quite cheerful. "I'm going to have lunch with Henry Fisher next week, and I'll see how he feels about the lease, so that when he next talks to Ms. Wystan, he can offer her some very good advice. How does that sound to you?"

"I think you're pushing, not that you care," Ross said, toying with his pencil and frowning out the window.

"If I left it entirely up to you, you might get around to talking to her next October, after the vintage is in. One of us has to be practical, and Henry Fisher is a sensible man with a good understanding of the kind of money running a place like that requires." From the slightly more rapid speech, Ross knew that his brother was getting angry, and as always, it saddened him.

"Could be," he said noncommittally. "I'm not going to do anything more demanding until I've at least talked to her at dinner. There's no point to it. If I learn that she needs something I can supply so that the lease seems more like a favor or an exchange than a bribe, we might get somewhere. You can be aloof from the sordid details living down there in your Embarcadero highrise, but you're talking about a woman on the land next to mine, remember?"

"Ours," Ian corrected him.

"If you prefer. Jennifer Wystan and I are neighbors. She has a right to expect a certain degree of courtesy from me."

"So send her a bouquet of flowers on her birthday and a case of champagne at Christmas. You don't have any obligation to her beyond that. She isn't expecting anything like that from the sound of it, and it's probably just as well. You know that you can be taken advantage of in these situations."

His brother's cynicism disturbed Ross, but he said nothing more. "I'll talk to you in a few days, Ian. Don't put too much pressure on Fisher, will you? I know that you're eager to move on this, but if you give him a bad time, it will make it more difficult in the long run, and wine is a long-run proposition. I don't like bargaining from a position of weakness."

"That sounds better," Ian approved. "I look forward to hearing from you. Be a good boy, Ross. Keep your nose clean." He chortled as he hung up.

Ross sat and worried for a few minutes. He knew from long years of experience that his brother could be pushy to the point of out-and-out bull-headedness, and he sensed that this was one of the times that Ian was determined to have his own way. Most often, Ross was willing to ignore his brother's behavior, but in this instance, with Jennifer Wystan involved, he could not. He thought that he would be taken to task for that by his directors, but that did not bother him as much as it might have under different circumstances. He decided to give Ian a call in a few days and find out exactly what his ambitious younger brother was doing. It was little more than a sop to his conscience, but it allowed him to return to his work.

Drew had teased Jennifer for taking such pains for the impossible Mr. Ross Benedetto, but she was glad that she had decided to wear the fine silk dress she had chosen. The color, a delicious shade of raspberry, tempting as a sherbet cone, made her pale skin seem rosier, which pleased her because she had been shocked to see how pale she had become. "Here I own a resort," she said to her face in the mirror, "and I haven't a trace of a tan to advertise the place." Her makeup had been applied with more care than usual, and she had taken the time to brush her hair to a glossy sheen. She felt a bit awkward in the two-and-a-half-inch heels she had not worn often in the past few months. It was time to get used to them again, she told herself, since she wanted to present a professional appearance that would, in part, compensate for

her obvious youth. She hoped that her manner, learned at the
restaurant, would help. This evening, spent with Ross, would
be her first test. She chose a small linen handbag and debated
whether or not she should carry enough money to pay for her
meal herself. At the last minute, she tucked two twenty dollar
bills into her purse, along with a tube of lipstick.

Ross arrived ten minutes later, and when Jennifer saw him
come up the wide sweep of the front steps, she was glad of the
care she had taken. Ross was wearing a three-piece suit with a
silk shirt and tie that were all the more elegant for their
restrained good taste. He smiled as he caught sight of her. "I
don't want you to think I didn't like you the other day, but
this is impressive."

"Thank you," she said as she opened the door to the inner
lobby. "Let me show you around."

"I can see how much you've done already. Most of the
paneling was dingy, and you've got it glowing. And it's good
to see Samuel's portrait hanging again. He took a good deal
of pride in this place."

"So do I, Ross," Jennifer said with quiet determination. "I
love this resort, and even if you and the rest of them don't
believe it, I want to make a go of it." She did her best to keep
from sounding defensive, but she could hear the tension in
her words, and could find no way to disguise it.

"Hey, don't come after me like that," he protested, holding
up his hands in mock surrender. "I want you to make a go of
it, too. Partly because I like the place and it pleases me to see
someone caring for it, and partly because you haven't gone
into business to play with it."

She was almost convinced by what she heard, but could not
forget how skillfully, how sincerely George had wooed her.
She was determined not to be taken in again, and so she
steeled herself. "We'll see," she said with a tight showing of
teeth. "I know that there are those around who don't have
such high hopes for me. Do they?" If she expected him to
deny this, she was disappointed.

"Sure. And there are those who expect anyone who comes
from the city to be too high-and-mighty to be able to live as
we do in this part of the world, but there are those who
manage, aren't there?" He had followed her toward the bar,
but stopped in the hallway. "I like that picture. If the rest of
the decorations are up to that standard, you'll have a
showplace here."

She would not have been able to mask her pleasure at what

he said. "Yes. It is quite beautiful, isn't it? The artist was a friend of my . . . ex-husband's, and he paid for a lavish dinner with it. I . . ." She broke off, not wanting to remember the bitter words she had exchanged with George over the painting.

Ross saw the faint wince that crossed Jennifer's face, but chose not to mention it. Instead, he stepped into the bar and gave it the same appraising look. "Very attractive. I can see that you're taking time to do this right. So many places open up, and they look dreadful. Is there a bar attached to the restaurant, as well?"

"A small one. We're hoping to put more emphasis on wine than on hard liquor in the restaurant, but it will be possible to order regular drinks there." She was aware that he approved of her plan, but determined not to pursue it at present. "I've done some of the wines, but most of them are in the hands of my chef."

"Your chef? Does he know what he's doing?" Ross laughed, adding, "There are a lot of wine snobs out there, but it doesn't mean that they know a damn thing. They learn labels instead of trusting their palates. That's how some of the weird fads develop. You don't want to run into that, if you can help it."

"I make full allowances for your bias, Ross," Jennifer said, starting to leave the bar, and addressing him over her shoulder. "But admit that I know my business. I wouldn't have a chef who was an idiot, and he would have to be if he had no understanding of wine. At least in this part of the world."

"Touché," he conceded. "Who is this gem?"

"His name is Drew Usher, and he used to be the chef at the restaurant I . . . was part-owner of. He was the strongest asset we had." She relaxed as she thought of Drew, who had been so steadfast in his loyalty. "When I came up here, he came with me. I'd be lost without him."

"A rival?" Ross asked in comic dismay.

Jennifer laughed outright. "I think you'd better meet Drew."

"What—is he ancient? Crippled? A hopeless idiot about anything but food?" Ross inquired theatrically as he followed Jennifer toward the stairs to the lower floor.

"Not exactly. He's a little younger than I am, healthy, sane and fairly handsome. We're excellent friends." She had reached the bottom of the stairs and motioned down the hallway. "He has his own rooms there. Shall I introduce you?"

"Is he the one I've talked with on the phone?" He saw her nod. "Yes, I would like to meet him."

"This way," Jennifer said, indicating the way down the hall. As she neared Drew's door, she called out, "Drew! Visitors!"

"Mercy," Drew responded, coming out of his quarters. "Is this the great Mr. Benedetto? I was beginning to think you were only a disembodied voice." He propped one hand on his hip.

"Drew, stop it," Jennifer said indulgently, and turning to Ross, she went on, "Drew enjoys being outrageous every now and then."

Drew grinned, but said perfectly seriously, "It helps to pass the time. And I find that there are times being outrageous can be very instructive." He gave Ross a short, intense stare. "You weren't shocked or repelled. You don't look as if you've seen a freak. That's reassuring."

Ross simply held out his hand to Drew. "I understand you're a good chef."

Drew took the hand. "One of the best."

"I'm looking forward to finding that out for myself." Ross glanced from Drew to Jennifer and added, "I'm beginning to think that this old place is going to turn out all right."

"Thanks," Jennifer said ironically.

"He's pulling your leg," Drew informed her rather grandly. "Don't let him get to you."

Jennifer very nearly smiled. "You're both being impossible," she said with as much dignity as she could. "I don't want to spoil your fun, but do you want to complete the tour now or after we eat?"

"Why? Are you hungry?" Ross asked politely.

"I'm famished," Jennifer said at once. "I've been running around all day, and only stopped for a sandwich."

"But it was an excellent sandwich," Drew interpolated, and stepped back toward his rooms. "Go on. I've got plenty to keep me occupied." He looked again at Ross. "It's been a pleasure to meet you, Mr. Benedetto."

"You too, Mr. Usher." Ross waited until the door was firmly closed before he took Jennifer by the elbow. "Since you're hungry, we'd better get going. It's twenty minutes to the restaurant. You should have said something earlier."

"Not with Drew standing there, I couldn't. He would have tried to make Steak Diane or Beef Wellington for us." She permitted him to take the elevator instead of the stairs, and as they rode up, she said, "I'm glad you think I've done right by the place. I know that Uncle Samuel hoped I'd make the attempt."

"And you've done him proud, if the rest of the hotel is like the first floor." As the door opened, he stood aside for her, and once they left the elevator, followed her across the lobby.

"If you'll wait a moment, I'll get my coat." She had put it in the small closet on the south end of the registration desk. As she walked across the newly-laid carpet, she could feel Ross's eyes on her, watching now the turn of her leg, then the curve of her hip. It was an invigorating sensation, to be so much the center of his attention, but she could not entirely abandon the guarded attitude she had adopted from the first. She got her coat from the closet, and out of habit, pulled it on before Ross could help her with it. It was a fine ecru wool with a wide shawl collar and elegant wooden buttons, and she knew it was attractive on her. As she came back toward Ross, she experienced again that exciting silent approval, and her smile widened.

"Very nice, but next time, let me do the honors," he said, offering her his arm. "They do teach us manners, you know, even though we're miles into the country. I gave up eating peas with my knife years ago."

Jennifer flushed slightly, and was not aware how flattering the additional color was to her pale face. "Sorry. I'm not used to the courtesy."

His expression was sympathetic. "So I understand. I'm sorry."

"Don't be," she said at once, enough to keep him from making further inquiries into what was still a very painful subject. "It's better this way."

"Good." He made a point of walking ahead of her and holding the door open. "It won't worry me if you're not pleased with the place I've chosen. When it's good, it's superb, but they do have off nights, and you must not feel that you have to make compliments you don't believe."

They were on the porch now, and she gave him a startled look. "I wouldn't think of such a thing."

"Of course you would," he countered as he preceded her down the steps to his waiting BMW. He opened the passenger door and held it for her. "Anyone in your business should. Keep that in mind. And remember that Benedetto Wines owns a restaurant, too."

She got in, tucking her skirt and coat around her legs. "All right; you'll get a full critique."

"That's more like it," he said as he closed the door and went around to the driver's side.

"Now, then," Ross said when the waiter had brought the cognac and dark French roast coffee. "What about the critique?"

Jennifer stirred the coffee absently and smiled. "If you insist."

"I do," Ross told her, leaning a bit closer. He resisted the urge to touch her, but knew it was an effort not to. "A full evaluation."

She thought a moment. "The appetizer was good but not well-presented, and the plates should have been thoroughly chilled. The soup had a bit too much fennel for my taste, but the texture was excellent and the rest of it was good. I liked the Colombard with it, but something a bit dryer would have done as well. The duck was fine, but the sauce lacked tang. The vegetables were wonderful—not over-cooked and not too bland. I thought the garnishes were unnecessary, but that's a matter of personal style, and Drew would disagree with me. The Gamay Beaujolais was very good, and properly young. The salad was unobtrusive; still, I would have liked a little watercress in it because I like watercress. The house dressing is a bit too robust, but not overwhelming. The chocolate decadence was slightly too sweet, but using fresh raspberries makes up for a lot. The coffee is,"—she sipped at it—"a little too bitter for my taste, but not impossible."

Ross listened attentively, enjoying her comments. When she fell silent, he said, "Very good, although I don't agree about the house dressing."

"You're Italian," she said, as if this explained it.

"Half," he corrected her. "But I won't dispute the point. You do know what you're doing, no doubt about it, and that's reassuring."

Some of the pleasure she had been feeling evaporated. "Was this a test, Mr. Benedetto? Have I passed? Is there more to come?"

Ross realized at once that he had made another mistake

with her. "Nothing like that. I know that you owned a restaurant, but that doesn't always mean . . ."

"What you're saying is that you think most of the success was due to my husband and I was only there for color? Well, you're wrong." She kept her voice low with an effort. "I know what I'm doing. It took a lot of work and a lot of heartache, but at least I can judge good food. Is there going to be a quiz on architecture next? I ought to warn you I'm not very good at anything but turn-of-the-century buildings. My history is a little shaky, too. Math I can do pretty well, but I need a calculator if you want speed." Her eyes were bright and angry.

"No, no, no," Ross objected, feeling himself a complete ass. "Nothing like that, Jennifer. I don't mean to sound like that. If you think I'm being condescending, just say so. I don't mean to be. Look, I've told you that there have been places here that stay open a year or so, and then collapse because the owners don't know what they're doing. I don't want that to happen to you, that's all. When I met Drew, I was concerned that you might be relying too much on him, using his skill to carry you. It's happened before, and you know it has."

The memories of just such arguments with George were too fresh for her to deny this. "Yes, it happens. But the reason Drew is here is that he knows I'm not like that." She finished her coffee and lifted the small snifter. "The cognac is very good, by the way, with good age on it."

"Thank you. It's our private reserve." Ross let himself grin and measured her surprise by the length of time it took her to say something more. He gauged the reaction at half a minute, which pleased him very much.

"My compliments. It's marvelous." She meant what she said, but she felt awkward in giving him this respect. "Is the rest of your line up to this?"

"Not all of it, no," he answered her at once. "For one thing, the cognac is forty years old. For another, not all our wines are up to the standard I would like, but most of them are a couple cuts above average at least. Does that sound like I'm boasting? Why don't you come by and test out what we make? I've discussed a few matters with Drew, but you're the one who has to pay for what you order. And I should tell you that we do give restaurant discounts." While this was true, he had already decided to make an extra allowance for Jennifer.

He also knew that he would not be able to tell her this without raising her suspicions again.

"Okay, I'll think about it." She was certain that she would take him up on his offer, but did not want to appear too eager, for fear he would use her enthusiasm to his advantage.

"What about next week—say, Tuesday? I have a meeting in San Francisco on Monday, but the rest of the week is open." He admitted that this was an excuse to see her, that if it had not been the wine, he would have found another reason to make such an offer. He wondered if Aunt Rosa could be persuaded to invite Jennifer to dinner.

"I don't know yet. I'll call you." She wanted very much to see him again, but did not trust herself to be properly cautious. "We're getting supplies in, and that means a lot of work. And I have to hire more staff. I'm doing pretty well, but I'm not ready to open my doors yet, and the day is coming up quickly."

"Which is one of the things we ought to talk about," Ross said, grateful for the opportunity to bring up a matter very much on his mind. "What plans have you made for that opening? Are you having a special event?"

"Of course," she said, a bit affronted. She had to keep reminding herself that this man wanted the use of her land, and that his interest was more powerfully occupied with grapes than with her.

"What sort, may I ask?" He could see her bristle, and did not know how to reassure her. Jennifer baffled him, and at moments like this one, he could sense her suspicions of him and wished he knew how to counter them.

"A buffet, very lavish, so Drew promises me. A dance in the evening, if I can find a decent dance band who aren't too expensive. As grand a show as I can manage." She lifted her chin in a minor show of defiance.

"And the name-the-elephant contest?" he asked.

"I'm still thinking about it. I like the idea, but I don't know if I want to live with the choice of the judges—who must not be me. I'm still trying to find a way around that, because I do want to have some sort of contest to stimulate business." She knew that the cognac was having more of an effect on her than it usually did, and considered ordering another cup of coffee to counteract the light-headedness she felt.

"Don't worry," Ross said, watching her closely. "You can relax. I'm driving, remember?"

"But you're drinking cognac, too," she pointed out, then flushed for no reason that made any sense to her.

"True. But I've eaten more than you have, and I had more for lunch than a sandwich. Besides, every cop in the county knows my car on sight, and unless I do something inexcusably stupid, we won't get stopped. If it makes you feel better, I've never had an accident and the cops have never escorted me home. Go on. You could use the break."

She was tempted, and for a little time, she stared down at the liquid in the snifter. "Maybe," she said, setting the snifter aside.

"As you like." Ross again had the feeling that he had bungled. He wished he knew what made her so elusive, and why he was so determined to find out what made her at once so self-possessed and so skittish. "I was going to offer to make a special deal for the wines for the buffet, if you're willing." He saw the guarded expression come back into her face, and went on quickly, "Of course I'll want to get publicity for it, and as we're neighbors, this is a good gesture. You might not be aware of it, but around here, this is exactly the sort of thing that gets paid attention to. If I *don't* supply the wines, there are those who will take it as a sign that I'm not pleased to see the . . . White Elephant open for business, and that's the kind of ill-will neither of us can afford."

"You've out-maneuvered me," she said when she had heard him out. "You've anticipated all my objections, and you're being so damn reasonable that there's no way I can reasonably refuse your kindness without being a complete . . ."

"Boor," he supplied with that smile that so disarmed Jennifer.

"Yes." She stared at him a moment, her face not as unreadable as she would have thought. "You're being kind to me. Why is that?"

"Politics. Neighborliness. Whim. Interest. Take your pick." He finished his cognac and set the snifter aside. "More coffee? It might make you feel less reckless."

"You're right," she said with a sigh. "That was exactly how I was feeling. This is the first time since . . . in months that I've been out and . . ."

"And you're nervous. Stagefright." He was pleased to see her smile again, and so pressed his advantage. "But I'm not such an ogre, am I? You haven't thought that, have you?"

"No," she said, and then frowned. "Ross, I know that you're interested in leasing my land, and it's easy to believe that you're willing to be nice to the newcomer, but . . ." She faltered and took refuge in another sip of cognac she had not intended to have.

"But?" he prompted.

"I don't know what it is you want, but I'd prefer you didn't romance me for business advantages." She breathed deeply and thought, *Thank God I've said it*.

"Good Lord, Jennifer!" Ross said, genuinely shocked. "Do you think I'm trying to get better lease terms? I could do that by talking to your attorney. Sure, I want your good opinion, and I admit I like to get on with my neighbors. But that isn't why I asked you to come to dinner with me, not really." His voice had softened and he brushed her hand with his. "You're sensible—how is it you can't see that I'm interested in you?"

Jennifer stammered a few disassociated words and glared down at the tablecloth. "I wish you wouldn't say that."

"Why not? You're not a child, and I'm not a child, so why must we behave as if we were sixteen years old? Let me tell you what I've found out about you, and before you start asking questions, yes, I have taken the time to find out about you. You're twenty-eight years old, divorced, no children. You and your ex-husband owned a restaurant in South San Francisco which was relatively successful. Your father died of a heart attack six years ago and your mother is remarried and lives in Chicago. Your Uncle Samuel left you his hotel because he said you cared for it, and he's right. He also left you a trust fund to get the place back on its feet again, but it isn't as much money as you would like, which is probably the only reason you'd consider my offer of leasing acreage. Is that about right?" He had tried to keep his manner disinterested and matter-of-fact, but he could not help wanting to touch her again. He let his hand rest beside hers, not quite against it, but close enough that he could feel the warmth of her skin.

"That's right. You've been . . . busy." She was angry and flattered at once, and more on her guard than she had been.

"I want to know who I'm dealing with, that's all." He signaled a waiter and asked for more coffee.

"And you're satisfied that we can do business together?" She had not meant to sound so sharp with him, and thought that if she had not found his smile so fascinating, she would be able to deal with him—to use his own phrase—more easily.

"I don't know about that. I do know that I want to take you out to dinner again, if you think you can stand it." The light from the soft, overhead fixture made the white streak in his hair glisten. There was the first faint blue shading of stubble along his strong jaw and stubborn chin. He lifted his hand and brought it, feather-light, over Jennifer's. "Do you think you can?"

"I don't know," she said in a small voice as she looked down at their hands, chiding herself for being so attracted to this man, wanting to find a way to move away from his disturbing presence without being obvious. It had been more than a year since she had felt so strong an attraction for a man, and it worried her. She was aware that after the long period of work she would be looking for someone to make her feel more complete. It was possible that this man could do that, but it was equally possible, she reminded herself, that he was used to using women to his advantage. If only he had not admitted he had so much to gain from her, then she might be more willing to accept him at face value. In the next instant, she doubted that, for she recalled bitterly that she had accepted George in such a way, and the scars were still fresh and tender within her.

"But you're not telling me a direct no, are you?" Ross said with a somber turn of his expressive mouth.

"Not that," she said, and finished the cognac just as the waiter brought more coffee.

"Then I'll call you. And you can tell me you're too busy, or waiting for deliveries, or hiring staff, or having a sandwich, and I'll call again later. Is that all right with you?" He moved his hand to stir cream and a touch of sugar in his coffee, but when that was done, again rested it over hers.

"That sounds reasonable," she admitted, trying to find an objection that would not sound lame. "But I doubt I'll have much free time for the next several months." That caution was as much for herself as for him.

"I'm persistent and not easily discouraged," Ross told her, and drank his second cup of coffee.

When they arrived back at the White Elephant, it was quite late and Jennifer was embarrassed to find herself stifling a yawn. "It's not the company, it's the hour," she said automatically as Ross turned his BMW in the drive.

"If you're relaxed enough to yawn, that's great," Ross said. He was beginning to feel tired, too. "I want to get some

numbers from Drew for the opening, and then I'll come back
with a figure. Will you have him call me?"

"Tomorrow morning. Or is it this morning?" She was not
wearing a watch, and it took her a moment to find the one on
the dashboard.

"This morning." Ross rounded the shoulder of the hill and
came up the drive to the front of the hotel. "It's almost one.
High time you were in bed."

Jennifer shot him a quick, suspicious look, then realized
there was no double meaning in his remark. "Yes. And if I
sleep late in the morning, Drew will never let me hear the end
of it."

The car came to a halt and Ross turned off the engine. The
silence of the spring night rushed in on them, making them
feel suspended in the vastness of the land under the butter-
milk sky.

"I love it here," Ross said dreamily as he looked out at the
faint rolling hills and wide expanse of darkness.

"It's beautiful," Jennifer agreed quietly, thinking again
that this was one of the loveliest spots in the world.

The ceiling light of the car was glaringly distracting. Ross
got out quickly and closed his door before coming around to
help Jennifer out. He closed the passenger door as soon as she
stood beside him, and took her hand. "I would like to have
time to walk home tonight, so I can watch the sky. And I'd
have an excuse to come back tomorrow, to collect my car.
And if I rode over, I might leave my horse so that I'd have to
come back for it later on." He saw that his bantering tone was
distressing her, and stopped at once. "Jennifer, I don't know
what is frightening you, but I wish I could help."

"It's just the uncertainty of opening a new business and
starting my life over," she said, trying to get the same
lightness he had and failing.

"I'd like to think that was all," he said, and started up the
stairs. On the second step, he turned back to her, and as she
came up to the same tread he stood on, he took her gently by
the shoulders and drew her near enough to him to touch her
lips with his. It was a tentative kiss, sweetly awkward and
deeply disturbing.

Jennifer stepped back, flashing an uneasy smile that was
not easily seen in the dim light. "Thanks."

"Thank you," Ross said, releasing her shoulders and giving
her a long, puzzled look. He had not thought it would mean

so much to him, to kiss her. In the years since Rosemary's death, he had known a number of women, had indulged in half a dozen light affairs, and often used his charm deliberately, but this was nothing like any previous experience. To his baffled amazement, he discovered that he wanted this woman, that he was more drawn to her than he had been to anyone since his wife died. It was frustrating to recognize that Jennifer was not as greatly attracted as he, and he tried to convince himself that when the cognac had worn off, her spell would fade with it. He took a step backward, almost tripped, and then started toward his BMW. "I'll talk to you in a day or so."

"Good," Jennifer said, watching him fumble for the door handle. "Thank you again for a . . ."

"Pleasant evening? Your mother must have had the same etiquette book that mine did." He opened the door at last and was about to get into the car when another thought occurred to him. "Should I see you into the lobby? I don't know what's correct when returning a hotel owner to her hotel."

"I'll manage. But it was a nice thought." What surprised her was her feeling that he was concerned for her. Just for an instant, she longed to respond to him, to have him return to her for a second kiss and the nonchalant flirtation he had been conducting most of the evening. Then her good sense reasserted itself, and she waved as he started the BMW and drove off. It was foolish of her to be interested in Ross Benedetto, she told herself sternly. He was a good businessman and a charming host, but she knew better than to put too much importance on a single kiss. She was not in high school any more, and if all the years with George had taught her nothing else, she had learned that a man was capable of using charm and pleasant manners to achieve his own ends.

When the car was out of sight down the curve of the road, she went into the hotel and for once took the elevator to her room.

Ben Cory did not much resemble his father. At sixteen, he was all gangling limbs and energetic starts. He sprawled rather than sat in the chair on the far side of Jennifer's desk and gave her a pleading look. "I can't work full time, not even during the summer. Dad insists that I take summer courses, and I don't like to argue with him."

Jennifer remembered her encounter with Wilbur Cory and

felt sympathy for his boy. "Well, there aren't too many part-time jobs available, and the pay isn't as good as for the full-time jobs."

"I know that," Ben said with the seriousness only teenagers possess. "But I want to learn about resorts and hotels. Most of the places around here are sewed up tight, and unless I want to scrape plates, there's nothing much I can do. But if you've got chores and odd jobs, I'd like to do them."

A frown of concentration appeared on Jennifer's brow. "We do need someone to run things into town, and I'm short on grounds security. I can't pay you a great deal, as I've said, but if you're willing to run the errands and do the evening patrol, I think we might be able to work something out. That is, of course, if your father doesn't object."

"He wants me to get work experience," Ben said carefully.

"I'd need you about twenty-five hours a week, and I don't think I can pay more than minimum wage for the work. But you can have access to the pool, and we can throw in lunch for you."

"That sounds fine," Ben said with a relieved smile. "I want to have a look around the place, if that's okay."

"Fine. You'll be doing a lot of that later on." She thought a moment. "Do you have a dog? A good one?"

"Well, he wouldn't win any ribbons, but he's smart and I've trained him well," Ben said with a mixture of embarrassment and pride. "Why?"

"It might be a good idea to take him on your grounds patrol. We can throw in food for him, too, if that would make it better." She was not quite sure why she suggested this, but her recent concern for the size of her land had grown, and she was aware that a little more attention to the inner recreational boundaries of her holdings might be wise.

"That'd be fine, Mrs. Wystan," he said. "You won't be disappointed. I'll work hard, and I won't do anything too stupid if you warn me about it." This last sounded like the rehearsed speech it was.

"Good," Jennifer said.

Ben shifted in the chair and said, "When do you want me to start?"

"Well, this is March twenty-fourth. We open next month. Let's say that you start your patrols and learning your responsibilities the first of next week. That way, you'll have your routine established by the time you have to deal with guests."

"Hey, that's great." He stood up. "Is there anything else I have to do?"

"See Muriel Wrather on the way out to fill out your tax and insurance forms." She also rose and extended her hand. "We don't have uniforms here, but I expect you to be neat at all times, and we'll provide you with identification. You'll have to check with your insurance company about driving the van, and I'll add your record to our insurance."

"It sounds awfully official," Ben said with a shy chuckle.

"It is," Jennifer answered, thinking of the many explanations she had been giving to the various men and women interviewing for jobs at the White Elephant. So many of the words made no sense anymore. There were three more people to see today, and already she was beginning to feel overwhelmed. "I'll expect to see you at ten o'clock on Monday, if your high school approves the work-study hours."

"They will. Dad will see to that." He ambled over to the door, a boy with more legs than he knew what to do with. At the door he turned back to Jennifer. "I really appreciate this, Mrs. Wystan."

"Tell me that in six months," Jennifer said to him, both cordial and professional. It was only when she was alone again that she stared down at her desk, at the letter from Henry Fisher mentioning that Mr. Benedetto had had lunch with him and had indicated that he was determined to get those acres for the winery. Henry advised her to consider the offer seriously and to be willing to strike a bargain with Benedetto. She very nearly crumpled the letter and threw it away, but that, she knew, was irresponsible. So it was the land that Ross was interested in, not her. The little warm place that had begun to glow at the junction of her ribs turned cold, and she felt once more that small, grinding ache at her heart.

"Jennifer?" Muriel Wrather said as she tapped on the door. "There is a Mr. Gossman to see you."

"The bartender?" Jennifer asked, shocked out of her self-pity. "I'll see him now, and then, will you let Drew know that I'm ready for lunch?"

"Of course," Muriel said, and opened the door to admit the next job applicant.

∽ April ∽

The phone call came as a complete surprise to Jennifer, and as she put aside the first reservation assignments, she said, "*Who* is it?"

"Ross Benedetto," Muriel said quietly, though her hand was protectively over the receiver. "He said he'd call back if it wasn't convenient."

Puzzled, Jennifer said, "No, that's all right. I'll take the call." She had spoken to him only once since their dinner out. Then he had seemed to be breezily polite, and she had not expected more than that. As she lifted the receiver and punched her office line into life, she subdued a sense of anticipation. "Hello?"

"Jennifer, this is Ross. Look, I know you're up to your ears in work and the last thing in the world you need is another good idea from someone on the outside, but have you thought of contacting the press about your opening? It's only nine days away, and there might be some interest in the restoration work you've done."

"We've sent out press releases," Jennifer said in a neutral tone, not adding that there had been very little response to the announcements.

"What about television? The reason I ask," he hurried on, "is that I know Gregory Lennard slightly, and he occasionally does stories on projects like yours. Have you kept a record of the restoration you've done?"

"Yes," Jennifer said with some pride. Every step of the way, in fact, she said to herself, thinking of the many rolls of film that had been used to document all the changes and repairs that had been required to make the White Elephant the gorgeous building that it was. She had been told by Henry Fisher that should her taxes be called into question, such a record would be invaluable. "Why?"

"Well, if you don't mind, I'd like to call him up and suggest that he cover your opening with all the usual hoopla. He's been a good sport about such things in the past, and I think he'd be interested. The attention wouldn't hurt you, either. And I know Greg well enough to know that he would do it right." Ross did his best to be pragmatic, outlining the advantages, but was inwardly aware that if Jennifer said yes, it would provide another excuse to seek her out. He fiddled with the papers stacked on his desk and waited for her comments.

"I'm interested," Jennifer said carefully. "But I don't want to turn this into a circus."

"Of course not," Ross said, relieved. "Let me put in a call to him, and if you like, I'll give him your number and suggest that he get ahold of you today. Would you be able to take time off to talk with him?"

"If it means television coverage, I'll make the time," she said, feeling more enthusiastic than she had in the last few days. She had needed a break very much, and this might be the means to discover one at last. In spite of the doubts she felt at being indebted to Ross, she knew that the advantages outweighed the disadvantages. "I'd love to talk to him, if he's interested."

"He'll be interested," Ross assured her, finding himself oddly disappointed that she never showed such eagerness to deal with him. "I'll contact his office at once and give them the details. You should hear from him or one of his staff before the day is over, or first thing tomorrow."

"Thanks," Jennifer said impulsively. "I'm glad you thought of me. We're not doing too well on our advance registrations, and a little favorable publicity would mean a lot right now." In the next instant, she doubted it had been wise to admit so much to him, but the damage had been done. "We want to start off as full as possible, of course, so that we generate more word of mouth."

"Good idea," Ross said, and began to scribble a note to himself on the pad at his elbow. Gregory Lennard would want as much information in as terse a form as possible. "The opening is on the tenth, is that right?"

"That's right. Begins at four P.M. and goes until two A.M. Buffet supper, dancing and all the rest of it. Drew told me you gave us a great price on the wines, so that part will be easy. I still haven't made up my mind about the rest of the bar. I'd like to have an open bar, but that can run into money, especially since it's going to be such a long evening. A cash bar doesn't look as good, but if there's wine and champagne for the asking, it might be okay to charge for the hard stuff. The only other alternative is to open the bar later and have drinks for free before then, but that bothers me." She had not voiced these concerns to anyone but Drew, and did not expect Ross to give her his serious opinion.

"Better to have a cash bar the whole time. The other looks more judgmental. And there are those who will appreciate your emphasis on wine." He had seen other occasions turn out well with the same arrangement. "You might get a reputation for wine snobbery, but around here there's nothing wrong with that."

"Particularly from your point of view?" She regretted her asperity and added, "I don't mean to be sharp with you. It's just that I've got so much on my mind and . . ."

"And the last thing you need is another good idea being shoved down your throat. I won't keep you. Besides, I'll have to call Greg's office pretty soon if I want to catch him before he begins getting ready for his evening program." He was pleased that she had softened her last remark, and he determined to be more persuasive with Greg than he had planned at first. "If there's any trouble, I'll call you back. If not, then expect a call from Greg's office. Okay?"

"Yes. Thanks." She could think of nothing else to say except, "Well, goodbye," before she hung up the phone. She could not help being puzzled by this new generosity, and now that the offer had been made and accepted, she thought it might not have been wise to let him do so much for her. All the doubts that had lurked in her mind rushed in on her, and she was on the point of calling him back and declining his help when the door opened and Muriel came in with a stack of figures for her.

"Advance registrations?" Jennifer inquired hopefully.

"Not all of them. They're the breakdown on the operating expenses. Nothing too overwhelming, but you said that you'd want to have these for Henry Fisher. I don't doubt that they're important from his point of view as well as yours."

"How do they look?" Jennifer asked, not wanting to go over them just yet.

"Steep. You'll do okay, of course, but we'll have to keep a close eye on things." Muriel looked over the two sheets again. "Henry called to say that he planned to be at the opening, incidentally, and wanted to know if he could bring a few friends. I told him I was sure you'd welcome them. He'll have a party of four with him."

"Good, I think," Jennifer said as she thought the matter over. "Fine. I'm pleased that he wants to be here, but it means that there will be more questions to answer once he's seen how things are set up around here."

"That's all right. It will give him a better understanding of how the . . ." Muriel broke off as the telephone rang. Automatically, she picked it up and said, "White Elephant." Then she paused and an excited smile came over her face. "Just a minute, please. I'll get Ms. Wystan." She put her hand over the receiver and said, "Lois Chatham for Gregory Lennard. You'll take the call, of course."

"Of course," Jennifer said, somewhat surprised and pleased that the newsman had responded to Ross's call so quickly. As she took the receiver, she said to Muriel, "I'd rather not be interrupted until the call is through."

"I'll make sure of it," Muriel said, smiling with anticipation.

As she watched Muriel leave the room, Jennifer said into the phone, "This is Jennifer Wystan, Ms. Chatham."

The voice on the phone was young and precise, almost fussy. "Good afternoon, Ms. Wystan. Gregory Lennard asked me to call you. About the opening of your resort?"

"Yes?" Jennifer said, not certain what more the woman required of her.

"Can you give me some details? Mr. Lennard is interested in covering the event." From the sound of the woman, she was ticking off notes to herself as she spoke.

"Well, the opening is on the tenth, a buffet and evening

dance affair. The resort is called the White Elephant, but when my uncle, Samuel Wystan, owned it, it was known as the Empress. The building was willed to me by my uncle and I've done what I can to restore it and bring it up to the former standard." As she said this, she thought she sounded like some sort of prerecorded message, but she went on. "The restoration is almost complete except for three of the detached cabins on the grounds. The main hotel is in full readiness, and every improvement has been made, but not so as to interfere with the building's authenticity. There are hotsprings as part of the hotel. We have swimming and tennis and lawn bowling. In the summer we will also have a trout pond stocked and open, and next year there will be equestrian trails and horses available. The old stables were burned in sixty-one and have not been properly rebuilt. What else can I tell you, Ms. Chatham?"

"I hear you've got photographs of the restoration process?" Lois Chathem said as if she were conducting a quiz.

"Yes. All aspects of the restoration have been covered, from the exterior to the smallest interior details. Where modifications have been made, every step in the process has been recorded. The bar is the best example of that, because it's the one part of the hotel that has been significantly changed. When my uncle owned this place, the bar was a reception room, catering mostly to afternoon teas. There is a lovely terrace beyond the room which is an extension of the covered porch that fronts most of the building, and in the old days, women retired there after croquet for a sandwich and lemonade. Although I want to keep much of the flavor of the Empress, I don't think there will be as much use for watercress sandwiches as there will be for piña coladas. We've hired two excellent bartenders, by the way, one from Napa and one from Greenbrae. We have a third man to serve as back-up. Our kitchen is superb, and our chef has a great deal of experience and a well-earned reputation for haute cuisine." Listening to herself, Jennifer thought it might be wise to make a tape of what she was saying and incorporate it into their advertising.

"Mr. Lennard should be able to do something with this. . . ." Ms. Chatham said, but with an underlying doubt.

Jennifer sensed the ploy at once. "Naturally, if Mr. Lennard is interested in covering our opening, he and his staff would be more than welcome for the entire festivities. If it's necessary to arrive earlier than we begin, we'll be sure that you're fed and housed. Mr. Lennard may have the use of two of the grounds cottages for himself and his staff for the day and the night. It would be my pleasure to have you as my guests." It would also mean that there would be two fewer cabins to rent out, but in this instance, she knew that the loss of immediate revenue would be worth it.

"I'll inform Mr. Lennard of your offer. We'll be getting back to you tomorrow or the next day. We may send someone up there to check out your location before the tenth. How would the eighth be?"

"Fine," Jennifer said, thinking of how frantically busy she would have to be on the last few days before opening. "Let me know when your people will arrive and how many of them you'll be sending. We'll attend to the rest of it on this end." She made a note to herself to take a tranquilizer the night before, little as she liked them, so that she could meet the newsmen with some degree of serenity. "We're looking forward to having you with us," she said automatically, as she had said before when taking banquet reservations for the restaurant. How easily the old habits reasserted themselves, she thought as she said her goodbyes and hung up.

Muriel Wrather came bustling back into the inner office. "Well? What happened?"

"Block cottages eleven and nine for Gregory Lennard and crew and staff," Jennifer said with a smirk. "And make sure that there are complimentary baskets of cheese and wine in both of them early on the morning of the tenth. Ask Ben to give the grounds around those two cottages special grooming, since that's going to be their main impression of the place. Also, better arrange for Fred Jenkins to get the ceilings painted in both those cottages. I know that he's supposed to be working on the hotsprings building, but this is more important. If I have to pay him extra," —she sighed again— "so be it. We don't want a single note of disappointment to come from Gregory Lennard and company."

"Everyone here will be thrilled!" Muriel predicted.

"I don't care about that—what matters now is that Lennard is thrilled." She picked up another set of papers and began to read through them, determined not to set too much stock in the advantages of having Gregory Lennard cover her opening.

Jerry Baxter arrived on the afternoon of the sixth, when Jennifer was covered with potting soil and aggravated at

Carlo Donati, the gardener she had added to her staff the week before. Her old sweater had bits of earth clinging to it and her dark hair was tied back at the neck with a green ribbon. She viewed the newcomer with dismay. "Excuse me, but . . . "

He held out his hand, then seeing how muddy hers were, shrugged and beamed at her. "I'm not supposed to be here until five-thirty, but it was such a pleasant day that I talked Greg into letting me take off early. I'm Jerry Baxter, Gregory Lennard's scout."

"Hello. I suppose someone told you I'm Jennifer Wystan." She wondered which of her staff had sent the man to her without warning.

"Yes. It's a change to see an owner doing manual labor," he said. "How many more of those do you have to get into the ground today?"

Jennifer looked at the neat row of cans filled with small azaleas. "I'd like to get them all in, but I don't think it's going to be possible. Carlo has two kids down with the flu and can't leave them until his wife gets home. I don't argue with his priorities, but it isn't the most convenient time for this to happen." She did her best to give a philosophical shrug. "But it wouldn't be the usual opening, would it, unless something went wrong?"

"I guess not," Jerry said, watching as Jennifer brushed the bits of earth and loam from her knees. "If you want a little more time, I can walk around on my own."

"No, I'm glad of the excuse to stop. My hands are getting ruined, and that will never do if I have to be presentable on the tenth." She also had no intention of letting this brash young man wander around her grounds unescorted. "If you'll come in, I'll arrange for a snack for you in the bar while I shower and change. Then I'll be happy to answer any questions you may have, and show you around the place." She scraped her boots clean on a brick, and then made her way up the steps of the porch. There she took off her boots before entering the lobby. "The janitorial staff would shoot me if I tracked mud on the carpets or the floor," she said as she padded in in her stocking feet.

"Nice place," Jerry said as he looked about the lobby.

"I hope so," Jennifer said devoutly. "Excuse me while I ring the kitchen and arrange for a bite for you. Would a chicken sandwich hold you until supper?" Anything else would have to be specially prepared, but she would not tell Jerry that.

"Sounds great," he replied while looking around the walls. "That's your uncle, is it?" he asked, pointing up at the portrait.

"Yes." Jennifer went to the reservations desk and leaned over to pick up her house line. "Drew," she said when at last he answered the persistent ring.

"What?"

"Jerry Baxter of Gregory Lennard's staff has arrived a few hours early and requires a sandwich and a drink of some sort to keep him going. If you'll take . . ."

"What the hell is he doing showing up here now?" Drew demanded.

Jennifer kept her voice as low as she could. "He's trying to catch us off-guard, of course. And he's done a good job of it. It can't happen again. So whip up a sandwich and get Johnny to serve it as prettily as possible. In the bar. And provide a split of something tolerable but not too special for him. Coffee to follow. I'll need twenty minutes to make myself presentable. Can you handle it?"

"Sure, boss," Drew said, sounding slightly chagrined. "I didn't mean to bark at you, but you ought to see what we're running into down here. I thought we had the egg order taken care of, but there's been a foul-up, if you'll pardon the pun, and we're going to have to scrounge for them. But never mind about that." He paused to shout an order across the kitchen and then said, "One scrumptious chicken sandwich, served ever-so-nice, coming up. And you get yourself into shape for this guy, so they'll say nice things about us on the magic telly."

"Thanks, Drew," Jennifer said, and put the phone back behind the desk. She turned to Jerry Baxter with an assumption of calm that was far from her actual feelings. "Mr. Baxter, the bar is down this hall. Let me show you how to get there, and then we'll have the kitchen bring up something for you."

"Great," Jerry said with such smug self-assurance that Jennifer longed to be able to yell at him.

"This is the part of the hotel that has been altered the most. Originally, this wall was further over, and the diagonal paneling is modern, of course." As she conducted Jerry down the hallway, she kept up this informative patter while she tried to think of how best to proceed with the man.

"I'll be fine here, Ms. Wystan. Or do I call you Jenny?"
Jerry found himself a table near the window and sat down.
"Nice view. I like those trees and the ferns."

"Enjoy it. I'll be back shortly." She turned back down the
hall at once, and though appearing not to hurry, went quickly
to the stairs and began to climb to her quarters on the third
floor. As she hastened up the stairs, she tried to figure out
what she should wear. Nothing too fancy, or Jerry would take
it as more of a compliment than she intended to give him.
Nothing too plain, or he would dismiss her out of hand.
Finally, as she opened the door to her rooms, she decided
that a pair of gray woolen slacks and her best sweater, which
was a deep teal-green, would be best. As she slammed the
door, she was already throwing her boots across the room and
tugging off her dirty, ancient sweater.

The remnants of a chicken sandwich were on the plate in
front of Jerry, and an empty wineglass stood beside them
when Jennifer returned. Jerry was making notes on a small
pad of paper, but he closed this as soon as he heard the tap of
her shoes. "You're quick," he said as he tucked his pen into
the pocket of his tweed jacket.

"I thought it would be best not to waste too much of one
another's time," Jennifer said cordially. "You've got your
obligations, just as I have." She knew that she looked much
more attractive than when he had arrived, but was not
prepared for the frankly appreciative look in his hazel eyes.

"All work and no play and all the rest of it," Jerry said, but
got up from the table. "It was good, the sandwich. I hear you
have a good kitchen staff."

"At a place like this, Mr. Baxter, it's absolutely necessary." She opened the sliding door onto the narrow terrace.
"Let's go this way, and I can show you some of the original
work done on the hotel, and where we've had to restore it."
She closed the door behind them and pointed up at the
elaborate woodwork overhead. "That gingerbread is original,
but that next section of it, with the curlicues coming down
along the door-frame, that's restoration work. The man who
has done a great deal of it is named Fred Jenkins and he has a
business in Sonoma. He specializes in these old places and
does superior work."

The next two hours went rapidly, with Jerry asking a few,
cogent questions, and Jennifer providing clear answers and all
the volunteered information she could think of. By the time

they had seen the work going on and been over the photographs of the work in progress, Jerry's attitude had changed from that of one doing a favor to genuine interest.

"I'll tell Greg that he'll need two pieces for the story, and that should get you a bit more time on the tube." He was standing in the front drive as he said this, preparing to return to the studio. "It was a real treat, Jennifer. Greg will call you tomorrow. He always says ten, but he doesn't get into gear until ten-thiry or so, so don't worry if it's any time before lunch."

"Thanks. I won't." Jennifer was more kindly-disposed toward Jerry than she had been at first, but was careful that her approval did not go beyond the proper reserve her profession required. "Will you be at the opening?"

"If I can wangle it."

"Fine," she said, and waved before going back into the hotel. She did not wait until Jerry drove away to hurry down to the kitchen and pull Drew aside.

"So how is the great world of video?" Drew asked as he took a break from shaping rye loaves on the narrow marble slab he had been delighted to discover in the unrenovated kitchen, and which was now his greatest pride. "We're half an hour behind in here, but these loaves won't raise any faster just because I want them to."

"How's it all going?" Jennifer asked, wanting a bit of a break herself.

"Well enough. Johnny has made an arrangement with one of the locals to get us fresh mushrooms—strictly okay and very commercial—and is trying to arrange for other fresh-off-the-vine veggies for the dips. I can't stand dips, but what are we going to do?" Drew wiped off his hands and looked at Jennifer closely. "You still haven't said how the TV type reacted."

"It could turn out pretty well," Jennifer told him, not wanting to sound too optimistic. "Toward the end, he was beginning to take me seriously, and that's something, I suppose."

"And they're going to cover the opening." He picked up a damp cloth and draped it over the loaves.

"So it seems." She rubbed her forehead. "I don't know what to do with myself. I have a whole two hours unaccounted for."

"Then check over the new reservations and find out what the maids are doing in the upper rooms. The third floor needs a good going over, and that cupola of yours could stand a cleaning. I was up there earlier for a couple aspirin, and it looks like a disaster area." His hectoring tone did not conceal his affection for her, and he reached over and grasped her shoulder in his strong, blunt fingers. "You're going to have to keep yourself going on all burners for a while longer, and it won't do anyone any good if you find yourself running out of steam. Go do the reservations and take a breather."

"You're probably right, but I don't like the rest of the staff to be working while I've got my feet up. It's a bad example." She could not forget those many times that she had seen the resentment at the Savoia when George would saunter in long enough to be sure everyone was working and then leave for an afternoon of conversation and drink with his friends who had more leisure time than he.

"No one is going to think it wrong of you to get some rest. They all know how hard you've been working, and they're depending on you to run the show. It isn't being self-indulgent to be prepared to do your job. Remember that." He looked at her carefully. "You're letting yourself get run down, and you don't want to look exhausted when we open. You have to think ahead."

"All right, Drew, you've convinced me. I'll take a nap after seeing to the registrations." She looked down at the rising loaves. "How far over budget are we, do you know?"

"Not far," Drew said with his most soothing smile. "Not enough to worry about. The price we got on the wines sure helped. More than twenty percent under what I was expecting to pay. A few more breaks like that one and we'll be right on the button."

Jennifer kept her own opinion to herself, but was troubled to know that Ross had done her another extravagant favor. What if, in the end, she decided not to lease him the land he wanted? Would he be offended? How could she refuse when he had done so much for her? She saw that Drew was giving her a worried look again and tried to smile. "I'm looking for the fine print," she explained.

"Are you finding any?" He did not sound too concerned, but he kept his undivided attention on her in spite of the sudden crash of a stainless steel bowl and the swearing of one of his underlings.

"I don't know. That's the trouble."

"You know what I think the trouble is?" Drew asked. "I

think you're taking on so much that you can't see the forest for the trees. You're spending all your time anticipating things going wrong, and you're wearing yourself out to no purpose. Haven't you been listening to me? Do you need a flashing neon sign?"

"Probably," she said. "Rest. Relax. Do nothing for a couple of hours. Have I got it right?"

"Pretty much. I wish you could get away from here, though, because if you don't you'll end up doing just one more thing and then another one more thing." He looked around the kitchen, saw something that made him click his tongue in annoyance. "Steve, that is not the way to mince ham. A good part of food is the appearance, particularly this kind of food. It can't look as if we were going to feed it to the cats." He regarded the other cooks steadily. "If you're wondering why I don't put all the things through the food processor, it's because we do not serve flavored paste for appetizers here. This is a grand hotel in the old tradition, which we will have to live up to. Do you understand?"

There was a tired, annoyed round of agreement, and Jennifer shook her head.

"I don't know why they put up with you," she said affectionately.

"Because I'm a master and they know it." He pointed to the door. "Go on. You've got some serious resting to do. Or take a walk. But do something other than standing around inventing new things to worry about."

"Okay. I'll talk with you later, Drew. And thanks." She went out of the kitchen to the sound of chopping and the sliding of trays.

The day before the opening, Jennifer woke with a sore throat and stuffy head. She swore comprehensively and got out of bed reluctantly. In addition to her regular morning vitamins, she took a couple aspirin and doubled up on the vitamin C. Determined to let this be enough, she arrived at the front desk at eight-thirty to find the new reception clerk all but crowing with satisfaction.

"What is it?" Jennifer asked, hating the thick sound of her voice and knowing her eyes were heavy.

"Another reservation, for two weeks." He held the letter up. "See who it's from."

Jennifer took the paper without much interest, but quickly

found herself smiling as she read the name. "Eric Bush," she said with pleasure, thinking of the few times she had heard the great pianist. "Does he want a piano made available, I hope?"

"He said, at the bottom of the letter, that he'll make arrangements. That's why he wants one of the cottages, probably." He took the letter back like a trophy. "If he likes it here, we might have a lot of those concert people coming. That would be terrific."

"Don't count on it, Dean," she warned the clerk. "But it's good to have Bush coming. I didn't know he was interested in the wine country." She was about to go on when Dean stopped her.

"He says that his wife is in a wheelchair. Can we handle that?"

Jennifer had been vaguely aware of Mrs. Bush's tragic accident of a decade before. At the time, there had been headlines, because the operators of the ski-lift from which she had fallen were found to be negligent, and it was revealed that two other skiers had fallen and been hurt before. "The state requires it. Just make sure you let them know that the handicapped parking is on the south side of the building. There are no steps that way." She went into the reception office where Muriel Wrather was working this morning. "How's it going?"

"Very well. I've had a warning call from Henry Fisher, but I think his feathers are less ruffled than they were. He said that the Benedetto offer has been renewed." She looked closely at Jennifer. "Are you feeling okay?"

"Just a stuffy head," she said rather gruffly, not liking the idea that her malady was so obvious. "It'll clear up by mid-day I think."

"Better let me call Dr. Robb, just in case. Let him have a look at you. We can't have you down with a cold now." She was already reaching for the telephone, and Jennifer could not bring herself to protest.

"I'm going to be in the bar with Hugo for part of the morning, and if you really think it's necessary that I get checked, tell the doctor that I'll be free in the early afternoon. We've got too many deliveries coming for me to be gone before then." She sighed as the telephone rang. "Have Sandra get it. It's her job."

"You *aren't* feeling well, are you?" Muriel inquired. "Ordinarily, you'd have that receiver up before the second ring."

"There are other things on my mind," she said somewhat grumpily, and left the office.

"First," said Dr. Robb with a warning shake of the finger, "you're badly run down. I don't know how much sleep you've been getting, but it's probably not enough, and from what I've heard, you're eating on the fly as well. No one can keep that up for as long as you have and not pay for it one way or another." He rubbed his blond hair back from his forehead. "I'm going to give you an injection and leave a prescription for you. I want you to spend the rest of the day in bed, and I am telling your staff that it's necessary. And if you have some idea about working in bed, let me remind you that passing a cold to the people working for you is not the best idea just now." He was putting his file aside as he said this. "Be glad that Muriel called me. You have to be in presentable shape tomorrow. I understand that. But without this now, you wouldn't have been able to get out of bed." He began to scribble on a prescription pad as he went on. "I don't want to hear any objections. You want to argue with me, you can do that after you're back on your feet good and proper."

"But . . ." Jennifer began.

"I don't want to hear it. Take these. And wait a moment until my nurse has your injection ready. It's antibiotics and a hefty dose of vitamins. I'm also giving you a mild tranquilizer, and I want you to take that as soon as you've had a light meal. No more excitement for you until tomorrow, or I won't be responsible for it." He handed her the prescription.

Jennifer took the proffered sheet of paper. "There's a pharmacy in the next building. They'll fill it quickly. And then get home with you. I've got a woman in labor waiting for me, or I would stick around to see that you do this, but babies don't wait. When Betty comes in, have your sleeve up and don't give her a hard time." He was out of his chair and pulling on a jacket. "I got an invitation to the opening, by the way, and I said I'd attend, but late. If I see you looking haggard then, you'll hear about it." He gave her a sudden wink and went to the door. "Chin up. There's nothing really wrong with you but exhaustion, and that's curable."

"Thanks," Jennifer said forlornly.

Dr. Robb's smile was irresistible, and he waved breezily as he went out the door.

"Is he always like that?" Jennifer asked the nurse when she came in five minutes later.

"Never seen him when he wasn't," she said. "Ready for the shot? And you've got the prescription."

By the time Jennifer got home, she was feeling slightly disoriented, but the worry that had taken possession of her was reduced, and for once she went meekly to bed while the sun was up, allowed Drew to fuss over her, and welcomed the sleep that claimed her quickly. Her aching head felt as if it had floated free of her body, and that alone soothed her until there was a light shaking of her shoulder and she looked up into Drew's freshly-shaven face and heard him say, "Time for breakfast."

At quarter to ten, Gregory Lennard arrived with his staff and crew. Jennifer was able to meet them as they came into the outer lobby, her smile firmly in place and the worst ravages of her appearance skillfully concealed with unobtrusive makeup.

Gregory Lennard was in the forefront of his entourage, a tall, handsome man with glossy brown hair and deep green eyes. He was dressed in what an expensive men's magazine might call country casual—a light-weight suit, ascot under a fine linen shirt, and loafers. He beamed at Jennifer. "You're Jennifer Wystan, aren't you? I'm Gregory Lennard. Jerry there told me all about you."

"Hi, Jennifer," Jerry Baxter said from his position in Gregory's ranks.

"Hello, Jerry. Good morning, Mr. Lennard. If you'll come with me, we'll get you checked in to your cottages." She led them toward the registration desk. "This is Mr. Lennard, Dean. You have cards for him and his staff, don't you?"

Dean swallowed hard and recovered himself. "Of course. We need names and addresses, and the license numbers of the cars, and we can get you settled in no time."

"Fine, fine," Gregory said, exuding goodwill and charm.

As Dean got busy with the registration cards, Jennifer excused herself long enough to follow Dr. Robb's instructions, and took one of the prescribed pills before getting caught up in her day.

For the next three hours, she gave Gregory a guided tour in much the same way she had given one to Jerry, but this time there were cameras and lights following her, and when she showed him the photographs of the improvements being made, there was more commotion as displays were arranged and adjustments made. Finally, Gregory pronounced himself pleased with the first stages and decided to take a lunch break followed by a nap so that he would be fresh for the opening festivities.

Jennifer would have liked to follow his example, but both Muriel and Drew were in urgent need of her, and so she wished the newsman and his staff a pleasant break, suggested they try the pool, and went off to her duties.

Between setting up the full buffet, arranging for the hot dishes which would be served later, and establishing the serving line, Jennifer did not get to see Muriel for more than an hour, and by that time the accountant was feeling harried. "We've had calls all morning. Sandra has taken as many as she can, and I've tried to handle the rest, but we're still way behind. Why is it that everyone waits until the last minute to phone in, or to ask questions?" Muriel handed over a stack of notes. "These are the last acceptances, and you can see there are a lot of them. We'll have at least sixty more than we'd thought."

"Sixty!" Jennifer cried in dismay. "Have you warned Drew?"

"Oh, yes, more than an hour ago. He had a few choice words to offer on the matter, and then he said that he had to make a few calls." Muriel looked at her records. "Oh, the delivery from Benedetto got here an hour ago and is being decanted now; it will be set out as soon as Mike is satisfied with it." Mike was the wine-steward, an amiable Dutchman with a wide smile and a passion for wines.

"I'll go check on him." Jennifer started to rise. "Anything else?"

"Dr. Robb called to remind you to continue your medication. He claims that he'll know if you stop taking it." Muriel smiled a bit. "Have you taken it?"

"Not the noon dose, no. How is Caroline holding up, by the way?" She had not spoken to the housekeeper since yesterday, and was worried that there might be some difficulty there she had not discussed with the woman.

"She's doing fine. You're the one who has to watch out for now. Why don't you go get changed? You've got a couple of hours, but you don't want to be away at the last minute if guests start arriving a bit early, which is possible." Muriel looked down at her neat pantsuit. "I've got something a bit fancier for myself, as well. That way I won't be expected to curtsy." She made a motion as the phone rang. "White

Elephant, Mrs. Wrather speaking. Just a moment." She held out the receiver. "For you. The local paper."

"Okay." Jennifer took the phone. "This is Jennifer Wystan. May I help you?"

There was little more than half an hour to spare when Jennifer at last broke away from the preparations and hurried up to her cupola to change. She had wolfed down a bowl of soup somewhere in the confusion and had taken the medication Dr. Robb had prescribed, but her head was still whirling, more from excitement and anticipation than the cold she could still feel when she permitted herself to notice it. She hurried into the shower, and was in and out in less than three minutes. She forced herself to take particular care with her makeup and hair, knowing that both would have to last most of the evening and night.

She had chosen a beautiful silk dress with a sheer paisley pattern, which she wore over a slip of thick Belgian lace. A necklace of rose quartz beads with an amethyst pendant was her only jewelry, but she knew it was a fine piece and properly elegant. On occasions like these, when she knew she would be on her feet for hours, she wore support pantyhose, the sheerest and silkiest she could find. Wine-colored shoes with moderate heels completed her outfit, and when she rose to look in the mirror, she felt fairly pleased with the results. She made a last adjustment to the clip that held back her hair, and then dusted a bit more color into her cheeks before going down to the main floor to greet her arriving guests.

Gregory Lennard was already setting up on the porch. He, too, had changed, this time into a beautifully-cut tuxedo which he wore with a silk cummerbund and ruffled shirt. His crew looked very much the way they had that morning. "Ms. Wystan. You look lovely."

"Thank you," she said with her most polite smile. "So do you."

"This is a classy event, so I've decided to be classy." He smiled at his staff and looked around the lobby. "We'll set up here and get shots of all the guests arriving, which we can edit for the Sunday evening show, where we can give you more time." He nodded to the others. "How does that sound?"

"Good," said one or two of the staff.

Jennifer could not help but ask, "More time? What does that mean? How much time will we have?"

"Oh, six, seven minutes. A good slice," Gregory said in his most off-hand way. "On the evening show, we couldn't give you more than two minutes. This way, we can expand the story." He beamed at her, and Jennifer made an inane remark about how lucky she was before a signal from the bell captain caught her attention and she excused herself to attend to the newest arrivals.

Two minutes! she thought to herself as she went through the automatic rituals of receiving guests. But because it's the weekend, they might get six or seven minutes. She felt oddly outraged, though she knew she was fortunate. Grimly, she was aware that the length of the segment would depend partly on the number of well-known people who showed up for the opening. Was it worth it, she asked herself, having the television crew here, with the disruption and fuss? She was certain that commercially it was, but at the moment she resented the intrusion. Then she saw Henry Fisher's Granada pull up, and her spirits began to lift.

"You're looking well," said her attorney as he got out of his car and relinquished the keys to the parking valet.

"Thank you, Henry. So are you." She came down the steps to meet him, and stood while he introduced her to his guests. "You know Melinda, but I don't think you've met the Winnstons. Elaine and Bradley. This is Jennifer Wystan."

"It's a pleasure to meet you," Jennifer said, thinking that she would say that a great many more times before the evening was over.

The Winnstons murmured something to her and Elaine expostulated on the fine job of refurbishing Jennifer had done. Then they were gone into the hotel and another group of guests were coming up the steps.

"You've taken the medication I gave you?" Dr. Robb asked as he arrived an hour later.

"Not this evening's, but yes, the earlier ones. Thank you. I do feel much better." She had greeted more than fifty guests, but the greatest number had not yet arrived. "I thought you said you'd be here late."

"This *is* late. And I won't be able to stay too long. I just wanted to look in on you and see this place everyone's been talking about." He ran his hand through his blond thatch again. "You're going to have your hands full. Come and see me again next week when the worst of this has blown over." He went on through the lobby toward the bar.

Jennifer was greeting the next guest when a tall, statuesque woman in a gorgeous peach-colored cocktail dress swept in. "Gregory! How wonderful to see you!" she called out.

Gregory had been interviewing the oldest son of the local lumber baron, and frowned when he looked up. This was banished at once by an expansive grin. "Helene! Don't you look marvelous!"

Most of those guests who were in the inner and outer lobbies turned to stare at the newcomer, and Jennifer had to resist the urge to ask someone who she was. She did not want to walk up to the woman and introduce herself when she so clearly felt completely at home.

The woman looked around, and after a moment, she spotted Jennifer. "You must be Jennifer Wystan!" she cried out. "You look *so* much like your uncle."

Her face ached from smiling, but Jennifer managed to broaden the one she wore. "Yes, everyone in the family says so," she agreed.

"I'm delighted to meet you. I'm Helene McClennan. I can't tell you how excited I am about you reopening the Empress. Everyone's been talking about it for weeks." She came over to Jennifer, exuding friendship and Shalimar. "Gracious, you're so *young*."

If there was one thing Jennifer loathed, it was being reminded of her age. She looked at the other woman. "Not as young as Uncle Samuel was when he took over the Empress. I'm twenty-eight and he was twenty-five."

Helene laughed as if Jennifer had said something very witty. "You're very much like him. It's just wonderful you could do so much work here." She gave an expansive gesture to the lobby. "Magnificent. I can't tell you how impressed I am."

"Thank you very much," Jennifer said, wishing that someone else would arrive and give her an excuse to break away from this oppressive woman.

"Oh, we should thank *you* for setting such a fine example of what can be done with these old buildings. Don't you think so, Gregory?" She turned away from Jennifer and bore down on him. "Aren't you impressed?"

"Always, Helene," he declared. "With this place, too." He was glad to join in her laughter as she came within range of his cameras.

Jennifer watched them greet each other again, more effusively, as each jockeyed for center stage. Good manners, Jennifer thought, would give Helene the advantage, but she thought that perhaps the woman could not be entirely wise to treat Gregory that way.

"Penny for your thoughts," said a quiet voice behind her, and she turned to see Ross Benedetto less than a foot behind her.

"I didn't hear you drive up," she said, flushing for no reason.

"That's because I rode over. I figured I'd have an easier time finding a place to put a horse than a car tonight. Also, the horse knows the way home." He smiled at her, and she answered with a genuine grin.

That smile! What was it about that smile? "Your wines are a great hit," she said because she felt suddenly giddy and awkward.

"Of course. They're superior wines. And I know that Mike will treat them properly. You've done quite a job here," he said, with a knowing look at the various decorations and ornaments that had been put in the lobbies.

"We've all worked very hard," she said, and was about to go on to compliment her staff for all they had done when he interrupted her.

"You, Jennifer, if you'll excuse my mentioning it, don't look as well as . . . No, don't worry. You're fine to look at. Makeup perfect, hair beautiful, and that's a wonderful dress. But there's a white line around your mouth, and your eyes aren't as bright as they should be. Is something the matter?" In another setting, he might have touched her, but not here, and not now.

"Oh, I have a touch of a cold. Nothing to worry about. Dr. Robb says I've been working too hard." She was torn between satisfaction that he had observed her so closely and irritation that he should have noticed she was not at her best.

"Sensible man, Sheridan Robb. You listen to him." He gave her a pat on the arm and was conscious of the desire to do more than that.

"I'll try, but you . . ." She was cut off by a sudden joyous shriek from Helene.

"Ross! What a delight!" Helene broke away from Gregory with a blithe gesture and came toward Ross with determination. "I haven't seen you for *weeks,* you wicked man. And no excuses, when you know how things are piling up. You must come to my kick-off dinner. It wouldn't be any fun without you."

Ross relinquished Jennifer with a reluctant smile. "Hello,

Helene. So you're going to become a state senator and take over Sacramento, are you?"

Jennifer did not hear the rest, for there was another arrival, this one the Downs from San Francisco, who had often come to the Savoia and were going to stay for a few days to get more of Drew's good food. When Jennifer had shown them the way to the dining room, she caught a glimpse of Gregory and Ross standing on either side of Helene as she made a statement for the camera about her intention of running for state senate. "Not that it's official yet," she cautioned, "but I'm very encouraged by the support I've had. I'll make up my mind in the next month, and then we'll see what Elwood Roberts has to say."

Both men made approving noises, and Gregory bent to kiss Helene on the cheek in the full glare of the television lights. "You'd certainly make a nicer-to-look-at senator."

"I'd make a better senator in every way." She touched her honey-blonde hair with a flick of her finger. "It's true, unfortunately for this area." Then she laughed again, and put her arm through Ross's. "But I don't want to talk politics tonight. That's for later. Tonight I want to enjoy this beautiful old hotel and see my friends and neighbors. I've put in my work hours for the day."

As she strolled off with Ross, Jennifer watched them with a disappointment that was as startling as it was sudden. Firmly, she told herself that it was the effect of the medication and fatigue that influenced her, that she did not have any reason to care what went on in Ross Benedetto's life. She knew that he could not have lived as a celibate, and she reminded herself forcefully that it was none of her business if he showed an interest in Helene McClennan or anyone else.

"You're Jennifer Wystan, aren't you?" a tall, lean man in a light blue leisure suit said to her as he came through the door. "You've got the look of Old Samuel."

Jennifer was heartily bored with hearing remarks on her resemblance to her uncle, but dutifully she acknowledged this. "Welcome to the White Elephant."

"That's what it is, all right," said the man. "I'm Ted Hatfield, and I'm crashing your party."

"Oh?" Jennifer looked a bit askance. "For any particular reason?"

"Well, I heard this was going to be a real do, so I figured I should be here. And I've wanted to meet you for quite a while." He chuckled. "You might wonder why I haven't come by before now, but the reason is that I've been working on another project and I couldn't get away."

"Another project?" Jennifer echoed, feeling somewhat baffled.

"Oh, I do construction. Land development, that sort of thing. I've been putting in condos over in Napa, but my headquarters are in Rutherford. You'd be surprised the number of people buying condos in this area. It's expanding, and not just because of the wineries. There are a lot of companies moving out of the city, and where they go, their employees go, and they need housing. They need recreation, too. You must be counting on that." He smoothed the polyester lapel of his leisure suit. "A place like this is mighty expensive to keep running, I should think. You ever consider going in for shared use?" He reached into his pocket and pulled out a card. "You might want to think about it. I know people who'd jump at the chance to develop this place. Wouldn't interfere with the hotel, of course, that would be the draw. Fine old spa provides the social activity rooms, and all that kind of thing. You've already got the pool and the hotsprings and the rest of it. Those hotsprings are worth something, as well, what with the interest in geothermal power. You could turn them to real advantage." He held out his hand to her. "Hope you don't mind my introducing myself this way, but I didn't want to pass up such a good chance."

Jennifer stared at the card in her hand. "Thank you, Mr. Hatfield. I'm not interested in doing business with you, but you're more than welcome to enjoy the party, whether or not you got an invitation." She wanted to get away from him, and was pleased to see two old friends from Sacramento come up the steps. "Al! Marcie!" She gave Ted a perfunctory smile. "Excuse me. I must say hello to these people."

"You do that. But don't forget what I told you." He sauntered away, humming softly and rubbing his hands together as he looked around.

After greeting her friends, Jennifer found herself with a few minutes' privacy, and she took advantage of it to duck into the ladies room and take her evening medication. She was beginning to feel tired already, and there were hours more to go before she was through for the night. It would not be wise to drink while on the medication, but she had arranged with Hugo to keep her supplied with iced tea. That way, she could have a glass in her hand without doing any real damage to herself. Once she was back in the lobby, she

discovered that more guests had arrived, and she made
herself smile again as she shook hands with the newcomers.

At eight o'clock the band arrived and began to play in the
Grand Ballroom. A third of the guests went upstairs to dance
and enjoy the second buffet which Drew and his harried staff
had just set out. The crush in the dining room diminished and
the patronage in the bar became somewhat greater.

"I'm going to need a sling for my tootsies all week," Drew
complained as he stopped to talk for a moment with Jennifer.
"I've got a blister on my big toe that's *killing* me. And there
are still the hot foods to go. Oh, for the simple pleasure of
doing dinners." He put his arm around Jennifer's shoulder.
"You're doing great, Jenny. Pay no attention to my complaints; though I *do* have blisters."

"Thanks, Drew," she said wanly, then adjusted her dress
and smile. The sound of Helene's laughter reached her from
the ballroom and she winced.

"That the blond bombshell who traipsed in earlier?" Drew
asked with an arch smile. "Subtlety is not her style, is it?"

Jennifer, who had not been at all pleased to see Ross
dancing with Helene not long ago, gave a little shrug. "She's
well-thought-of, I gather, but no, she is not subtle."

"Her charm is a tad obvious," Drew said, dismissing
Helene. "I hear my friends Eric and Elvira Bush are going to
come up for a visit. You'll like them, and besides, they're
simply *oozing* class and prestige." He looked closely at
Jennifer. "You *sure* you're all right?"

"It's just a cold. I'm fine." She took a deep breath. "We've
got all but two of the rooms full for tonight, and Dean says
that there have been twenty-six reservation cards turned in
this evening. We're doing damned well, if I say so myself."

"Good. Now go back in there and wow them." He patted
her flank and headed off toward the elevator, wishing he
knew what it was that was troubling Jennifer, for it was not
her cold that had made her eyes shine with tears.

With a resigned gesture, Jennifer walked into the ballroom
and made her way from one group of people to the next,
exchanging a word here, a compliment there, being the
gracious hostess she had learned to be while running the
Savoia. It took her more than an hour to complete the circuit,
and when she was finished, she found Helene standing in the
ballroom door, deep in conversation with Henry Fisher and
Wilbur Cory.

"Ms. Wystan . . . Jennifer," she called out suddenly. "Do let me call you Jennifer, and you must call me Helene. Anything else is too stuffy for neighbors, isn't it?"

Jennifer did not quite know what to say to this barrage, but was spared from having to say anything when Gregory Lennard approached the group and took Helene by the arm. "You'll have to forgive me, but I want to find out more about your plans. Strictly off the record, of course, but I don't want to be caught off-guard when you make your announcement."

Helene preened under his attention. "I wouldn't want that. But we were talking and I hate to . . . well, Jennifer, you know how to keep these two gentlemen amused, don't you? How can I resist the media? But I don't want to offend Henry and Wilbur."

"Oh, I know when I'm out-classed," Wilbur said with an indulgent nod. "Go on, Helene. You're itching to have a go at Lennard, anyway. We've got plenty of other times to argue about zoning ordinances, and I won't interfere with your fun." He held a glass in his hand, which appeared to contain scotch. After a long, reflective pull on it, he stared after Helene as she entered the crowd with Gregory.

"They make a handsome couple," Henry said with almost no inflection.

"Yes, they do," Jennifer said equally neutrally.

"She's certainly well-liked." Henry turned to address a further comment to Wilbur, but he had already strolled away toward another group of local officials.

"I don't doubt it." Jennifer made an effort to change the subject. "Are your rooms satisfactory, Henry?"

"They're wonderful. The view is splendid and the restoration is perfect." He saw some people he knew and motioned to them. "I didn't know the Wedicks would be here. I ought to say hello to them." He patted Jennifer on the shoulder and walked away.

By ten o'clock, the first departures had been made, and those who remained settled in for determined partying. Jennifer went to Caroline's room to find out if the housekeeper was getting any complaints. Caroline assured her that all was well, and tranquilly predicted that the opening would be the most successful of any that had been undertaken in the area for a long time.

"You're looking a trifle run-down. Can you take a short break?" Caroline added as Jennifer turned to leave.

"I don't think so. Besides, it's only a cold." The momentary concern of the other woman unnerved Jennifer, and she choked back an irrational impulse to cry. It was the apprehension and excitement, she told herself, and there was no reason to let that throw her.

Back upstairs, she found Hugo arguing with Ted Hatfield, and stepped in to intervene.

"It's just that he won't take a check," Ted complained.

"That's my policy," Jennifer said with as cordial a smile as she could bring herself to give. "We take all major credit cards."

"But that's just it. My wallet was stolen last week and I haven't got replacements for the credit cards yet, and there's a stop on all of them. I'm supposed to get the new cards next week, but that doesn't help me tonight. It's a local bank, and the vice-president of the bank is upstairs. Let me introduce you, and he'll vouch for me. I know you don't want to get stiffed, but I'm in business here, too, and it would be bad for me to stiff you. Or doesn't that make sense to you?" He was a bit flushed, partly with anger and partly with alcohol.

"This is a special evening, Hugo," Jennifer said with a sinking sensation. "We'll allow Mr. Hatfield to pay by check. But in future, Mr. Hatfield, we have to request that you use either credit cards, cash, or arrange to pay by check in advance." Not only did this man crash the party, she thought, but he caused more trouble than the other, legitimate guests.

"What about if I make the check for fifty, and that will cover my drinks and those I might buy for my friends?" Ted said, taking immediate advantage. "That way, if there's extra, Hugo, use it as a tip."

Jennifer was offended by Ted's slick attitude. "I think it would be best for the amount of the drinks, Mr. Hatfield. It makes our bookkeeping easier and saves any future confusion."

"All right, but I've only got five with me in cash to leave for a tip. The waitress and Hugo aren't going to like that." He raised his brows in a conspiratorial way toward Hugo.

"I'm doing well enough tonight," Hugo answered, crossing his heavy arms on his chest. "Leave the five for Andi. If you think you owe me something, come back next weekend and leave it off."

At that moment, Jennifer could have hugged the barrel-chested, middle-aged man beside her. She knew that Hugo was good with drinks and was not easily over-awed by anyone, but he earned her lasting gratitude in these few minutes. "By then, you should have straightened out your credit card trouble, or will have had time to go by the bank for more cash. I know what a problem it is when credit cards are stolen." She smiled once more and said, "You know how it is for a new operation, Mr. Hatfield; we have to be pretty conservative until we're a bit more established."

"Good idea," Ted agreed, to Jennifer's surprise. "Good idea. A sensible attitude."

Jennifer felt more baffled than ever, but she concealed this as best she could. "I'll tag the check for you, Mr. Hatfield, when you're ready to leave, or Hugo can do it."

"I'll take care of it, Mrs. Wystan. You've got your hands full already." There was a touch of grimness about Hugo's mouth as he said this, and Jennifer was confident that the amount would be paid.

"Thank you, Hugo," she said with real warmth. "And I hope this straightens things out to your satisfaction, Mr. Hatfield."

"Fine," was Ted's answer, with an accompanying glare at Hugo.

At midnight there was a special late supper, and the guests who had been dancing attacked it with voracious appetites. Helene was squired down to supper by Ross and Gregory, and she made the most of the attention she received to remind everyone around her that she was going to run for office if she decided it would be beneficial. Jennifer went and took another pill and felt a degree of guilty satisfaction that Dr. Robb was not around to check up on her.

She was just coming down from her quarters when she met Ross standing by the elevator nearest the ballroom.

"I wondered what had happened to you," he said as she stepped out.

"Just taking a break," Jennifer said lightly. "Enjoying yourself, Ross?"

"Pretty much, yes." He fell in beside her, looked at the darkness under her eyes that had been partly eliminated with expert makeup. "Are you all right?"

"Getting tired. It's been a long day in a long week. You know how some weeks go—Monday, Tuesday, Wednesday, Tuesday, Wednesday, Thursday, Wednesday, Thursday, Friday—an old friend of my uncle's used to say that. It's been like that this week. We're somewhere about the third

Wednesday, I think." She attempted to make light of this with a casual shrug, but at the last moment did not chance it. Ross's eyes were too intently upon her for such prevarication.

"Is there anything I can do?" He meant it, and they both knew it.

"You've done a great deal already. Your wine has been wonderful, and sending it over when you did made everything much easier in the kitchen." She hoped that she sounded sincere, but she had been making pointless conversation for so much of the evening that she could no longer tell.

"Drew and I worked that out in advance. When I heard that Greg and crew would be here, I thought we'd better work out our timing." He put his hand on her arm. "You haven't answered my question. Is there anything I can do?"

"No, thanks. Have a good time. That's what this opening is supposed to be about." She hated to admit that her eyes were beginning to feel heavy and that the thought of another two or three hours of this were about as joyous a prospect to her as having her tonsils out.

"I think you need a little respite, Jennifer," Ross said, choosing to ignore her brush-off. "You're worn out. Did you take the medication Sheridan gave you?"

It took Jennifer a moment to realize that Sheridan was Dr. Robb. "Oh, yes. A little late, but I am getting it down. I'm grateful for it, too." Belatedly, she remembered where they were. "We're holding up the elevator. Either you get in or I'll get out."

"I'll get in. And then we'll find a quiet corner somewhere and get you off your feet for a few minutes. It's bad business to have the owner looking half-baked. Don't argue with me, Jennifer," he warned her as he saw her chin come up. "I'm not in the mood for it. Someone has to take you in hand and Drew is up to his ears in work. I know you'd listen to him, but for now, you have to listen to me."

"But, Ross, there are people here . . ." she began.

"Yes, whole bunches of them, and they can manage without you for a little while. Let them entertain each other." He pressed the button for the main floor and for the sake of making conversation said, "When does the band quit?"

"Two o'clock, when the bar closes. We'll be putting them up for the night, in one of the cottages, just down from where Gregory has his staff." The elevator doors opened, and Jennifer hesitated before stepping out. "There are a couple of tables at the end of the porch, outside the smaller meeting room. I doubt anyone's out there right now." She had not intended to make such a suggestion, or so she told herself, but Ross nodded and said, "Now you're being sensible for a change," and asked which door would give them access.

"Second on the right," she said.

"And straight on till morning," he answered, and was delighted at her surprise. "I was a child once, you know, unlikely as it sounds."

"I always liked *Peter Pan* and *Mary Poppins,*" she said with sudden nostalgia. "Uncle Samuel would read them to me, out on the back lawn."

"This is the best setting in the world for that," Ross said at once as he held the door open for her. They crossed the quiet meeting room and fumbled for the latch on the sliding glass doors in the dark.

"I've got it," Ross said, but did not move to open it. One hand was on the latch, and in the dim light from the spill of the ballroom above, he reached out to touch her face. "I've wanted to do that all evening," he confessed, and then cupped her face in both his hands as he kissed her.

Jennifer was at first startled, and then she felt her own need answer his. She put her arms around him, and as his hands dropped away from her face so that he could wrap her in his arms, she let herself enjoy the first giddy stirrings of desire. This was not like the first kiss—now his mouth was firm and insistent, and as her lips parted, his tongue probed her mouth. She had not always liked being kissed so, but now there was an awakening in her, an urgency that had not stirred in her for a long time. She pressed closer to him and took a curious pride as she felt his arousal through their clothes.

"My God," Ross whispered as they broke apart at last. "I knew there was fire in you, but . . ."

"But this is too much?" she finished for him, feeling a rush of shame come over her.

"No." He held her more tightly. "Don't be a goose. I thought you had banked it down so far that I'd never see more than a faint glow from it. If having a cold does this to you, I'll start growing viruses in my winecasks." He kissed her again, not quite as insistently, but with more ardor. His hands moved over her back, pressing her nearer, so that she was as close to him as it was possible without being naked.

His ignited passion surged through him, but he knew he must not be hasty with her, and with an enormous effort of will, he loosened his hold on her. "You're . . ." he hesitated, wanting to find the one right word that would tell her how deep the feelings were she had called forth in him. "You're splendid. No, that's not right." He kissed her again, quickly, almost roughly. "You're magnificent. You're incredible. You're . . ."

He was interrupted by the sound of breaking glass on the front steps, and both of them turned toward the window.

Jennifer's senses were swimming and the slumbering yearnings Ross had awakened brought turmoil to her thoughts, so that it was a moment before she was able to perceive what was happening.

"They're throwing wineglasses off the ballroom balcony," Ross told her when another sound of shattering cut through the night.

"Oh, hell," she said, breaking away from him reluctantly. "I'd better see to it before there's any real damage done." She started across the room, but his voice stopped her.

"Jennifer, this isn't the time, obviously, and it isn't the right place, but this isn't finished between us." He could not tell what her expression was in the dark, but he felt her breathe in sharply and silently.

There was another breaking glass and a peal of laughter, and someone said with fond indulgence, "Helene, stop showing off."

Hearing the name of the overwhelming blonde woman acted as swiftly as smelling salts to clear Jennifer's mind. "I've got to take care of my hotel," she said, and left the room quickly, adjusting her clothing as she went.

"What time did you finally get to bed?" Muriel asked Jennifer when she came heavy-eyed down to the office at nine-thirty the next morning. "I turned out the light at midnight, but that was at home. I hear this went on for hours."

"I saw the last ones off who were going at about three," Jennifer muttered, recalling that one of the last to depart was Ross, astride Nicodemus.

"And what are you doing up now?" Muriel asked.

"I have a hotel and resort to run," Jennifer reminded her wryly.

"It's running," was the older woman's placid remark. "And you're not, by the look of you. Why not take the morning off and do something about that cold? Dr. Robb's already called and said that he would prefer it if you'd stay in bed all day."

"I can't do that," Jennifer protested.

"Sure you can," Muriel told her. "Go on. You look like an old dishrag. Take the good doctor's advice and get rid of the cold. We'll ring your quarters if anything goes wrong. We've got nine people checking out this morning, plus the television crew, who are already gone, and this afternoon and evening, we're expecting eight to come in. That's not too bad, and Dean and I can handle it." She smiled up at Jennifer. "If I walked in here looking the way you do now, you'd send me home, Jennifer."

"All right," she grumbled, but could not disguise her relief. "If there's anything needing my attention, make sure I hear about it at once." It was an effort for her to cross the lobby, for there were several guests there, all wanting to congratulate Jennifer on her highly successful opening. She accepted this with as much grace as she could muster, and was overjoyed to take the elevator back to the third floor and climb the stairs to her private rooms in the cupola.

By the time she was over her cold, more than a week later, Jennifer began to let herself feel optimistic about the White Elephant. There had been spots on television—Gregory Lennard had been as good as his word, though his coverage seemed evenly divided between the White Elephant and Helene McClennan—and a few favorable reports in papers as far away as San Francisco and Sacramento. Reservations continued to come in, and the locals came to the restaurant and bar, which Jennifer knew was a good sign. Drew was pleased with the routine he had established in the kitchen. Aside from a problem with one of the maids, Caroline had her housekeeping staff in excellent order, and restoration of the hotsprings continued without a hitch. If there was one thing to trouble Jennifer, it was her unadmitted and acute disappointment at Ross's continued absence, for he had not returned to the White Elephant since the night of the opening, and Jennifer could not convince herself that it had nothing to do with her.

She very nearly gave way to despair when a letter from Henry Fisher informed her that Mr. Benedetto had been to see him again and was more insistent than ever about the leasing of the land. Why did it have to be the acres that tempted him? she asked herself late one night toward the end of the month. Why couldn't it be her?

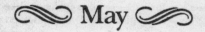 May

Ross faced his grinning younger brother across the dining table of their family home. "Dammit, Ian, I wish you'd leave well enough alone."

"But Fisher has said that he's advised her to lease. Look, the resort is getting guests, sure, but you know how hard it is for the first year, and they still have the trout pond and stables to put in, to say nothing of finishing the restoration of the hotsprings building. She needs the money, and she will go along with the lease if we pressure her." Ian cut himself another slice of ham and spooned Aunt Rosa's wine-and-raisin sauce over it. "It's good acreage, and we can arrange favorable terms. Fisher is certain that Ms. Wystan knows the advantages of such a contract, and it would mean money coming in for the slim months. Summer might be a good time, but the fall and winter are going to be mighty lean for her for the next few years."

"I know that," Ross said. All the flavor had gone out of his meal. He had not intended to argue with Ian, but when Jennifer had been brought up, all his resolutions fled. "I've been trying to get the Geyerville acres under better management these last couple weeks, and that's been bad enough. Whatever made you think that Standing was up to the job?

He's made a complete muddle of it." It was not entirely fair to strike out at Ian this way, but it gave him some satisfaction to be able to call Ian's judgment into question over more matters than Jennifer Wystan's acres.

"All the more reason to keep closer to home," Ian said quietly. "I'm glad that Nana stayed in San Francisco. She can't stand squabbles."

"This isn't a squabble, it's a battle," Ross said, then relented at once. "Sorry, Ian. But you've got to lay off. If you want her cooperation at all, you've got to leave dealing with her to me."

"But you aren't getting anywhere," Ian pointed out. "Aunt Rosa, what's the matter with wanting to get the best possible deal on land? It's not like we're trying to do her out of anything, but Ross acts as if it were his own acres we were trying to take over for some terrible purpose, like putting up condos or a miniature golf course." He chuckled at his own humor.

"Ross lives here," Aunt Rosa said in her sensible, steady way, "and you don't, Ian. He has more time and knowledge invested in his land. If he says that it might be best to leave the bargaining to him, you'd do well to listen."

"But he'll just have to deal with Henry Fisher in the end, and I'm already on good terms with Fisher. He agrees that this is a sensible way to manage the transaction, so that Ms. Wystan doesn't have anything more on her mind than necessary." Ian flashed a smile across the table at his older brother.

"Ms. Wystan isn't the village idiot," Ross said, and regretted it as he saw Ian's brows shoot up.

"So *that's* it. No wonder you don't want me trespassing. Well, I'm sorry to have intruded on your strategies, brother mine, but I was under the mistaken impression that this was a commercial venture." He laughed, not entirely pleasantly. "If you don't mind, I'll keep in contact with Henry Fisher, because you don't know how your little venture will go, and it would be wise for one of us to remember that this is basically a business arrangement we're trying to make."

Ross sat thunderously silent at his end of the table. "It is *not* what you imply, Ian. I admit to being attracted to Jennifer Wystan, and I'd just as soon not endanger the good feelings she may or may not have toward me, but if I have to put both your demands and the reputation of the family first in everything I do, I might as well install a computer in the office and fill my veins with icewater." He started to get up and then, seeing the tiny, warning shake of his Aunt Rosa's head, thought better of it. "Let me handle this, Ian. I'm not going to compromise the business over this, you can take my word for it."

"Well, you never have before when you were after someone, I'll give you that," Ian allowed. "But you haven't been dealing with next-door neighbors most of the time either."

"You're being nasty, Ian," Aunt Rosa said mildly. "You may think that Ross is wasting an opportunity, but it's my opinion—although neither of you has asked for it—that this is one of the best things that has happened to Ross in a long time." She met his startled gaze directly. "That's right, Ross. It was one thing when you were spending so much time with Helene—that was understandable, but I was worried for you. This is different. You're actually concerned about Jennifer Wystan, and you haven't shown that degree of interest in another person for too long." She got up. "Now that I've had my say, I'll see to the dessert. And if I come back in here and find you two bickering again, I will empty the strawberries into your laps."

When Aunt Rosa had left the room, Ross gave Ian a sheepish smile. "She means it about the strawberries."

"Yeah. I know."

Muriel had changed out of her jogging clothes, but her hair was still a bit wet. She came into the reception office with quick steps and smiled at Jennifer apologetically. "Sorry, Jennifer. I was out on the trout pond road, and turned my ankle. It was a stupid thing to do. I know that they're working on it, and I wasn't looking for things in the road, which I should have been doing." She sat down at her desk. "I'll stay after tonight, to make up the time."

Jennifer smiled a bit sadly. "It isn't necessary. I wish we had enough work to justify my asking you to do that. Take the time now and hope that we'll need the extra hours later on."

"Don't get down," Muriel said cheerfully. "We've been open less than a month and we're running about half-full. That's better than a lot of resorts do after years and years in business." She took a stack of daily charge sheets and glanced over them. "Who're the couple in 306 who use room service for everything? Newlyweds?"

"I don't think so," Jennifer said, glad for the distraction. "They don't behave like it. And they don't look very much like it. I think they're just unwinding."

"Let's not discourage them. The extra charges add up nicely," Muriel observed.

"We've got three new parties arriving tonight," Dean called out by way of encouragement. "Two for three and four days, one for a week. That's pretty good."

"Yes, pretty good," Jennifer said automatically. Her mind was not entirely on what Dean was saying to her. "What about Eric Bush? When is he coming in?"

"Day after tomorrow. Have you had the ballroom piano tuned yet?" Dean was smirking now, overjoyed at the thought of such a celebrity.

"The tuner is coming tomorrow afternoon. Have him do all three pianos while he's at it, but the grand is the one that will need the closest attention. We'll want him back twice while Mr. Bush is here, so that the tuning doesn't slip. I've already informed him why he's needed, so there shouldn't be any trouble with availability." She nodded to Dean and went off to the kitchen.

Drew was waiting for her, annoyance causing his pleasant features to look older and more unapproachable. "About time."

"You're mad at me, too?" Jennifer asked, a bit surprised.

"No, at David and Gary. They've screwed up the veggie order again, and we're still trying to get it fixed. I was going to offer a wilted spinach salad tonight, but I don't have enough to meet a reasonable demand, so I'll have to use it as a side-dish instead, and God alone knows what I'll do for a salad. Probably cucumbers, beets and sweet onions with dill and rosemary, but that is *so* dull."

"Is that the main problem?" Jennifer asked with some dread. "Or is there something else I don't know about?"

"No, that's it. You know I tend to get over excited about things like this. On the whole, we're doing as well as can be expected," Drew admitted. "If anything else goes wrong with ordering food, I might change my mind, but the freezer is well-stocked, and if we have to serve frozen food, at least there's enough of it. I want to do a special dinner in a month or so. Is there an occasion we can take advantage of coming up? A birthday or something?" His eyes grew bright and he became more animated.

"I'll think it over. Those shindigs cost a pretty penny, and at the moment I have to keep my eyes on the pennies, at least until the trout pond is stocked and paid for." She felt the heaviness return to her once again, and the relief of a few minutes ago faded.

"Worried, Jenny?" Drew asked.

"Sure. So are you, or you wouldn't be snapping at your staff. It's touch and go for at least a year, you know it and I know it. So far there's enough in the trust to maintain us, but we're not bankrolled indefinitely." She clutched her purse more tightly.

"You remember what I told you about . . . my friend. The offer's still there." He gave an odd smile, a softer one than Jennifer usually saw on his features. "He won't turn me down, or you. He's not like that."

Jennifer sighed heavily, putting one hand to her forehead. "It's not that I doubt you, Drew. I don't. But I don't want to be beholden to anyone right now. I am to you, but that's a special case. I'd rather take the offer from Ross for the lease than get involved in . . . oh, I don't know, obligations of so personal a nature." She rubbed her hands together nervously. "I don't dare cut back, but hiring quality help is more expensive than I thought it would be, and . . ."

Drew turned to her with a wicked chuckle. "I've just thought of something, and it might work. Listen to me a bit, okay, boss?" He saw her nod and took that as permission to forge ahead. "You need more here in the way of help. Not just serving, but doing chambermaid work and grounds-keeping and all that. I need people I can train, and we've got all kinds of chores that we haven't quite enough staff for. Well, how does this sound? We can offer jobs through the local high school and community college that provide not only training, but credit for minimum-wage pay. That means, though, that the kids coming in will have to learn to do *all* the jobs—kitchen, chamber, bar, grounds, desk work, billing, lifeguard, guide, all of it. Let me put together a program we can offer, something for the school year and something for summer. That way, we've got ourselves more of the help we need, and at the same time we're insuring that we can *continue* to get that help later on. What do you think?"

"It's a little rough, but you might have something there. Provided that the county doesn't decide it's a ripoff," she ended darkly.

"But how could it?" Drew protested. "Look, we offer the training, real training, with classes as well as on-the-job, lab-type experience, we do complete evaluations and skill development. If I find a good cook in that lot, you know I'm going to take him or her under my wing. Same thing with those doing other work. A kid going out looking for a job with a full file from us is going to have a better chance to get a decent start than one simply walking in the front door and hoping for the best. We can start with a dozen, say, and then increase if it looks like a good idea."

"And who is going to run these classes?" Jennifer asked, interested in spite of herself.

"You, me, Muriel, Dean, anyone who's in a position to teach. Hugo would do a good class if we could be allowed to teach minors bartending." He stifled a laugh. "We'll make sure we get the highly-motivated ones, like Ben, and give them a great deal of attention."

"It might be more trouble than it's worth," Jennifer said cautiously, thinking that having a hotel partly staffed by teenagers could be hazardous.

"Could be, but maybe not. If we get kids who are thinking about work, they'll want to know what we can teach, especially if they want to move up in the world, and you can bet that some of them do. Ben hasn't said anything to me, but I'll wager a pound of truffles that he doesn't intend to remain here the rest of his life. He can't be the only one, can he?" He clapped his hands together, pleased with the idea. "You know, if we do this right, we can get some very favorable publicity out of it. Let me have a couple of days to play around with it, Jenny, and I'll work out the details."

"Okay," Jennifer said. "But I'll have to check it out with Henry Fisher before we do anything final. You're right, though; it could work." She picked up her purse. "Is that all?"

Drew gave Jennifer a quick, impulsive hug. "Don't worry, boss. We're going to come through this just fine. In a year, you'll wonder what the fuss was all about."

Jennifer recalled that Drew had said something very like that to her fourteen months ago, at the time of her divorce. He had been right then, though she could still feel the dull, despairing ache under her ribs when she thought of it. But the anguish had retreated and was fairly tolerable now. So she regarded Drew without flinching. "I'm glad you're confident. Rub some off on me when you need to, will you?"

"Any time, boss." He grinned at her. "And I'll put that program together so that the schools will greet it with hosannas and laurel wreaths. That's a culturally-mixed metaphor, but you know what I mean." He pointed at the door. "You've got somewhere to go, so you might as well get going."

"Glad to," Jennifer said with a notable lack of enthusiasm. "Wilbur Cory and then Helene McClennan."

"What a charming combination," Drew said sympathetically. "Good luck, Jenny."

"Thanks." She shut the door behind her and went out the lower basement door toward the staff parking lot where her Datsun waited.

Two days later, Ted Hatfield showed up, this time in a sea-green leisure suit. He strolled into the lobby and asked at once for Jennifer. "She knows who I am. I met her at the opening."

Sandra gave him that swift, appraising look that is common among hotel staffs the world over, and decided that she was not overly impressed with what she saw. "I'll have to send word to Ms. Wystan," she said with great civility. "She's not in her office at the moment." Sandra knew very well that Jennifer was out at the trout pond, checking the drainage with one of the inspectors from the county planning office, but she was not going to admit this to her visitor.

"Well, I can't stick around just now. Why don't you tell her that I'll be back by about six and we can have a drink together? I've got a proposition for her, and I know she'll want to see me." He flashed a wide, meaningless smile at Sandra and went back to the elevator.

When Jennifer came in two hours later, she took the news of her impending meeting with some annoyance. "It's land again, I know it. When did Hatfield say he'd be here again?"

"About six." Sandra shook her head. "He's that developer, isn't he? Muriel told me about him. What are you going to say to him?"

"Get lost. As politely as I can." She grimaced. "Sorry, Sandra. I shouldn't talk this way, but after dealing with that self-important toad of an inspector for most of the afternoon, I think I'd take pot-shots at my own mother."

"Is he unreasonable?" Sandra asked, recalling the portly, autocratic figure of the inspector she had glimpsed earlier that day.

"Yes, and a great many other things, as well." She untied

the scarf that was holding her hair back. "Well, I'd better get into something more managerial than this if I'm going to have to be pleasant to Mr. Hatfield in . . . what? forty minutes."

"There's a call from Henry Fisher, too. He asked you to call back tomorrow before eleven." Sandra handed the slip to Jennifer.

"I'll do that. Who's handling the desk tonight, do you remember?" She had the list in her office, but she wanted first to go to her rooms in the cupola.

"Ivy. Do you want me to tell her something?"

"Just warn her that Hatfield's coming. You're doing a good job, Sandra, and try not to worry too much if I snap from time to time. It's no reflection on you."

"Thanks, Mrs. Wystan. I wasn't too concerned."

As she changed, Jennifer wondered again why she was able to handle her complex professional life with some degree of competence while her personal life was so chaotic. Whether her business succeeded or failed, she knew that she was doing as good a job as anyone, and there was some consolation in that. But her personal life! She paused in pulling on the light-weight plaid wool skirt and sighed. Her personal life dismayed her. She was not yet thirty, her marriage had ended in anger and bitterness. Would she have to spend the rest of her life alone? There was the resort, and she was grateful for and enjoyed the work it provided, but what else would fill the years to come? This last question was so depressing that she banished it from her mind and turned her attention to choosing a blouse that matched the skirt. She noticed as she did up the buttons that her hands were shaking slightly, and she reproved herself for this, but the shaking did not stop.

By the time she came down to the lobby, she had better control of herself, and was able to face Ted with a degree of good humor. The man was irritating, but he was also strangely absurd, and her humor armed her against him.

"Well, you're looking prosperous," he said to her, taking in the skirt and silk blouse. "Elegant, too."

"The White Elephant demands it," she said coolly, and permitted him to escort her to the bar.

"What do you want to drink?" Ted asked grandly, fully anticipating what came next.

"That's kind of you, but let me treat you. After all, this is my hotel." She hated being manipulated in this way, but she resigned herself to accepting the man's self-serving behavior. "What are you drinking?"

"Bourbon and seven," he said promptly, then went on. "It's real nice of you to do this. I'm flattered."

"Thank you," Jennifer responded obliquely. "What was it you wanted to see me about, Mr. Hatfield?"

"About the same thing we discussed earlier. You know, condos. That's my business, putting up developments. You've got one of the most perfect places around here, and there's a lot I can do for you." He leaned forward, his arms braced on the table. His face was not easily read in the muted light of the bar, but Jennifer continued to watch him, hoping to learn something from what she saw there.

"For instance, Mr. Hatfield?" There was not a great deal of encouragement in her tone, but she was not too off-putting, either.

"First off, a place like this deserves to be special, real exclusive. I don't know what else to say that would explain it any better. When I think of how this place could be developed, I know that we could have the hottest spot in the entire Napa/Sonoma area." His drink arrived and he gave the waitress an appreciative wink before he sipped it.

"Mr. Hatfield, the White Elephant is a resort, not a development. I don't intend to do anything with it other than what I am doing right now." Jennifer took the sherry which Hugo had sent over to her, but she did not drink immediately.

"Well, that wouldn't have to change too much. Look, we're talking about a lot of money here, not just a couple hundred thousand, but millions. There's no reason you couldn't turn that kind of a profit, and then you could open up any kind of place you wanted, almost anywhere. You wouldn't have any money worries, either. You'd be bankrolled from the start." He had finished almost half the drink, sipping between sentences as he tried to get closer to Jennifer as a way to convince her. "Let me see if I can explain it another way. You've got the knack of running one of these things, but you're strapped for cash, and that makes for trouble, doesn't it? Well, now you can get around that by selling this place and using the profits from it to get another one going, on the terms you'd like. Sure, there's sentimental value here, but this is business, and that means that we've got to watch out for the realities of the situation. You've got a rough road ahead if you don't get more money behind you, no matter what else happens. But you don't have to do it that way. Hell, we could work it out so that there was a resort section to the development, hotel, meeting rooms, restaurants, a mall, maybe, with shops, and could be we could tie in the wineries on this one. You'd be set up for life, and . . ."

Jennifer had listened with growing alarm. "Mr. Hatfield, I don't know if I can find a way to tell you this that you'll understand, but let me make it clear to you. I intend to run this resort. This one, not some other. This is my legacy from my uncle, and I want to continue the tradition within the family. I appreciate your offer, but I don't care to pursue the matter." She was about to rise when the tense smile on Ted's face stopped her.

"You say that now, because you think you can last out the year. Well, come fall, you'll see it differently. I'm not unreasonable. I won't take advantage of you then, no matter how broke you are. But you know that eventually you'll have to give this place up. These antiques are through! White Elephant! Damn straight!" He downed the last of his drink all at once. "You're playing at being a hotel owner, but the thrill won't last, and then you'll see what the real world is like. And when you do, you'll come around to my way of thinking so fast that you won't be able to wait to get your signature on a contract. I'll wait a bit, but don't think I can be patient forever. You think it over. You'll find out I'm right, in time." He signaled for another drink, and Jennifer did not countermand his order. "You'll see how it is when things get tight."

"Mr. Hatfield, I know how it is when things get tight. I was in the restaurant business for quite some time, and I've seen it. My financing here is not your concern. For the rest of it, be sure I will remember everything you've said. More to the point, I want no part of it." She did her best to put a little cordiality into her voice. "You're welcome to come here, but let me warn you, my answer is no, and will continue to be no. Even if the hotel should fail, I don't want to see this land subjected to the kind of treatment you've outlined. I don't mean to offend you by saying this, but it's precisely the sort of thing I want most to avoid. Enjoy your drink." She picked up her sherry and walked over to the bar. She could feel tears in her eyes, but how much was anger and how much worry, she did not know.

"Trouble, Ms. Wystan?" Hugo asked as he saw her take the farthest seat.

"Not exactly." She put her hand to her eyes.

"Whatever you say, Ms. Wystan. But we'll make sure that fella gets the treatment he earns for himself. How's that?"

Hugo nodded toward the waitress. "Lenore knows what she's doing. She'll make sure he doesn't try anything out of line."

"Don't make an issue of it," Jennifer said quickly. "Four drinks and a few kind words ought to be enough for Mr. Hatfield."

"You sound as if you're trying to convince yourself," Hugo said kindly. "Don't worry. We'll keep an eye on him for you."

"Thanks." Jennifer got up from the barstool. She had not quite finished her sherry, but she turned and left the bar, thinking that for once she might leave the hotel although it was nearing the dinner hour, and walk a bit. She did not want to take the chance of encountering Hatfield again for fear of arguing with him.

She was on the path to the trout pond when she came across a number of tools lying in the way, and remembered Muriel's mishap on the jogging rounds. Jennifer glared down at the trowels and shovels and considered calling the company doing the work that evening to complain. As she gathered up the tools and moved them to the side of the path, she shook her head in silent disapproval. She was glad that she had discovered this disorder instead of one of the guests. She had just finished her work when she heard the plop of hooves behind her.

"Everything okay?" Ross's voice asked.

Jennifer turned to see him astride Nicodemus. "It is now," she said rather pointedly. "What are you doing here?" It was not the most gracious of questions, but she had not had time to think of a more courteous inquiry.

"Taking a shortcut back to my place. I've been at the supervisors' hearings." He dismounted and brought the reins over Nicodemus' head. "It's the new codes again. You ought to be following that. It could affect you."

"So I understand. It isn't easy for me to get away during the day." This reminder added sharpness to her underlying worry. "How strict do you think they'll be?"

"Pretty strict, but there should be reasonable time to comply." He could see that she was not paying him a great deal of attention, and asked, "Is anything wrong?"

"Yes and no," she answered. "Some of it is megrims, but the rest . . . We all have periods of doubt, I guess, and this is one of mine."

"What happened?" He stopped walking and looked directly at her. "You can tell me, Jennifer. You might not believe that, but you can."

To her astonishment, she realized that she wanted to tell him. "Oh, it's all the little things." Her voice almost broke, and she swallowed hard before going on. "We're having the usual difficulties, but sometimes they're harder to deal with than other times. And Ted Hatfield—I suppose you know him?—came by this evening to talk to me."

"Yes, I know him. What does he want to do, build condos all over your hillsides? He tried to get me to sell him part of my land a couple years back. It took months to convince him I was not going to sell him one inch of Benedetto. He's persistent, I warn you. He's utterly convinced that condos are the future, and he tries to put them up everywhere. To give the devil his due, he has put up a lot of them and they do seem to be commercially successful."

"I don't know how much consolation that is," Jennifer said glumly. "He wants the White Elephant, and kept saying that the money I made from it would let me have any hotel I wanted. But *this* is the hotel I want. This is *my* resort and it's the place I want to run, as it is, not with shopping malls and all the rest of it."

"I know," Ross commiserated. "Benedetto has been here for five generations, longer even than the Empress. My blood curdles at the thought of condominiums where my vines are."

Jennifer nodded in emphatic agreement. "I'd hate that, having your vineyard gone. If that's what Ted Hatfield wants . . ."

"You can keep telling him no. That's what I did, and eventually he let it drop, but it took the better part of a year." He was distracted as Nicodemus, hearing an unfamiliar sound in the underbrush, shied, snorting. "Hey, there. Calm down." He patted the horse's neck and made soothing noises until Nicodemus' ears pricked forward again. "Sorry. He gets jumpy sometimes."

"Like all the rest of us," Jennifer said, and they walked on a bit in silence. Jennifer did not feel awkward as she often did when nothing was being said. This was companionable and easy. At last, as they neared the trout pond excavation, she said, "We're supposed to be stocking this for summer. I hope it's finished in time."

"It's nice. Do you have provisions for having the trout cooked?" He came to a halt and stared out across the large, muddy-bottomed hole.

"Naturally. Drew loves inventing new things for fresh fish. My main concern is keeping him from coming up here at night and fishing the place out so he can do trout almondine or pan-fried each lunchtime." She liked his chuckle as much as she liked his smile.

"You're going to have to keep an eye on the place, of course. There are kids in town who might try to get the fish at night, on a dare, and there are other poachers. To say nothing of the natural ones like raccoons and bobcats. You've got a grounds patrol now, don't you?"

"We have an evening one, but it might be wise to get night rounds going as well, once this is open."

"Saves doing things after the fact. That way, too, Ben can let it be known around town so that there is a patrol and can stop some of the trouble before it starts." He saw her concentration. "Ben's a good kid. They listen to him."

"I'm not surprised. He's been working hard, and I think he's interested in what he's learning. That's always encouraging. And it could be that we can work out a work-study program for other kids his age." She said this last tentatively.

"I hear that Drew is working out something like that. Very enterprising of him. And I think it's a good idea, if that means anything." He patted Nicodemus to give himself an excuse to look away from her. If he watched her too closely, he was afraid that the friendly atmosphere they had at last developed would fade and she would retreat behind her polite, reserved façade. He did not want that to happen.

"Well, it's good to know that you're not against it, anyway. I was afraid that there were people here who might think we're taking advantage of school kids." There were pockets in her skirt, and she thrust her hands into them. She also realized that she should have changed to better walking shoes. Her feet were starting to get sore from the two-mile walk on a dirt road in moderate heels.

"Nothing of the sort, not around here. Most of the parents are eager for their kids to show an interest in something other than television and beer. And sex, of course, but they'd worry about that, no matter what." He did not know how to warn her that there might be couples in the summer who would think the grounds of the White Elephant the perfect parking place.

"Hell," Jennifer said amiably. "I worry about that with staff people, sometimes. But I don't like to interfere unless it gets in the way of business. It might be trickier with teenagers, but I doubt it." She walked on a little way, to the end of the trout pond where the spillway had been built. "It's pretty out here at dusk."

"This is a beautiful spot, Jennifer." He wanted to come near her, to take her in his arms again, but he held back. She might be frightened or think he was amusing himself, making a pass because they had said something about sex. Helene was that way, he recalled with a twinge of inner discomfort. Helene had liked to talk suggestively before starting to make love. He had gone along with it while they were having their affair, but it had never caught his fancy much. With Jennifer, he did not know what to do. "I like your outfit, by the way."

"Thanks. It isn't too practical for this walk, I was just thinking. I intended to impress Hatfield with it." She gave a quiet, self-conscious laugh. "I don't look forward to the last half mile back to the hotel."

"No worry. I'll put you up on Nicodemus and we'll get you there in fine shape." Ross was oddly pleased at this opportunity to make a gesture that she could not want to examine as suspiciously as she usually did.

"I'm not exactly dressed for riding, either," she pointed out, but did not want to object any more. The ride was much too welcome an offer for her to question it.

"So you sit sidesaddle. Nicodemus won't mind too much." He hoped this was true. He had never put anyone up on the horse in such a fashion before.

"I hope so," she said dubiously. "I'm not much of a rider, but I guess it's better than blistered feet."

"Very likely," Ross said promptly. "How's everything going for you?"

"Pretty well," she said, and looked away into the darkening evening. "We're not in as bad shape as I was afraid we might be, but it could be a lot better and I wish it were. I suppose that's natural."

"Yes. There are times like that with grapes, too. One year you don't get enough rain and the crop comes in shy, or it comes at the wrong time and the wine is more acidic or doesn't hold enough iron or it turns frosty early and the later harvest is blighted or it stays hot too long . . . oh, there are thousands of things that can go wrong. And each time it goes right, really right, you want to look over your shoulder to find out what disappointment might be following along. We're always watching the weather, as superstitious about it as medieval shepherds, really. We have techniques we can use to handle a lot of the problems, and there are more coming along every day, but vines are strange things. Nothing alive is all that predictable." He laughed suddenly at himself. "I didn't mean to go philosophical on you."

Jennifer was captivated by what he said, and she did not stop him. "I'm flattered you're talking to me this way. I don't know all that much about what you do."

"I don't know that much about what *you* do," he countered at once.

"But you can see what I do," she said, with something very near a giggle.

"You can see what I do, too," Ross told her. "There are vines on the hillside, there are vats in the winery and there are bottles of wine. That's what I do." He smiled at her with real warmth.

"And there is a hotel with people in it. That's what I do." She looked up at him and could not keep from thinking that he was really a good-looking man, and when he was not trying to get something from her—such as a lease on her acres—he was quite charming. It saddened her that she could not have more such times with him.

"What's wrong?" he asked, seeing the melancholy that touched her features.

"Nothing. Just random thoughts." She did her best to put her doubts from her mind. It was nice to talk with him as if they were old friends, having a moment's respite from the business of life.

"Care to tell me?" He could sense her subtle withdrawal and felt helpless. He wanted to recapture their intimacy. "When there are waiters and reservations clerks and guests all around you, you don't have much chance to talk, not really talk. And when I have grapes to look after and a winery to run, most of my conversation is about bottling, vintage, labor disputes and marketing. My Aunt Rosa thinks that I let the business run me far too much. She could be right."

"I'm glad there's a business to run," Jennifer said. "I don't know what I would have done without it. Just thinking about what the last year has been like, if there hadn't been the White Elephant I don't know what I could have done."

"It's impressive," Ross said with true admiration. "Have you named the elephant yet, by the way?"

"No. I'm going to have a suggestion box out for the entire

summer season, and at the end of it, we'll pick one. The winner gets the New Year weekend with us, completely on the house. That gives me a little more time and it means that we can use it for publicity at the slowest time of the year, which can help a lot."

"Sensible. And you're right about the slow time. The papers around here will give you more coverage in winter than in summer." It was almost dark now and he felt the touch of a chill at the end of a warm day. "Do you want to get up? I don't want to get you back to the hotel too late."

Reluctantly, she said, "It would probably be best. It's been fun, talking." As she said this, she had to quell the impulse to hug him. Her past experience said that he might well misinterpret her actions. She did not want this to happen, not after so pleasant an interlude.

"I'm glad we had a little private time," Ross said, and she was startled that his thoughts so closely mirrored her own. "Maybe we can do it again before too much . . ."

"I'd like that," Jennifer said, startled that it was so.

"Then I'll call you." He thought now that it might indeed have been best to hold off coming to see her, because now she was genuinely interested in his company. "Let me help you up onto Nicodemus. He's well-trained, and he won't give you any trouble. If you'll let me give you a leg up."

"What do I do for that?" she asked, trying to remember what she had been taught more than a decade ago when she had taken riding lessons for almost a year.

"I'll make a cup of my hands, you step into it and I'll toss you into the saddle. Nicodemus isn't too tall for you. You're what?—five-seven?—and he's just under sixteen hands. A piece of cake." As he kept up this reassuring blather, he joined his hands and bent so that Jennifer could step into them. When she did, he swung her up with practiced ease and said, "Grab the horn and get yourself set. If you turn so that you're sitting three-quarters forward, you'll balance a little better."

"Fine," she said, trying to make herself comfortable in the strange position in the saddle. At last she found a way to be fairly secure. "I think I'm ready."

"We'll start down the hill. I'm going to keep the reins so that I can lead. You sit up there and look regal." He gave an amused chuckle. "I don't have a suit of armor, but I do have a foil left over from college fencing. Next time I'll bring it along if you'd like."

"You fenced in college?" Jennifer said, favorably impressed in spite of herself.

"Not very well. I was on the second team, and we had a few matches with other colleges and universities, but I never did terribly well. I didn't lose a lot, either, or I wouldn't have been on the team, but I wasn't the kind of fencer who drives hard enough to put my opponent off, so it was only recreation." He had enjoyed the fencing, he thought, and missed those hours spent in the fencing room of the gymnasium. "I took it up because the girl I was dating then did it, and when I saw her in those white fencing togs, I thought it was the greatest looking outfit I'd ever seen for a sport. She had another boyfriend by the end of the semester, but I was hooked on fencing."

"I fenced for a semester, but didn't stick it out. I was in the middle of my junior year." She was not quite certain why she was telling him this, but it was so nice, so ordinary, that she welcomed it.

"What was your major?" He walked more slowly as they came to one of two small groves of redwoods. It was dark under the trees and he was not familiar with the path.

"I wanted to do architecture, but ended up with commercial art as a compromise. I think I might have switched, had I stayed. What about you?" She could not see him clearly in the night, but had a sense of him, his shoulder not far from the toe of her shoe.

"B.S. in organic chemistry, M.S. in viniculture. Minor in industrial design. Undergraduate work at Stanford, graduate at Davis." He had got used to reciting his academic credentials over the years, so he paid very little attention to them himself. "I didn't like the routine of college, but it paid off."

"Sounds like you were in line from the beginning to run the winery. Didn't that ever bother you?" Jennifer thought that in similar circumstances she would feel stifled by such expectations. As it was, even the minor pressure she had encountered about architecture had seemed intolerable to her.

"Not in the least. No Benedetto has ever been forced into making wines. My brother is in advertising in San Francisco. My nephews are all given plenty of choice as to what they want to do. Matt likes the business and so does Tony, but their mother—that's my sister, Jeanne—wants them to take their time in making up their minds. If I had a couple of kids, it might be different, but since Rosemary died . . ." He always found it difficult to speak of his dead wife.

"You're not ancient. You can still have lots of kids, if that's what you want," Jennifer said with a degree of defensiveness in her voice.

"Not lots of them, I don't think, but two or three, that would be nice. I wouldn't want to try it when I'm too old. I doubt I'd want to have to raise a passel of teenagers when I'm in my sixties, but my Uncle Angelo has done it, so I suppose that I might change my mind." He stopped, seeing the irregular waver of a flashlight down the trail a way. "Is there supposed to be someone out at this hour?"

Jennifer looked up, then said, "It must be Ben. He makes the rounds at sunset and I think the trout pond is the last thing on his route."

As if in confirmation, the young man called out, "Who's there?" His dog barked vigorously.

"It's Jennifer Wystan and Ross Benedetto and a horse," Jennifer called back. "I thought you'd been out already, Ben."

There was audible relief in Ben's voice as he called back, "Mrs. Wystan! Good. I was looking for you. Drew couldn't find you and he's getting worried."

"Your mother hen," Ross said quietly. "We'd be glad of the flashlight, Ben," he called out.

"I haven't been up to the trout pond, Mr. Benedetto." He had come up to them, and his dog was busily sniffing at Nicodemus' hooves.

"But we have. This once you can cut your rounds short," Jennifer told him. "Why are you so late?"

"Nothing major. I found a gap in the fence on the north side, and I wanted to put a couple boards across it. I think it's just local kids using it, but you said that I shouldn't let anything like that slide. I'll tell Julio where it is and he can get to work on it in the morning." Ben directed the flashlight·up the trail and the narrow beam of light picked out the tools Jennifer had stacked at the side of the path. "Nothing much happening around here, I guess."

"I guess," Jennifer echoed, thinking again that it was strange the tools had been scattered in the road. Perhaps, she suggested to herself, if there had been local kids coming through the fence, they might have toyed with the tools. Then something else occurred to her and she asked Ross, "Where did you get through the fence?"

"There's a gate on the north fence. It's an old access road. Samuel used it for a shortcut, and let both my father and me do the same. There's a lock on it, if that's what you're worried about. I've got a key." He glanced toward Ben. "Have you ever checked that gate?"

"I know about it, but I haven't been up there. It's a way beyond the trout pond, and aside from the trail there isn't much up there but trees and a couple of soda springs."

Jennifer had seen the gate three times and had been satisfied that it was properly secure. Now she wondered, "Did Uncle Samuel give the key to anyone else?"

"He said that he had given out one other than ours, but he never mentioned who had it, and I've never known anyone else to use the gate," Ross said. They were within sight of the hotel now, and he felt more than a touch of regret that their friendly, stolen moment had to end so soon.

"Maybe I'd better get down now, Ross," Jennifer said, thinking that this was not an entirely appropriate way to arrive.

"All right." The hotsprings building was not more than a hundred yards ahead and the most distant of the cottages was little more than that. He pulled Nicodemus to a stop and reached up to lift Jennifer down. He had to swallow against the woolly feeling in his throat as he touched her. He caught her just above the waist and brought her to her feet between him and Nicodemus' flank. Her nearness tempted and disturbed him, and he recalled Ian's mocking laughter when they had last talked.

"Thank you," Jennifer murmured self-consciously, not knowing what to say to Ross or how to behave.

"My pleasure," he said, stepping back. "Ben, see that . . . Ms. Wystan gets into the hotel all right, will you?"

"Sure, Mr. Benedetto," the youth said, grinning. "Mr. Usher is sure going to be glad to see her, that's certain."

Now that she was back on the ground, it seemed to Jennifer that reality came back to her in a rush, and she was at once worried and confused. "I'd better find out what's worrying him. Thanks again, Ross. I'd probably have had to soak my feet for the next three days, if you hadn't come along."

"Glad to be of help," he said. "And if I call you in a week or so, do you think you might find a couple spare hours? We wouldn't have to do anything fancy, just both get a break from work."

"That sounds very nice," she said, thinking that there would be no gracious way to refuse him—nor did she want to, really.

Ross got onto Nicodemus and gathered the reins. "Take care, Jennifer," he said, and then clapped his heels to his mount's sides.

As he rode away, Jennifer had the oddest sensation of loss. Then, reprimanding herself for senseless romanticism, she turned and went into the back door of her hotel, picking her way carefully because of the soreness of her feet.

Eric Bush was tall and rangy, nearing sixty with flair. He sat at the grand piano in the ballroom, running through scales and exercises. Jennifer watched him respectfully from the door.

"It's not a bad instrument. For what it is and where, it is quite good." He smiled at his wife who sat beside him in her wheelchair. "I think it will be quite satisfactory. I have played on worse, much worse." He began a gentle Brahms waltz, picking out the lilting melody with the finesse born of long practice. "I won't need the instrument very much, Ms. Wystan. Probably no more than three or four hours a day, since this is a vacation. And as you arranged for the tuner to come while I'm here, I know it will go well." He stopped playing long enough to give Jennifer a careful look. "If there's any difficulty, tell me at once, and I will accommodate you to the best of my ability."

"There is only one party booked in here during your stay, Mr. Bush," Jennifer said hastily, "and they are an evening event with a small rock band, so the piano will be removed from the room and tuned the next morning when it's moved back in." She did not say that she was relying on his fame to work to her advantage for the hotel, though she doubted he was unaware of this.

"Then there is no conflict whatever. How very kind of you." He put his attention on the keys, and while he was engrossed in Brahms, his wife turned and rolled her chair across the room to Jennifer. "Drew said that you were a fine person, which is high praise from him. Eric might not mention how much he values your work on his behalf, and so I'll do it for him."

"Thank you very much," Jennifer said quietly. "It's an honor to have you both here."

"You're more than welcome," was the gracious answer before she turned and wheeled back to her husband's side.

The sound of the piano followed Jennifer downstairs, where she found Dean sitting in respectful silence at the registration desk.

"Sounds so easy when he does it," he remarked to Jennifer as she came up.

"That's forty years of playing you hear making it sound easy," Jennifer said. "Who's coming in today?"

"A Mr. and Mrs. Ashe from Marin County. They're in 214. They both look terribly fit. Mid-forties, prosperous. There have been a couple of calls for you, by the way. A Ted Hatfield called this morning, and Wilbur Cory wants to talk to you about the new ordinances that are being considered by the Board of Supervisors." He handed slips across. "I've been taking the calls while Sandra is at the dentist. She lost a cap on one of her teeth last night."

"Poor kid," Jennifer said with real feeling, remembering the time the same thing had happened to her on a busy night at the Savoia. George had been furious when she had insisted on getting treatment.

"She said she'd be back tomorrow morning. Muriel is doing her best to cover the phones, but she's also working on the billings. We're . . ." He stopped as the phone rang. "White Elephant."

Jennifer left him to deal with his work, and went into the office where she saw Muriel bent over the file of receipts from the day before. "How's it going?"

"Terrible. But at least taxes are out of the way for a while. I hate doing those figures every three months." She looked up. "Bar business is up a little, the restaurant is about the same. We're holding our own, but not too much more. And there's due to be an increase in paper costs next month, so printing will go up, to say nothing of the napkins in the bar." She closed the file.

Jennifer took her seat at her desk. "How would you assess our condition, then?"

"I'm cautiously optimistic," Muriel answered. "We're running a little high on expenses and supplies, but that's to be expected early in the game. If there were a little more money coming in, we wouldn't be quite so guarded, but as things are . . ." She looked down at the ledger.

"Well, we haven't fallen flat on our asses, have we?" Jennifer asked, intending to shock the older woman.

Muriel laughed. "No, we haven't done that." She opened the file. "And we're not going to."

Betty Ashe was dressed more for running than for tennis, but she and her husband, Jim, faced each other across the net, and she was winning their second game of the day. "Faster!" she called out delightedly, and sprang to return the ball. It was warm and windy, spring was ripening around them in the hills, and the slopes were still a soft green instead of the golden-brown they would turn in the summer. The tennis courts, newly resurfaced, were standing ready for use, though only the Ashes had come out to play that morning.

Elvira Bush watched them from the swimming pool, a wistful smile on her pain-sharpened face. She had played a lot of tennis before the ski-lift had snapped a cable and ended all of that. There were others in the swimming pool, and Ben was acting as lifeguard.

"That's the second time you've missed!" Betty caroled as she rushed to continue the volley. Jim chuckled and slammed the ball back toward her.

The accident happened so quickly that almost no one saw it clearly. One moment, Betty was running across the court, yelling at the ball, and the next, she was skidding along the edge of the court, her warm-up suit tearing, and her racket cast away by the impact of her fall.

Jim came around the end of the net at once, calling out to her in distress. At the pool, Elvira shouted for someone to help.

Although Ben knew he was not supposed to leave the swimmers, he hurried to the tennis courts. Two of the swimmers vaulted out of the pool behind Ben and followed him toward the courts.

"One of you!" Ben shouted over his shoulder. "Go into the hotel. Get Mrs. Wystan and tell her what's happened." He was into the court and running up to Betty as he gave the order, wishing now that the poolside telephone had been installed.

"Oh, damn!" Betty said as she tried to roll onto her side.

"What did you do?" Jim repeated for the third time as he knelt down beside his wife and tried to keep her from moving. "Don't get up. You're cut."

"I *know* I'm cut," she shot back. "Everything from my toes to my scalp knows I'm cut. What the hell did I trip on?"

"You didn't trip on anything," Jim said reasonably.

"You bet your life I did," she said through gritted teeth. "Dammit! Somebody get a doctor!"

"I think you'd better do that," Jim said with a cool, meaningful look at Ben.

"We're trying to get one, Mr. Ashe," he said, turning red under the hard stare.

"And soon. My wife has been hurt. She is cut and bleeding." His usually easy-going manner turned steely. "If there is a significant delay, I'll take that into consideration when I decide what is best to do."

Betty swore comprehensively and began to cry. "I hate it when I do this!" she declared between sobs.

Ben was growing more embarrassed and flustered by the moment, and wanted nothing more than to flee. But there was no one else to take charge of the emergency, and he knew that he could not leave the pool area, or the tennis court. He was about to shout for one of the gardeners working on the new lawn being put in for croquet when he saw the lower door open and Jennifer came hurrying out.

"Mr. Morgan told me there was some sort of accident out here," she said as she came up to the court. One quick look had told her that the situation was indeed serious, and she was glad now that she had put in an emergency call to Dr. Robb's office before coming out to the court.

Jennifer came up to Betty Ashe at once and said in as calm a voice as she could manage, "The doctor has been called and he'll be here shortly." She was confident that Dr. Robb would respond quickly. "Since we're a little way from town, it takes a few minutes for help to get here. Is there anything I can do for you?"

"You can find what the hell I tripped on!" Betty said. "I don't want to lie here for the next hour. . . ."

"Tripped?" Jennifer interrupted.

"She says she tripped," Jim said, with no hint of apology. "She's not the sort to think she did when she didn't."

Jennifer felt her whole body go cold. There could easily be a lawsuit, and after that, a loss of insurance, or rates so high that she could not afford to keep the hotel open without charging disastrous rates. "Are you sure?"

"As sure as I can be," Betty said. She was not crying as much now, but her face had taken on the set, white look that was the onset of shock. "There's something under my hip, I tell you, and that's what tripped me."

"Do you want to turn . . ." Jennifer began, then stopped.

"No, you'd better not. Dr. Robb's office said we shouldn't move you at all. He'll be here shortly. They said he wasn't far from here and on his way in. They'd get him on his CB." She felt she was babbling, but she dared not stop. "As soon as he arrives, we'll make sure that everything that's necessary is done for you. He's an excellent doctor."

"Do you mind if I go back to the pool?" Ben asked. "I really ought to be on lifeguard duty there, but when this happened . . ."

"Fine, Ben," Jennifer said gratefully. "You did very well. But you're right. You should be at the pool." She found herself thinking that they needed a second groundsman of some sort to relieve Ben or anyone else, should an emergency arise again. And it would be essential to put in the poolside phone, no matter what problems the phone company encountered. Had there been a poolside phone for Ben to use, he would not have had to ask one of the guests to go find her.

"What if Betty did trip on something?" Jim said distinctly.

"Then we're at fault and we'll have to make proper restitution." Jennifer felt so utterly defeated as she said this that her voice dropped to a near-whisper and she found it hard to meet the man's eyes.

"Well, at least you realize that," he said, reaching down to touch Betty's shoulder with a reassuring gesture.

"I know what my legal responsibilities are," Jennifer said flatly. "And you know that I will do everything that's necessary. I'm deeply and truly sorry that this happened, and I hope that you can believe that."

Jim was about to answer, but Betty said, "I don't think you did anything deliberately. No, Jim, I don't."

"Betty, wait until the doctor gets here, please," Jim said, holding her hand more tightly. "We'll settle this once we know how seriously you've been hurt."

That last phrase rang like a death knell in Jennifer's mind, but she kept up her front of resolute competence. "Good."

Jim was about to say something more when a call came from the kitchen door and Drew hurried out. "Dr. Robb just pulled up in front. Dean's sending him on back."

"Thank goodness," Jennifer said, and got rather unsteadily to her feet.

"Heard there was trouble," Sheridan Robb called as he came in his long-legged stride up the path to the tennis courts. "What is it? Twisted ankle?"

"More than that," Jennifer said reluctantly. "There's an

abrasion and . . ." She did not finish. Dr. Robb brushed past her and looked down at Betty.

"From the look of you, that was quite a tumble." He dropped onto his knee. "You're bleeding, aren't you?"

"Some," she admitted.

"Doctor," Jim said firmly, "I want to know precisely how badly hurt . . ."

"So do I," Dr. Robb interrupted him as he knelt down beside Betty. "Jennifer, go in and call my office. Tell them I'm bringing this patient in for x-rays."

Jennifer, glad for something constructive to do at last, rushed to do as he asked.

Betty returned in state and triumph a little after five, and at six, with her installed once more in her room, Jennifer went up to speak to her.

"Was it negligence on our part?" Jennifer asked when the basic questions had been answered.

"There was a wrench, a little one, lying near the net. It wasn't the kind that the net fittings use—more like something for plumbing. Dr. Robb has it at his office in case there are any more questions. If you want to see it, just call him." She looked down at the ruined warm-up pants. "Jim's getting my robe for me, but I hate to have to change. I'm comfortable in these pants. Oh, well."

"We'll take care of Dr. Robb's charges, of course, and the cost of your room for the length of your visit," Jennifer said.

"Thank you, Ms. Wystan. That's decent of you." She rubbed at her leg. "He gave me one of those painkillers, you know? Only now it's wearing off, and it tingles something awful. I wish it were an itch. Then I could scratch it."

Jim came in from the dressing room, a velour robe of electric green in his hands. "Here you are. Good afternoon, Ms. Wystan."

"I suppose I'll have to put it on." Betty sighed in an exaggerated manner, then turned back to Jennifer. "I know that this is your first month open, and there are going to be problems. From everything I've heard, you're conscientious and serious-minded. I don't know how that wrench got there, but I'm satisfied that it wasn't shoddiness on your part, or on the part of your staff. If there are further complications, I will expect you to pay for them, and if there were serious damage, it might be different, but Dr. Robb assures me that the cuts, though painful, are superficial, and that I should be up in a couple of days. There were only two stitches, and I've had worse than that from cutting myself with a kitchen knife." She held up her hand as Jennifer started to speak. "Also, I don't like to abuse responsible people, particularly those new in business. You're doing a tough job well, and I appreciate that."

"Thank you," Jennifer said, humbled. "I hope this hasn't given you a distaste for the White Elephant, because there is no one I would rather have as a guest here." She got up rather unsteadily, emotion threatening to overcome her. "I'm grateful to you, Mrs. Ashe. I can't say how much."

Jim cleared his throat portentously. "Now, about this robe . . ."

Jennifer left the room as Betty began to pull off her top.

"I heard about your lucky escape," Ted said to Jennifer a few days later when she encountered him outside Wilbur Cory's office.

"Lucky escape?" Jennifer said, not understanding.

"No lawsuit. That was a lucky escape if I ever heard of one." He grinned at her. "You're not in any position to sustain that kind of suit."

"Is anyone?" she asked rather pointedly.

"Well, let's just say that you're more vulnerable than most." He glanced down at his watch. "You've been to see Wilbur?"

"Yes." She had no intention of volunteering any more to this man, and was thinking of a graceful way to leave when he cut into her thoughts.

"What would you do, if you had to pay out that kind of money?"

"I don't know. But I have some errands to attend to. If you'll excuse me . . ." She started away down the hall.

Ted called after her, "If you get tired of taking those risks, remember that my offer is still good."

Jennifer would have liked to turn around and yell at him, for no reason other than the simple release of yelling, but she kept her head high and her eyes straight ahead and ignored Ted Hatfield until she was out in her Datsun, where she could curse to her heart's content.

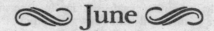

June

Helene McClennan stared around the ballroom critically. "I think it will do if we open up the Silverado Suite as well. That will give everyone a place to talk business if they want to." She grinned over at Jennifer. "This is a much better place than the usual hotel meeting rooms. I think I can get real enthusiasm here, don't you?"

"I hope so," Jennifer said quietly. She had spent the better part of this warm morning with Helene, and was beginning to feel worn out.

"You know, when I left my law practice for commercial real estate, everyone thought I was crazy, but they don't say so now. Now I'm the most forward-thinking woman in northern California." Helene laughed aloud. "There's no reason I can't go as far as I want now. The state senate is just the beginning. Our district senator is not doing his job properly, and everyone knows it. If I show that I can and will do a better job, there'll be support and some changes."

Jennifer had heard the same sort of talk most of the morning and was running out of appropriate replies. She put her hands behind her back and followed Helene around the room a third time. "We can have the buffet set up in the parlor of the Silverado Suite, if you like. That will give you more area for dancing, and will encourage circulation. You'll need two waiters to handle the buffet if you're serving anything hot—which I suggest you do."

"It's more expensive, isn't it?" Helene said cannily.

"Yes. It also is better if you're going to have a gathering of any length. People who have something worth eating don't get quite as drunk and you can do more business over the course of the evening. It's up to you, of course, but considering what you want to accomplish, it might be best . . ." She left the rest unsaid.

"You've got a point. I *don't* want anyone to think of my candidacy announcement as a bash. A great party, yes, but not one of those brawls that happen." She thought over what Jennifer had said. "Okay, we'll do a buffet in the parlor of the Silverado Suite. With something hot. Any suggestions?"

"Naturally," Jennifer said, smiling for the first time. "You'll have to discuss it with Drew, but I think if you have hot chicken, which can be kept warm in serving trays, then beef or ham, whichever you prefer, and something like hot crêpes; four or five kinds of salad, perhaps a cold glazed bass for those who like fish. I know that Drew will give you sensible advice. He wants to have his food appreciated, and he won't recommend dishes that would not go well in such a setting."

"I've heard a lot about Drew Usher this last month, and I had the food at your opening. I'll leave the details up to him, after he and I work out the main things to be served. I'll want a band, too, but nothing too modern or loud. I wish I could get some good Dixieland players up here. *Everyone* likes that, and this is a good place to have it, all period pieces." Helene hummed a little of *The Cascades* and shrugged. "See what I mean? It's contagious. But let me know what you can come up with. And prices. I want this to be grand, but I don't want to break the bank doing it. My campaign is going to be expensive enough."

Jennifer regarded Helene speculatively. "Will you give me some idea about what you're prepared to spend? I won't hold you to it absolutely, but if I have an estimate of the figures involved, it would make it easier for me to plan within those limits."

"I'd rather not go over eight thousand, but if necessary, ten is okay. Do you think that will be enough for the kind of evening I have in mind?" She was dressed in a pin-striped pantsuit with a blouse of frothy lace under it, and she smelled of *Shalimar*. To hear her speak so uncompromisingly and extravagantly was somewhat bewildering, but Jennifer heard her out, doing some arithmetic in her head.

"I think we can bring it in for that. Will you want to reserve other rooms in the hotel for the occasion, or is that going to be left up to individuals?" Jennifer walked over to the small platform provided for bands. "I'm willing to block, say, ten rooms for your guests, so that there will be space for them. If that's satisfactory?"

"It's probably a very good idea. I know that Greg will be back, with part of his crew, but not the whole gang like last time. He'll want to stay over, but he might prefer to come to my place. He wouldn't want the others along, of course, but we can work that out later. I don't know how Ross would feel if I sent a couple people over to his place. He has *tons* of room, but it's been a while since he and I . . . you know. And you never know exactly how old lovers will react when you ask favors." She tossed her blonde hair and smiled. "Have I *seen* the Silverado Suite yet?"

"Yes. That's the one at the end of this wing, that overlooks the trees. Two rooms, a dressing room and a bath." Her thoughts were jumbled, as she heard Helene's words ring in her ears. *I don't know how Ross would feel . . . you never know exactly how old lovers will react when you ask favors.* Jennifer tried to tell herself that she was not truly surprised, and certainly not upset, but she had to bite the insides of her cheeks to keep from making a sound that would give her away—even though she did not know what the sound would be.

Helene was going on, making a sweeping gesture, and Jennifer forced herself to concentrate on what the other woman was saying. ". . . decorations, but so near the Fourth, they ought to lean toward red, white and blue, don't you think?"

"It couldn't hurt," Jennifer said, trying to pay attention to Helene.

"Can I leave that up to you, or should I arrange to have it done?" She was coming back toward Jennifer, a cordial, practiced smile on her face.

"If you will tell us how much you wish to have done and what you want to spend, we can take care of it for you, if that would simplify your plans."

"Sounds wonderful. You're a wonder, Jennifer. I wish it were as easy to deal with all the rest of my associates. I'll

check back with you next week, and you can give me the hard
figures then. In the meantime, I'll start thinking about a guest
list on a scale with the party." Helene strode for the door,
whistling as she went. "Is the bar open yet? I'd like a Bloody
Mary before my next appointment."

Jennifer glanced down at her watch. "It opened twenty
minutes ago." She went to shake Helene's hand and see her
down to the lower floor.

"I'm glad I thought of you. And I will talk with this Drew
Usher of yours. Everyone says he's a genius." She clasped
Jennifer's hand firmly and gave her a bright, direct look.

Jennifer was relieved when Helene relinquished her hand.

"You're lucky to have him in more ways than one." She
motioned to Jennifer, implying a closeness that Jennifer could
not reciprocate. "Women in business, we have to stick
together. It's so easy for things to . . ."

"Go wrong?" Jennifer prompted when Helene broke off.

"Not just that, but it's part of it. Don't you ever lose heart
and want to chuck it all for the lives we were all trained to
live?" As if shamed by this candor, she forced a giggle. "I'm a
fine one to talk, aren't I? Come on, show me where the bar is
and we can have a drink together."

"I'll come down with you, but I've got things to attend to in
the office. Not the least of which is getting figures for you."
Jennifer led the way to the stairs. She put her hand on the
covered bannister. "When I was a kid, these were polished
and I'd slide down them, but the insurance likes it better if
they're a less slippery grip."

Helene nodded to show that she had heard, but her
thoughts were clearly far away. "I think you'd better have
your Drew call me next week, when you've got the figures. I
want to be sure we understand each other perfectly."

"All right." They had reached the registration desk and
Jennifer was secretly relieved to end their difficult conversation. She nodded in the direction of the bar and pointed out
the new sign that had finally arrived, a stained-glass represen-
tation of her White Elephant with its beautiful trappings. *The
Howdah,* it proclaimed.

"Oh, that's very nice," Helene enthused. "Keeping up the
image. That's got class. I saw your stationery the other day,
by the way, and I really like it." She waved as she went off
under the stained-glass display.

"Quite a lady, that one," Dean said from his place at the
registration desk.

"That's one way to describe her," Jennifer said, wishing she could keep from making remarks about Helene. It was unprofessional of her, and she thought it was silly of her to feel such jealousy of the woman.

"She does seem a little rich for the blood," Dean said wistfully. "You know that the Bushes leave today. They asked you to meet them here before they leave."

"I hadn't forgotten," Jennifer said, although she had. "What time do they want to see me?"

"Three-thirty. In the meantime, Drew wants the usual conference with you." Dean looked down. "Kind of slow today."

"Yes," Jennifer said thoughtfully, feeling somewhat troubled. "I'm going down to the kitchen. I'll be back up in fifteen or twenty minutes."

Jennifer paused at the kitchen door, listening for Drew's light, precise voice, but heard only Johnny Chang talking with the two assistants about vegetables. She glanced in, and did not see Drew, and so on impulse went down the hall toward his rooms. She was thinking of the questions he had left for her, and was formulating her answers when the sound of a man's voice stopped her.

"But Elvira would be delighted if you would come back with us," said Eric Bush. "Drew, please consider."

Drew's answer was low and filled with more hurt than Jennifer had ever heard him express. "Eric, I can't. It's one thing being with you occasionally and . . . But I couldn't do that to her. Or to you. Or to me. Don't ask me to be your pet boy, please, please, Eric. It would kill me."

Jennifer stood absolutely still in the hall, afraid to move. This was much too private for her to hear, and any intrusion would be unforgivable. She moved at last back toward the kitchen door, listening to the now-indistinct words that came from behind the closed door. When she got to the kitchen, she stepped inside and went up to Johnny. "Where's your master?" she asked, as if she had not known. "I peeked in here and in the loading bay, and I can't find him."

"I don't know," Johnny said, not overly concerned. "He went out about twenty minutes ago and said he'd be back in time to do the luncheon omelettes. Give him another ten minutes or so."

"He wants to talk to me. Tell him I was here. There are some things I have to attend to upstairs. I'll see him after lunch unless he has to talk to me before then." She wanted to give Drew as much time as possible to compose himself. "Thanks, Johnny."

"Okay, boss, sure." He waved her away and went back to work.

Jennifer was glad for the time this gave her for reflection. She had wanted to know who Drew's adored lover was, but now that she had learned the truth, she felt distressed and awkward with the knowledge. She could not betray by any actions or innuendoes on her part that she had learned so much. Drew, she had learned long since, was acutely sensitive and perceptive: she could not lie to him, or dissemble. She would have to keep herself on guard where that part of his life was concerned, or Drew would be deeply wounded. Jennifer sighed deeply as she returned to her office. She might as well take the time to go over the billings with Muriel now. It would take her mind off her disturbing discovery—and she would be all business by the time she had to speak to Drew after lunch.

By the weekend, Jennifer was feeling more optimistic, for the reservations were coming in with greater frequency, and the stays were in general longer. She sat over coffee with Muriel on Sunday evening, looking over the week's billings and beginning to think that the summer would go better than she had hoped.

"I'm grateful you were willing to come in for these extra hours," she told Muriel. "I wish I could give you a bonus beyond overtime, but you know as well as I do that it isn't possible yet."

"As your employee, I thank you for the gesture; as your accountant, I would scream bloody murder if you tried to give bonuses right now. Overtime is what's required, and that's all I want." She hesitated. "Besides, I'm going to be meeting someone here in half an hour or so. . . ."

"Oh? Who?" Jennifer had not been aware that Muriel had much of a social life. She wondered whether Muriel was meeting a man or a woman or perhaps family members, but could find no diplomatic way to ask more than she had.

"Sheridan Robb," Muriel said, and flushed slightly. "He and I have had a couple meals together. He said that so long as I was going to be here anyway, he thought he'd come out and we could have dinner. . . ." She closed the ledger she had been studying. "So I said fine."

As soon as Jennifer got over her surprise, she nodded her approval. "Very good, Muriel. I'm glad for you." Saying it, she felt a slight twinge of disappointment that she had not been out recently herself. Absurdly, she wanted to blame Ross for this, and immediately reminded herself that it was unreasonable to expect such attention from him. But it was his attention she wanted, and the more fool she, she railed inwardly, for being so unwise in her choice.

"Thank you, though there's nothing much to be glad about yet. In time, perhaps, but for the moment it's a pleasant interlude." She said this firmly, as if he had been pressing the argument privately. "It's early days to be building up hopes."

Jennifer could not help blurting out, "But you are."

Muriel turned away, saying quietly, "I'm trying not to."

This was not a comment Jennifer knew how to respond to, so she held her peace and decided to let the matter take its course, which is what would happen in any case. "Have a nice dinner, then. Ask for Dave's station. He's the best waiter on the Sunday crew and you know he'll take the best care of you. Besides, he has three tables by the back window, and the view is nice, even at night."

"Thank you. I will." Muriel stood up. "Do you mind if I go freshen up?"

"Not at all. In fact, with my blessings." She gave Muriel a victory sign, and as the other woman went out of the office, returned to her work.

But her thoughts strayed. She could not help but wish that she, too, had someone to meet that night for reasons other than business or hotel goodwill. It would be so nice, she told herself, to go upstairs and change into her long silk dress with the graceful, flattering lines and deep neckline, to put on perfume and makeup, her sheerest nylons and her brocade evening shoes, and meet someone in a quiet, elegant place for a long, romantic evening. To her annoyance, the man she pictured was Ross, but she could not block him from her mind. "All right," she said aloud, "if you're going to be that way . . ." What would it be like having such an evening with Ross? It was her fantasy, and she could do with it what she wished. It would not be here, then, but in San Francisco. She would be staying at the St. Francis or the Stanford Court— let's really do this right, she reminded herself—in one of the best suites. They would meet for drinks, he picking her up right on time, driving—what?—a Porsche turbo was okay, or a vintage Bentley—and they would have an hour, just at sunset when the city was at its chiaroscuro best, for cocktails. Then to the Opera House to see the ballet. They would sit—why not go all the way?—in Box L or M or one of the other central ones, and they would see Nureyev in *Don Quixote,* which she loved. Then they would dine, graciously and lingeringly, at D'Oro's, or some place equally good and private, and there would be no question of a closing hour, only their convenience. After that, it would be back up the hill to the hotel where they . . . would they part? Would he kiss her tenderly and help her from the car, then wave and drive away? Is that what she wanted? Or would they return to her suite together, holding hands and laughing in whispers as they rode up in the elevator, to embrace as soon as the door was closed behind them? Try as she would, she could not quite remember how his kisses had felt, and she could not imagine another lover at this stage . . . Lover! Her face reddened and she was glad that no one could see her. But, her visions persisted, his hands would move over her back as they stood together, and then the zipper at the back of her dress would slide down and she would shiver as his fingers began the first caresses to excite her, and he would kiss her in that way that she could not remember. His jacket and tie and shirt would be flung aside as they made their way toward the bedroom. . . .

The shrill sound of the phone was at once welcome and disconcerting. Jennifer did not answer it until the fourth ring, so uncertain was she as to what she should do. When at last she did lift the receiver, her voice sounded odd, even to herself. "White Elephant."

"I'd like to talk to Ms. Wystan, please. This is Henry Fisher."

"Oh, hello, Henry," she said, trying to sound more jaunty.

"Jennifer? I didn't recognize your voice." Some of the formality left his.

"Took a sip of too-hot coffee," she improvised. "You caught me just after."

"You're all right?" He was asking for form's sake, and Jennifer did not bother to answer. "I've spent part of the afternoon talking with Mr. Benedetto. He wants me to tell you that he's still interested in leasing part of your acres. The offer is the same as the one I outlined in my letter, and the terms haven't changed. He's seriously interested, and I do think it is in your best interests to give him your serious attention. You haven't added those acres to your expansion plans, have you?"

"No, Henry, I haven't." Why did she have to be reminded of Ross's business so soon after that ridiculous, impossible, delicious fantasy? It was like a dash of cold water in the face.

"Well, I do think you can stand to part with some of the acreage for a lease if you're not going to include them in the expansion. You're pretty much holding your own, but as you told me yourself, a few setbacks now and you might have need of a better cash flow. I've told Mr. Benedetto that I'd inform you that his interest is still active. And, that aside, I do want to make reservations for myself and my wife for weekend after next, Friday, Saturday and Sunday." He said this last in a jovial way.

"Cottage or room?" Jennifer asked automatically, reaching for a reservation card as she spoke.

"A room would be preferable. On the back side of the hotel, if one's available. We'll arrive about six in the evening. Do you want my American Express card number?" He gave a long chuckle to let her know that he was enjoying the joke, teasing her.

"Oh, I think we can trust you that far," she said, going along with it. "We're running about sixty percent full for the summer, judging from advance registrations, and if we can bring it close to seventy, that will be good for a first year." She hoped that he made a note of this, so that if there were questions later from that damned Mr. Benedetto, Henry would not feel that he had to represent her as being in precarious financial straits.

"That's quite commendable. But I can't help being concerned about you, Jennifer," he said, in one of his rare expressions of affection. "You haven't had the support and assistance you deserve."

With the impressions of her interrupted fantasy still fresh in her mind, Jennifer did not want to get into a discussion of her woman-alone status, and so she said nothing.

Henry coughed and said briskly, "We'll be seeing you shortly then. I'm looking forward to seeing how the trout pond is coming. I expect you to stock a couple fifteen-inchers for me."

Jennifer knew she had been less than polite, but was relieved that Henry changed the subject. "It would be my pleasure. And with a little luck, you'll be able to have a try for one." She finished filling out his reservation card and stuck a VIP tag in the upper righthand corner. "Thanks for calling, Henry."

"You're welcome, Jennifer. Remember that my good wishes are with you." With this assurance, he hung up.

It was more than an hour later when Jennifer finally left the office and took the elevator up to her rooms in the cupola. As she waited for Drew to send up a sandwich, she began to indulge in a bit more optimism than she had permitted herself for several months.

Four nights later, the outermost of the cottages caught fire. Shortly after one in the morning, the alarm was sounded.

Jennifer, who had been lying back reading the latest spy thriller, was roused almost at once by the penetrating emergency beeps from her desk in the room below. She raised herself on one elbow as she listened to the code. "Oh, no!" she gasped as she realized it was the outer cottages, for they were some little distance from the hotel itself and largely hidden by trees. She got out of bed at once, and pulled off her robe and nightgown. There was a pair of jeans in the lower drawer of her dresser, and she pulled these on at once, then found one of her ancient, shapeless sweaters to drag over her head. Before the code had rung a tenth time, she had slipped boots on and was rushing for the stairs, feeling intense relief that the signal would be sounding as persistently in the County Fire Department. There would be help on the way at once.

When she had got to the basement level, Drew was already waiting for her, dressed much the same as she was, and still half-asleep. "I rang Hugo and asked him to clear the bar so that we won't get gawkers and sightseers. What about the other cottages?"

"Well, the signal is from one of the furthest pair." She started out the door. "I don't know if we have to clear the others yet, but if the alarm *just* went off, we have a little time. There's no one in either of them, or the next two pairs down from them. Fred Jenkins was working on them yesterday, in fact." She doubted that she was making much sense, but had to talk, as if speaking would be of help.

"Yeah. I called the Benedetto Winery, too. They've got some equipment of their own, and Ross told me we could use it, if we ever needed it." They were hiking past the swimming pools and going toward the path. Suddenly, Jennifer stopped, listening. "Well, that's something," she sighed, and resumed walking, this time more quickly.

"What?" Drew asked. "What's that sound?"

"The emergency sprinkler system," she said. "I didn't know they'd been connected at those outer cottages yet. Thank goodness for that."

There was a roar of an engine on the service road behind her and a van with Benedetto Winery on the side came racing toward her. "Mrs. Wystan!" shouted the driver of the van.

Jennifer and Drew turned and ran toward the waiting vehicle.

"Mr. Benedetto sent us," said the driver as they scrambled into the van, indicating the three men in the back. "We've got some pressure tanks and regular extinguishers. How many extinguishers do you have in the nearby cottages?"

"Ten," Jennifer answered when she had run a quick mental check. "Two are in the last cottage, so they're probably lost." The van was hurtling up the road now.

"How long has the fire been going?" the driver asked.

"I don't know. The alarm began . . . " Jennifer checked her watch—"eight minutes ago."

"A fire can go a long way in eight minutes. What's in the cottage?" They could see the fire through the trees now, an uneven, sputtering light that trembled beyond the branches.

"Nothing much. The last four here aren't open yet. They're being restored. There isn't much but painting supplies, carpenters' and plasterers' equipment in them. The furniture was supposed to go in next week." A spatter of water flicked across the windshield.

"A sprinkler system?" the driver asked.

"Yes," Jennifer said. "It was put in because of the break on insurance. I'm glad I had it done now."

"I'll bet," said the driver and pulled up beside the cottage nearest to the one that was burning. He leaped out of his side shouting orders, and a few minutes later he and the three men accompanying him were shooting protective foam on the trees near the cottage. Luckily, none of the branches were flaming yet, though one or two were smoking a bit. "That's it. And the ground around the cottage, too. It's got to be contained!"

Jennifer, holding one of the middle-sized extinguishers, turned to Drew, who was also working at spraying the boughs of the trees. "When does the county get here?"

"Don't ask me," he shouted back, but put a degree of

enthusiasm into his words that he did not sound disparaging.
"Soon, I hope. My arms'll give out if I've got to keep this up
much longer."

"Mine, too." The extinguisher was heavy, and holding it to
aim took more strength than Jennifer had anticipated.
"How're the others doing?" The glare from the fire made it
difficult for her to see what the rest were doing.

"Pretty well, I think." Drew turned suddenly. "Here
comes the county, in full sail," he called to Jennifer.

Even as he spoke, two small, blocky fire trucks came
barreling up the road, red lights turning and sirens moaning
down from full scream. The men in the trucks set about their
work at once, pulling out their hoses and starting to pump
from their self-contained water supply. One man, obviously
in charge, came over to Jennifer while he shouted orders.

"You the owner?" He bawled at her, to be heard over the
confusion and noise.

"Yes. I'm Jennifer Wystan," she said, grateful for the
excuse to put the extinguisher down.

"I see Benedetto sent his hands over. Good. How'd this
start?" He pulled her back toward the rear of the second
truck.

"I don't know, Mr. . . ." She was slightly offended by the
tone of his voice, but controlled her reaction. She did not
want to argue with the man.

"Bright. Lieutenant Bright." He shook her hand in a
no-nonsense way. "How did the fire . . . ?"

"Get started? I haven't any idea, Mr. . . . Lieutenant
Bright. I was in my own apartment when the alarm sounded.
So far as I know, there was no one near these cottages. They
aren't quite finished, you know."

"Lucky thing you have those sprinklers. We can save the
shells, anyway. Was there anyone on grounds patrol?" He
had flipped open a small notebook, and as she answered, he
scribbled in it with the stub of a pencil.

"Not since shortly after sundown. I have a patrol around
midnight, but the groundsman doesn't come this far. Well,
these cottages aren't occupied yet, so it's not to be expected
that there would be any reason . . ." She was cut off by the
older man.

"That means anyone could have got back here and not
been discovered." He stared at her. "Right?"

"As far as it goes, yes." She turned as she heard the
throbbing of the fire trucks' pumps decrease. She saw that the

fire was less active, and starting to gutter under the combined onslaught of water from the trucks, the sprinklers and the extinguishers.

"What does that mean?" Bright demanded.

"It means that with painting supplies in the cottage, it's possible that this was an accident. You're talking as if you suspect arson." She put her hands on her hips.

"Well, it could be. A place like this, it's always a consideration."

"How do you mean, a place like this?" Jennifer asked tightly.

"A new place, not quite making it, maybe. This is one way to get insurance money to keep going and you know . . ." He saw her expression and broke off. "Look, I have to examine every possibility, and that *is* a possibility."

"No, it is not," Jennifer said, so angry that she did not care now if the good lieutenant was shocked for the rest of his life. "You're accusing me of starting or causing to be started a fire that would destroy my property and endanger my guests. Do you have any notion of how repugnant that whole notion is to me? Do you?" She saw Drew turn toward her, with a gesture of caution, but she no longer guarded her tongue. "Since you're so quick to think that I'd burn my own property and put the lives of innocent people in danger, what makes you think that I wouldn't have tried it on something bigger, like the hotsprings building? It's larger and more ornate and would present less of a hazard to the rest of the resort. You're not only saying that I'm criminal, but *stupid.*"

"Mrs. Wystan, you can't blame me for . . ." Bright began.

"Yes, I can, and I do. You're being insufferable. Do you say that to every resort and hotel owner in this valley when there's a fire? Or is it just me? And what's this idiocy about insurance? No matter how much they eventually give me, it won't pay for the fine plaster work Fred Jenkins was doing. That isn't the kind of thing I've got covered. So before you decide that you're going to haul me off for breaking the law, check your facts, Lieutenant Bright, and be damned sure you know what you're talking about before you make rash statements!" She stalked away from him toward the Benedetto Winery van.

Lieutenant Bright hurried after her. "Mrs. Wystan, I didn't mean this the way it sounded. If there is arson, we have to investigate. Maybe there are kids coming in, using the empty cottage for their meetings, smoking a little pot and other things, and maybe that's what caused it. They might know that the patrol doesn't get this far, and that would make these outlying buildings doubly attractive. Think about that. Or it could be something else. But I don't want you to think that you were our only consideration for . . ."

"How flattering," Jennifer said at her most icy.

The fire was much lower, crackling and whooshing as the water soaked into it. The three men from the van stood back and began to gather up their extinguishers. The driver had the door open, waiting to pack up the equipment.

"Mrs. Wystan," Lieutenant Bright said doggedly, "I apologize if I insulted you. But if it turns out that this *was* a set fire, I'm going to expect you to apologize to me."

"If it was a set fire," Jennifer said sternly, "I'm going to expect you to help me find out who did it, and how, and why."

Bright stared at her. "That would mean the police would be involved."

"Can you think of a reason they shouldn't be, if this is arson?" Her challenge was so open that Lieutenant Bright felt a bit shocked. Now that her fear was gone, she was able to feel angry—angry at the lieutenant's suspicions, angry at the fire for happening at all, angry at herself for the fear she had felt.

"Hey, lieutenant," one of his men called out, "we've got most of it out. Give us a hand . . ." He gestured and Bright nodded.

"I'll talk to you later, Mrs. Wystan. After we've made sure the fire isn't going to start or spread again. And you can count yourself lucky that this is all that happened. You were smart to put in the sprinklers." He gave her a brief handshake, but Jennifer detained him with one question.

"Lieutenant Bright, assuming that I did want to burn down a cottage, why would I bother to install and connect the sprinklers? The building codes don't require outside sprinklers, and the insurance only recommends them. Think about it, before you answer me." She saw him frown as he walked away, and hoped he'd be up all night with a headache over that one.

Drew was standing near one of the foam-lathered trees, his face sooty and his clothes a mess. "What a night. And I still have to think about doing breakfast."

"Take a nap afterward and let Johnny handle the slack."

She began to feel dispirited almost at once. "You deserve something for all you've done."

"A couple hours extra rest sounds about right," he agreed. "And maybe a couple of days off, mid-week. I'd like to go down to the city for a little change of pace." He rubbed his hands on his jeans, but since there were cinders clinging to both of them, it made little difference.

"I think we can arrange that. But for a lot of the summer, we'll need you here. There's that political reception that Helene McClennan is throwing. That's going to take a lot of time and energy. But if it goes well, it means a boost for the Elephant, and that's going to be necessary if we have to put more money out to get these cottages open for guests. I was going to have another three built, but since this . . ." She sighed. Just when she was becoming confident that she could get through the summer in pretty good form, the fire had to come along.

"It's lousy," Drew said with a nod. The dark circles under his eyes were not entirely from ashes.

"That it is, my friend, that it is," Jennifer said. She saw the Benedetto van start up and motioned to the driver to hold on for a moment. "I'll be back," she said to Drew, then crossed the foam and gravel to where the Benedetto men were getting ready to leave.

"What is it, Mrs. Wystan?" the driver asked.

"I wanted to thank you before you left, that's all. It would have been a great deal worse if you hadn't been here, and I know it. I'll call Mr. Benedetto in the morning to tell him how much your timely arrival meant in saving as much of the cottage as we did. I can't tell you how much I appreciate this, your being here, all you've done."

The driver grinned at her. "Our pleasure, Mrs. Wystan. We're glad to help out."

"You're very kind," she said, and stepped back from the van. Behind her, the cottage was smoldering, but no more flames spurted from it. She waved as the van rolled away, and tried to think of an appropriate gesture to let the men know that she was truly grateful. After all they had done, she thought, they deserved something more than a dinner on the house.

"We're almost through, Mrs. Wystan," Lieutenant Bright said, coming up to her. "We'll be back in the morning to sift the ashes, and in the meantime, no one—and I do mean no one—is to come near this cottage. If you have to put a guard on it to prevent the site from being disturbed, then do it. Your compliance is important, Mrs. Wystan. If you're not cooperative, it looks suspicious." He braced his hands on his hips, as if expecting an argument from her.

"That will be fine with me," Jennifer told him. "The insurance people will probably be in contact with you early in the morning. No doubt you'll want to coordinate your efforts."

"Very likely," Bright said at once. "Someone is going to have to shut off the sprinklers. They're still operating."

Jennifer studied Lieutenant Bright. "Are you sure you don't want them left on, so that all the fire is soaked out completely? I was planning to keep them on, but if you would rather not . . ."

"It wouldn't hurt to have them on for another hour, just in case," Bright conceded with some irritation. "But if you soak it down too much, evidence might be destroyed."

"Fine. An hour it is." She refused to let this man irritate her further. "And I'll expect to hear from you before . . . shall we say ten-thirty?"

"I'll call you." He turned abruptly and strode away toward the trucks.

Drew ambled up to Jennifer. "Who's the charmer?"

"Lieutenant Bright. He thinks this was arson." She almost choked on the words now, and her composure threatened to desert her. To her horror, she realized she was on the brink of tears.

"It might have been. So?" Drew said, looking toward the firemen as they began to gather up their equipment and stow it away in their square-bodied trucks.

"He hinted broadly that I might have wanted it started," she declared.

Drew laughed. "You're kidding."

"No." Jennifer folded her arms and sighed once more. "No, I'm not. He figures that I need the insurance money."

"That's ridiculous," Drew said, beginning to feel indignant. "If he's carrying around that kind of misconception, maybe I'd better go straighten him out about . . ."

Jennifer caught Drew by the arm. "Please don't," she begged him, fighting to control the emotions that filled her with turmoil. "I don't want to have anything else go wrong tonight, and if you argue . . . Drew, let him find out for himself."

"Oh, all right," Drew said after a moment. "But you know I'll talk to him any time you want."

"Fine. Good. But not right now." Her head was beginning to ache fiercely and she discovered her hands were shaking badly. "Do you mind if we go back to the hotel? I could use a little brandy and sixteen hours of sleep."

"I can do something about the brandy, but the sleep is your problem," Drew said, allowing her to start him down the path away from the burned shell of the cottage. "I think I could use the same prescription myself."

Jennifer crossed her arms, thrusting her hands out of sight in the crooks of her elbows. "We'll have to make some kind of statement for the guests, won't we?"

"It would probably be wise," Drew said. They had begun to walk past the occupied cottages, and by tacit agreement their pace increased.

"And if there are questions from the outside, we'll have to respond so that there's no undue excitement." Terribly tired now, she was aware that this was not the time to make complex decisions. "I'll have to take care of that in the morning, I guess."

"You're right." They were past the swimming pools, and looking up they could see the last, die-hard patrons in the bar staring out the windows a floor above them toward the place in the trees where the fire had been and where now the firetrucks were starting to wind their way down the slope.

"Do you think you could charge them extra for entertainment?" Drew asked with an attempt at cheekiness.

"I doubt it, but they'll dine out on the story for a while." She felt despondency settle around her like a sodden blanket. "I wish the fire had come after the bar closed. It might have caused a stir, but nothing like this."

"But you might not have got the help as fast, either," Drew reminded her, and patted her on the shoulder. "Buck up, boss. This isn't the end of the world."

"No, just two cottages and some of our survival money." She tried to smile. "Don't pay any attention, Drew. It's the hour speaking, not me."

"And the brandy will help both those things," he said at his most heartening, and held the door open for her to pass into the basement area.

Ross had already spoken with his men who had gone to assist at the White Elephant, and so when Jennifer's call came, he was not surprised to hear her sound chastened and weary. "I'd send the van for any of my neighbors," he assured her, cutting off her long and somewhat convoluted expression of gratitude.

"But you sent it here, and it made all the difference in the world," Jennifer said with heartfelt sincerity.

"I'm pleased to be of help," he said. "I hear from Bob that the damage was pretty extensive."

"I don't have the full report yet," she said, wishing that she could see his face rather than talk to a telephone receiver. "But from what I saw last night, I'd guess that the cottage will have to be rebuilt."

"That's a pity," Ross said. "That was the one Fred Jenkins was working on, wasn't it? He was doing fancy plasterwork and carpentry."

"You seem to know as much about it as I do," Jennifer said, not sharply, but with some apprehension; she was still not used to the degree of familiarity country-dwellers had with their neighbors' business.

"Well, Fred's brother works here, after all," Ross said, noticing the slightly critical sound in her voice. "Fred takes a great deal of pride in his work, and so does Ben. The two of them live right next door to each other."

Jennifer had not realized that, and felt oddly abashed. "I'm not used to how things are done here yet, I guess." She twisted the phone cord. "I do think you've been more generous than a lot of my neighbors would be, though. The others didn't send rescue vans over, and you did."

"The others don't have wineries, and I do. I have to keep emergency equipment around. I have a lot to lose." He chuckled in the hope that it would dispel some of the tension which had so unaccountably sprung up between them.

"Well, I'm grateful it was on hand, for whatever reason." She tapped her finger on the reservation pad beside the phone without actually seeing it.

"Are the investigators there yet?" he asked, trying to discover why she was being so remote.

"Not yet. The fire marshal was out earlier, but the insurance people haven't shown up yet. They're supposed to arrive this afternoon. What worries me is that Helene McClennan has doubts about her reception now." Jennifer bit her lip. She had not intended to blurt that out, especially to Ross. But she brought her head up defiantly—though he could not see this—and went on. "At a time like this, that's quite a blow."

"You can always let me lease those acres if you want," Ross said, and then knew he should not have made such an offer, for he could hear Jennifer grow cold through the phone lines.

"That's not what I meant, Mr. Benedetto. I'm not quite that desperate." But she knew that she was desperate. When Henry Fisher called her in the evening, she would have a better idea of just how desperate.

"Don't take it amiss. I wasn't planning to plant right now, anyway," he soothed, hoping to undo the damage he had done.

"And I'm not quite a candidate for charity," she said more pointedly. "I know that you mean well, but it isn't necessary to do this. I am grateful for your fire equipment and men, but . . ." She stopped awkwardly, not knowing precisely why she was so reluctant to take what he offered, and thinking that it might be because it was another painful reminder that Ross's considerable charm had its roots in business rather than personal attraction.

"Jennifer, you're being overly cautious. I'm not trying to put you at a disadvantage. Look, if there had been a fire here at the vineyard and you could send a van over to help, or could have offered rooms to those who had trouble in the fire, you would have, wouldn't you? As to the acreage, I won't mention it again until you bring it up. How's that?" Why couldn't he find the key to this woman, he wondered. What was it about her that made it so impossible for him to be as at ease as he usually was with women? Jennifer could make him feel the worst kind of sixteen again, and though he was vitally interested in her, he wasn't sure he liked the responses she generated in him. He cleared his throat. "I know you've got your hands full, but in a couple of days, why don't you drive over here for a couple of hours? Aunt Rosa will make lunch or something and we can have a quiet talk."

"Aunt Rosa?" Jennifer said.

"My father's youngest sister. I was named for her, in a way—Ross, Rosa. It was as close as my mother would come. Anyway, she'd be delighted to have someone new to cook for. Say you'll think it over." He tried to find a way to make his wish become her wish, to drive it down the phone lines from him to her, so that she would accept.

"I'm sorry, Ross, but I don't know how much of my time is going to be tied up in this investigation. But maybe later on . . ."

"Well, don't forget that the offer is there, any time you

want to take me up on it. Aunt Rosa would be very happy to have you here, and when you think of the size of this place I rattle around in, company is always welcome, even though we can absorb a dozen or so guests without getting too much in each other's hair." Again he tried to put an easy-going sound in his voice.

"It sounds great, but . . ." There was that *but* in her mind always, and nothing she could think or do would drive it away. If she accepted his hospitality, then the next time he asked her, oh so charmingly, to let him lease her acres, she would not want to have to disappoint him. "Maybe later," she repeated.

"I won't stop asking," he said with a friendly growl.

"I wouldn't want you to," she declared at once.

"That's encouraging." He made light of it, but he felt his pulse quicken. Damn the woman! he cursed delightedly.

"And I am grateful. I know that I owe you and your men in the van a great deal, and I don't want you to think that I'll forget it." It seemed to her to be very important to emphasize this. "I want to do something in appreciation, remember."

"Yes. We can talk about that after you've gone around with the insurance people and know a little better where you stand. But I think that anything you plan would be welcome if you have Drew do the cooking. You have a treasure there." He felt himself back on safe ground again, and was less likely than before to be thrown by her responses again. "In any case, I'll talk to you later."

"All right," she said, vaguely unhappy to have the conversation come to an end. "I'll keep what you said in mind. And I do want you to convey . . ."

"Your gratitude. Yes, I will. Have a good afternoon. I hope that the news is good."

"Thank you, Ross," she said quietly, and finally, "Well, goodbye."

"Goodbye, Jennifer." He hung up quickly, then glared out the window before he began to dial another familiar number, and began to order his thoughts to deal with the next conversation.

"It appears that there was a pipe left near one of the paint cans," the insurance inspector told Jennifer three days later. "Does Mr. Jenkins smoke a pipe that you know of?" He was a tall, angular man with slitted eyes and a beaky nose, and Jennifer could not repress a shudder when he looked at her.

"I believe he does," she said coolly. "I haven't inquired too closely. It seems unlike him to leave a burning pipe near a paint can. This man has been doing work of this sort for almost forty years."

"Everyone can forget. And if, as you say, he had a young assistant with him, it is possible he may have forgotten it." He rubbed thoughtfully at his lower lip. "Mrs. Wystan, I don't mean to pry, but is there any reason Mr. Jenkins might *want* to burn that cottage?"

"Mr. Dortmund!" Jennifer said, coming straight up in her chair. "Fred Jenkins is so involved with his work that for him to destroy one of his buildings would be like a mother killing her child!"

"That has happened more than once, Mrs. Wystan," Dortmund reminded her. "It is not impossible that this was a very cleverly constructed case of arson made to look enough like an accident so that the crime could not be satisfactorily proven and tried. If Mr. Jenkins is all you say he is, then we must assume he was careless in a way that you insist is out of character. Well?" He leaned forward and braced his arms on the desk.

"I don't believe that Fred Jenkins would willingly burn down a building," Jennifer insisted. "I'm more willing to believe that he was careless, as unlike him as it is. He's not a young man and his temper is a bit short. If he was arguing with his assistant, he could have set his pipe aside and forgotten about it. It surprises me, but not as much as the possibility that the fire was deliberately set, as you're suggesting."

Mr. Dortmund gave a reluctant glare. "There's no hard evidence of deliberate arson, none that would mean anything in court, or to the company. Not everyone agrees that it was an accident, however," he appended significantly.

Jennifer could not help but wonder how much Lieutenant Bright's theories had contributed to Dortmund's insinuations. She met his eyes limpidly. "If there has been arson, I hope that you and the police and the fire marshal and all the rest of them will make every effort to catch the person or persons responsible. I don't want my hotel to be the target of any more . . . mischief. I have a business to run, and no matter what you may think about insurance payments, they aren't nearly as important to me as a continuing number of paying guests."

"I'll tell the front office," Dortmund said woodenly.

"Thank you. I would appreciate it." She reached for the phone as it rang, saying, "Excuse me."

"Sure," Dortmund said heavily.

"White Elephant." Jennifer was surprised to hear Helene's voice on the other end of the line.

"I've been thinking it over, Jennifer, and I've decided I've been rash. You do have the best location, and anyone can suffer a freak accident as you have. Figure that we'll do the reception as planned. What I said was pique, nothing more. I get that way when things aren't going quite the way I'd like them to. You know how it is." She gave a brittle laugh and went on, "And my campaign manager is sold on the White Elephant. He says it reminds everyone of the great traditions of this district, and who am I to argue with him? I'll be by in a couple of days to discuss the final arrangements with you. How does next Wednesday at three sound to you?"

Jennifer had looked at her engagement calendar on her desk and said, "Wednesday at three is fine. Do you want to talk to Drew as well?"

"The man of the hour!" Helene declared. "That's a great idea. But I don't dare have too many samples of his work if I'm to keep my girlish figure." Again she laughed, and then said, "I'm looking forward to it, Jennifer. I think we're going to have a great success."

"Thank you, Helene. I hope we will." She scribbled down Helene's name and added Drew's next to it.

"See you then. Sorry about the fire. These things do happen." With a third, airier laugh, she hung up.

"Business still doing okay?" Dortmund asked with heavy sarcasm.

"Well enough, providing there are no further mishaps," Jennifer said. "The fire very nearly cost me that reception as well. You might keep that in mind."

"I'll keep in mind that you said it," Dortmund responded as he picked up the file folder he had put down. "They'll be getting ahold of you from the front office in a couple of weeks. And the fire marshal and the building inspector have to look at the shell before any sort of compensation can be made. You understand that, don't you?"

"Of course," Jennifer said. "If there are any questions, don't hesitate to ask them."

"We won't," he promised, and left the room.

A few moments later, Jennifer began to dial Henry Fisher's number in San Francisco.

Drew grinned at Jennifer. "I *told* you not to worry, boss. And you see, it turned out okay. We'll have that ravening horde of politicians ecstatic about this place, and then we'll be so busy that there won't be a vacant room until November." He was just putting the finishing touches on a plate of curried chicken. "Then you can put in the extra cottages and the stables and you'll be one of the marvelous little places that everyone always raves about."

Jennifer was still recovering from Helene's whirlwind visit and didn't quite know yet if she was satisfied with the outcome. The reception was on and Helene had announced that she was thrilled at the prospect of the entertainment and menu, but with Helene it was not always an easy matter to sort out the politician's acceptable phrases from the genuine compliments. "I guess so," Jennifer sighed, unable to join in Drew's enthusiasm.

"I'll talk to you later, Drew. Dean wants to leave early this evening, and I told him I'd fill in until Ivy gets here."

"Good enough, Jenny. I'll talk to you tomorrow." Drew smiled and gave her a comforting pat on the back.

As Jennifer climbed the stairs, she began to work out in her mind how she would handle the ebb and flow of Helene's enormous reception. There were so many things to consider, she thought, and was somewhat abstracted when Dean gave her a handful of message cards. To her surprise, one was from Ross. She tried to figure out what he wanted from the few scrawled words, but gave it up when the Stantons from Yreka arrived—husband, wife and three teenage kids. For the moment, she put Ross out of her mind.

◈ July ◈

"I can't get *over* how nice the weather is. Isn't it perfect?" Helene enthused as she came up the front steps of the White Elephant. It was not quite eight in the morning, and the sun was hanging in the eastern sky like a bright bauble. The air was warm enough to make heavy garments uncomfortable, and Helene had taken off her linen jacket, revealing a light blue silk camisole over her linen slacks. She looked glossy; a supple, tanned goddess waiting for her acolytes.

"We're getting the Silverado Suite in order for you now." Jennifer was not so elegantly rigged out, and she knew that she was facing a day of hard work before Helene's reception began. The one luxury ahead in the otherwise grueling day was the hair appointment she had made, which would take her away from the hotel from three until a bit after four. By then, she would be grateful for the tranquility she often experienced in the beauty shop.

"Well, I can see that you're unflappable," Helene said as they went through the door into the lobby. "I wish I had your calm. These events always drive me wild, but what can you do?" She was wearing some expensive, flowery perfume that surrounded her like a cloak. It had not been particularly noticeable outside, but now Jennifer could not ignore the pungent presence of jasmine and rose and hyacinth.

"I'm not unflappable," Jennifer countered. "I'm just not awake."

Helene laughed, and as they started up the stairs, she preened under Dean's admiring glance.

At the entrance to the ballroom, two of the housekeeping staff were setting up a few tables. "This is for your protection, of course," Jennifer said, showing the prepared lists that were put out. "Crashers aren't in your best interests."

"Most of them aren't," Helene said with a quiet laugh. "I've seen a few I wouldn't mind having back again. But not when I'm making political hay." She looked down at the lists. "How many of these people are staying over?"

"About thirty," Jennifer said promptly. "When were you planning to arrive?"

"No later than five-thirty. That lets me get my business done at the office and puts me here before most of the guests arrive. When's the band coming?" She walked across the ballroom and stood looking out of the large bow window toward the distant road.

"Seven. They're scheduled to start playing at seven-thirty. We're keeping on a good portion of the work-study kids, so you'll have the staff you need." Jennifer did not approach Helene, but stood her ground near the doors.

"That's good." Helene began to pace, a smile on her lips that had more ambition in it than she usually showed to the world. "What about the flags? How many do you have to hang up?" Helene had turned away from the window and was continuing to pace toward the bandstand. Once there, she turned again and went back toward the window.

Jennifer did not like the heavy-handed patriotism of the decorations that Helene was requiring, but thought that in this instance she would be wise to remain silent. "There are thirty of the large flags, forty-five of the small and a dozen California flags. Most of them are going up in here and in the Silverado Suite, but there will be two in the lobby, over the arch between the inner and outer lobby. Our own flags will be up, of course, so that should get the point across."

"You're droll," Helene said, laughing a bit. "I wish I could come up with one-liners the way you do. I know that I give a great speech and there are all kinds of ways to deal with social contacts, but I've never had that knack of being able to toss off a good one-liner. Everyone is always saying how well you do it."

"Really?" Jennifer asked. She was genuinely surprised.

"Yes, didn't you know? That comment you made to Dr. Robb about herringbone stitches is still going around." Helene shrugged. "Sheridan tells it himself."

Jennifer could vaguely recall making polite conversation with Dr. Robb while he waited for Muriel to finish her work. That this had led to a reputation for repartee baffled her and even made her feel slightly uneasy. She decided to change the subject. "How many people are coming for sure, do you know?"

"Not precisely," was the blithe answer. "But I don't think we'll be too far off the estimate. I've been told that this is being touted as something of a political event, which could be of great benefit to you, of course, as well as to me. I want to be sure that no one forgets this little bash." She chuckled. "I'd like to see what's going on in the Silverado Suite."

Jennifer tried to head her off. "We haven't really got those rooms ready yet. If you'd like to see it, fine, but don't expect much. We had a meeting of the mineral water bottlers there day before yesterday, and aside from housekeeping, there hasn't been a great deal done with it." Jennifer led the way down the short hall to the suite.

Helene waited while Jennifer opened the door to the Silverado Suite. "I *do* like this room. It's got that beautiful view and it's so *big*. In a lot of hotels now, if you get more space than three phone booths, you can think yourself lucky, but in these old places, they always made sure there was a lot of space."

Jennifer began to grow impatient. She had spent far too much time already with Helene, but she concealed the urge to rush her, and tried instead to think of a way to distract her. "Look, I have a few things to do around here, to take care of the other guests before your bash begins. If you don't need me to show you the kitchens, perhaps you can induce Drew to part with some of his goodies. He's already at work on the canapés, and I know that you'll like what he's done."

"Of *course*," Helene purred. "I shouldn't be monopolizing your time like this. But I worry about these things. When I'm doing something so *big* with my life, you know how that can take over. Well, I guess you *do*," she added with a wink. "This place is a pretty big thing in your life, isn't it?"

"Yes, it is." Jennifer did not apologize for her brusqueness. "I must get my jobs done early today, so that we won't have anything in the way this evening. Your reception is by far the largest function we've held since we've opened, and I want everything to go without a hitch."

"So do I," Helene said emphatically. "Go on, and I'll have a word with your precious Drew. If there are any difficulties, give my office a call at once."

"Certainly. But I hope there won't be any," Jennifer said as she escorted Helene from the Silverado Suite and paused to lock the ballroom door.

It had been with difficulty that Jennifer had persuaded the hairdresser not to give her an overly-formal, upswept style. At last the hairdresser and Jennifer had compromised, and the results were more flattering than Jennifer had thought possible. The crown and front sides of her dark hair had been drawn back to make a little Gibson Girl pouf, and below that the rest of her hair, shining and softly curled, hung to her shoulders. Looking in the mirror in her room, Jennifer was still startled to realize how much this style emphasized her eyes, making them spring into prominence. She decided to use a bit more makeup than she normally did, to take advantage of this.

At five-ten she was dressed except for her shoes, and looking critically in the mirror again, she felt for the first time in more than two years that she was a reasonably attractive woman with something to offer a man beyond her skill in business. Her dress was long and tunic-like, falling in gentle folds that seemed to conceal her body at one moment and reveal it the next. The color was somewhere between jade and turquoise, and the sheen of the silk flowed over her like a caress.

"Gracious!" Drew said from the door. "Don't you look scrumptious."

Jennifer smiled at him in the mirror. "Thank you."

"Helene might find you a thought too attractive tonight, boss, but I think you're just grand." He did not look bad himself, with his immaculate chef's whites.

"Flatterer!" Jennifer said, embarrassed by his praise.

"Not a bit. It's high time you started looking good again. It drives me nuts to see you wandering around looking drab. Are you going to wear the agate pendant?" He had gone over to her dresser and opened the elegant little jewelry box there.

"I didn't think I'd wear any jewelry . . ." Jennifer said tentatively.

"But you're wasting a terrific chance," he protested. "No, not the agate, I think. It's a bit too bold for all that silk." He opened another one of the little drawers. "Aha!" He lifted out a long strand of lapis beads. "If they're not the wrong shade with the dress, they'd be perfect. Just the right touch of class, but restrained. Are there earrings to go with this?"

Resigning herself to Drew's insistence, Jennifer said, "In the third drawer. Two teardrops. But they might not go with this color."

"Then I'll think of something else. For the moment, let's see how it looks." He came over to her and held the necklace against the silk. "Yummy. Makes you look like a moon goddess or something." Drew fastened the necklace around her throat and adjusted the hang of the strand. "You can do the earrings. I have to make sure that Johnny is ready for setting up the carving trays."

"Fine," Jennifer said, staring in the mirror. Drew had been right. She looked much more attractive than she had permitted herself to be. And what, she asked herself, would Ross think of it? She banished the thought immediately, but could not forget that he was the first man to come into her mind.

From the door, Drew blew her a kiss as he left.

Jennifer regarded the disorder around her and decided that it could wait until morning to be neatened. She dared not delay any further. Muriel had already warned her that Gregory Lennard had arrived with a crew of four and was getting ready to interview people arriving in the lobby.

She left a light burning, as she always did, and closed her door. She had a feeling it would be a very long night.

"And there's the glamorous owner herself," Greg said smoothly as Jennifer came into the lobby. He was basking in the intense lights his crew trained on him, and the mellifluous tone of his voice indicated that he was speaking for his audience and the microphones.

"Good evening," Jennifer said, wishing she could avoid this.

"And to you, Ms. Wystan. It's quite an evening you're having here at the White Elephant, isn't it?" His expression told her that she was required to agree.

"Yes. Events like this are always exciting for us." She was

able to smile, but felt like a carved doll speaking through a ventriloquist, not herself.

Greg beamed his approval. "I know you and the rest of the staff are doing everything you can to make this a perfect evening."

Jennifer forced herself to smile at him, and said so sweetly that she felt a bit sick, "Why, yes. Those of us who work in the hotel business always try for that."

This seemed to be precisely what Greg wanted to hear. He turned back to the camera with an incandescent smile. "That was Jennifer Wystan, the gracious and charming owner of the White Elephant where this gala reception is taking place." With that, the bright lights faded and the cameraman muttered something about moving up to the ballroom in an hour.

"Let them take care of it," Greg said to Jennifer, taking her arm. "Why don't you and I have a drink while they're attending to the scut work."

"Well, I have . . ." Jennifer began, but they were interrupted by Muriel, who stepped out of the office behind the reception desk with a sheaf of papers in her hand.

"Jennifer, do you mind if I talk to you a moment? We've just got a large reservation from the Makepeace Corporation and there's a question of blocking rooms." Muriel looked harried and shook the paper at her.

Jennifer turned to Greg. "I'm sorry, but I've got to attend to this." She did not allow him to protest, but turned away and entered the area behind the reception desk. When the door to the office was safely closed, she looked at Muriel and said, "Thanks. I don't think I could stand much more of that man."

Muriel chuckled. "I just grabbed a handful of paper and came out. I could see that you were in a bind." She dropped the papers on the desk and sat down. "Sheridan will be here this evening. Do you mind if I . . . ?"

"Stick around?" Jennifer suggested. "It's fine with me. You can stay over in room B-6 if you like. No one is using it at the moment, and it might make things easier. You don't have to drive home late."

"Thanks," Muriel said, color flooding her face. "I don't think I'd be staying alone." This last came out in a rush, and Muriel clasped her hands as she said it.

"Really?" Jennifer beamed at her. "That's great!" She meant it, too, though she felt a pang of sadness. Her own life seemed suddenly so busy and so empty.

Muriel looked up. "Do you think so?"

"I sure do," Jennifer assured her. "It's wonderful. I've been hoping that you'd get the chance to . . . be closer than you were."

Now Muriel did not know what to say. "Well. That's a relief. I . . . Oh, hell!" And quite suddenly, she began to weep.

"Muriel," Jennifer said, surprised.

"Oh," Muriel said shakily as she dabbed at her eyes, "there's nothing wrong . . . nothing at all . . . I'm so . . . I'm so happy, that . . ." She wiped her eyes with determination. "There," she announced. "I think I've stopped. What I was trying to say, before I went and broke down, was that I didn't think you'd be so . . . understanding. Sheridan said that you'd be supportive, but you know how it is—women don't always act the way men think they will, even the most sympathetic women—and I was afraid to mention what has been going on." She blew her nose and put her handkerchief away.

"It's terrific," Jennifer said firmly. "I can't help wishing it was me."

"You and Sheridan?" Muriel asked, bemused.

"No. Me and somebody." She knew that familiar forlorn sense and she forced herself to overcome it.

Muriel sighed. "You can't think like that, Jennifer," she said as she rummaged in her purse for her lipstick. "You know that you won't be this way all your life."

Jennifer's laugh was shaky. "I want to believe that, but I can't always convince myself. And considering how things worked out with George, sometimes I wonder if I want to try again. Those are the bad days." She coughed to clear her throat. "What are we bothering about this now for? There's a reception to run." Her expression was deliberately resolute and she made herself smile charmingly.

"Yes. And Helene McClennan expects the very best we can provide," Muriel said with a moue of distaste.

"Her money spends as well as anyone's," Jennifer said, as if reciting a lesson, "and we could do a lot worse than have Helene announce her candidacy from this place."

"That doesn't mean that she's easy to take," Muriel said wryly. "All right. I'll spend my time with the books and leave the guests to you." She looked at Jennifer again. "You're looking fetching tonight."

"I hope so," Jennifer said, and waited while Muriel put her face in order.

In the hall outside the Silverado Suite, Wilbur Cory was in the middle of an argument with a square, meaty-faced man in an expensive but ill-tailored suit.

"You're doing it again, Wilbur and Mark," Helene admonished with a wag of her finger as she swept out of the ballroom, a vision in swirling layers of filmy red organza. She put her arms through each of theirs and led them toward the ballroom. "Come along. If I leave you out here, you'll be at it again in less time than it takes to say lawsuit."

Both men gave appreciative chuckles and allowed themselves to be propelled through the wide doors of the Grand Ballroom.

Jennifer watched this from her vantage point by the tall window in the lounge. She could not help but marvel at the ease with which Helene manipulated those around her. Helene made it look so simple, and Jennifer often found it impossibly difficult. She shook her head as Helene vanished into the crowded ballroom.

"Penny for your thoughts," said a voice in her ear, and she turned to find Ross standing beside her, looking positively dashing in a tuxedo and ruffled, cream-colored shirt.

"I . . . they aren't worth so much," Jennifer said, wishing that she were not so very grateful to see him.

"They're probably worth a lot more," he said, and held out a glass of champagne to her. "Go on. One drink isn't going to hurt you, and you look as if you could use a touch of the bubbly."

In general, Jennifer made it a policy not to drink while working, but she was glad to be persuaded at this moment. "All right; one glass won't make that much difference."

"And besides, you're not driving," Ross said as he touched the rim of her glass with his. "To . . . to what?"

"To the White Elephant," Jennifer said at once.

"If you insist," Ross said, and sipped at the sparkling wine. "Quite a mob scene you've got here."

"It's Helene's mob, I'm just managing traffic," Jennifer said lightly. The reception was little more than an hour underway and less than half the guests had arrived, and already she was beginning to feel tired. She could ill-afford to leave so early in the festivities, and she knew that with the band playing underneath her room, she would not be able to sleep even if she left at once.

"You're doing a great job of it. I've been having a look around and I'm impressed." He wanted to see her smile again, so he said, "You know, you're the best-looking woman here tonight."

Jennifer wished the idle compliment did not make her pulse race, since she was determined not to allow herself to be taken in by her attractive neighbor. "That's nice of you to say, Ross, but next to Helene . . ."

"Next to Helene you stand out like a Renoir next to a Corn Flakes box." He finished his champagne and watched while she did the same. "If you want a refill, let me know."

"I will," Jennifer said, thinking that she would abstain for most of the evening.

"Good enough," Ross said, trying to think of something to say that would keep her with him a bit longer. "How many are coming?"

"I don't know exactly. Neither does Helene." She touched the strand of lapis beads around her neck. "We'll manage the best we can. I think we can put up another twenty attendees, but that will fill us up completely." There was a touch of pride in her voice as she said that.

"Congratulations. A full house," Ross said, genuinely pleased for her. "That's the first time, isn't it?"

"Well, it hasn't happened yet, but it very well might, and that's worth something, I guess." She felt a bit like an actor saying, "Break a leg" instead of "Good luck" so that she would not jinx the show, or her performance.

"Why so cautious, Jennifer?" Ross asked quietly, leaning a bit closer to her to be heard over the roar of conversation from the ballroom and the Silverado Suite.

"Because I have to be," she answered bluntly. "This is my hotel and . . ."

"And you're doing a great job with it. So why worry about the twenty guests? You know this reception is a success already and . . ." He stopped when he saw that Jennifer was staring toward the elevators on the far side of the lounge.

"I don't believe it," Jennifer said in a hushed voice.

"What's wrong?" Ross asked, for something was certainly very wrong, judging from the tension she was so carefully concealing.

Jennifer just shook her head. Her face was pale under her makeup.

Ross glanced away from her once toward the party of people who had come up the stairs. There were eight of them, all talking enthusiastically, a few of them joking with the portly older man who was clearly in charge of them. Jennifer, he saw, was looking intently, briefly, at a man in his early thirties, with tousled fair hair and crinkled eyes. "Who is he?" Ross asked Jennifer in a low voice.

"George Howard," she answered quietly, wishing that she could disappear.

"Who's George Howard?"

Jennifer sighed and looked ruefully at Ross. "My ex-husband."

Ross resisted the urge to stare at the man, to try to see what he had that had attracted Jennifer, or what he had done that made her skittish now. He kept his eyes on hers and said, "I gather you didn't know he was coming."

"No, I didn't. Helene said she didn't have a complete guest list, but I never thought that George would be one of . . ."

"Hello there, stranger," said a voice behind them as George sauntered over to Ross and Jennifer. "A friend told me about the party, and I couldn't resist coming along. You look great."

Jennifer forced herself to smile. "Hello, George. I didn't know you were interested in politics."

George shrugged. "Who am I to pass up a party at the White Elephant?" He leered suggestively. "Who's your friend?" he asked, giving Ross a quick, curious look.

"Pardon me," Jennifer said, feeling terribly flustered. "This is my neighbor, Ross . . ."

He interrupted her, thrusting his hand out to George. "Ross Benedetto. I've been told you're George Howard. You own a restaurant, don't you?" He wanted to give Jennifer as much time as possible to regain her composure, and he watched her covertly as he went on. "I don't recall your restaurant being on our lists. Don't you buy our wines?"

"Wines?" George echoed. "Benedetto. Benedetto Winery?" He beamed at Ross, suddenly very cordial. "I know your wines well. They're very popular at the Savoia."

Ross decided he had to be polite to the man. "Thank you. We try to keep our quality at a high standard. I don't think I know the Savoia."

"It's in South San Francisco. It's been in operation for eight years, and we're doing pretty well." He looked down at Jennifer. "You're smart to keep in good with *this* neighbor. Make him give you a discount on his wines."

"He does," Jennifer said shortly. "Excuse me, please. I want to be sure the buffet is prepared." She turned away from the two men and hurried down the hall to the Silverado Suite, hoping Drew would be there.

He was. He had taken his place behind the long tables, and was frowning down at the curried chicken which had just come up from the kitchen. He looked up sharply as Jennifer came through the door. "You look like you've seen a ghost, Jenny," he said with a grin.

"I think I have," Jennifer said, putting her hands to her face.

"Anyone I know?" Drew asked, concealing his concern behind his flippancy.

"George," Jennifer answered. "I hoped I wouldn't have to talk to him again until the next time I was in San Francisco." She lifted stricken eyes to Drew's. "I didn't think he'd ever come here. I don't know what to say to him. Drew, I want to run away and hide."

Drew left his chicken and came around the end of the table. "Jenny, don't. You've given him enough of your time and worry. You can't let it go on." He put an arm around her shoulder.

"You should have seen the way he smiled," Jennifer said, trying to keep from shaking. "You know the way he used to grin when he was about to do something awful. It was that kind of smile. I wanted to scream at him." Her hands were clenched into fists.

Drew remembered all too well the way George had treated Jennifer when they were married, and his eyes grew flinty for an instant. But he knew there was nothing to be gained in discussing the past. "You can handle it, and you can handle him. This is your place, boss, not his, and you're the one who makes the rules."

"But I don't know if . . ." she began.

"Let me take care of the staff. You have all those guests to worry about, and that's what you should be doing. George can't pull any numbers here: this isn't his place, and you're the one in charge." He tightened his grip and then let her go, crossing the room to the large champagne dispenser at the side of the inner door. He filled a glass for her and brought it back to her. "Here."

"Oh, Drew, I shouldn't. I've already had one glass," Jennifer protested.

"That was before you knew that George was here. This is prescribed by Dr. Usher, and you damn well better drink it." He held the glass out forcefully and glared at her until she gave a resigned shrug and took the glass. "Fine. And I don't want to find that sitting on an end-table with only two sips gone and somebody's cigarette floating in it. Got that, boss?"

"I've got it," Jennifer said, and took some of the champagne. She had to admit that it was pleasant, and she knew it would help relax her. There was a great deal to do yet, and she solaced herself with the knowledge that two glasses of champagne would not make her tipsy.

"Good. Now finish that up before you go outside. I've got to get these doors open in the next ten minutes, or Helene will be outraged. Quite a handful, isn't she?" Drew went back to his chicken and stirred it experimentally.

Jennifer was almost finished with the champagne. She knew she was drinking it too fast—already she felt the bubbles fizzing along her veins. "That's got to be all I have," she said to Drew. "Otherwise, I might not behave with proper decorum, and you know how careful I have to be."

"Well, I know how careful you *think* you have to be, but that's not the same thing." He winked at her. "Go out there and knock 'em dead, boss. You look gorgeous. Your dress is stunning. There's nothing out there, and no one, that you can't handle."

"Whatever you say," Jennifer said with a sinking feeling as she put the champagne glass aside and reached for the doorknob.

"Come back in an hour and I'll feed you." He waved and motioned her out of the room.

As she closed the door, she saw three of the work-study waiters hurrying down the hall toward her, and stood aside for them as they went into the Silverado Suite to assist Drew. Left to herself, Jennifer stood indecisively for more than a minute until she saw that Ted Hatfield had seen her and was heading in her direction with a determined smile. Then she permitted herself to be distracted by the confusion at the tables where the guest lists were. She turned toward them quickly, as if she had just recalled some imcomplete task. As she neared one of the tables, Muriel came up to her and smiled. "More cars are coming. Sheridan said that it took him ten minutes longer than usual to get here."

"I suppose Helene will be delighted," Jennifer said. "She's proved she can muster the troops."

Jennifer stiffened as she saw George coming toward her.

"What's wrong, Jennifer?" Muriel said as she saw Jennifer's expression.

"Nothing," she answered, and tried to look cordial as George strolled up to her.

"Nothing what, Jen?" he asked with a nod to Muriel.

"Nothing to be done about the parking situation," she said, ignoring the curious look Muriel gave her. In the years she was married to him, Jennifer had learned how to distract George.

"Probably not. You're getting more people here than usual, I guess." He gave Muriel a quick scrutiny. "Who are you?"

"Muriel Wrather. I'm Ms. Wystan's accountant. Who are you?" Muriel knew that Jennifer did not like the man, but could not account for the almost fearful way she regarded him.

"I'm George Howard. Jen might have mentioned me; I'm her ex-husband." He shook hands with Muriel as he said it, and grinned at her bafflement.

"George surprised me," Jennifer said to Muriel.

"I haven't seen her in a couple months at least—more like three or four, so when I got the chance to come here, I thought it was too good to miss." He saw Sheridan Robb coming up and gave him his practiced smile.

"I've been looking all over for you, Muriel," Sheridan said, with a quick, curious look at Jennifer and the newcomer.

"Jennifer was just introducing me to Mr. Howard." She had taken the doctor's hand in hers, and her tightened fingers warned him that something was amiss.

"Mr. Howard?" Sheridan said, offering his hand. "A pleasure to meet you."

Muriel tugged once at Sheridan's hand. "I'm afraid there's something I forgot to show Ms. Wystan in the office. Would you excuse us for ten minutes or so?"

Sheridan nodded. "Sure. It's turning into a madhouse, so you'd better get the business done now."

The quick smile that Muriel flashed him told the doctor that he had said the right thing. "Thanks. We'll be back up in a little bit." She motioned to Jennifer and went at once to the stairs.

Gratefully, Jennifer followed her, and when they were at

the reception desk, she said, "That was beautiful. I don't know what I'm going to do for the rest of the evening. I've been thinking of going upstairs to my room, but that's no answer."

"What's he doing here?" Muriel wanted to know.

"I don't know. I wish he were almost anywhere else." Jennifer put a hand to her brow. "I need a couple minutes to figure out how to handle this. I wish I knew what George is up to."

"Why does he have to be up to something?" Muriel asked. She had not seen Jennifer so upset before, and was not certain how to help her.

"Because that's his style. He wants things out of balance. That's how he seizes control. I don't know if I can explain it, but he's the kind of man who can tell you that you look marvelous and have you wondering what's wrong." Jennifer gave a shaky laugh.

"Would you like Sheridan and me to run interference for you?" Muriel offered.

"I'd love it, but it would be a trifle obvious. I think I might spend a bit more time in the Silverado Suite than I'd intended. Drew's in there, and George doesn't want to tangle with him." She put her hand to her hair absent-mindedly. "I wish I knew . . ."

"Don't let it worry you. Sheridan and I will keep an eye on you, and we won't be clumsy about it. We won't leave you alone, and that might help."

"You know," Jennifer confided, "I'd rather talk to that smooth-talking Hatfield than spend ten minutes alone with my ex-husband. Pretty poor-spirited of me, isn't it?"

"Maybe it's just sensible," Muriel said.

"It might be," Jennifer conceded. "In the meantime, we'd better get back upstairs. I don't want anybody to come looking for me. That would make it more awkward than ever."

"There's always the ladies' room," Muriel said philosophically as she fell into step beside Jennifer.

"I can't spend the entire evening cowering in one of the stalls. Come on, Muriel. I've got to do better than that." She tried to chuckle, but did not succeed.

"That's fine, but you don't have to go it alone," Muriel reminded her as they reached the top of the stairs.

"Did you find out what the matter was?" George asked as he came over to Jennifer and took her arm possessively.

"I think so," she answered, doing her best to extricate herself from his grasp.

"Do you think you can relax a little? You and I haven't had much time to talk in the last year. I want to know how you're doing." He was guiding Jennifer away from Muriel and Sheridan, his face a mask of hearty goodwill.

Jennifer tried once more to break free of him. "I can't, George. This is a major reception, and this is my hotel. I have obligations and responsibilities. I can't spend time away from it."

"If you're running this place the way you ran the Savoia, you could be gone all night and the thing would still go like clockwork. You know that as well as I do." He leaned one hand against the wall by her head, crowding her back against the wall.

"That was after the place had been open a few years. George, I have work to do." She hated the way he was treating her and wanted to scream at him, but here, with the ballroom near at hand and the Silverado Suite beginning to fill up, she could not bring herself to make such a show of her private life. That she realized that George was counting on just this prudence made her even more annoyed.

"Not right now." He reached forward with his other hand and tweaked one of the curls that brushed her shoulder. "You look lovely, you know that? Even prettier than you did before."

"George, don't," she said sharply.

"Can't a man pay a compliment to his wife? Pardon me, his ex-wife?" He leaned a little closer to her. "I miss you, Jen. I know that I acted like a fool the last year we were married. I've tried to tell you before that we could make it work now." He was smiling now, that professional, persuasive salesman's smile that Jennifer knew only too well. "You can ask around, if you like. You'll find out that I'm different. We wouldn't have all those problems we used to have. You could go your own way more, and I'd see that there was plenty of extra help at the Savoia. You and Drew made such a difference in the place. . . ."

Jennifer's eyes hardened. "Thanks for the compliment." She could not bring herself to touch him to push him away, but she compromised by folding her arms on her chest. "Will you move and leave me alone?"

"Aw, come on, Jen. Loosen up." His eyes crinkled at her

and she had to resist them. "You know we could make a go of this."

"Of this? You mean to take on my hotel in addition to your restaurant? You think big, George, I give you that," she said, not able to keep the bitterness out of her voice. Why did he have to do this? Why did he insist on making it worse between them?

"It isn't just the hotel, Jen, it's you. I know it was a mistake for us to split up, and I want to fix it." He smiled again, this time with more warmth. "I haven't met anyone who can touch you. And you know there were times when we were great together."

"I know there were times we were awful, too. Leave it alone, George." She kept her voice low with effort, and had to fight down a sense of panic rising within her.

"But why? You know you need someone . . ." He reached to touch her hair again and she jerked her head away.

"Stop it."

"You don't really want me to, do you?" He had taken on that teasing, wheedling tone that he had often used when he wanted his way, either in bed or in the restaurant.

"Yes. Yes, I want you to stop." She was becoming angry with him, but dared not show it, recalling how well he used her anger against her.

"But you've always liked . . ." George began, and was interrupted.

"Hello, George," said Drew as he came out of the Silverado Suite. "I hate to interrupt this little tête-à-tête, but we have a problem with the food, boss, and I need to make some quick adjustments."

"Hello, Drew," George said with false warmth. He started to say something more, but Drew reached out and grabbed Jennifer's arm and abruptly pulled her away from George.

"I don't have time to talk just now," he said over his shoulder as he spirited Jennifer down the hall. "Excuse us."

"Oh, thank God for your problem," Jennifer said quietly to Drew as they went into the Silverado Suite.

"The food problem is spelled G-e-o-r-g-e. Muriel came in all riled up and saying she didn't know what to do. Dr. Robb offered to take you away, but I said I'd handle it. What does he want?" Drew said this in a rush as he returned to his place behind the serving tables.

"He wants the White Elephant and me, in that order." She

looked around, belatedly recalling that there might be others in the room.

"Don't worry. I've closed this section off for ten minutes. I said that we're bringing up the second trays, which is true. Go ahead and talk." Drew gave her a kindly smile. "Whatever possessed you to let him get you alone like that?"

"I wasn't watching, I guess. I was avoiding someone else, and George showed up." She sighed and shook her head as Drew held out a glass of champagne. "No. Thanks a lot, but I'd better not."

"It won't hurt you," Drew insisted. "If you put on a lampshade and start singing *She's Only a Bird in a Gilded Cage*, then I'll send you off to bed, but you're looking like an overstretched rubberband. George wants to do that to you, and you're letting it happen."

"All right, I guess," Jennifer said, taking the glass reluctantly.

Half an hour later, Ross found her near the bandstand. "I've been looking for you, Jennifer. Muriel said you'd had some trouble."

Jennifer felt a quiet thrill from his concern and tried to rationalize it to herself. It was simply that a man other than George Howard was going through the motions of being concerned for her. Or, she thought, it might be the champagne. "Nothing drastic."

"Your ex is up to something?" Ross asked. He had seen George accost her in the hall, but had not known how to interrupt without causing Jennifer further embarrassment.

"In a way. It's not important." She had to speak louder, but now the band was starting up with *The Pineapple Rag*.

"Let's get away from here. I can't hear myself think, let alone speak," Ross said. He held out his hand to Jennifer. "Come on. Isn't there a balcony or a terrace or a bend in the stair where we can talk?"

She felt his fingers close around hers and very nearly sighed. "Nothing but my quarters. And they're pretty loud," she added, thinking that he would refuse to go there.

"That's okay, so long as it's private and not too noisy." As he passed one of the young waiters, he grabbed two glasses and a bottle of champagne off the boy's tray. "It's from my winery," he said airily, and continued toward the stairs.

"Ross, someone may notice." It was the last concession Jennifer was prepared to make to propriety.

"In this mess? Even if they do, they'll figure we're going where there's less noise. And they'd be right." He saw Jerry Hasslund and waved to him. "Jerry, Ms. Wystan and I are stepping out by the pool."

"Sensible," the younger Mr. Hasslund shouted at them. "I might wander out there myself a little later."

They were out of the ballroom in four more hasty steps, and Ross tugged her toward the elevators. "Less conspicuous than the stairs, believe me." He pushed the knob and looked toward Jennifer. "We won't be gone any longer than you want to be. How's that?" As he said it, he hoped she would want to spend more than a few minutes with him.

The elevator arrived and half a dozen people got out, leaving the cab empty. Before the doors could close, Ross stepped inside and pulled Jennifer after him. As he pushed the button for the floor above, he said, "See how easy it is? Up we go." He tucked the bottle of champagne under his arm. "This is a terrible way to treat sparkling wine, and if the whole thing goes off like a Roman candle when I try to open it, it'll serve me right. But I didn't think you'd want me to call room service for something to be sent up."

Jennifer shrugged. "I don't think we'd get much attention from room service in any case. Johnny has one assistant in the kitchen tonight and Drew wanted to discontinue the room service altogether, but I said no. And you're right. It wouldn't be very . . ."

"Discreet?" Ross finished. "Not if we're supposed to be taking the air out by the pool, it's not." The door opened and they were on the third floor.

It was deserted and eerily quiet, with the distant sound of the band muffled by the floor between them, almost as if they had not changed levels so much as buildings. No one walked in the hallway, and the muted lights set into elaborate wall sconces looked more like gaslights than the electric bulbs they were. It was precisely the effect that Jennifer had striven for, but now she found it disquieting.

"This is great," Ross said, just above a whisper.

"Do you think so?" In spite of the strange sensation she felt, his praise pleased her. "I wanted it to be right."

"You did fine." He looked around. "Which is your door?"

"Third on the right, at the end of the alcove. My office is on this level and my own apartments in the cupola above." As they walked toward the door, she added in a rush of confidence, "Sometimes, when I wake up in the morning, I

look out my window over my land here and see your
vineyards beyond. Your place is very beautiful."

"Thank you," he said with warmth. "I think so, too."

She took her key from where she had tucked it into her bra,
hoping that he did not see too clearly. As she opened the
door, she warned him, "I haven't done any straightening up
for days, and it shows."

"You should see my office," Ross said with a self-
deprecating laugh, knowing that Aunt Rosa kept it well-
ordered at all times. "I get knee-deep in papers sometimes."

The office was not too formal, more like a reception room
than the usual desk-and-files cubicle that most offices were.
There was Uncle Samuel's large oak desk at one end of the
room, flanked by four elegant wooden filing cabinets. At the
other end of the room, two low, plump sofas were set at right
angles to each other against the wall. There were two tall
bookcases and a low coffee table to complete the area, and a
fine Oriental carpet on the floor. The colors were muted earth
tones relieved by blues and greens to match the colors in the
carpet.

"Very nice. I like it." Ross smiled. What a difference
between his smile and George's, Jennifer thought. He went
on. "You've done wonders with everything here, Jennifer. I
didn't think it was possible to do so much in so little time."

"Well, Uncle Samuel left a trust fund for the refurbishing,
and it's made the difference. I couldn't have done it any other
way." Now that she was in her own quarters, she asserted
herself as hostess. "Would you like to sit down?" She chose
the nearer of the sofas and sat down.

Ross chose the other sofa but sat as close to her as it
allowed. He put the two glasses on the table and began to
open the champagne. "Where should I aim it if it goes off?"

"The table can stand it better than the carpet," Jennifer
said, and hesitated before adding, "I don't know if I should
have any more of that."

"Of course you should. I'm going to have some." He had
had just the one glass and knew his tolerance for wine to the
last sip. "You don't want me to drink this heavenly stuff
alone, do you?"

"No." Jennifer watched as he expertly removed the cork
with only the faintest of pops, and began to fill the two
glasses.

"Neither the carpet nor the table will suffer," he said as he finished pouring. "Here." He handed her a glass. "To the most beautiful woman here."

"I'm the only woman here," she pointed out as she took the glass; their fingers touched and she shivered.

"In this entire hotel." He gestured his toast and took a sip. "All right. It's your turn."

Caught off-guard, Jennifer said, "To the best neighbor I've ever had."

Ross watched her. "Really? Then thank you. I was afraid that we'd got off on the wrong foot and were still there."

"But you've been a great deal of help," Jennifer said, and resisted the thought that he had a great deal to gain from being helpful.

"I haven't, you know. I've done a few little things, which were largely as advantageous to me as to you, and sent over my men when you needed them. In this part of the world, that isn't a whole hell of a lot." He leaned nearer to her, his china-green eyes intent on hers. "I'd like to do something special for you, not yeoman service." Without haste he touched her lips with his, no more than a light brush, but one that stirred him.

Jennifer drew back, quivering slightly. "Ross . . ."

"I'm not going to apologize. In fact, I'll probably do it again." He had another sip of champagne and watched her.

"Ross, I don't . . ." She had some more of the champagne and wondered if it was the wine or his presence that was disorienting her. "I don't . . ."

He touched her face. "You don't what?" He forced himself to draw back from her a little. "Are you worried about being alone with me? We're both old enough to know what we're doing, if we're doing anything. For the time being, we can enjoy each other's company and the—relative—quiet." He poured champagne into their glasses again.

Jennifer drank automatically, and quite without warning her vision swam. "Oh, dear." She put a hand to her head and thought that she had let herself get tipsy. "I'm sorry, Ross. I don't usually have . . ."

Ross heard the slight slurring of her words and was puzzled by it. "How much have you had to drink, Jennifer?"

"These glasses, and the one you gave me earlier. And Drew gave me two." As she totaled them up, she was faintly shocked. "This isn't like me. I don't do this."

He cut short her protestations. "When did you eat last?"

"Eat?" she repeated. "I had . . ." —she thought about it carefully, trying to bring her very busy day back into focus— "I had a sandwich about eleven."

"That was almost twelve hours ago," Ross said. "No wonder the champagne hit you." He got up from the sofa and crossed the room. "What's the extension for the kitchen?"

"Five," she said automatically. "But they're so busy down there. Don't bother them."

Ross paid no attention. "Hello? This is Mr. Benedetto. Ms. Wystan and I would like a light supper in her office. Just a little of whatever you're getting ready for the buffet. Bring it up when you can."

"You don't have to do that. Johnny's got his hands full," Jennifer objected. "In a couple of hours, I can call down for a sandwich, or . . ."

"It'll be up in ten minutes. That's what the kitchen said." He leaned back against the desk. "How much weight have you lost in the last month, Jennifer?"

She giggled. "I don't know. Eight, nine pounds. Why?" She had not thought about it much, and had attributed it to her constant busy schedule.

"Because it isn't good for you, that's why." He had folded his arms. "Look, Jennifer, what good is everything you do here if you let it run you into the ground? You've done a magnificent job, and you deserve a lot of credit. But what good is that if you're flat exhausted? Enjoy what you're doing for a change." He saw the confusion in her face, which she could not disguise. "Jennifer," he said, more fondly.

"But it's all that I have," she murmured, and then pressed her hand to her mouth, as if to shut the words in again.

"That's nonsense," Ross said, but wondered what life she had beyond the hotel. He had assumed that she had chosen to throw herself into her work. But what if there were no alternative? He wished he had enough confidence to ask her more questions, but he could not bring himself to trespass on her when she was so vulnerable. For the time being, he changed the subject. "Is the band likely to get any louder?"

"It depends on how much of a sing-along they end up with." She gave a lopsided smile. "I'm glad you brought me up here. I don't think I could cope with the band and the reception and George and all in the condition I'm in."

"I shouldn't have given you that extra champagne," he said with a shake of his head.

"Yes, you should. I know it's the wine, but I feel great."

She flung her arms out on the back of the sofa. "I feel like I own the world. And half an hour ago, I thought everything was falling in around me."

Ross almost set aside his scruples and went to take her in his arms; holding himself back from that was more of an effort than he had thought it would be. "You're fine," he said, thinking it idiotic, but hoping she might decide to talk to him. "You're doing fine."

"God, I hope so," she said with a sigh. "I shouldn't be saying this. Don't pay any attention to me. I'll try to keep from blathering." Jennifer looked across the room at Ross and shrugged. "I don't know what to say."

"Anything you like," Ross told her, thinking how sensual she looked now, so relaxed and languorous. There was a part of her that was warm and passionate and exciting, and most of the time it was concealed behind her cool professional competence. Now, with the help of the champagne, he was getting a glimpse of the fine creature she might be, and he was not entirely surprised to feel an intense desire grip him.

"It's not important. Ancient history, as Uncle Samuel would say." She put her hand to her hair. "Have I messed it up?"

"No, it looks fine. You look beautiful." It was harder than he had thought possible to keep his distance, for he could feel his desire quickening. It was not advisable or wise to take advantage of her, he knew. To pursue her now, while she was not quite herself, or so much more herself, would be a Pyrrhic victory. He might be able to take her to bed, but it would be once only, and the precarious trust that had been built up between them would be damaged beyond repair. He wanted Jennifer, but he wanted her more than once, more than for an evening's amusement.

"I feel like I'm trying to get out of a cellophane skin. I'm like a snake, trying to shed, or moult, or whatever they do." She fingered the shoulder of her silken dress as if it were foreign to her. "I don't like the way this . . ."

The knock at the door startled them both.

"I'll get it," Ross said, and went to let in Johnny Chang with their supper.

"I truly am feeling better now," Jennifer said a little more than half an hour later. The remains of the meal were strewn about on three trays, and the pot of hot coffee was nearly empty. Jennifer sat with her feet on the coffee table, and Ross sat beside her trying to decide if he wanted to eat the last bit of pickled cauliflower. "Thanks for insisting I have this," she said as she ate the last of the deviled eggs. "I didn't realize how hungry I was."

"You were too busy," Ross said. He drank down the last of his coffee and turned toward her. "They're getting a little rowdy downstairs, aren't they?" The band was louder, and there was a more emphatic sound of clapping and dancing feet.

"It's not unusual. Especially if they've had as much champagne as I had." She looked over at him. "You were very good to me, Ross."

"It's easy," he told her, and put his arm around her shoulder. He knew he could do this safely now, without the overwhelming need for her overruling his good sense. He liked the feel of the silk under his palm, and the presence of her skin beneath the fabric.

"I want you to know that I appreciate . . . everything." She felt suddenly awkward. How could she say thank you for not taking advantage of me when she was not entirely certain that he wanted to do so in the first place?

"It's nothing." Then, before he had time to think about it, he pulled her close to him and kissed her long and thoroughly. He could sense the passion slumbering within her, and he was suddenly determined to revive it. As her lips parted, he touched her tongue with his, gently at first and then more forcefully.

It would be folly to give in to the need that rose, tempest-like, within her. Jennifer tried to keep this in mind even as she felt her nipples grow taut and her body become pliant. She could not trust Ross or his motives. He was primarily interested in her land, not her. Desperately, she clung to these bits of caution, but all the while she was aching for him to seek more from her, to make her aware again of what it was to be desired—she could not let herself want to be loved.

With a long, shivering breath, Ross took Jennifer by the shoulders and held her off from him. His groin throbbed, his pulse leaped, and he knew that if he did not leave quickly, he would want more from Jennifer than ardent kisses. "I think I'd better go."

"But . . ." Jennifer said, unable to conceal her disappointment. "What have I done?"

"Nothing . . . nothing wrong. It's . . ." He gave an abashed shrug. "Jennifer," he said, as he saw doubt cloud her features, "I want you. If I stick around, I don't think I could entirely ignore it."

Jennifer paid no attention to the burst of noise from the ballroom below. "I wouldn't mind," she said, thinking how pleasant it was to have him with her, and taking unexpected pride in his admission. So it was not only those acres that brought him back to the White Elephant.

Ross very nearly grinned, but he knew he had to make it plain that he did not wish to be led on. "I mean I want to make love to you." He still held her by the shoulders, trying to convince himself that if she refused him, it would be easier to leave if he did not permit himself the luxury of another embrace.

"Yes," Jennifer said. "I understand that."

"Is that the champagne talking?" His hands were not as firm, and he felt her interest in him sharpen.

"Not after supper and three cups of coffee. I know what I'm saying. I'm not going to reproach you for taking advantage of me." She was able to laugh a bit, and he knew from that, more from her words, that she was serious. "It's been more than a year, though." To her amazement, she felt herself go scarlet. "I'm a little out of practice."

Ross pulled her tightly against him. "We'll improvise," he whispered as he kissed her. He did not know what perfume she used, but it was more intoxicating than the champagne. His mind reeled with the impact of their kisses.

As they strove to press more closely together, Ross knocked one of the empty trays with his knee and it upset one of the two empty coffee cups with a clatter. They broke apart, startled by the intrusion.

"Maybe we'd better go upstairs," Jennifer said when she had righted the overturned cup. "It's quieter." She did not want to be reminded of her hotel and the reception that was continuing at a more riotous level below her. For once, she wanted time to herself, so that she could revel in the joys of the moment without thinking of the myriad demands that might impinge on her. Was she irresponsible? The question nagged at her. If she were needed suddenly, what then?

Ross sensed her worry, and drew back from her. "What is it?"

"It's . . ."—she made a helpless gesture—"business." Saying the word aloud seemed absurd, something that an inexperienced girl might use for an excuse with an overly-impetuous boyfriend. "It's nothing."

However, Ross understood. "You're used to putting that first. I know." He kissed her hair, her forehead, her eyelids, her cheeks. "But it's time to put *you* first."

Jennifer nodded, and yielded her lips to him. Then, when he had managed to let her go long enough to get to his feet, she looked somewhat dazedly around her office. "The stairs . . ."

"On the left." He held out his hand to her, and brought her up beside him. He could not resist holding her, kissing her. He let his hands brush her breasts in anticipation, but would do no more until they were able to go on without interruption.

Jennifer led the way up the stairs, knowing with each step that this was what she wanted more than anything else in the world. By the time she reached her room, she was aflame with desire, longing for the satisfaction she had once been able to achieve in making love. That the satisfaction had ended two years before her marriage, and the emptiness of those years still haunted her, fueled her need all the more intensely.

As Ross closed the door behind them, he looked around the room briefly. One bedside lamp was burning and the curtains were open on a clear, starry night. There was a slight disorder in the room which only made it more appealing, more truly Jennifer's. He was vaguely aware that the predominant colors were a muted apple-green and sandy-gold, but forgot the room when Jennifer turned toward him, one hand loosening the pouf of hair atop her head.

Slowly, she took out the pins, then ran her fingers through the hair, shaking her head to let the dark tresses flow freely. She gave him a questioning look, then could not keep from smiling as he undid his velvet bow-tie and dropped it. "Do you want to undress me?"

"Yes," he said hoarsely, and took three unsteady steps toward her. His touch was eager, but he moved slowly, savoring the movement of the silk as he slid it off her lifted arms, chuckling once when he could not find the way to unfasten the shoulder closing. He gathered her necklace in his hand and set it and the dress on her dressing table stool.

She was nude now but for bra, pantyhose and earrings. Ross stared at her as he unbuttoned his shirt and took it and the tuxedo jacket off together. One of his gold cufflinks went flying as he dragged his hands through the cuffs, but neither paid any attention. Ross was deep-chested and solidly-muscled without being bulky. He had a fair amount of dark hair on his chest and lower arms, and there was a sprinkling of gray in that, as there was a white streak over his right brow. He reached out for her again, running his hands over her shoulders, and then to the fastening of her bra. The hooks resisted, then separated, and he felt her breasts against his chest.

Jennifer shivered as his hands cupped her breasts. He bent his head and kissed her nipples, exciting them to hardness with quick flicks of his tongue. He did not stop this as he hooked his thumbs in the waistband of her pantyhose. As he peeled the nylon down her legs, he moved further down her body until he knelt before her, and gently, almost reverently, touched the petal-folds between her legs. Jennifer trembled at his delicate probing, and the breath caught in her throat. It was all she could do to continue standing.

A minute later, when Ross stood again, he was naked and wholly aroused. He lifted Jennifer into his arms and carried her the few feet to her bed, setting her down and lying beside her with almost a single motion. "You're glorious," he said as he looked down into the molten blue of her eyes. He held himself back, not wanting to rush her, sensing a last remnant of doubt behind her anticipation. He soothed her, caressed her, brought her to a higher pitch of desire than she had known in years.

"Oh, now, Ross. Please, please, now." The soft glow of the bedside lamp showed the need in her from the line of her body to the curve of her mouth. She was open to him, shivering even in her bones for want of him. As he moved over her, she stared up at him, hoping she would not disappoint him. "Let me," she whispered, and reached to guide him into her.

He penetrated her slowly and deeply; he would not be rushed. He kissed her open mouth, his tongue moving in concert with his manhood. She moved with him, rocking with his deliriously-prolonged thrusts, carried by their passion as by an inexorable tide. She surrounded him, holding him with her legs, her arms, the deepest part of herself. There were no bells, no stars or comets—they were too remote, too impersonal for this closeness between them. She needed nothing more than this intimacy to sustain her rapture. The first restless twinges of fulfillment quivered through her, and she shook her head in protest. Not yet! Not yet! She strove to hold it back, but the force built in her, and the dizzying spasms shook her like a willow tree in a storm.

"Good," Ross breathed as he held himself within her and let her climax engulf him. When it had passed, he continued the long, slow thrusts. "Good."

Jennifer opened her eyes and stared up at him. "You're . . ."

"I want more," he said, and pressed closer to her, catching the lobe of her ear in his teeth and encountering her earring. The disruption was momentary, and both of them were more amused than annoyed. "Next time, take them off," Ross whispered to her as he bent his head to her breasts.

This prolonged gratification was new to Jennifer, and she required a little time to respond. As she was increasingly aroused, she explored him with her hands, touching his back, his face, the little nipples hidden in his chest hair—"Does that feel good?"—"Yeah."—"Does that?"—"Ummmmm."—his arms, his buttocks, the top of his legs. She liked the way the muscles slid and tightened under his skin, the scent of him, the fleeting taste of his sweat.

The end came in a long crescendo of passion that approached a blissful frenzy. First Ross increased the speed of his movements, and then his mouth sought her lips, her breasts, her shoulders, even her fingers, with more demanding kisses. Jennifer met his desire with her own, drawing him into her with all the strength of her release, laughing with him as they clung together in the tempest of completion.

"I should leave," Ross said for the sixth time, but made no effort to rise from the bed, or to move Jennifer away from the pillow of his shoulder.

"Not yet," she said, and kissed him lingeringly. It was almost four in the morning, and the last of the reception guests had tottered off to bed. The hotel was unusually still, and only the distant call of an early-waking bird disturbed them.

"You'll have people up and around in a while. They might notice the tux." He brushed her hip with gentle, tired fingers.

"You've been at the reception, or a room party, or something." She sighed. "You're right, but I wish you could stay." This was much more of an admission than she knew she could make, and saying the words aloud shook her.

Ross held her closer. "I can come back."

"Soon," she whispered.

"Tonight?" He kissed her before she could answer. "Tonight?"

"Yes . . . but not until after eight. We have a party of union negotiators coming in for a seminar and banquet, and I have to make a few special arrangements for . . ." She stopped. "I didn't mean to talk business."

"That's okay," Ross said with a smile. He did not want to move. He did not want to go away from Jennifer, from her nearness, her warmth, her promise. "Tonight we can both forget about business again." He stared out at the night sky, knowing that it would begin to lighten soon.

"I want to do that." She could not entirely believe what had happened to her, and she feared that if anything came between her and Ross, the pleasure and satisfaction they had shared would turn out to be ephemeral, one of those once-in-a-lifetime chances that could not be accomplished more than once. "Ross?"

"Umm?" He brushed the dark hair back from her face. Earlier, he had held her as she dozed in his arms, and he had marveled then, thinking that she could not possibly be more beautiful than she was in sleep; now that she was awake, seeking him, he decided he was wrong, that now she was lovelier than ever.

"Will you . . . ?" She did not finish. She knew better than to ask all the questions that jumbled inside her—Was it special? Will you continue to want me? Was this an accident? Or was it an amusement? And most forbidden of all: Was it love or lust?—but it cost an enormous effort to keep silent. She contented herself with kissing the corner of his mouth, and felt the rough stubble of his beard against her face. She touched his jaw, loving the scratchy feel of it under her fingers.

"Will I what?" he asked when she did not go on. He was stirred by her nearness, and experienced the first tug of desire, but sternly repressed it. There would be time tonight. It did not seem enough.

"Oh, nothing important." She snuggled on his chest, content to be there and disappointed because she knew, as he did, that he could not remain much longer.

"Which means it's too important to talk about now. Okay. Tonight then." He wrapped his arms around her and kissed her, leisurely, tenderly. "Tonight. Eight o'clock."

"Here," she added, and opened her lips to his.

Drew garnished the omelette with sprigs of watercress and added a ramekin of buttery cumin-and-lemon-flavored sauce to the plate. "How many times have you been out with Ross in the last two weeks, now?"

"Six," Jennifer said. "Why?"

"How's it going?" Drew asked, not answering her question. He put the plate on the tray for the dumbwaiter.

"Pretty well," was her guarded answer.

"How serious is it?" He reached for another plate and began to assemble his cold chicken salad with walnuts.

"I don't know yet. It's too soon to tell," Jennifer replied.

"Don't try to kid me, Jenny. I've never seen you this way about a man." Drew's face was serious and he watched Jennifer steadily. "I'm not going to tell you to go slow—that's foolish. People go at their own paces in any case. I'm not going to tell you not to get hurt—we all get hurt when we lose things we care about. But . . . look, Jenny, take it from me, because where this is concerned, I'm an expert. Love it for what it is, not what it could be." He deftly finished the salad and gave Jennifer another penetrating look. "Are you happy, Jenny?"

She nodded, feeling a tightness in her throat. "Yes, for the most part."

"That's good then." The salad joined the other dishes bound for the dumbwaiter.

She hesitated. "He's got a passel of nephews and nieces coming day after tomorrow, so we won't have . . . as much free time together." Her attempt at lightness was not successful. "It's probably just as well."

"How do you figure that?" Drew asked dryly.

"Well, I've got to find out who's been breaking into the trout pond, and get the thermal spring pump repaired again. It broke down again, and until they okay it on inspection, I can't open the hotsprings building for our guests. I've been neglecting that, and it's time I got my mind back on business," she said, sounding forlorn.

"Have one of your staff attend to it. That's what you pay them for. Besides, Fred Jenkins would rather work with Dean than you any time of day. Let him handle it, if you want a little time to yourself. It's good that you're getting a little enjoyment for a change. Jenny, this place isn't supposed to be a burnt offering. Don't get into the habit of thinking like that. You're not expected to commit suttee on the pyre of your hotel. Got that?"

"Yes," Jennifer said, feeling shamefaced. "You're too damn perceptive sometimes, Drew, do you know that?"

"So I've been told," he said, and reached for another plate. "I've got four cheeseburgers to prepare, so get out of my kitchen. I can't bear the thought of anyone seeing this." He waved her toward the door and was pleased that she laughed at his silliness. Only when the door closed behind her did the faint frown return to his face.

"Oh, Ross, I'm sorry," Jennifer said to the receiver. "I've got to do something about the trout pond in any case."

Ross heard the disappointment in her voice, and he shared it. "What about the trout pond?"

"We're getting a little casual vandalism," Jennifer said. "The cops think it's some of the local kids who need a little summer excitement and don't like the tourists. I've hired a couple extra patrollers for the groundsmen, got a new bolt for the gate, and I'm looking into an electronic surveillance system for the pond. I don't like the idea, but it might be the best way to go."

"Could be," he agreed. "Look, what about next Monday? I've got most of the afternoon free. We could have lunch or take a picnic off into the hills or just talk over iced coffee." He wanted to be with her, to see her, listen to her laughter, touch her. They had not been able to spend more than one evening together in the last week, and he discovered that he missed her, though they were only three miles apart.

Jennifer looked at her calendar and set her mouth in annoyance. "We've got a tour group coming in. German tourists doing the wine country, and that means a full special banquet. And a lot of your wines, incidentally."

He cursed under his breath. "Well, I can try for Thursday night, but it couldn't be until nine-thirty or ten." He was afraid that he sounded pushy and that she would resent his insistence.

"Call me Wednesday, and I'll see what I can arrange." She didn't like the way she was talking to him, as if they were trying to fit a little sex into a busy day. "I do want to see you, Ross. I want to see you now."

"I want to see you, Jennifer." He looked up at a rap on his door. "Just a moment!" he called, then said to the phone, "Aunt Rosa is doing a big dinner tonight, but why don't I call you afterward, okay?"

It was better than nothing, Jennifer thought. "Maybe I can drive over late for a glass of port." She heard the rap again over the phone.

"Tonight might be awkward. I'll call you." He hated to say that. He wanted to tell her to come over now, and the hell with it, but he could not. His irritation showed in his voice and he could not disguise it.

"Sure," Jennifer said wistfully as she hung up.

Henry Fisher looked very fit in his tennis whites, but his manner was entirely professional. "If you want to get the hotsprings building open, it's going to cost another five thousand dollars, and that would make your reserve fund dangerously low. Mr. Benedetto's offer is ideal to your purposes. Lease out that far acreage and permit him to pay for the construction. You're not doing badly, but the thermal springs . . ."

Jennifer glared at him. "When did you get this most recent offer? Right after the vandalism, you say?" She stared out the window toward the hotsprings building and felt her eyes mist over.

"Mr. Benedetto phones me quite regularly. I've told you that he's adamant about his offer. He's a very persistent man, Jennifer, and it might be easier to let him have what he wants."

Henry's choice of words struck her deeply, and she had to turn away from him or lose her composure. "Very persistent," she agreed bitterly. And why did Henry have to remind her that Ross wanted her fields for his wines? Why could he not leave her the illusion that he was courting her for herself? She blew her nose. "Sorry. I seem to be allergic to something that's blooming," she said by way of excuse for her moist eyes.

"You're letting yourself get over-tired," Henry said in his rather pontifical style. "You should take a little time off."

"The cobbler's children don't have shoes. The hotel owner never takes a vacation," Jennifer said, and faced Henry again, a determined, bright smile affixed to her mouth.

"And what shall I tell Mr. Benedetto?" Henry asked. "I have indicated that I'm advising you to take the offer."

So he doesn't have to court me anymore, Jennifer thought. He's got what he wants, or so he thinks, and there's no need to romance me. Dammit, dammit, dammit! she screamed inwardly. "Maybe I should just sell him the acreage and leave it at that," she thought aloud.

"Well, I wouldn't recommend that. If the lease works out, it could prove more profitable in the long run." Henry said this in carefully-considered and well-measured tones, a man making a proclamation. "There's no reason to break up any of the holding. With the price of real estate what it is in this area, you would be wise to keep as much of this place intact as you can." He beamed at her. "You've worked nothing short of a miracle here, Jennifer, and I want to see you continue from strength to strength." For Henry, this was a major admission, and Jennifer might have been more moved by it if she had not felt quite so hurt.

"Thanks, Henry. But we're not in the clear yet." She wanted to have half an hour to herself, to try to sort out her hurt and confusion, but the buzzer on her desk sounded and she heard Muriel's voice say, "Ted Hatfield on the phone, Jennifer."

Jennifer looked up at Henry. "Excuse me, Henry. I have to deal with this."

Henry's demeanor changed. "I wouldn't recommend any direct dealings with Mr. Hatfield. Keep that in mind."

"I will," Jennifer said, and wished miserably that Henry had given her the same terse warning about Ross Benedetto.

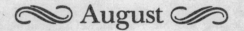

August

Muriel had changed her hairstyle and looked very attractive as she came in from jogging. "The figures are on the desk," she said to Jennifer as she blotted the sweat from her face. "A day like this can take it out of you. It must be over ninety out there."

"The radio said ninety-two," Jennifer murmured as she took the pages and looked over them. "Not bad. We haven't had to use the reserve fund in two months. That's promising, considering how long the place has been open. How's the elephant-naming contest coming? Do we have any more entries?"

"Three or four. I think it was great of Eric Bush to agree to be the judge. It makes it sound classy as all get out." She ran her hands through her short hair and grinned. "I'll have to shower before sitting down to work, or no one will be able to stand being in here with me. Do you mind?"

"Use the one in my quarters," Jennifer suggested. She was both pleased and slightly envious of Muriel's blooming good looks. She remembered her Uncle Samuel saying that there was no cosmetic in the world that could beat love for making a woman pretty.

"Thanks." She smiled at Jennifer.

Jennifer opened a file on the desk and offered the contents to Muriel. "You'll be glad to know that the insurance company will pay for all the repairs on the cottage. They've decided that even if it might have been arson, we're not to blame and they are responsible. That's *one* thing we won't have hanging over us."

"I understand that Lieutenant Bright still thinks that the fire was set deliberately," Muriel remarked. "That's not easily ignored by the insurance company."

"But so far he hasn't been able to prove his allegations. My only worry now would be what the reaction might be if we had another accident of any major significance." It had bothered her more than she admitted, but Jennifer had been telling herself for weeks that there was no point in borrowing trouble. She turned as the door opened and Drew came in. Drew and Muriel exchanged greetings as the older woman left the office.

"Hi," Jennifer said. "Playing hooky?"

"No, I'm bolting," he said with a smile. "Mercy, Muriel's looking spiffy. I wonder what kind of tonic the good doctor is prescribing for her." Drew sat on the edge of the desk, one leg dangling, the other braced on the floor. He bent a bit lower. "I don't like to mention this, Jenny, but you're looking peaked." He pronounced the last with two syllables. "Have you been getting run down again?"

"It's just that we're busy," she answered evasively. "I don't have much spare time right at the moment."

"And I haven't seen Ross around as much." He gave her a quick, canny stare and saw her flush. "Problems there?"

"Not really. It's a busy time for him, too, and his family is around. It isn't easy to get an hour or two alone, and . . ." She did not want to say she hated to make love on a tight schedule. It made her feel like a convenience, not a woman with a lover.

"It's always tough sometimes, Jenny. I know, oh, brother, do I know. You don't have to kid me, or yourself, about that." He put his hand on her shoulder. "If you want to talk, just come down to my room."

"Thanks, Drew," she said, feeling moisture in her eyes. "But I don't think it will be necessary. Besides, when will either of us have the time? We've only got another six weeks of summer, and then what? Sure, there are the Thanksgiving and Christmas seasons, but we've got to have some business between now and then or we're going to have . . ."

"Boss, boss," Drew interrupted her. "Stop worrying, for God's sake. Worry doesn't turn out reservations. You're doing everything you can to make this place run right, and you've got some excellent bookings. There are more and more people coming up on weekend wine-tasting tours. We've already got some of those coming over from Benedetto. I think Ross recommends the place. That slacks off a little in the fall, but not too much, and that will help out."

"But the costs are so high," she sighed. "And we're going to have to hire regular union help in the fall when the work-study kids go back to school."

"We'll manage. You're doing great, but you won't believe it. Well, *I* believe it. I won't let myself get side-tracked by a lot of gobble-de-gook about empty rooms and union contracts. And you shouldn't, either."

Jennifer smiled. "Thanks, Drew. I get distraught sometimes, and you make a difference." She stood and gave him a kiss on the cheek.

Studiously, Drew traced an invisible design on the desktop with his finger. "It wouldn't hurt, also, if you'd swallow that stubborn pride of yours and call Ross."

"And if he doesn't want to talk to me?" she countered, more sharply than she had intended.

"He'll want to talk to you. He's nuts about you."

"But what if he doesn't want to be? What if he's trying to withdraw from . . . what's going on between us?" The breath caught in her throat and she coughed to cover it.

"Then he's fighting a losing battle," Drew said. "Jenny, you can trust him. You shouldn't think he's using work as an excuse to stay away from you."

Drew's notion was so close to the very thing that Jennifer had been fearing that she lifted one hand as if to protect herself from a blow. She laughed a bit unsteadily and did her best to make light of it. "I shouldn't let it get to me, I guess, but I don't seem to be able to keep from feeling, oh, I don't know, abandoned, or forgotten." Saying her fears aloud brought another spurt of tears to her eyes, but she forced a calmer expression onto her face. "It's fatigue, I know. And all the pressure. Given a little time and a few days' rest, I'll have a better sense of perspective again. As soon as the summer is over, I'm going to give myself a few days in San

Francisco and do some shopping and other entertaining things."

"Why not do it right now?" Drew suggested. "Come September, you'll be caught up in getting the new cottages built and the hotsprings ready for their expansion and all the rest of it."

It was true, Jennifer admitted to herself. "I'll think about it."

"Which means no. What if Ross were to kidnap you for a weekend, what then?" He was still worried about her. He had seen the smudges under her luminous blue eyes deepen and darken, and now there was a strain around her mouth that had not been there two weeks before. "You need time off, Jenny. The rest of us can manage without you for a few days."

"But . . ." Jennifer began.

"All I ask is that you think about it, not as something that would be nice to do someday when you aren't so busy, but something that you can do right now. Okay?" He leaned forward. "Okay?"

"Sure, okay. I will think about it. I'd like to do it." She could not bring herself to say that she would hate to spend so much time alone now. She wanted company, the company of a man who would be concerned for her, would take care of her wants and her pleasure. The thought of sitting alone in a hotel room, or visiting her friends by herself, was more depressing than her occasionally panicky fears late at night that she would always be single, isolated.

"I'm not going to let this drop, Jenny. I'm keeping an eye on you." Drew wagged his finger at her as if she were a recalcitrant child. "Remember that."

Jennifer gave him a gentle smile. "Thanks, Drew. Really."

Helene turned on her most devastating smile and purred at Ross, "Don't you think we should close the door? What if Aunt Rosa should come in?"

"I think we should leave the door open," Ross said pleasantly, indicating the sofa on the other side of his desk. "It's been quite a while, Helene."

She pouted prettily. "And you haven't forgiven me for taking up with Greg?"

"That's your . . . affair. What puzzles me is why you're here now." He toyed with a pen, hoping to keep himself distracted from her intense sensuality.

"Nothing very important," she said, sitting and crossing her legs so that the superb line of her thigh was clearly outlined by the soft drape of her skirt. "Hasn't it been hot?"

"Very," Ross agreed, waiting.

"Well," Helene said after a minute in a more businesslike tone, "I'm worried about my running. We're getting opposition from the anti-feminist types. Not that I'm much of a feminist, but these are the ones who insist that a woman's place is solely in the home, and they feel that I should not be running for public office."

"That's a problem," Ross acknowledged. "But what am I supposed to do about it?"

"Put in a word here and there that I'm not an irresponsible mother or flagrantly immoral or any of those things. It's better said to men, of course, but if the chance arises to talk to some of the local women, the ones who are fence-sitting, then . . ." She touched her hair and smiled warmly.

"What good would that do? Why should they pay any attention to me?" Ross felt an unwanted pang of desire as he looked at Helene. His affair with her had been straightforward and uncomplicated, not like his continuing fascination with Jennifer. For a moment, he longed to have that simplicity again, the lack of worry and general involvement, but the impulse was gone as quickly as it came. His relationship with Helene had been shallow, and now that it was over, he rarely thought of it but in passing. With Jennifer, it was different. He found in her some of the same compelling involvement he had had with his wife, Rosemary. But he had been a decade younger then, a man who had yet to prove himself, and his love for his talented, elfin wife was a young man's love. Until she died, he had not known what it was to be lonely, or to be bound by the power of a memory. That had tempered him the way no other experience could, and he was grateful for it, and could not deny the impact his learning to live with loss had had on his life. He did not want to endure such a loss again, but through it, once, he had learned how to value what he had while he had it. He liked Helene, admired her ambition, but that was all. Jennifer had broken down the barriers he had made around his life with her bravery and strength, and he had not been the same since he met her.

". . . but you never know who might be listening, and you're good with people, as well as being respected."

Ross realized he had not been listening, so engrossed was he in his own thoughts. "I doubt my word carries all that much weight," he said, hoping that she would not know he had let his attention wander.

"Come on, Ross," Helene protested sweetly, "you know better than that. No one will ignore what you say, even if it's only a word or two after dinner. I need to change the direction of those women without making it too obvious." She folded her arms and there was nothing coy about her now, and though she was still stunningly attractive, she did not appear to be out to sweet-talk him any longer.

"That's good," Ross said. "I'm all for it. But do you think, considering what has gone on between us in the past—which is not the best-kept secret in the Napa Valley—that my word would count for much with the women you're trying to reach? What about finding women's groups and seeing if they'll support you?"

"Thanks, but no thanks. Feminism, closely-espoused, is a touchy issue right now." She started to pace. "What am I going to do, Ross? I want to win, but believe it or not, I don't want to sell out to anybody. I've got this far clean, and I intend to stay that way."

"I believe you," Ross said, knowing how fierce Helene's pride was. "What about any businesswomen's associations? Surely, they're in the same boat you are?"

"I'm doing that, but it isn't enough. I'm going to need more contacts and I haven't any idea where to start. Dammit!" She stopped and looked at Ross. "I have to try every avenue that's open to me, and you're one of them. No hard feelings?"

"Of course not," Ross said, and got up. "If I can do something, I will. That's not lip-service. I'll tell anyone who asks that you're a capable and competent woman and a fair sight better than the jerk we've got in there now. If that's enough, then you're welcome to it. But I can't promise to deliver more than that." He admired the way she moved, swiftly, sensually but with a predatory grace that was at once attractive and unnerving.

"That's better than most of the answers I get. Thanks." She swung her purse and gave him a roguish grin. "You're a plain-dealer, Ross, and I can't say that about most of the people I know. It's a shame we never worked things out."

"Not so much a shame as a stroke of good fortune. You don't want to spend the rest of your life being a vintner's wife, Helene, and you know it. You weren't cut out for the life I lead. We were lucky enough to recognize the differences in us so that we can stay friends. We don't do badly as friends." He held out his hand to her. "I'm pleased you came by, and flattered to think you wanted my help."

Helene gave a feline shrug. "You can't blame me for trying the best I can."

"No, I can't. I expect it of you," Ross said pleasantly. "And I wish you all the good luck in the world. For what it's worth, I think you'll win the election."

"Thanks. I'm *counting* on winning. I'm spending almost everything I've saved over the last six years to get me through the campaign, and it bothers me to have such problems come up now. I don't like being caught up short so close to my goal." She held Ross's hand a bit longer than necessary and gave him another melting smile. "Maybe later?"

"Maybe," Ross said, showing her to the office door. There was nothing in his manner to offer her encouragement.

Helene knew the signs. "There's someone new in your life, isn't there?"

"Not exactly," was his careful answer as he reached for the doorknob.

"Ah. It must be very special this time. Good luck with it, Ross. Another time, I might have tried to change your mind, but at the moment I've got other fish to fry. Whoever she is, I hope she knows what a good man she's getting." She flashed him her wide grin that the photographers loved so well, and then went quickly down the stairs so that she would not have to see Ross close the door.

"It's the bikers," said the deputy sheriff as he stared down at the dead trout floating on the surface of the pond. "We've had a lot of trouble with them this summer. We do what we can, but . . ." He gave Jennifer an exasperated look.

"But there are only so many of you, and you don't know how to handle them without creating an incident that might escalate hostilities," she finished for him. "I do understand, Deputy Sayer. The Hasslunds told me about the vandalism at their place year before last. What I don't understand is why they wanted to come up here and kill all my fish!" She had been told about the poisoned fish two hours before, and she was over the worst of her outrage.

"That's the truth, Ms. Wystan. Unfortunately, until we catch them breaking the law, we can't do much." The deputy wiped his forehead with a swipe of his arm. "Hot day."

Jennifer stared down at the dead fish floating on the

stinking water and nodded. She had already called her groundsmen to come and start the messy business of cleanup. "We'll have to drain the pond and have the soil checked before I can stock it again," she said, looking at Deputy Sayer. "When do you think your team will be out to finish their investigation? I want to get this taken care of as soon as possible."

"Well, I've got a couple dozen photos of the place, and there are those bike tracks up on the hill. The team should be out of here by three in the afternoon, and that means you can start cleaning the fish out now, if you think best." He sniffed the air, knowing that in a few hours it would be redolent of decaying trout.

"Good. And I've got to call in to the insurance company," she said this glumly, knowing that a second claim coming so soon on the last would not be well-received. "Do you think they'll be . . . reasonable?"

"They should. You aren't the only place that's had trouble with them this summer." He looked at the trout pond again. "It's too bad this had to happen. I been hearing good things about this place, and I know that there are customers who want the whole package or nothing at all."

Jennifer had not yet had a reservation canceled or cut short, but she knew that there were a few guests who were muttering about this latest crisis, and it would not surprise her if they left before their stay was finished. "It's the kind of problem we all face," she said as philosophically as she could. It was not easy to keep that attitude, given the time and money she had put into the trout pond.

"If you need me to put in a word for you, with the hatchery or the insurance," Deputy Sayer said, "you just give me a call. I don't think you'll have any difficulties, but I just want you to know that I'll do what I can for you." He winked at her. "And I wouldn't say no to a free drink when I'm off duty. Not a bribe, naturally, but a kind of gesture."

"Any time," Jennifer said.

"It won't be for a month or so, with my schedule the way it is, but I'd take it kindly if you're willing to do that." He put his hat back on. "Well, I got to get this film into the lab and get back on my patrol. I'll tell the investigation team to hurry it up. They aren't going to like smelling dead fish any more than anyone else." He began to walk away from her toward the fire-break road he had used as access. "Any trouble, you remember to call me."

"Thanks, deputy," Jennifer called after him, and waved as he got into his squad car and drove off in a rooster-tail of tawny red dust. Deputy Joe Sayer, she thought, was a far cry from Lieutenant Bright of the Fire Department. She did not try to hide her relief, but it was short-lived. Within the hour she had a call from Henry Fisher, and her spirits fell.

"Even though it's an accident, I think it would be best if we modify the claim on it." He spoke crisply and with a great deal of emphasis.

"But if I can't afford to file another claim, why do I have the insurance in the first place?" Jennifer protested.

"You're very new to the business. This is clearly a case of vandalism, but you know as well as I do that the insurance company was reluctant the last time, and this second claim, coming on top of the last, may cause them to raise your rates. At the moment, you can better afford to clean, drain, test, refill and restock the trout pond than you can afford a twenty-percent jump in insurance premiums. Ask Muriel Wrather, if you doubt me." He was sounding huffy again, and Jennifer knew he was offended that she should question his judgment.

"Twenty percent?" she echoed, horrified. "They couldn't do that, could they?" Jennifer's voice rose with anger. "Henry, I have insurance for just such instances as this. You've negotiated the contracts for my coverage. Now, I know you're one of the best there is, but I wonder if you aren't being over-cautious. Look, isn't there a way to put a proviso into a contract, even an insurance contract, that keeps the amount that the premiums can be raised at any one time within limits?" She wanted to sound sensible and pragmatic, but she could hear the annoyance in her voice, and she gritted her teeth.

"It can be done," Henry said even more stiffly, "but you're hardly in the best position to bargain. Within half a year of opening, you have had two significant claims. Now, Jennifer, if you were in their position, how would you feel?"

"Worried," Jennifer said, and wished that she had not. "But it's a different case than most. We're not taking stupid risks." She had to bite back her sarcasm once more. "Henry, please, do me a favor. Talk to the insurance company and see what they have to tell you. If you can discuss the matter off the record, so much the better. I know that you're telling me what you honestly think is best, and I trust you. I know that you would not deliberately misguide me, because you've helped me so much already. But I also have to be able to make my own decisions. The White Elephant is my place, my business, my home, and I have to do everything that I can to protect it."

Henry sounded humbled. "Of course, Jennifer. I'll do what I can for you. You're certainly entitled to know where you stand, but I warn you that you may not like what they tell you."

"I'm prepared to deal with that," Jennifer said, hoping it was true.

"And if you would only accept Mr. Benedetto's offer and lease the acres to the winery, it would not be a problem. . . ." Henry ventured.

"Damn Mr. Benedetto!" Jennifer snapped, and had to restrain herself to keep from hanging up without another word.

"Jennifer!" Henry objected. "He's being both patient and reasonable."

Jennifer wanted to add that he was being more than that. But the thought of Ross distressed her, and she sighed instead. "Sorry, Henry. I've spent a good part of the day with a couple hundred dead fish. I'm sorry I snapped at you, but you can appreciate, I hope, why I'm a little testy."

"Better than you know," Henry answered. "I'll let you go for the time being and we will talk again tomorrow. Would three in the afternoon be a convenient time for me to call?"

"I'll make a point of being in the office," Jennifer answered, looking up sharply as a knock sounded on the door. "Just a second, Henry," she said to the receiver and called out, "Who is it?"

"There's a gentleman from the *Dispatch* to see you," Muriel called through the door. "If you can spare a few minutes."

"There's a reporter wanting to see me, Henry," Jennifer said, adding to Muriel, "Just a moment. I'm on the phone."

"That's to be expected," Henry said ponderously. "I'd advise you not to avoid him. An unkind remark in the press right now would not be a great deal of help to you."

"That's what I thought," Jennifer concurred. "No matter what I sound like, Henry, I really am grateful to you. Don't be put off by my . . ."

"You have a great deal on your mind, and I know that

times like these are quite difficult for anyone. Tomorrow at three." He hung up without further comment.

Jennifer took a couple of minutes to prepare herself to meet the reporter, running a comb through her hair and checking her mirror to be sure she did not look as if she had been wading in mud—which she had—or smell too much of decaying fish.

"This is David Howell," Muriel told Jennifer as she came out of her private office. "Ms. Wystan."

David Howell stood up and smiled in a tired, cynical way at her. "Hello, Ms. Wystan."

"David Howell is a good Welsh name," Jennifer said to the older man with a determined charm she did not often employ, and was pleased to see him thaw a bit. "You're with the *Dispatch?*"

"Yes. I heard about the vandalism of your trout pond on the police radio." He held up a tape recorder. "You don't mind if I use this, do you? My handwriting is terrible." He had obviously said this so often that he did not think about it at all.

"Certainly," Jennifer said, sensing that any refusal would be construed as subterfuge. "We're still in the middle of things here, so I don't know how much I can tell you just yet."

"Tell me anything you like. From what I heard, bikers broke into your grounds and poisoned the fish in your trout pond." He motioned toward the chairs. "Would you prefer to sit down?"

Jennifer took advantage of this. "Why don't we use the smaller conference room? It's empty today and that way we won't be disturbed."

When they reached the conference room she closed the door and motioned Howell to a chair.

"About the bikers . . ." he prompted.

"Well, that's not been established, that bikers were responsible, I mean. There were tire tracks found that looked as if they were made by a pretty big motorcycle, but it hasn't been confirmed. I'd appreciate it if you'd make that clear in whatever you write, by the way." She could see that this was not what Howell wanted, but she was determined not to be lured into making rash statements.

"Bikers have done similar things before," he said, and waited.

"So I understand." She sat down on the opposite side of the oblong table that was the focal point of the room. "But I think it's best to leave that aspect of the question to the police."

Howell frowned. "And the bikers, or whoever it was, killed off all your fish?"

"That's right," Jennifer said with a bit more spirit. "All of them. At the moment, we're trying to clean up the mess."

"What are you planning to do about it?" Howell asked, pouncing on the question.

"Do about it? I've made extra security provisions for the rest of the summer, of course, and increased the number of patrols at the pond." It was going to cost a great deal more than she wanted to have to pay, but at this stage she knew she had little choice if she wanted to convince her guests that everything was being done to ensure their protection and enjoyment.

"You seem fairly calm about the occurrence." His tone was insinuating.

Jennifer was able to chuckle for Howell, though it was more of an effort than she cared to admit. "Now, yes." She lifted her hands to show her resignation. "When I first saw the trout pond, I wanted to throttle someone. Anyone. But that solves nothing, and I'd rather turn my time and energy to something constructive."

"You're acting more sensibly than most of the folks around here. Something like your trout pond happen to them and they'd be up in arms, demanding a stricter enforcement of the law, and policemen at the gates."

"And they're not running resort hotels. The circumstances are different. Also, it's much too early to start casting blame about. Suppose it wasn't bikers at all? Suppose it was someone else? Why should we create ill-will for no good reason?" Much more of this, she thought, and she would hire herself out part-time to Helene as a speech writer.

"Are you going to reopen the trout pond?" Howell asked, returning to his prepared questions.

"I hope so. It's been very popular, as I'm sure you know. But first we have to find out what sort of poison was used and how much of it has leaked into the soil. If the amounts are small enough to be safe, then of course it will be opened again. Those decisions will be made in the future, when I have the information I need and the permission of the Board of Supervisors. Check with me in a couple of weeks and I'll be able to tell you something about how it's going." She trusted that she sounded optimistic.

"You're not willing to go out on a limb now, are you? No guesses, no speculation, is that it?" Howell teased her, familiar with all the usual tricks of evasion that people used with the press.

"I don't even know which tree we're on yet, let alone which limb," Jennifer replied with a touch of asperity. "I'm not trying to hold out on you, Mr. Howell—I simply don't know where I stand." She made a move to rise. "In the meantime, I have a hotel to run, and I should get back to it."

"Just a couple more questions, Ms. Wystan. I won't be much longer." He had that look, one that Jennifer had seen before in newsmen, that indicated Howell had saved the best for last. "I heard a rumor that someone is trying to sabotage your operation here. What do you think about that?"

Jennifer stared at him. "You're kidding." She wasn't quite able to laugh. "That's absurd. Who would want to? Why?"

"You're sitting on a lot of valuable land, and land is at a premium here. If you think that people aren't willing to try a prank or two, you're being naive, Ms. Wystan." He looked at her expectantly.

"Perhaps I am," she said, bristling. "But I don't know what else I can believe. You might doubt what I tell you, but I can't think that poisoning fish is a good way to run me out of the Napa Valley."

"You've already had a fire here, haven't you? One of the cottages burned down." He watched her closely, seeking for that tell-tale shift of the eyes.

"Have you been talking to Lieutenant Bright?" Jennifer said with a shake of her head. "It was an accident. Hotels have accidents. That was the last cottage on the road and the fire started from a pipe that should have been out and wasn't. I agree that it was foolish, but hardly a plot to bring me to my knees." She put her hands on her hips as she rose. "Mr. Howell, if you unearth some fiendish conspiracy to drive me away from here, I hope you'll let me and my attorney know about it. If you don't—and frankly I doubt it's likely that you will—then I trust you'll use a little discretion about how you report the matter."

Howell nodded. "You're damned cool, Ms. Wystan, and I say that as a compliment. Not many people in business would be so willing to extend the benefit of the doubt the way you do."

"I don't see that I have anything to gain from being suspicious all the time, Mr. Howell. There are difficulties enough in this business without that."

David Howell grinned at her. "Would you mind if I came back here, maybe in a couple of days, for a drink and some talk? Off the record, of course."

Jennifer was at once flattered and annoyed. "Mr. Howell, are you asking me for a date?"

"In a way," he answered, trying to smile openly. It was something he had not done in a long time and he did not do it well.

"Call me on the weekend and I'll let you know how it's going here. This is the busiest we've ever been and I simply don't know how much, if any, time I'll have free." It was crazy, she told herself. And there was every chance that Howell only wanted another chance to pump her for information when she was more off-guard.

"I won't tell my boss, if that would make you feel better," Howell volunteered.

What difference would that make? Jennifer thought. He could always tell his boss later, when he had the information he wanted in hand. It was an effort to be polite, but Jennifer had had long years of practice and she used all of her experience now. "That's kind of you, but I wouldn't want to put you at a disadvantage, Mr. Howell. And if you'll excuse me, I do have work to do. I hope that this has been some help. I'm sorry I haven't anything more to tell you." She was about to shake his hand, but thought better of it, and gave him a nod as she went back into her office.

Jennifer had just got away from an embarrassing conversation with Ted Hatfield, who was still trying to convince her that the White Elephant should be turned into an exclusive condominium enclave, when Wilbur Cory approached her with a tall, spare man at his side.

"Good to see you at the Board of Supervisors' meeting, Mrs. Wystan," Wilbur said by way of opening. "You're not listening to all the schemes Ted Hatfield is trying to sell, are you?"

"No, Mr. Cory, I'm not," Jennifer informed him. She had done her best to look rigidly professional. Her hair was pulled back off her face and she had worn the most severe summer-weight pantsuit she possessed. But she had seen two of the men at the meeting give her a speculative look that bothered her. The man with Wilbur had such a look, and she wondered if she would have to be polite to yet another boor.

"Good thing. This is Mr. Bronson. He's the local administrator for the power company. He's been wanting to meet you." Wilbur looked at his companion, obviously convinced that he had completed his obligations to him. "This is Mrs. Wystan, the owner of the White Elephant."

Bronson leaned down. "It's a pleasure, Mrs. Wystan. Or is it Ms. Wystan?"

"I prefer the latter," Jennifer admitted. "What may I do for you, Mr. Bronson?"

"It's more of a question of what I can do for you, Ms. Wystan. I was listening tonight to the various problems you claimed you'd face when the new zoning regulations go into effect. It appears that your hotsprings, except for the swimming pool you've attached to them, will have to be redesigned and structurally altered to be in accordance with the regulations." He paused, giving this time to sink in.

"Yes, that was my understanding," Jennifer said.

"Well, that can get pretty expensive, from what I hear, the way costs are going up and the interest rates are climbing. You might want to think carefully about what you do." He had a smooth, deep voice and a manner so wonderfully bland that it was tempting to agree with him without question; these assets had carried him a long way.

"I have funds for improvements, Mr. Bronson," Jennifer said, becoming stiff with him.

"All the same, you might want to give a little consideration to what I have to say. You mentioned at the meeting tonight that at the rate the supervisors are going, it won't pay you to keep that old spa building open. Which is what I wanted to talk to you about, Ms. Wystan. That building and the hotsprings." He paused, giving her a chance to speak before he launched into his comments.

"What about them, Mr. Bronson?" Jennifer asked, knowing he expected it of her.

"Well, as you know, we're very interested in developing more geothermal installations in this area, and we're very interested in the hotsprings on your property because of the speed of flow of the springs. You have a high-temperature spring, and a good rate of flow. We'd like . . ." His prepared speech was interrupted by Jennifer, who shook her head impatiently.

"Mr. Bronson, I know you're not going to believe this, but I don't want to sell any part of my land. . . ."

"We're interested only in the hotsprings, and we could negotiate an extended lease instead of an outright sale." His face was set for maximum ingratiation, but it was still not enough to change Jennifer's mind.

"You're not hearing me, Mr. Bronson," Jennifer said, surprised that she could be so forceful with the man in public. "I do not want to sell, lease or otherwise surrender one foot of my land."

"Actually, we would only need a couple of acres at the very most, Ms. Wystan. . . ." Mr. Bronson said, ever-hopeful.

"A couple of acres sounds pretty big to me. And I doubt you'd be willing to keep up the old spa buildings, or allow the guests access to the hotsprings, would you?" Jennifer's blue eyes were bright with temper now.

"Well, no, that wouldn't be possible. But think of the advantages. There would be the financial security of the lease or sale, to say nothing of the added security of our patrols to protect you and . . ."

Although Jennifer knew it was not entirely wise, she cut short Bronson's assurances. "Mr. Bronson, I doubt very much my guests would like to be next door to an armed camp. It might be to the power company's advantage to have the land, but it is not to mine to give it up. I'm starting to make a go of the place, and you're showing me a new way to forfeit everything I've gained. I do not want to have your installation in my backyard."

"Ms. Wystan, I seem to have offended you. That wasn't my least intention, believe me." Bronson did everything but bow to show how distressed he was.

"She's got a lot of spunk, this young lady," Wilbur put in. He had been listening with interest. "Don't you give her a bad time, Larry. She knows her mind, and I don't think you're going to change it at this stage."

Jennifer had never thought she would be grateful to Wilbur Cory for anything but his boy Ben, but at the moment she could have kissed him. "That's high praise, coming from you," she contented herself with saying.

"Well, little lady, you've shown that you're not here to play, but to work. We respect work in this part of the world. It's just too bad that you're getting caught in the code changes. If there were a way to give you a variance, I'd see that you got it, but frankly, you're exactly the kind of setup we're trying to bring up to date, and about all I could arrange would be a reasonable extension of deadline." Wilbur put his hand on her shoulder in an awkward way, as if to make amends for his earlier, harsher words.

Larry Bronson cleared his throat and once again molded his features into an expression of maximum geniality. "Well, naturally, we didn't mean to impose upon Ms. Wystan. Of course, there's no question of forcing anyone to cooperate with us, and coercion is completely out of the question. We want to be on the up-and-up from square one. Anything else is . . ."

"Bad for business," Jennifer finished for him.

"That's a factor, but it's not all of it," Bronson said uncomfortably. "We're a public utility, and we have an obligation to provide power to our customers. It's just something we'd like you think over, Ms. Wystan," Bronson continued, game to the last. "In case you find you have to . . . rethink your position. We'd be interested later on as much as now."

"So I supposed," Jennifer said rather sharply.

Wilbur looked over at the other man. "No more of this, Larry. She's given you her answer, and you can tell those bosses of yours that she declined."

"Of course," Bronson said sourly.

Jennifer thought they were both being absurd. But she sensed that behind all the polite phrases and the good manners, there was iron determination in Bronson, and that worried her. As she left the high school auditorium where the meeting had been held, she could not shake the uneasy feeling that she should keep an eye on Larry Bronson and his bosses at the power company.

"I heard that the Fish and Game Commission gave you the go-ahead to restock the trout pond," Ross said to Jennifer as they finished the last of the omelettes Drew had insisted on making them, though it was three in the afternoon and in theory this was slack time in the kitchen.

"Yes. I had the call yesterday morning." She finished her coffee and smiled at Ross, thinking she was very pleased he had taken the time to stop by.

"That's good news, isn't it?"

"Yes. And I hadn't thought to have any. It's been such a tense period, waiting for the results and watching to see what the investigation came up with. We're still not sure who it was who broke in, but at least the cops aren't insisting that it was bikers." She felt pleasantly full now, which was not a sensation she often enjoyed with the demands of her schedule. It was good to be able to sit for a few minutes with nothing more to do than talk to Ross.

"And why do you say that, Jennifer? What bothers you about blaming the bikers?" He was intrigued with her stubborn refusal to join the general hue and cry against the motorcyclists.

"I don't like to see anyone made the scapegoat. If they did it, then they should take the blame. If they didn't, there's no good reason to give it to them except that it's easier than continuing a dead-end investigation." She moved her plate aside and brought her coffee cup nearer.

"That's commendable, but don't you think you're bending over backward for them?"

"No, I don't think so. If someone could give me real proof—and a set of tire tracks isn't enough—that the bikers are responsible for the fish, then fine. Ross, you don't want to punish the wrong parties, do you?" She watched him as the waiter filled her cup and then Ross's.

"Put it that way, and no, I don't." He reached for the cream and added a touch of it. "But you aren't going to find a lot of sympathy for bikers around here. We've had too much from them already. They ruined three acres of my grapes—during a bad drought year, too—and that puts them beyond the pale for me. I'm not fair about them, but, well, I have reason to feel as I do."

Jennifer heard him out with a great deal of sympathy. "If I had gone through that, I'd probably be a lot more ready to suspect the bikers right off. Who knows? I might be this cautious because I don't want them to get *really* mad at me and come back to do some serious damage."

Ross smiled at her. "You're not the kind to knuckle under. I don't think that's your reason, whatever you believe." He was glad to be in her company. After the long, exhausting time he'd spent with his brother the day before, he liked having a few tranquil minutes alone with Jennifer. The dining room of the White Elephant was not quite as private as he would have preferred, but he would not complain.

"Thanks. I could use a vote of confidence along about now." She was delighted that Ross, of all people, said that to her. "You're embarrassing me."

"Come on, Jennifer. I haven't said anything that isn't true." He reached out and touched her hand. "You're doing great."

She was not able to say anything for a moment, and then she cleared her throat. "I'm very glad you think so."

"I do. And so do a lot of other people around here. When you first took over, there were some doubts, and I admit that some of them were mine, but that didn't last." This time Ross did not release her hand. "I'm proud of you, and not because you're an attractive, desirable woman, but because you're doing your business well. Some of the other resort managers could learn a few lessons from you."

It was almost more than Jennifer could stand. She loved to hear praise, but so much, and coming from Ross, made her feel she did not deserve it. The other side of that coin, which was harder for her to admit than the first, was that she loved it, that she thrived on Ross's good opinion. "Well, I want to do the best job I can," she forced herself to say as lightly as she could. "And things are going well," Jennifer admitted with satisfaction. "Henry Fisher—my attorney, I think you know him—has said that he's fairly certain that if we continue this way that we can get along without Uncle Samuel's additional funds from the trust he left. Of course, if the autumn and winter are very slow or we run into other problems, everything could change, but at the moment, it looks pretty good."

Ross beamed at her. "That's great! It's good to hear you being optimistic for a change."

Jennifer smiled enchantingly at him, her mouth curving warmly, and she had to resist the urge to ask him to stay longer. She knew he had work to do, as did she, and she was determined that she would not use her job as a lure. "In a month I may be singing a different tune, but for the time being, I think that I can make a go of it."

"I hope it keeps up, and I hope that you make all the progress you want through the off-season." He said it with genuine feeling, but could not help adding, "And I hope that you'll still have a little time for me."

"I hope I will, too," Jennifer admitted, and flushed. "I . . . I'm sorry that we're both so busy just now, but there is a slack period coming up here. I don't know how it is at the winery, but maybe you'll want to . . ." She could not bring herself to say the rest.

"Oh, God, I do want to," Ross said, holding her hand more tightly. "And I won't have the time to spare for another six weeks or so, or not a great deal of it. Maybe if you don't mind having . . ." He knew that anything he suggested would sound cheap, and it was not what he wished to convey. "Maybe we can get together later in the evening, when most of your work is over for the day and they don't need me at the winery. We could have a late supper and anything else that you'd like." He had not felt so awkward since he was starting college. How could he make Jennifer understand that time with her, no matter how brief, was precious to him?

"It might be possible," she conceded. "But I don't know exactly when would be a good time. I'm not trying to put you off, but . . ."

"Suppose I give you a call a couple mornings a week for the next few weeks and we'll see how things are shaping up?" He was not certain the idea would work out, but he was determined to try it.

"Fine." Jennifer got up reluctantly. "Call me tomorrow?"

"If I can. I'll try, Jennifer. And thanks for taking time for me. I'm very happy for you." He wanted to find an excuse to ask her to stay with him a bit longer, but that would not do. She had her work to attend to, and he was needed back at the winery. He watched her walk across the room with a sense of disappointment, and promised himself that he would make sure they got together at least once a week until the end of September, when their time would be more flexible.

"Well, dammit," Jennifer said to Drew with more heat than usual, "if he didn't intend to call, why did he say that he would? I can't figure it out. I don't know why I'm wasting my valuable time trying to figure it out. It's idiotic!" She flung her hands into the air and cast a smoldering glance at her chef.

"Maybe he's got things he can't get away from," Drew suggested mildly. "He's not playing games with you, Jenny. I know when a man is serious, and believe me, Ross Benedetto is serious about you." He moved a colander of fresh vegetables away from the chopping block.

"He's got a peculiar way of showing it!" Jennifer declared. "Look at it! It's almost two in the morning, and I have to be up at seven. What the devil am I doing down here complaining to you like a lovesick teenager?"

"Jenny," Drew said kindly, "it's okay to feel hurt because he hasn't been able to see you. I'd feel the same way in your position. And believe me, I have been in your position, more than once. You want to bash him over the head while you kiss every inch of his body, right?"

Jennifer flushed. "Something like that."

"That's natural. What's bothering you is that he might . . ."

Jennifer cut him off. "That he might be using me. That's exactly it, and I hate it!" She tossed her dark hair. "Listen to me. I'm worse than, oh, I don't know. I can't think straight. I'm searching for something that probably isn't even there."

"It's there," Drew said quietly.

"I wish, oh, Drew, I do wish I believed that! I know you're telling me what you believe is true, but I don't know. When Ross is around, I feel myself falling into all those rosy dreams again, and I forget all the pain and anger and hurt that . . ." Jennifer made a helpless gesture that almost upset the colander.

"Ross isn't George," Drew told her as he moved the vegetables out of harm's way.

"That wasn't what . . ." Jennifer stopped herself. "No, that's exactly what I've been afraid of. Every time I begin to respond to those lovely, lovely words and the attention, I keep thinking, in the back of my mind, that George was good at those games, and I was such a sucker about him that I let him take advantage of me before I could get up the nerve to make him stop it." She let herself sob once. "I won't go through that again, Drew."

"You won't have to with Ross," Drew pointed out, then added, "Jenny, you'll have to take a chance someday. Ross won't take you for the kind of ride that George did, and he won't . . ."

"Please," Jennifer said in a stifled voice. "Drew, forget it. I'm going up to bed and get some rest. I'm tired, and I'm magnifying things all out of proportion. It's silly for me to bother you this way." She could not bear to talk about Ross and George at the same time, not even to Drew. She gave an artificially bright smile to her friend and nodded once. "I'll see you at ten in the morning, isn't that right?"

Drew's eyes were sad as he answered, "Sure, boss. At ten." He watched Jennifer leave with growing concern. He did not know how to nurture her fragile hopes, and that knowledge pained him.

❦ September ❧

The last of the Labor Day guests had checked out that morning, and Jennifer looked at the totals with a touch of pride. For more than two months, the White Elephant had been paying for itself. That the winter months would not be so fortunate did not bother her as it might have, since she had been prepared from the first to lose money from the middle of October until the end of May.

"Not bad, is it?" Muriel asked as she brought Jennifer a cup of coffee. "You're doing damned well for a new hotelier."

"That's what I think, too," Jennifer said.

"Think you can stand some more good news?" Muriel asked. "You can add one more reception to the bookings we have for November."

"Oh? Who?" There were two private parties reserved for that month, and a gala for Thanksgiving. Another good-sized party would offset the lack of room reservations.

"Sheridan and me," Muriel said, smiling. "We're getting married on the fourteenth, and we want a great big party on the fifteenth."

"What?" Jennifer set her papers aside and looked at Muriel with undisguised delight. "How wonderful! When did this happen?" This was news she had not anticipated. "Tell me all about it." She stopped. "Oh, dear, I can never remember which of you I'm supposed to wish happiness to, and which I'm supposed to congratulate."

"I'll accept them both, for both of us," Muriel said emphatically, "the happiness and the congratulations. I never thought this would happen to me, not at my age, with everything I've gone through. And I thought that Sheridan wanted amusement or companionship or all the other excuses you hear, and all along, he wanted a wife. I can't believe it!" This last was a whoop of joy, and Jennifer wanted to cheer with her.

"It's terrific!" Jennifer said with real pleasure. "I'll see you have the best party we've ever thrown here. And I'll get Drew to fix you a masterpiece."

Muriel shook her head. "I don't think we can afford . . ." she began, but Jennifer got up and hugged her impulsively before she could say much.

"Afford has nothing to do with it. It's time we had a party for the hell of it, and this is the best reason I've heard all year for a party. We'll arrange to do everything just the way you want it, and that will be my wedding present. How does that sound?" She was already thinking of what she could do, and how; of the dishes she would want Drew to serve; of the preparations she could make and the rooms to be used.

"As your accountant, I think it sounds extravagant and possibly a bit foolish. But as your friend, I'm . . . overwhelmed by your generosity, and I love the idea." She sniffed once and put her hand to her eyes. "Oh, goodness. I thought I'd stopped doing this." She laughed once in a watery way, saying, "When Sheridan proposed, I ended up crying because I was so happy. And when I called my brother, I cried again. And when I talked to Sheridan's mother on the phone, I cried *again*. And all because I'm so happy."

Ordinarily, Jennifer would have felt embarrassed by this display of affection and emotion, but she had come to know Muriel well enough that she felt deeply flattered that the older woman would be so confiding. "Hey, there's nothing to worry about. You're going through what every bride goes through, or so they tell me."

"I don't want to . . . you know, remind you of things that went wrong," Muriel said when she had brought herself under her usual good control.

"Just because my marriage didn't work out doesn't mean

I'm against it. I'm still hoping that maybe I'll have one that works, someday." She gave a wistful smile. "When I see you, it makes me hopeful."

"Good," Muriel said firmly. "I'm very happy that you're not . . . put off." She looked toward the telephone as it rang. "Oh, no."

"I'll get it," Jennifer said, and gave her attention to a travel agent in Los Angeles who was looking for reservations space for October for a two day wine-country tour he was arranging for a large party of German tourists. Jennifer sighed and began once more to attend to business.

"Mr. Benedetto is really quite adamant," Henry was saying to Jennifer two days later. He had already declared he was pleased with the way things were going at the White Elephant, but he pointed out that her plans for the next year were ambitious and she would require a bit more money than she had on hand. "Unless you want to exhaust the trust completely, and I would have to advise against that."

"But we're a bit ahead," Jennifer protested, dismayed at the thought of turning over any of the acreage.

"You know that the Benedetto offer is by far the best, in many respects. Unlike Mr. Hatfield, Mr. Benedetto wishes to make no alterations in the resort itself, and the money he has offered is generous. You're a sensible and practical woman, Jennifer, and I think you would prefer to make what is a short term compromise for a long term gain. It's true that you might be able to manage on your own, but you would have to keep yourself dangerously low in reserves." His voice, as always, was dry and rather cold, but Jennifer knew that he was doing his best to show concern, and that he was truly worried about her.

"Henry," she said with a great deal of care, "I know that the Benedetto offer makes the most sense, but until I feel that it's absolutely necessary to do so, I would prefer not to give up any of my holdings. It might not be entirely wise, and if it's my stubborn pride getting ahead of me, so be it. Don't you see, Henry? If I keep this place going by cutting off a bit here and giving up something there, it won't be mine any more."

Henry cleared his throat. "Jennifer, I will do what I can, but I advise you, as your attorney and the executor of your Uncle Samuel's estate, to give the most careful consideration to the Benedetto offer."

"All right," Jennifer sighed. "I will. Anything more?"·

"Yes. I thought you might want to know that George has taken on a partner at the Savoia. George is not likely to tell you, but I believe that where businesses are involved, it is best to keep reasonably well-informed." He paused. "I'm looking forward to spending a couple weekends with you at the White Elephant. How is your contest to get a name coming?"

"Eric Bush and his wife will be here in a few weeks and he'll make the selection then. He's also agreed to play an informal concert on the twenty-second, so you might want to plan to be here. He's trading the concert for the week between Christmas and New Year's. His wife likes it here, she says, and he wants a bit of a vacation." Privately, Jennifer wondered how much Drew had to do with Eric's return and his generosity. She felt occasional qualms about Drew and Eric, but knew that both men were strongly committed to one another, and, being adults, would resent her intervention.

"You're very lucky to have interested a man like Bush," Henry said, with just enough reserve in his tone to inform Jennifer that he was impressed.

"Yes. I'm aware of that." Jennifer said nothing more, hoping Henry would change the subject. He did. "I'll talk with you tomorrow about those letters you mentioned. I've put in a call to Wilbur Cory, and he should give me an answer about the variance then. You will be able to make plans after that."

"Thank you, Henry," Jennifer said, grateful that she would not have to deal directly with the Board of Supervisors until their policy had been established. There were times, she thought, when Henry Fisher was worth his weight in gold, or at least in guest receipts.

"It's nothing, Jennifer. And your payment to this office ought to guarantee you my attention at all times." Apparently, this was as close as Henry could come to a joke, because he laughed a bit and bid her good day before hanging up.

Jennifer sat still for a time, paying little attention to the smoldering autumn sky outside her window. It was a drowsy, hot day, with the first, illusive hint of fall in the still air. In the distance, she saw the ordered rows of vines on the Benedetto land, and Jennifer tried to imagine what her own acres would look like with vines on them, the russet-colored earth showing between the rows. She could admit that she liked the vineyard, and that if it weren't her land, the gently rolling hills around her would be as pleasant and orderly with vines as with a resort. But it *was* her land, and she had no intention of seeing it change to vines or condominiums or geothermal power stations. With renewed determination, Jennifer got up and marched out of her office.

In the next three days, she sustained visits from both Larry Bronson and Ted Hatfield, so when Ross came to pick Jennifer up for a late lunch in Napa, he found her in an unusually belligerent mood.

"What's wrong with everyone?" Jennifer demanded as Ross turned away from Calistoga. "Don't they understand plain English? I tell them that I do not want to sell, lease, rent, lend, give, or in any other way part with any section, bit, inch, foot or other portion of my land." She had folded her arms and now sat glaring at the road ahead.

"You're sounding pretty plain to me," Ross said, determined to make the afternoon a pleasant one.

"Do you think so?" Her voice had turned sweet, and she gazed at him limpidly for a moment. "But you're up to the same thing, aren't you?"

"You know what my offer is, and it stands. If you want to act on it, you will. If you don't, you'll do nothing. Isn't that the way it works?" He gave his attention to the road as a truck carrying two trailers laden with lumber roared up behind them.

"I want to do it on my *own*," Jennifer said intently. "Why can't anyone accept that?"

"I'm not objecting," Ross pointed out. He turned off toward a street lined with trees. "You'll like this place. Their chef isn't Drew, but he's good, nevertheless. Besides, Drew doesn't make Mandarin cuisine and Tom Kua does."

"A Chinese restaurant?" Jennifer asked, interested in spite of herself. Suddenly, she realized how much she had missed Chinese food. "Mandarin cuisine? That's marvelous. I haven't had a Chinese meal since I left San Francisco."

"Whew!" Ross said in mock relief. "The way you've been talking, I was beginning to think I'd have to find something more . . . exclusive."

"Stop it," Jennifer said ruefully. "I didn't mean to sound so . . . condemning. But you don't know what it's been like, spending so much time working for this and having so many people tell me, indirectly, that I'm going to fail at it. That's what it feels like when I get another offer on the land—that it's expected that I won't be able to keep running my business without help from someone."

"That's not how I mean it," Ross said with a short chuckle. "I know you're going to do fine. I'm worried about getting enough acres planted so that I can keep up with the expansion program we're supposed to be in the middle of. We've got every bit of land we own under vines and have leased another six hundred acres, but it's nowhere near enough, given what my brother has projected." He turned into a parking lot surrounded by fig trees. The restaurant was low and unassuming, its wood façade beautifully kept up without looking artificial. "Here we are."

But Jennifer was struck by what Ross had said. "Do you mean that?" she asked.

"About what?" Ross paused, the door half-open.

"You want the land because you're short of acreage? You don't mean to lend a helping hand to the niece of an old friend?" She was amazed that he might not be offering to lease her land as a misguided act of charity, but because he was looking for badly-needed acreage. "Why didn't you mention that before?"

"Mention it? What do you mean? I thought you understood my problem with land and production." He got out of the car and locked the door, then came around to her side. "I've got to have more land producing grapes, Jennifer. We're smack in the middle of an expansion program, and we're not producing enough to keep on the schedule we've established." He held the door for her as he spoke, and slammed it as final emphasis.

"But . . ." Jennifer frowned. "Ross, aren't you looking anywhere else? Why the White Elephant?"

"Of *course* I'm looking anywhere else." He opened the restaurant door and paused as the scent of hot sesame oil and star anise drifted to them. "Ah, I love that smell."

"Hot and sour soup? On a day like this?" Jennifer inquired.

"You'll like it. It stimulates the mind, or something like that." He nodded to the Chinese waitress who came up to them. "Benedetto. Reservations for two-thirty."

"This way," she said, and led them through a largely-empty, tastefully-decorated dining room to a table in an alcove fronting on a formal Chinese garden seen through a moon door.

"This is beautiful," Jennifer said as she took her seat. "How's the food?"

"The best thing about the restaurant," Ross assured her, then went back to what he had been discussing in the parking lot. "The reason I'm interested in the White Elephant is that it's close, for one thing, and it isn't under any option I know about. It would be possible to tend the vines without driving twenty miles to a new plantation. That's always a difficulty, and we've got two of those going already. We know the soil chemistry and microclimatology of our immediate area, and don't need to pay for costly tests and reports as well as being able to take advantage of what we know already to get the best production out of the land. And besides, I like the White Elephant. It would be fun having an in with it. Or does that make any sense to you?" He had not yet opened the menu, but when the waitress returned, he said to Jennifer, "Will you trust me to order?"

"Sure," Jennifer answered.

"Good. We'll have steamed bao and spring rolls for an appetizer."

"Steamed bao will take a little time to prepare," the waitress warned him diffidently.

"That's fine. Then hot and sour soup for two, princess prawns, kung pao beef, bok choy with black mushrooms, steamed rice, tea and a split of champagne. If we have room, eight precious rices for dessert, but check with us before you start." He handed the menu to the waitress and looked expectantly at Jennifer. "Does that meet with your approval?"

"It sounds marvelous," she said, meaning it. "You know, about the only Oriental food I've had in the last five months is Johnny Chang's infernal kim-chee. This is balm to the senses."

Ross laughed. "Good. And you *will* think about that lease, won't you?"

Stung, she retorted, "Is that what this lunch is for? To butter me up enough that I lease land to you?"

"Well, I wouldn't mind if that were one of the results, but the reason I asked you to come here with me was that there hasn't been any other way I could find to have a little time alone with you. We've had just three nights alone in the last four weeks and I'm eager for the privacy. It probably wouldn't be a good idea to make passionate love on the table, but we can have a quiet conversation without the worry of constant interruptions." He was looking at her, noticing the way that the curved shadow of the moon window fell on her glistening hair, the way the soft folds of her dress clung to the slim curves of her body. Her blue eyes were distant, not quite dreamy, but full of depths he longed to sound.

"We're private here, true enough." She frowned slightly. "I can't help thinking that they might need me back at the hotel."

"They might, but whatever happens, it will keep until you're back." He braced his elbows on the table and leaned forward a bit. "You have to get yourself some private time, Jennifer. You're so caught up in that hotel that you've shut out most of the rest of your life, and that isn't a good idea. It's not just that I want to spend time with you, though I do, but I see you shutting out so many things that you enjoy and need. You don't even go out to have your hair done unless there's a special function at the hotel. You haven't done any shopping that I know of. . . ."

"I can't afford it at the moment, and I have an extensive enough wardrobe for my work. . . ." She stopped, seeing him nod at the word *work*.

"What about a dress for the hell of it? You should indulge yourself, give yourself an occasional reward for what you've accomplished. You can't go on being completely practical and wrapped up in work. You're not that kind of woman, thank goodness." He had not intended to say so much to her. He had planned an afternoon of light flirtation to take her mind off the various problems she was facing. "I don't want to tell you how to run your life. . . ."

"You don't?" she said quietly.

"No. But it bothers me to see you live the way you do, so shut off from all the delightful things you make possible for others. You probably don't see it that way, but looking in from the outside, I do." He was speaking sincerely, his voice low but firm with emotion. He wanted to reach for her hand, but was afraid she would think he was giving her a line to win her over. "You're a beautiful, desirable woman. I'd be lying if I said that wasn't a factor in what I'm saying, because it is. But it wouldn't matter if you had warts, you're still doing your best to wear yourself out. I don't want that to happen to you. It would trouble me a lot." He looked up suddenly as the waitress approached their table with a plate of spring rolls.

"The steamed bao will be ready in ten minutes. You have

these first." She put the plate between them, then set down a small cup of reddish sauce.

"Thank you," Ross said automatically, distracted by this interruption.

Jennifer put her napkin in her lap and picked up her chopsticks. "Ross, I do appreciate your . . . concern, but you know as well as I do that if the White Elephant is going to be the kind of resort hotel I'm trying to make it, I have to devote a lot of time to it. I *would* like to go on a shopping spree and have a couple days off by myself, but it isn't possible yet, and it won't be for a while. And it would be foolish to spend money on myself when I'm not sure I can afford to make the improvements on the resort that I want to have ready by next season."

"Listen to yourself, Jennifer," Ross said as he took half a spring roll. "You're doing it again. I know what I'm saying. After my wife was killed, I did the same thing, and it isn't worth it. I *know* what it does to you when you shut out everything but work. If my Aunt Rosa had not made a point of hectoring me almost out of my mind, I'd *still* be shut up in my office, poring over figures and projections and all the rest of it, pretending that nothing else mattered to me. It's not the same thing when you're divorced, probably, because there's the constant, nagging fear that there was something you might have done to change things. When someone dies, the chances are over. But you're letting this get to you, Jennifer, and it isn't a good thing. Believe me." He stopped long enough to eat the spring roll.

Jennifer had taken up a spring roll, too, and used the time it took to eat it to think how she wished to respond. Nothing suggested itself to her that she could say aloud. It was flattering to think that Ross cared that much for her, but she still could not believe that his affection was much more than convenience. Some of the things he said to her hit uncomfortably near the bone, and she did not want to get into a discussion of such painful topics. At last she put her chopsticks down and said, "I'll make time for a little more entertainment now that the summer season is over."

"Some of it with me," Ross said around the food he was chewing. "I'm putting in my bid early."

"I'd like that," Jennifer said, feeling a light-hearted, irrational happiness burgeoning within her. "You sound as if you could use a little rest, too."

"But my busy season is just getting started," Ross said.

"That might make timing a bit tricky, but I know that if we're going to get anything done, we should make plans now and do our best to stick to them."

The waitress came with a plate of steamed bao. "The soup is coming very quickly," she said quietly, and turned away from the table at once to leave the two alone.

"These are very good," Jennifer said as she tasted one of the puckered white buns stuffed with meat and vegetables. "They do them well."

"I think so, too," Ross agreed. "When are you free next week?"

"I don't have my calendar with me. . . ." she said, suddenly reluctant to commit herself to any plans beyond this pleasant afternoon.

"Then I'll stop by your office when we get back to the Elephant," he told her, and dropped another bao on her plate. "I hope you're hungry. We're going to have a big meal."

"The smell would make me hungry even if I weren't," she said, knowing that she was, in fact, quite hungry.

"Well, it's a change from sandwiches, soup and omelettes," Ross said lightly.

Jennifer looked up, startled. How had he guessed what she usually ate? She tried to make a joke of it. "Drew despairs at my habits."

"As well he might. You're not taking proper care of yourself, and you know it. So does he." He offered her another bao and turned his head as the scent of hot and sour soup wafted to them. "Hurry up with that."

Obediently, Jennifer did as she was told, then she paused, wondering why she had been willing to go along with him. "If I have much more of this, there won't be any room for lunch," she warned him. "I'm not used to having large meals."

"I know. And that's one of the things that worries me about you." He grinned as the waitress ladled out the fragrant soup into small bowls, then tactfully withdrew. "They make it very hot here, lots of sesame oil and pepper."

"Good," Jennifer said, strangely elated at the thought that he was worried about her.

By the time they finished the meal, more than an hour later, they were on better terms than they had ever been. Between the excellent food and the easy conversation, fueled in part by champagne, Jennifer was no longer wary or nervous with Ross, and if she suspected that he had gone to a great deal of trouble to make this so, he did nothing to confirm her suspicions.

"We'll start back in about ten minutes," Ross said when they had finished the last of the eight precious rices. "How does a picnic sound, say, next Thursday? I know I have that afternoon free, and someone will cover for you if you need it."

"I'll have to see if I have any appointments," she said cautiously. She could not admit to him that she wanted the chance to spend more time with him. As much as she had tried to put it out of her mind, their nights of lovemaking were disturbing her, awakening desires she had forgotten she had, and the deep fulfillment he had given her strove for greater expression. His large, sensitive hands, his mouth, all of his body spoke to her of abiding, secret delights that she had known for the first time with him. Her face flushed and she averted her eyes, afraid that he could see the need she felt in them.

"Then a picnic it is," Ross said, getting up and coming to hold Jennifer's chair for her. "I'll call you the day before, just in case."

"All right," Jennifer said, rising and smoothing the front of her dress as she dropped the napkin on the table in front of her. Was it her imagination, or did his hand linger on her back a bit longer than was called for? She did not want to delude herself with transient dreams that could not be realized, but neither did she want to turn away from sincere affection because she was afraid of disappointment. She wanted to ask a few direct questions, but balked at saying anything, knowing she would be unutterably ashamed if he laughed at her.

Outside, the sun had sunk toward the west and the air was still, sweet with the scent of figs and foliage. Jennifer stood with the sun full on her face and let the welcome heat sink into her. She felt as contented as a spoiled cat, and she found herself hoping that there would be more days like this one. "Do you have anything to do this evening?" she heard herself ask Ross.

"Why?" he asked as he opened the car door.

"I thought that we could get together later. That is, if you want to." She wanted to bite her tongue for making the suggestion as soon as the words were out of her mouth, but she let it go. She'd have to take a risk sometime—might as well do it now.

"How much later?" Ross asked, a gleam in his china-green eyes.

"That's your choice," she said, wondering how she found the nerve to be so brazen. It was ridiculous to feel badly about such an offer, she reprimanded herself. This was the time when women could be as forthright as men. But she quaked at exposing herself to ridicule or rejection, and her inner fears were stronger than her more recently acquired liberation.

Ross held the car door for her. "How does ten o'clock sound to you?"

"Fine. Ten would be fine." She did not know what else to say, and her relief as well as her triumph was so great that it was all she could do to keep from giggling with glee.

"Then that's when I'll be there. With bells on." He hoped that the afternoon was a promise of things to come.

"That would disturb the guests. Just come yourself." She began to feel happier as Ross closed the door on her side and went around to get in to drive.

"Ten o'clock. No bells," he said as he got into the BMW. His intention of breaking through some of Jennifer's reserve had turned out far better than anything he had imagined. He had not dared to hope that she might initiate a night together; the most he had assumed possible was a promise to spend more time with him. He shut the car door and put the key into the ignition. He was whistling.

Ross arrived ten minutes early and met Jennifer as she was getting ready to leave the main level of the hotel. "Should I wait in the bar, or what? What's discreet?"

"Go up to the third floor and I'll meet you there as soon as I check on something in the bar." She pointed in the general direction of the elevators and hurried off toward the Howdah.

Ross watched her go, admiring the brisk way she walked even at the end of a busy and demanding day. He guessed she would move that way always. With a nod to a couple he knew slightly who were leaving the dining room, Ross ambled to the elevator and went to the third floor.

A quarter of an hour later, Jennifer arrived. She glanced at her desk and sighed as she looked at the paperwork piled up on it. "We've got taxes coming up and Muriel is doing her best to have everything ready," she said, sounding harried.

"Would you rather work? I can come back another night," Ross suggested, but did not hide his disappointment.

Jennifer turned to him. "I'd much rather be here with you than anything else. I should leave the work behind when I close the door."

"But since this is your office, that doesn't make any sense," Ross said with some amusement. "If we go upstairs, you won't be in your office anymore."

"True enough," Jennifer said, then added, "I don't know what it'll take to get me ready tonight." She felt herself blushing. "What I mean is, if you want something fast and sweet, it's probably not the best time for it, since I've got all wound up since lunch. I hadn't planned it that way, but . . ." She knew she was apologizing and it bothered her. She had spent most of her marriage apologizing for one thing and another, and this reminded her of those uncomfortable years.

"That's fine. I'm really not much of a hit and run artist. I prefer to take my time." He approached her and wrapped his arms around her shoulders. "You've never worried about this before."

"But I have," she confessed. "I never said anything. I didn't want to disappoint you." She rested her head on his shoulder, enjoying the scent of his aftershave and the more elusive scent of his body.

"Well, in the future, you can tell me anything you wish to and I won't feel threatened. What matters is that we enjoy ourselves. We're not putting on a performance, Jennifer." He kissed her brow, then her cheek and, finally, her mouth. "I think we'd better go upstairs, unless you want to try mixing business and pleasure."

"I think so, too," Jennifer said, and was startled to realize she had become eager to be alone with him, though she was not yet sure she wanted to make love. If only that pleasant closeness of the afternoon had lingered through her hectic evening, she would want nothing more than to lie back and welcome him into her. But there had been other demands and the moment had passed and now she was edgy. She stepped into her room and switched on the light. She sighed a bit and turned to Ross. "Come in. Have a seat." As she spoke, she kicked off her shoes, then put them conscientiously into the rack at the bottom of her closet.

"Take off your hose," Ross said as he sat on the foot of the bed.

"And everything else," Jennifer said, not quite eagerly.

"In a bit. For the moment, I want to massage your feet for you. If you're like me, at the end of the day your feet are worn out." He patted the bed. "Come on."

"You're kidding," Jennifer said, but she smiled.

"I'm dead serious. You can't feel romantic if your feet ache. You see, I admit my ulterior motives from the first. Take off the hose." He gave her a genial, easy grin.

Jennifer shrugged and bent to take off her pantyhose. She tossed them aside and got onto the bed, where she did her best to lie primly straight. "I ought to warn you that sometimes I'm ticklish."

"Then I'll be extra-firm. That's the way to keep from tickles." He reached out and took her right foot in his hand. "If you feel jittery, tell me. This is supposed to relax you, not send you off in convulsions."

Jennifer nodded, thinking the whole thing was a little silly. But there was something quite soothing in the pressure of his thumbs on the sole of her foot, and almost without being aware of it, she began to relax. By the time he finished her left foot, she was feeling blissfully limp, and the tightness in her legs, which was so familiar that she had not noticed it, was fading. "I'm a dishrag, an old, soft dishrag," she said as he put her foot down.

"That's what you're supposed to be," Ross said. He had observed her closely as he worked on her feet, and he had seen her let go of the tension she had built up during the long day. Now she was at ease, the knots taken out of her, the tightness gone. He reached out and slowly began to stroke her leg.

"I'm aware of what you're up to," Jennifer murmured without opening her eyes.

"Good. It's always best if you know what's happening." He continued the slow, sure strokes. "No, don't wiggle like that. . . ."

"I'm ticklish at the back of the knees, too." She snickered, then yawned. "Sorry. I didn't mean to do that."

"It's fine," Ross said. Skillfully, he unfastened her skirt and, in a surprisingly deft maneuver, slipped it down over her hips and off. As he rubbed the top of her hip, he noticed that she had lost perhaps another five pounds since that first night they had made love. He put his hand over the prominent crest of her hip and rubbed lightly.

"You can press harder. I'm not made of glass," Jennifer said quietly.

"Possibly, but you don't have much between skin and bone there, and if I press too hard, it's not going to feel very good. You ought to let Aunt Rosa cook for you once or twice a week. You're getting too damned skinny." He did not know how else to tell her that he worried about her.

"Don't do that," Jennifer said with irritation. "I am the way I am. If you don't like it, you don't have to stay." She was aware that it was not fair to burst out at Ross this way, but she did not say more, because she had too many humiliating memories of times when George had complained that her hips were too narrow or her thighs too heavy or her breasts too small. It was difficult to have Ross complain as well.

"Jennifer, Jennifer, I didn't mean to criticize." He stretched out beside her and began to unbutton her blouse. "All I meant is that I become worried when I see you so thin. I don't care if you're built like a tank or an ironing board, I want you to feel strong and healthy, and at the moment, I think you're nervous, over-tired and run-down. I can't ignore it when a woman I care about is wearing herself out. I thought you understood that." He opened her shirt and eased it off her left and then her right arm.

"Oh, Ross." She sighed and shook her head. "I didn't mean to snap at you like that. And you're probably right—I could stand to gain a few pounds and sleep a bit more and all the rest of it—but . . ."

He silenced her with a kiss, his mouth warm and open on hers, but as always, unhurried. He seemed content to continue the kiss all night, for he did not move or caress her.

Jennifer shifted restlessly, then closed her eyes and let her world become that kiss. She opened her lips, thinking that he would deepen the kiss, and when it did not happen, she tentatively entered his mouth with her tongue. Only then did he respond, and Jennifer felt a shiver of pleasure, for she liked the opportunity to waken his feelings as much as she enjoyed his evocation of hers. Curious, she moved enough to be able to put one arm across Ross's side, and almost at once she was pulled into his arms. Jennifer discovered that leading Ross was stimulating to her the way patient acquiescence would not have been on this night. She propped herself on her elbow and began to open his shirt, chuckling as she ran her fingers through the hair that curled down his chest toward his groin.

"You're going to be the undoing of me," Ross said, half-seriously, as Jennifer fumbled with his belt.

"Good. You can't imagine what you're doing to me," she retorted, emboldened by his passivity. "How do I get you out of your pants, anyway?"

"I'll do it," he offered. "Otherwise, you're going to turn this into a wrestling match instead of . . ."

"Of what?" She paused in the act of hooking her thumbs in the elastic of his briefs.

"Making love," he finished, and made a strange sort of half-somersault as he tugged his pants off and flung them away from him.

Now that he was naked, his excitement wholly apparent, he did not seem as quietly receptive as he had been clothed. Jennifer hesitated, then held out her arms to him, turning just enough to bring him close against her.

"God, you're sweet," Ross breathed, his lips at her ear-lobe. Gradually, he covered her and entered her, and as they rocked together in the tumult of their passion, he thought he heard her cry his name as her climax gripped her, but his own rushed on him an instant later, blotting out everything but the fulfillment of their union.

"I don't understand how it could have happened," Muriel said to Jennifer on Thursday morning. "Caroline has talked to the housekeeping staff, and no one has any idea how it occurred."

"But the fact remains that fifty blankets and over one hundred sheets have been ruined, and we have to find a way to replace them in the next eight hours," Jennifer finished for her. "I don't want to sound discouraged, but that's the kind of thing that makes me want to give up." She saw the shocked look on Muriel's face and shook her head. "I didn't say that I *would* give up, only that it makes me *want* to."

Muriel nodded. "I know what you mean. Ever since that tour cancelled yesterday, I've been waiting for the other shoe to drop."

"I thought disasters were supposed to come in threes," Jennifer said in an attempt at levity. "Never mind. I don't want to know if there's something else going to go wrong. For the time being, phone the supplier and order replacements for the blankets and sheets. It could be worse," she added. "This could be July, when we were so full that we would have had to borrow blankets and linens from the neighbors. As it is, it's merely expensive and inconvenient. And at the moment I can be grateful for small favors."

"I suppose so," Muriel said quietly.

"God, what's all this going to cost? Don't tell me," Jennifer hurried on with a glance at Muriel. "I'll find out soon enough, but for the present, I'd rather remain in ignorance."

"Ignorance is bliss?" Muriel asked.

"Well, it's better than worry, anyway," Jennifer said. "How could such a thing happen? What was plastic solvent doing in the delivery van, anyway? Who here uses it?"

"I don't know. I've been asking around, and Fred Jenkins is the only one who does, and he has his own truck. The only thing that occurred to me," Muriel went on in a slightly apologetic tone, "is that perhaps one of the groundsmen saw Fred's things sitting out and put them in the van, but it doesn't seem very likely."

"No, it doesn't. And Ben has always been conscientious about what he carries in the van, so I don't think we can assume that he made this mistake. Damn! I wish I knew how it all happened."

"It couldn't change anything, Jennifer," Muriel said, shaking her head. "But it would settle a few questions."

"Yes, it would," Jennifer said. "And it might make things a little easier when I try to explain to Henry. Which I'd better do pretty soon." She felt a headache begin just over her eyes and found herself looking forward to the picnic that afternoon. There were so many things demanding her time, and she so much wanted to have a couple tranquil hours before the evening began.

Half an hour before they were supposed to meet, Ross called the White Elephant. "We've had an equipment failure and the replacements haven't arrived yet. I can't get away for a couple of hours at least." He sounded apologetic and Jennifer could hear angry shouts in the background.

"We're having a bad day here, too," she said, thinking that this would take the worst of the pressure off him.

"And here I was hoping for good news," he said with a wan attempt at humor. "What's wrong at your end?"

"Oh, nothing overwhelming. A bunch of blankets and sheets got wrecked." She did not mean to minimize the problems she had encountered, but, somehow, talking on the phone, with no way to read his expression or to gauge his reaction, brought back all the defensive patterns she had learned years ago. "We're taking care of it."

"Good," he said with feeling. "I wish I could say the same

on this end. So far, we're trying to get by with what we can cobble together from old equipment, but we're not getting very far. It's the bottler. Have you ever tried to advance bottles by hand?" He made a groaning sound. "Look, would you mind very much if we postponed the picnic, Jennifer? I'd like to get over there this evening. . . ."

"I'm going to be busy with a private party," Jennifer lied, not knowing why, but unwilling to admit her disappointment.

"Then tomorrow or the next day," Ross persisted. "I want to see you. I wish I were with you right now instead of working with all these damned bottles, but there's no way I can leave just at present." Even speaking to her, he felt a poignant desire to have her beside him, her long, coltish limbs reclining beside his, her laughter in his ears. He turned as he heard another bottle smash on the floor. "I've got to get back."

"It sounds like it," she said, trying not to sound petulant.

"Thanks for understanding, Jennifer. I'm sorry this came up, but . . ." He tried to think of ways to tell her that he did not want to make her feel bad, but the breaking of another bottle distracted him.

"It sounds like things are getting worse," Jennifer said, choking back her hurt. "You can tell me about it later, when everything's fixed."

"Good. I will. Tomorrow or Saturday." He heard a shout, and in the next instant the shattering of glass. "Later."

Jennifer hung up, thinking that more than glass was breaking.

At the end of the weekend, Jennifer was more exhausted than she had been since mid-summer. The trout pond had at last been refilled and stocked, her staff reductions for the off-season were going on successfully, and the sheets and blankets had been replaced at as reasonable a cost as Jennifer could expect. She still had not seen Ross, and this tended to make her more depressed than any other consideration— though she denied it to herself—and the one glimpse she had of him turning onto the road to the Hasslunds' place made her want to scream.

Monday passed quietly, and she was thinking that if the week stayed calm she would call Ross herself and suggest that they take time to have a meal. But what, she asked herself traitorously, if he said no? So she did not call Monday or

Tuesday, and submerged herself in dealing with the plans for bringing the hotsprings building up to code.

It was almost eight in the evening when Ivy buzzed Jennifer's office from the front desk. "Ms. Wystan? There's a gentleman here to see you."

"A gentleman?" She hoped it was Ross, but knew that Ivy would identify him. "Who is he?"

"He says you know him." Ivy sounded doubtful.

"I'll be right down," Jennifer said, puzzled. She set the blueprints aside and began to straighten her hair. Pausing only long enough to apply a touch of lipstick, she hurried down the stairs, still puzzling who would be calling at that hour, particularly someone Ivy did not recognize. Ivy knew Ted Hatfield on sight, and Larry Bronson. Who was this man and what did he want?

"Hi, Jen. You look great." George came to the foot of the stairs, smiling at her as if they were simply old friends.

Jennifer stopped stock still. "George." All other words failed her.

"I was going to call you, but then I thought I'd surprise you. You're always so busy that I decided the only way to get a little of your time was just to show up and take it." He held out his hand to her, still smiling.

"Hello, George," Jennifer said woodenly, pointedly refusing his hand.

"Well." George made an expansive gesture, negating the signals she was sending him. "You're doing a great job here, aren't you?" He indicated the hallway leading to the bar. "Can the owner's husband—pardon me, ex-husband—buy her a drink in her own place?"

"You can ask them to serve me a spritzer, but that's about all I'm good for. It's been a long day and I'm tired," Jennifer said, hoping that George would be willing to make his visit a short one.

"If that's what you want, that's what you'll have," he said, and pointed the way down the hall, but was wise enough not to offer his arm to her. "I've been meaning to get back up here for weeks, but the restaurant has been so busy that I haven't had time to read the papers, let alone get out of South San Francisco. I haven't been into the city for more than a week."

Jennifer, walking beside him, could not think of anything to say. She paused in the doorway to the Howdah and looked around at the tables. She wanted something near the bar, so that if she had to get away, Hugo would be near at hand. Just as she found a suitable table, George said, "What about that table in the corner? We won't be disturbed there." And before Jennifer could protest, he was starting toward the far corner of the L-shaped room.

"I'd really prefer to be where my staff can find me," Jennifer said, but George shook his head.

"That's what I mean. You're always putting business first. You've been like that all the time, Jen, and I know that it isn't good for you." He looked up as the waitress approached. "Yes. We'll have . . . whatever your boss-lady usually has, and a Tanqueray martini, very dry, for me."

The waitress gave a curious look to Jennifer, then wrote down the order with a smile at George. "I'll be right back."

"You do that," George encouraged her, and turned back to Jennifer. "Where was I?"

"You were trying the old snow job," Jennifer said patiently. "You're after something, George. I know you well enough to see that."

"Clever girl," he approved, leaning forward on folded arms. "I *am* after something. I'm after *you.*" He laughed at her look of consternation.

"Your drinks, sir," the waitress said as she returned, still curious about the man with Ms. Wystan.

"Good. Here's a ten. Keep it until I ask for the bill, and we'll go from there." He handed the bill over and turned back to Jennifer once more. "Well, here's to old times."

"Thank God they're gone," Jennifer finished, determined not to let George's flattery and nostalgia get to her.

"Well, the bad parts, certainly, but you've got to admit that we had good times, too." He tasted the martini. "You've got a good bartender. Tell him I said so."

"What's this all about, George?" Jennifer asked, wishing she had a means of escape.

"About you and me. I told you that already." He paused. "You're going to say that I've had more than enough chance to think about this, and I know you're right. I should have thought about a lot of things before now, but I couldn't. When you left, I was simply in shock. I didn't know what had happened to me or how much it meant to me. I know I was acting like a bastard, but . . ."

"You'd done that before," Jennifer said without much emotion.

"But don't you see, I'm trying to let you know that I appreciate what you were trying to do for me. I know that I made a mistake back then. I probably should have swallowed my pride before now and found a way to say something to you so that you wouldn't think that I was . . ."

Jennifer watched his handsome, open face and wanted to scream at him. There had been so many times before when she had listened to him, wanting desperately to believe the lies he told her. But she had learned the truth and could not forget it. She had not touched the drink at her elbow, and she had to resist the urge to take a deep swig of it. "George, cut it out, will you?" she pleaded. "I've had a long day, I'm tired, and I have to be up early tomorrow."

"But, Jen, don't you know what I'm trying to say? I want you to know that I've come to my senses. I'm not mad at you anymore, and I know it was wrong to let you walk out like that. I should have found a way to let you know how much I care about you." He finished the martini in two more sips. "You're not going to make me believe that you're through with me, not after the way we've talked over the last couple months."

"We haven't talked at all over the last couple months," Jennifer corrected him, shocked at what she was hearing.

"Not a great deal. But we've said the important things." He signaled for another drink.

"George, in the last three months we've had four brief conversations at the most. You might have thought the conversations were important, and they might have been in a practical sense, but if you've been building up a picture in your mind of me pining away for you, forget it." She had felt that way at first, in the first desolate months of their separation, but that had faded gradually, and now she could not bring herself to feel more than a mild, irritated frustration where her former husband was concerned. She knew she had loved him once, that she did not hate him now, but it was hard to deal with him this way, to be reminded of the failure and pain and loneliness that had been the legacy of their divorce.

"You're a brave girl, Jennifer. But I can see you're twenty-five pounds thinner than when we were married, and those circles under your eyes aren't entirely from overwork." He reached to touch her face and gave a pitying smile as she drew back abruptly. "See? I know you better than you know yourself."

"George . . ."

"Now you should listen to me a minute. I've let you say your peace, and now it's my turn." He grinned as the waitress put a second martini on the table. "I know you can make it on your own, and I admit that I should have been fairer to you, but I'm going to change that." He lifted the glass in a toast and drank half of it, then beamed at her.

Jennifer was so aghast that she almost got up from the table. "George, I don't know where you got the idea that all that I've done was to show you up, and that I wanted your attention. If you had said this a year ago, I might have thought it was wonderful and gone along with whatever crazy ideas you had, but no more. I have a life of my own now, and I don't intend to give it up. Getting it and keeping it has cost me too much."

"But I don't want you to give it up. We can work this place together, you and I, the way we did at the Savoia." He snickered. "And we can go back to those other things we did together, too. You must be pretty horny by now, Jen."

"You just want to chat up the customers and get laid regularly, by me or someone else," Jennifer said, losing all her reserve. "I don't want to hear any more of this, George. I don't care what you've made yourself believe, I don't care what you think you can get out of me. You've had all that I can give you, and now I've got something of my own and it isn't yours to tamper with." She started to rise, hoping that she had kept her voice low enough to avoid being heard.

"What's with this strong woman stuff, Jen?" George demanded, reaching out and catching her arm. "I thought you'd got over that. You've been on your own long enough to know that you can't keep a man that way."

"I don't want to keep a man," she shot back, knowing it was not entirely true.

"Bull!" George downed the rest of his drink and glared at her. "Sit down and listen to me." He pulled hard on her arm and smiled as she sat down.

"All right. Say what you must, and then leave." Jennifer folded her hands in front of her, hoping that she could avoid a scene here.

"Come on, come on, don't pull that on me. I know how to handle people, and a place like this needs someone who can make it run smoothly. You know how I can do that, Jen, and you know what it's like having me around regularly. I won't neglect you. I know I used to, but I've come to my senses. Let me have a chance, Jen, to show you how much you mean to me." He gave her his most persuasive smile. "It's been a while. I've learned some things you'd like, I think."

"George, for heaven's sake, *will* you shut up?" Jennifer said plaintively. "I don't want to have you here. I don't want you around. Don't you understand plain English?"

"Jen, Jen, don't fight it. You'll be a wrinkled-up prune of an old maid if you let yourself act like this."

That was the most malicious dig George knew. Jennifer had heard him say similar things when he was provoked before, but now, instead of striking to the quick, it only disgusted her. "All right, George. Maybe I will be a wrinkled-up prune, but I'll be my own woman, and that's worth a wrinkle or two."

George's veneer of charm dropped away again. "You *bitch!*" he hissed at her.

Jennifer sat still and let the abuse wash over her as if George were speaking a foreign language. He had said it all to her at one time or another before, and she had ceased to listen to him. In a remote part of her mind, she was curious to know why he had decided on this ridiculous attempt to win her over. George was not often so inept, she remembered. She reached for her drink and then thought better of it. If she were depressed now, a drink would only make it worse. She put her hands to her face and hoped that George would keep his voice down a bit longer so she could think of a way to get him out of the White Elephant.

"It isn't enough that you send me notes, but now you're being coy. Jen, you've got more nerve than . . ." George was interrupted by a pleasant, restrained voice.

"Hello, George," said Drew. "One of the staff mentioned you were here." He pulled up a chair to the table and sat down. "And up to your old delightful tricks, too, you naughty boy," he went on with campy politeness. "You always have to keep things in an uproar, don't you? You know, we're not used to that anymore." He did not quite put his arm around Jennifer, but his attitude was subtly protective and behind his ready smile there was implacable steel.

"Hello, Drew," George said with a brazen smile. "What brings you up from your infernal regions?"

"The pleasure of your company," Drew responded, with a grin that was as wide as it was insincere. "I don't know what you've been saying to Jennifer this time, but I've heard enough before to have some idea. As unexpected a delight as your visit has been, I think you'll have to pardon us if we can't encourage you to stay. Or to return." Drew looked over at Jennifer. "Why don't you go up and get into bed? It might be a little early, but you have to get up before six tomorrow and you're tired. Let me take care of speeding the parting guest." He rose as Jennifer did, and waited until she was out of the room. "Now, then, George, I'll walk you to your car and you can give me a lift to the crossroads."

"Faggot!" George said with quiet venom.

"Better a faggot than a man who has to abuse women in order to feel like a man," Drew said sweetly. "Don't take me on, George. Sober you're no match for me; half-smashed you won't even come close." He motioned to George. "Come with me. You ought to stop in Napa for coffee. Ordinarily, I wouldn't suggest a man in your condition drive, but this isn't ordinary, is it?" He waited while George got to his feet.

"I can stay here if I want," George announced as he started toward the door.

"But we're full," Drew said affably. "Not even a broom-closet."

George muttered, but grudgingly kept pace with Drew as he went toward the lobby.

Ross sat at his desk, his hands clasped under his chin, his china-green eyes fixed with superb abstraction on the opposite wall. There was a portrait of his parents there, but he might have been staring at a blank wall for all the expression he showed. He was supposed to be looking over the latest lease agreement he and the Hasslunds had come up with, but he could not concentrate on it. Three hours before, he had been having dinner with Jennifer. It was a good restaurant, not too fancy but far from plain. For the first part of the evening, Jennifer had seemed happy and animated. But under her gaiety there was strain, and as the evening progressed, she became more and more withdrawn and in the end had asked Ross to take her back to the Elephant and had given him a somewhat incoherent apology for disappointing him. It was true he was disappointed, but the evening was not the primary reason for it. He had begun to believe that Jennifer trusted him, relied upon him, liked him. Perhaps might come to love him. That last admission tightened his throat, but he no longer attempted to deny that he wanted more from her than erotic nights and pleasant afternoons. Until this evening, he had thought it was possible, but he was no longer certain, and it hurt.

A knock on the door jolted him out of his reverie. Ross looked up guiltily. "Yes?"

"Mr. Benedetto?" said a voice which was familiar, but which Ross could not quite place.

"Yes?"

"Your aunt let me in. I have to talk to you." The tone was polite, even deferential, but there was an underlying determination which Ross was quick to recognize.

"Just a moment," he said, and got up from the desk. As he went to the door, he glanced at the clock. Eleven-twenty. Who the hell would be coming here at eleven-twenty? he asked himself as he opened the door.

Drew Usher stood there, neat as wax and awesomely self-possessed. "I know it's late," he said, holding out his hand, "but I don't have a lot of free time."

Puzzled, and a bit worried, Ross held his office door open. "Come in, Drew."

"Thanks." He looked around the office, nodded his approval, then paced before taking a seat on the small sofa near the fireplace. "This is very awkward for me," he said, and lapsed into silence.

"Is something wrong with Jennifer?" Ross demanded, dreading the answer.

"In a way, but not the way you mean." He folded his arms. "You see, I make it a point, an absolute point, *never* to become involved in my friends' affairs." He fidgeted with his shirt collar. "I haven't done this kind of thing before."

"What is it?" Ross asked as he closed the door and came across the office to the chair on the other side of the fireplace.

"This evening, when you brought Jenny back, she went straight up to her room and didn't want to talk to me. That's crazy. She never doesn't want to talk to me. And when I reminded her of that, she started to cry and closed the door." He saw Ross stop in the act of taking his seat. "So I decided that one of you had better talk to me, and since she wouldn't, I came here. Does that make any sense to you?" He looked up sharply at Ross as he asked.

"I think it might. Why don't you explain a bit more?" He did not sound easy in his mind, but he kept a steady, calm gaze on Drew.

"That's what I'm trying to do," Drew responded, laughing uncomfortably. "I don't seem to be doing it as well as I thought I could."

"I'm listening," Ross assured him.

"Good. I don't think I can do this more than once. God, I hope you *are* serious about Jenny. If you're not, I should leave right now, before I make it any worse." Drew did not move, but he grew more tense.

"Stay," Ross said quietly.

Drew nodded. "I thought so. Jenny doesn't, but that's not your fault." He crossed his legs, then shifted and braced his ankle on the opposite knee. "I don't know quite where to begin. It's complicated. You know I worked at the Savoia while Jenny and George Howard were still married, don't you?"

"Yes," Ross said, still perplexed.

"Good. And I left about the same time Jenny did," Drew went on, seeing Ross nod. "When things get real bad, some people drink, and some of them sleep, and some of them gorge themselves on food or lovers or clothes or travel. Jenny works. Most of the time, she likes work. When she's idle, she goes nuts. But that's not the same as what she's been doing the last few years. And it has been years." He unfolded his arms and steepled his fingers, peering over the top of them. "I don't think I've seen her cry more than four or five times."

"She won't permit herself to," Ross said, knowing how much he wanted to offer the comfort she would not admit she wanted from him.

"That's true enough," Drew said, and was more relieved about Ross. "But that wasn't how it began. At first, her troubles appeared . . . trivial. Little things, and she told me that she'd blow them out of proportion. She believed it, too, for a time. You don't know what it was like, working at the Savoia and seeing what went on. Nothing obvious, of course, not at first. It took time to notice something was wrong."

"How do you mean wrong?" Ross asked.

"While Jenny was making sure that everything at the restaurant ran smoothly, working morning until night, George would come sashaying in about half an hour before we were supposed to open, all charming and enthusiastic, behaving as if he were the one really in charge, and Jenny was his lieutenant, carrying out his instructions while he was off doing the *important* work, but don't ask me what that was." His hands tightened into interlaced fists. "One of the things he'd do right off was to tell Jenny that she didn't look good, or that something wasn't right, or there were chores unfinished. It diminished her in the eyes of the staff, but not obviously, because he was always solicitous in his manner, at least when there were people around who could hear." He caught his lower lip between his teeth and closed his eyes for a moment. "For a while, I bought it. That was an assinine thing to do."

"But you changed your mind," Ross said, curious to know what had happened.

"We had a banquet one night. George had arranged it. There were forty-two coming, and George had forgotten to leave the dinner counts with us. Or maybe he never bothered to get them, I don't know. Anyway, Jenny ended up having to drive halfway to San Mateo to find the steaks we needed, which made the dinner late. She told us to serve both a soup and salad, just to give her enough time to bring back the steaks, though it meant we would lose money on the banquet. George showed up before Jenny got back, and at first he told the staff that Jenny had screwed up again. Then he went in to the banquet and showered charm all over the place and made sure that everyone understood that this little mix-up was because his wife wasn't really as good at this business as she ought to be. *This* from a man who hadn't bothered to ask where Jenny was or how we had managed so far. If that sounds insignificant, I don't know what I can tell you to let you see what . . ."

Ross broke in, "I know the kind of thing you're talking about. But why did she put up with it for so long?" He could not imagine his reserved, brave Jennifer tolerating such treatment.

"You don't know George. He's better at giving chops in the back of the knees than any man I've ever met. He also offered carrots. As soon as this is taken care of, then things will be better, or as soon as we make a certain amount a quarter, we can have a proper vacation. I heard a lot of that. And I remember dozens of times when he'd arrange to meet someone at the Savoia and would not come in until half an hour or forty minutes had gone by, and by then Jenny would have taken care of most of the business and all that was left was for George to come in and charm them. I give him this: he *can* charm." He cleared his throat, shrugging as if he carried a heavy burden. "That's one of the reasons I was taken in. George . . . you've seen him. He's not quite as good-looking as he was a couple years ago, but he's still one of the most gorgeous men around. That . . . misled me a little . . . a lot, at first. George uses his looks to . . . manipulate people. I've known other good-looking men like that. It isn't just a woman's trick."

"I met George. I can see what you mean." Ross did not think George was as attractive as Drew found him, but kept his opinion to himself.

"When they were alone, or thought they were, he'd call her a fool—or worse—depending on his mood. Maybe you've never seen how insidious that can be, making a person look inward when she should be looking outward, but I saw it up close for four years, six days a week, and even I learn, in time." He sighed.

Ross recalled the way his brother, Ian, dealt with his wife, the constant little "suggestions" that kept her in almost perpetual worry. "I've seen something like it," he said, squirming internally.

"Then you know what it does." He finally looked squarely at Ross. "After a while, when the worst of the pressure was off, things got better for a while, and Jenny brightened up, got more like the woman she ought to be. Then they got worse. George became involved with other women, or acted as if he were involved." He looked out toward the dark windows and nervously fingered his moustache. "He was cutting and abusive and critical, all the time, not just occasionally, and he has a knack for getting her where she's most vulnerable. He would accuse Jenny of being frigid after telling her that he'd spent the night with someone else. Making it her fault, you see. And for me, because we were friends, he called her a fag hag. She couldn't deal with that at all." He gave a humorless chuckle.

"Yes," Ross said, aching for her, and wishing it were Jennifer who was telling him this rather than Drew.

The other man sensed this. "Don't let her know you've found out about this, from me or anyone. She can't bear to be pitied. I wouldn't have said anything, either, if George hadn't come to the Elephant yesterday. It's the third time in a week he's just 'dropped in,' insisting that Jenny's been sending him notes. I don't know if that's a ploy or whether there's someone out there with a really warped sense of humor. All I know is that Jenny's wound so tight that she can hardly think, and all the old patterns are coming back." He got up and walked to the windows. "If she means anything to you, Ross, I hope you'll make the effort to . . . break through. I wouldn't like to see her get any more upset than she is. She does need your help, Ross. There's only so much I can give her." His smile was sad as he looked toward Ross.

"I understand," Ross said, trying to rid himself of the hope that rose in him. Perhaps, in spite of all his doubts, he had come closer to Jennifer than he realized.

"You won't tell her I came here, will you?" Drew asked, apprehensive now.

"I'll try not to lie," Ross replied. "But I won't volunteer, either."

"I'll accept that," Drew said, holding out his hand.

Ross took it. "I'm . . . pleased you trusted me," he said as Drew stepped back.

"Thanks." Drew started toward the door. "I hope it does some good." Then he stopped. "You know, I think it would work better between you if you didn't keep pestering her about the lease."

"On the acres?" Ross asked, puzzled. "I didn't think I *had* been pestering her."

"She sure thinks you have," Drew said. "She doesn't come out and complain about it, but whenever she gets one of those calls from Henry Fisher, she becomes very quiet and thoughtful, and that means she's trying to . . . control something."

"Calls from Henry Fisher? Her attorney? What about them?" Ross could make little sense of this. "I don't think I've talked to Henry Fisher more than three times."

"But he says you're pressing for an answer. . . ." Drew objected, stopping with his hand on the doorknob.

"I haven't said . . ." Ross stopped. "Oh, damn. Ian."

"Ian?" It was Drew's turn to be puzzled.

"My brother. In San Francisco. He's in advertising and promotion. I told him months ago to leave Jennifer alone . . . God, I should have known he'd . . ." Ross took a turn about the room. "I'll call him in the morning and find out . . . Better yet, I'll call Henry Fisher and see what he has to say. If it is Ian, well, I'm sorry about it. No wonder Jennifer is . . ." Ross did not like to argue with his brother, and often kept his complaints to himself, but this time he was certain they would have a monumental clash of wills. He had given his instructions to Ian, and Ian had ignored them.

"Fine. And if it *is* what's been happening, you'd better find a way to tell Jenny. I wouldn't be too obvious about that, either. She'd see that as another kind of pressure on her, and she'd feel she owed you an apology or something. Go gently with her, will you? She hasn't been gently used before, and it's time she was." He opened the door.

"I will. I want to. And the next time George shows up, give me a call. Insist that you speak to me, if they try to put you off. I'll have your name on my list tomorrow morning, and all they have to do is look at it. If you tell me George is there, I'll be at the Elephant in twenty minutes at the most." In an odd way, he hoped that Drew would call him soon, so that he would be able to put George Howard on notice.

"I will." Drew's serious face relaxed but his eyes were guarded. "Don't fail me. Or her." With that quiet warning, he left the room.

Ross sat by himself for another hour, trying to think of a way to mitigate the hurt Jennifer was feeling. When he at last went up to his bedroom, he had the first tenuous dawnings of a plan.

∾ October ∾

"I'm real sorry about this, Mrs. Wystan," Wilbur said over the remains of his salad. "I tried to get exemptions for all historic buildings, but that isn't acceptable, since they're the ones that often pose the greatest hazards." He smiled as the waiter refilled his coffee cup. "That hotsprings building is going to have to be changed, and there isn't much I can do about it. If it had been in use all along, you might have got that variance, but since it hasn't been, and you're already on file for restoring it, I have to go along with Board policy. They're understanding, and they know that you're not trying to get away with anything, but if we don't stick to our guns, there are opportunists out there who *will* take advantage of any laxity on our part. There's not a lot I can do."

Jennifer nodded and gave a pallid, appreciative smile. "Well, thanks for trying. I didn't think they'd go along with the request, but I had to try. There was always the chance, wasn't there? I'll just have to find a way to bring that building up to the new codes, that's all." That's all, she echoed in her mind, remembering the cost estimate she had got on the job from Fred Jenkins. The amount was staggering, and she could not imagine how she would come up with so much money.

Henry had warned her that she might not be able to get all she needed from the trust because there was an annual limit recommended and he was reluctant to exceed it, especially in the first year of business.

"I hope you can do it. And I'm still sorry I couldn't do anything to get you a better deal, Mrs. Wystan." He put his napkin back on the table. "I hear you're planning an Oktoberfest. Is that right?"

"We're trying for one. It's all rather short notice, but I think we can pull it off. We'll announce the name of the elephant and have polkas and waltzes. If it goes over well, I'll do it again next year." It gave her a sense of exhilaration to talk about plans being made so far in advance. If she kept thinking of what she would do in a year or two years, she was less bothered by the momentary setbacks.

"Sounds like the kind of thing that could catch on. Some of the wineries do their own little festivals, but you're plowing new ground here." He shook his head. "I still don't feel right letting you treat me to lunch, Mrs. Wystan."

"Don't let it bother you, Mr. Cory. You're one of the Elephant's biggest boosters, and this is small enough thanks for your support." She got up from the table and walked toward the lobby with him. "It's a pleasure to be able to make a gesture every now and then."

"Well, if that's the way you feel about it, I'd be a cad to refuse," Wilbur said as he pulled the lobe of his ear, a sure sign of nervousness.

"Yes, you would. And a male chauvinist, too." Her grin took the sting out of the reprimand, and he accepted it with good grace.

"I won't say it wasn't a pleasure, because it was, and I won't say it isn't appreciated, because it is. Your Uncle Samuel would be proud of the way you're doing business, Mrs. Wystan, and that's the best I can say to you." He held out his hand and shook hers awkwardly. "I know that I say things that go against the grain with you, but I'm not as young as you and I come from traditional folk who don't take to change too easily. Most of us try to be fair, though. We do try."

"That's all I ask," Jennifer said with a great deal of restraint. "That, and that I not be judged by any special standards." It was as tactful a way as any to let him know that she was aware of the prejudice that had greeted her when she first came to the White Elephant.

"Yeah," Wilbur said. "I know what you mean." He coughed and his eyes shifted around the walls and then down the hall toward the lobby. "Sometimes we jump the gun a little. We don't do it out of meanness, Mrs. Wystan."

"I know," she said gently. "And I don't think you'd be deliberately unkind. Besides, that's over and done, most of it." She came to the edge of the lobby and said, "I've got to get some work done in the reservations office. I'm glad we had the chance to talk, but now, if you'll excuse me . . ."

Wilbur nodded. "I didn't mean to keep you."

"You didn't. I have to take everything you've told me into account while I make plans for next year. If I have to bring that building up to the new code, I have to do it, and that means I have to shift my priorities a bit. I couldn't have done it as well without your help." She smiled and was glad to be able to move away from Wilbur. She had a great deal of thinking to do.

"I don't care what Wilbur told you," Ross said to Jennifer the following Saturday afternoon when he came to pick her up. "File for a variance, anyway. It will get you a little more time and that's important for you right now." He turned right at the Elephant and drove southwest.

"Where are we going?" Jennifer asked, still feeling slightly guilty that she had let him persuade her to take the afternoon and evening off.

"My place. I've been inviting you, and we've never been able to arrange things, so since Aunt Rosa is fixing a very special dinner tonight, I decided that the only way to make sure you could be here was to come and get you." He drove along the road at a good clip, and turned in smartly at his own gate.

Jennifer was too surprised to be indignant. She stared at Ross, wishing that he would turn to look at her. "I'm dressed. . . ." she began, putting her hand on the soft paisley-patterned wool of her suit jacket.

"You're dressed fine. My brother is up from San Francisco and he likes to be a bit dressy. Aunt Rosa likes it, too. She often gets after me for coming to the dining table in my working clothes." He was wearing fawn-colored slacks and a tweed jacket over an ivory shirt and ocher tie. "You're fine."

"Do you say that to put me at ease?" she asked, more curious than challenging.

"I hope it does, but it isn't why I say it." He pulled his

BMW in beside Ian's Mercedes and turned off the ignition. "Ian's a little younger than I am, and . . . well, you'll see. I don't want to influence you." He got out and came around to open the door for her.

"Am I on display?" she wondered aloud as she followed Ross toward the Victorian house ahead of them.

"Not display. I'm not even showing off. But," he said, stopping to face her as he reached the stairs to the porch, "I do want my family to get used to the idea that I spend time with you." He reached out and rested his hands on her shoulders. "Don't worry about it, Jennifer. If I thought this would be awkward or upsetting for you, I wouldn't have brought you."

Jennifer was dubious, but she gave Ross a guarded smile. "I'll try not to let it bother me. It's just that . . ." She did not go on, wanting to put behind her the memories of those dreadful meals with George's sisters. That was in the past, another time, another place, a different man; this was Ross, and she was learning to trust him.

Ross held the door for her as she walked into the front vestibule. A small woman with a square, emphatic body came bustling through the door of the front parlor. "High time you were back, Ross," Aunt Rosa declared, and turned to Jennifer. "I'm glad he finally remembered his manners and brought you over. Neighbors should know each other, shouldn't they?"

This brusque, no-nonsense greeting did more to make Jennifer comfortable than any show of courtesy would have. She felt herself become less taut, and smiled as she shook hands with Ross's aunt. "Yes, they should. I've had Ross at the Elephant so often that I forget I haven't met the rest of you. Bad form on my part."

"Don't be silly," Aunt Rosa said, leading Jennifer into the front parlor. "You have a houseful of people there all the time, and one or two extras aren't going to make that much difference one way or another to you. But here, when summer is over, there's just Ross and me and occasional weekend guests. I know what it's like to have an empty evening or two on my hands."

"Then have Ross bring you to the Elephant for supper. It would be my pleasure to have you as my guest." She liked this woman, she decided, and was sorry that she had not taken the time to meet her before.

"We'd like that," Aunt Rosa declared, and paused in the

doorway. "I don't think you've met my nephew Ian," she said to Jennifer, indicating the other person in the room. "This is Ross's brother."

"Baby brother," said Ian with a snide expression. He rose and offered a handshake. "So you're the stubborn Ms. Wystan."

This reaction puzzled Jennifer, but she said, "I suppose so."

"Suppose?" Ian echoed. "If your stance about the acreage lease is any indication . . ." he began, and was cut off by his brother.

"Not tonight, Ian," Ross said from the doorway. "You've done more than your share of that." He was able to chuckle, although it was more of an effort than he would have thought possible. He had hoped that some time during the evening Ian might let it drop that he was the one who had been dealing with Henry Fisher, but he had not intended this sort of confrontation first thing.

"Why not tonight?" Ian wanted to know. "From what Fisher tells me, it's about the only way to deal with her, and you refuse to do anything more." He gave Jennifer a wide, neat smile that had none of the devastating effect of his brother's, no matter how perfect his teeth and how well-shaped his mouth.

"And I refuse now," Ross said genially. "And so do you, Ian."

"Gracious, yes," Aunt Rosa interrupted. "And a good thing, too. When I take the time to cook like this, I want your undivided attention, and this nattering about business won't do." She stopped. "I hear a car. It must be the Hasslunds."

Jennifer sighed her relief. So the evening wasn't to be just Ross and his abrasive brother. "I didn't know they were coming," she said to Ross rather quietly.

"Yes. And there are two more guests beyond that. Not as large a gathering as we have during the summer, but quite nice for this time of year." He went to the bar at the end of the parlor. "What can I get for you? I warn you, in this household, we do not serve hard drinks before dinner. We're a wine-making family."

"Since you know what's for dinner, why don't you choose?" Jennifer suggested, and favored him with a more relaxed smile than she had shown earlier as she followed him across the room.

He chose a Colombard and poured out two glasses of it.

"This is something new for us in the last three years. It isn't bad, but I'd like it to be better."

"Now, no more of this canoodling," Ian said waggishly as he came up to his brother and Jennifer. "If I'm barred from talking business, I can still ask how the Empress is doing. You don't call it that, though, do you?"

"No. It's the White Elephant now," Jennifer said with her best company manners.

"And that's why the big statue. I've got to hand it to you, Ms. Wystan, that's a great gimmick. If you ever want to expand your advertising, give me a call. I'm sure we can turn that thing to real advantage. That's the best sort of identification there is, and you're using it just right. But with a modest advertising campaign, you could have real impact." He opened the cabinet under the bar and pulled out a bottle of Benedetto brandy. "Ross is always such a stickler for wine, but I find it a bit tame before dinner, don't you?"

"Well, not really, no," Jennifer said, not only because it was true but because she felt herself wanting to show this man that she was on Ross's side, not his.

"It's good wine," Ian agreed as he poured out a generous amount of brandy and then began his search for the soda.

"You're not being convincing," Ross said with a significant look at Jennifer. "If this is your approach to advertising, we're in trouble." He was bantering, but Ian's face darkened a shade as he splashed soda into the brandy and dropped in an ice cube.

"It's fine for you to take that attitude. You aren't the one who has to keep this company selling to the public: I am!"

"We sold wines long before ad campaigns," Ross said mildly.

"Just because we didn't start advertising until twenty years ago, you think that it's not important. But it *is*. And whom we reach is important. Our ads sell wine." Ian thrust out his chin as if expecting to fight.

"Sure they do. They cost a lot, too. So they'd better sell wine to pay for themselves. Now that doesn't mean that I don't think we should advertise at all, and you know it. Only I do think that the merit of the wines is more important than the advertising. And that's where we're always going to differ." He turned as Aunt Rosa came back into the room with the Hasslunds, Sheridan Robb and Muriel Wrather.

"Now we're all here, I'll bring in the rest of the appetizers. Ross, make sure people have what they want to drink, even if you don't agree with it." With this instruction, she went off in the direction of the kitchen, leaving Ross to attend to the newly-arrived guests.

"You don't have to leave," Ross said to Jennifer at the end of the evening when Ian had gone up to bed and the others had driven off. "You can stay over, if you like."

"Oh, Ross, don't tempt me," Jennifer responded. They were sitting side by side on the sofa, his arm over her shoulder.

"But it's going to rain," he said. "Think about the hazards of driving back."

"Three and a half miles. Terrible." She did not want to leave. She liked it here in this rambling, comfortable house, with the last scent of brandied custard on the air, like a lingering bit of melody. "It's after eleven."

"All the more reason to stay over. In the morning, we can talk about your Oktoberfest and make arrangements for the wines. Saves you a trip or a phone call."

"And they're both so difficult," Jennifer said, trying to keep her expression serious and failing. "Ross, don't. You're making me giggle."

"Good. I like your giggles," he said at once, then added seriously, "I'm sorry Ian's been pressuring you about the lease. I asked him not to some time ago, and I thought he had agreed; sometimes he takes things into his hands that he shouldn't. He said today that he thought I wouldn't pursue the matter and one of us had to. I didn't want you to think that . . ."

Jennifer nodded quickly. "I should have asked Henry one simple question, but it never occurred to me. He's very proper, is Henry, and he speaks with great formality. He always says Mister and Miss. He said Mr. Benedetto, and I thought . . . I knew there were more of you, but it didn't cross my mind . . . and you're the only one I really know." She faltered, then summoned up all her courage to add, "You're the only one I care about."

"I'm going to barricade the doors," Ross said, his voice lower and gruff with emotion. "After a declaration like that, you are *not* going back to the Elephant tonight." Then he did something he had been wanting to do all evening: he laced his hands through her hair, tangling them in the dark strands before he pulled her to him, kissing her long and tenderly.

There was no resistance in Jennifer, and no wish for any. It was marvelous to know she was so precious to Ross, to feel his desire and need in the way he touched her, the movements of his hands, his aroused state. There was no guile in him, no manipulation or deception. With Ross she did not feel constant anxiety that she would not satisfy or please, that she would in some inexplicable way disappoint him and have to face the crushing, sudden indifference that George had so often displayed.

"Something wrong?" Ross whispered, concerned.

"No." She sternly banished all thought of George from her mind. "A silly thing. Nothing important."

"Do you want to talk about it?" Ross asked. He wanted her, but he did not limit that longing to her body. As much as he desired her, he also cherished her, and to make love when she was troubled seemed offensive to him.

"Not really." She wanted to hold onto the awakening pleasure she felt. "Later, maybe. But now I . . . " She leaned forward and kissed him, and felt his response.

"Later," he agreed. "Come with me," he said as he rose.

His bedroom was on the second floor, a large chamber with redwood paneling, rosy-colored draperies pulled open with rust-silk braided cords. The comforter thrown over the bed was brick-and-beige, the lamps flanking it, brass. Underfoot, the redwood flooring was waxed and shiny where it was not covered by genuine Oriental carpets. Ross turned off the overhead light as he closed the door, and they were left in the faint glow from the two bedside lamps.

"A king-sized bed? For just you?" Jennifer asked, feeling a bit nervous in these elegant, unfamiliar surroundings.

"And you." He took her in his arms, but without urgency. "You might not believe this, but I haven't brought any woman here since Rosemary was killed. In fact, I did the room over, so that I wouldn't be always reminded that she was gone. I won't pretend I've been celibate, but I've never wanted anyone here with me until now." He kissed her eyelids. "I've slept alone here since Rosemary's death, but I've always hoped that it wouldn't be forever." His mouth opened over hers, and he fumbled with buttons, wishing her closer to him.

Jennifer was filled with stirrings that astounded her, for she had never felt so deep and essentially serene an arousal as

Ross evoked in her now. Her body was so sensitive that the touch of a feather would have set her shivering; yet there was none of the edginess that so often accompanied this state. A guitar being strummed must feel this vibrance, Jennifer thought dreamily as the brush of Ross's hand, even through the fabric of her bra and blouse, brought her nipples to standing points. The sliding of her clothes off her body was almost unbearably sensual. Jennifer felt as if her bones were melting when Ross at last picked her up in his arms and carried her to the bed. So much more than her body was open to him now, and so much more than her body received him, from the homage of his hands to the fervor of his penetration, that it seemed that their emotions, their very souls, were as linked as their flesh.

With someone less loving than Ross, the intensity of their lovemaking could have been shattering, but he gave himself without reservation, rejoicing in their shared elation. From the moment he entered her until the depth and force of her climax triggered his own, he rode the crest of passion like a boat running before a storm. It was exhilarating and triumphant in a way he had never known before. When he was spent, he could not bear to let her go, but held her close to him, one leg still resting between hers, his face in a cloud of her hair.

Jennifer sighed, feeling wholly comfortable. "One of us has an extra arm," she said quietly as Ross shifted beside her.

"I know. But we'll manage," he promised her, and moved his shoulder so that he could hold her even closer.

Drew looked at the assortment of sausages spread out in the kitchen and sighed. "I don't really have anything specific against German food, but I can't get that excited about anything wrapped up in used intestines."

"Drew, for God's sake," Jennifer said, laughing but exasperated. "We're going to have three hundred people through here tomorrow. Don't get me caught up in this now." She looked around the kitchen. "What else do we have?"

"Fourteen kinds of sausage, smoked ham, smoked fish, smoked eel, venison stew, five barley and bean dishes, three kinds of soup including one with apples, four cabbage dishes, eight kinds of breads, ten different sorts of mustard, twelve kinds of beer and ale, ten assorted wines, and sixteen varieties of pastry, including Black Forest torte. If that doesn't satisfy them, I can't imagine what would." He gave

Jennifer a very broad, very lascivious wink. "Everyone will find something to eat."

"Drew, you're impossible," Jennifer said, trying to look forbidding.

Drew gave her one of his puckish grins. "I try," he said. "But seriously, boss, we'll simply overwhelm them with German food, and they can drink up all the wine and beer and dance polkas all over the lawn." Drew picked up one of his omelette pans. "I'll sit down here and enjoy some French decadence while the rest of you indulge yourselves."

"We may not frolic on the lawn," Jennifer said. "The weather report isn't too encouraging. High clouds, some wind, and a chance of rain in the evening. I don't know how to arrange things for that, but I think I'll open all three function rooms on the main floor and the suites on the second, just in case. That way, we can't be rained out."

"Good planning, boss." Drew folded his arms. "Are you doing okay, Jenny?"

"Sure. I'm fine." She meant it, and knew that Drew believed her.

"What about George?" he persisted.

"I haven't seen him in the last few days. I think he's finally got the message." She was not as confident about that as she would have liked to be, but she refused to show concern about it. "You know what George can be like."

"Yes. That's what worries me. He's made up his mind he's entitled to a piece of your work here, and he hasn't given up yet. I can feel it in my bones. In a day or a week, you'll have to send him packing again. George can't stand the idea that you might make it on your own, without marvelous him to take the credit. He'll do everything he can to stand in your way, and don't you doubt it for a minute." Drew came closer to her, his eyes apprehensive and his good-looking features drawn with concern. "Jenny, George Howard is not a nice man. He doesn't like you. Don't ever forget that."

"You're talking to me as if I were five years old," Jennifer complained. "I know George resents . . ."

"I'm talking to you as if you're five because that's how you're acting. You're assuming that if you mind your manners and say the right things, George will get the message. I'm telling you that the side of a house dropping on him would not give him the message. Don't see him when he shows up again, all right?" Drew watched her, looking as if he would have liked to shake her.

"Drew . . ." Jennifer began in her most reasonable tone.

"Don't see him. Lie. Have Muriel or Ivy or Dean say you're out. Don't see him." He was so insistent that Jennifer wondered if the spur of alarm she had felt might have been well-founded, after all. "If you think it's necessary," she said slowly, surprised when Drew nodded emphatically and his features relaxed.

Johnny Chang approached Drew cautiously. "I have to work out something about the potato salad. How many gallons do you want Hilde to make?"

"She has the order . . ." Drew began, then lifted his hands. "Jenny, Hilde has to have at least four phone calls before she believes anything. I've got to go talk to her. I wouldn't bother, but if you've ever had her potato salad, you'll know why I take the trouble."

"What's so special about it?" Jennifer asked, pleased that they were talking about food instead of George.

"Did you ever go to the Alpine Chalet on Post Street?" Drew asked. "Not in the last four years, but before that?" The restaurant had something of a mystique in San Francisco and boasted a distinguished clientele.

"Once or twice, why?"

"Hilde was their soup chef. She also did the potato salad. Since she's retired, she only cooks when she wants to, for people she wants to cook for, period. It took me an hour to convince her that it was worthwhile to do this Oktoberfest. I'm a good chef, boss, and most of the time I'd shudder at the thought of asking anyone to mess with my menu, but when it comes to potato salad, Hilde is my master, and the master of half the German chefs this side of Munich." He grinned at Jennifer. "You'll *love* what she does to potato salad. It has onions and mushrooms and eggs and a dozen other goodies in it. Everyone will *adore* it."

"Fine," Jennifer said, and turned to leave the kitchen.

"Remember what I said about George," Drew called after her.

"I will," Jennifer answered, and put it completely out of her mind.

At seven o'clock the dancing began, and for once the older couples crowded onto the dance floor, bouncing energetically to an assortment of polkas and waltzes played by a six-piece ensemble.

"This is simply *fantastic*," Helene told Jennifer as she came off the dance floor with her partner, Victor Hasslund. "I haven't had so much fun in years." She looked very lovely with her cheeks pink and her blonde hair in disorder. The full-skirted dress she wore emphasized the narrowness of her waist and the shape of her breasts, and she preened in it. "I'm so pleased to be here." It was said with a politician's facile enthusiasm.

"I'm pleased you could be here, too," Jennifer said automatically, thinking that she did not like the way Helene had been cozying up to Ross earlier. "I'm a little surprised, what with the election coming up so soon."

"Well, I can't work all the time. And half the people I ought to be seeing are here, and this spares me the trouble of chasing after them." She laughed theatrically as a flashbulb went off, then turned to Jennifer. "Ross looks great tonight, don't you think?"

"I suppose he does," Jennifer said, hating to admit that she had been watching him covertly for most of the afternoon.

"He's a very attractive man. You might think about that, Jennifer. He's a competent lover, good looking, a reasonable age, and though he doesn't make it obvious, he's very rich. You could do worse." She gave Jennifer an encouraging grin. "If I hadn't so many other things going on right now, I might make a play for him again, for old time's sake, but I don't have the time to do it right, and you know how it is." She waved to three men on the other side of the Grand Ballroom. "Now I think I'd better concentrate on votes. The rest can come later."

Jennifer made some noncommittal noise which Helene was free to interpret in any way she wished. Why, she asked herself, did Helene have to remind her always that Ross had had other women? It was not that Jennifer wanted him to lie about it, or that she would have believed him if he had said that he had remained monkishly pure for the last decade. She did not want to think that she was picking up where someone else had left off, and nothing she could do could shake her feeling that this was precisely what Helene wanted her to think. She covered her conflicting emotions by watching the dancing—at the moment a spirited chain-gang polka—and doing her best to keep a professional hotelier's attitude toward the behavior of the guests.

"It's a good party, Mrs. Wystan," Wilbur said to her a little later when the energetic dance had ended and the little orchestra had taken up a more sedate schottish.

"Thank you, Wilbur," she said without much thought. "I hoped it would be."

"Just the kind of good time I'd expect you to provide," he continued with a more ingratiating smile. "You're showing all the others up."

"Good heavens, I hope they don't get annoyed with me then. I didn't intend this to be any sort of contest." She was a bit shocked, thinking that the competitive criticism of other hotel and resort owners was the last thing she wanted to achieve from this entertainment.

"Now, now, a little something new is good for all of us, now and again. Don't you get to thinking that you're handing anyone a bad time. Everything's good in business right now. If you'd done this at mid-summer, a few of the others might have thought you were grandstanding, but not now, during off-season. About the only grouser I've heard is Jack Warnor at Horseshoe Lodge. But he didn't get along with Old Samuel, either, so I wouldn't think much of him not liking you." Wilbur shook his head at the dancers. "When I was a kid, I could go on all night—schottishes, polkas, waltzes, hambos, you name it—and now I get tired just watching."

"So do I," Jennifer admitted.

Wilbur chortled and grinned. "Don't believe that for a minute, Mrs. Wystan. Now, if you'll excuse me, some liquid refreshment would hit the spot right now." He gave her an awkward bow and moved away.

Ten minutes later, as the musicians began a well-deserved break, Jennifer took the microphone and tried to contain the sudden rush of nervousness that consumed her. She stood in the center of the bandstand, feeling hot and cold at once and hoped that no one noticed that her hands were shaking slightly. "Good evening," she said, and was startled by the loudness of her voice in the speakers.

The guests turned toward her and the buzz of talk dropped to near silence.

"This evening, I'm pleased to announce the winning name of the White Elephant. As you know, we've been running a contest to name the White Elephant, our mascot out by the gate. Our judge in the contest is the distinguished concert pianist Eric Bush." She paused to allow her audience to applaud. "I have his decision to read to you tonight." She took the note from her pocket. "Let me read this to you. *It has been a great pleasure for me to choose the name of the White Elephant's mascot from the various suggestions you have been good enough to send. I have considered them all most carefully, and have made what is a fond and whimsical selection. I have long admired the Babar stories, yet Babar is much too obvious a name. However, Mr. and Mrs. William Dutton submitted the name Cornelius, and after careful consideration, I have found Cornelius irresistible, and have therefore awarded the Duttons the prize."* There were three or four lines of a more personal nature which Jennifer did not read aloud. *"With sincere good wishes to you, Cornelius and the Duttons, Eric Bush."* She smiled at the applause that greeted the announcement and was delighted to see Ross raise a wineglass.

"Well, then," he called out loudly enough to be heard over the rumble of comments, "to Cornelius!"

The other guests echoed the toast.

Jennifer nodded her approval, and made her last speech for the evening. "I'd like to thank all of those who entered the contest for their interest and enthusiasm." There was a ripple of applause. "My thanks also to Eric Bush for consenting to be our judge, and my congratulations to the Duttons. This is a very special evening at the White Elephant, and I'm glad you're here to share it with me and the staff. Thank you." She turned off the microphone and stepped away from the stand, feeling very pleased with herself.

By the end of the evening, Jennifer was giddy with fatigue. She had permitted herself just two glasses of wine and a good-sized sandwich, but these had not staved off her exhaustion. She was so staggeringly tired that she could not remember what she had said to any of her guests as they departed; she longed for ten hours' uninterrupted sleep. She had stationed herself in the foyer outside the Grand Ballroom where most of the departures could find her.

"At the risk of offending you," Ross said to her as he prepared to leave, "you look dreadful. Can't you leave the rest to your staff and go get some sleep?" He was looking his polished best, but Jennifer noticed that he did not move quite as briskly as usual.

"In half an hour, maybe. We're down to the last third. When a few more of them have gone, I can make my excuses and Ivy can take over." She had that headachy heaviness that often plagued her when she was so completely worn out. "Thanks."

"For what? For noticing you need rest? Anyone with two

eyes in reasonable working order could see that." He touched her shoulder and was puzzled when she seemed to draw away. "Is something the matter, Jennifer?"

"Nothing," she answered. "Really, it *is* nothing, but I'm so tired that I'm making too much of it. After a good night's rest, it won't matter to me at all."

"Helene said something to you, didn't she?" Ross guessed. "I saw you two talking earlier in the evening. What was it?"

"Good advice. How I should make a play for you. She recommends you." Her tone was more wistful than angry.

"Good of her," Ross said quietly. "Did you tell her it was too late for that?"

"I didn't tell her anything. I didn't know what to say. I don't know how to deal with women like that. Am I supposed to say thanks for trying you out, or what?" She pressed her lips together so that she would not say anything more damaging than she had already.

"Don't let her get to you, Jennifer," Ross told her. "Helene is always a little like that. She doesn't know any other way to be."

"I'm not arguing about that," Jennifer sniffed. "I just don't like it. I feel . . . so smirched." She touched her face. "I bet my nose is shiny and my eye-makeup has run."

"Your face is flawless. It's the way you're sitting that gives you away," Ross said. "Are you going to get some rest or not?"

"Shortly," she snapped. "Don't push me, Ross. I'm in no mood for it."

"I'm not pushing," he insisted. "If you think I am, then you're more tired than I thought you were." He frowned as she glared up at him. "Jennifer, believe me, you need to get to bed."

"Alone," she said, hating the bitchy sound of her voice, but too worn out to change it. "Don't listen to me, Ross. Forget everything I say tonight. None of it means anything. I'm tired." It was hard to admit it so succinctly, but his concern had worn her down. "Let me have another twenty minutes, and then I will get to bed."

"Alone," Russ agreed, but with sympathy. "Tonight what you need is sleep, and nothing else." He rested his hand on her shoulder for a moment, to indicate that he was not upset by her abruptness.

Jennifer sighed. "You know, Ross, I think it might be nice just to sleep but not alone. To curl up for the night the way those desert foxes do." Her voice became slightly dreamy as she spoke, and her eyes, she knew, were half-awash in tears. Oh, dear, she thought, if I don't get to sleep I'll make a complete spectacle of myself. "You're right," she conceded. "I'd better go up now." She waved vaguely at the group of departing guests, and said one or two polite words to them.

"Good." He offered her his hand, which she ignored, and accompanied her to the elevator. "I'll call you around noon. Maybe we can have lunch together."

"I thought you had more of the harvest to attend to," Jennifer said, a bit surprised at this suggestion.

"I do, but I don't have to be there every minute. You and I could both stand a break, and I, for one, intend to have one." He turned toward the elevator as the doors opened. "You've done very well with this Oktoberfest. You ought to be proud, Jennifer."

"I may be, in a day or two," Jennifer said, and stepped into the elevator. She tried to say something more, something to let Ross know how much she appreciated his care and concern, but the elevator doors closed before her dazed mind could supply her with anything appropriate, and then all she could think of was sleep.

George's smile slipped a little at the corners as Jennifer folded her arms and shook her head. "I've told you no before, and I'm telling you no now," she said flatly. "I'm fed up with this nonsense of yours." She was glad that her desk was between them this time, so that he could not lean nearer to try to touch her.

"Jen, don't be such a silly girl about this. You know I love you . . . " He braced his elbows on the desktop and did his best to give her an intimate look.

"I am not a girl, silly or otherwise. Please, George, why don't you simply leave? You say that you want to do something to prove you still care for me. If you really do, then go. Let it be over."

"You can't brush off our marriage just like that," George protested.

"I didn't brush it off just like that. It took me more than a year to get over it, and I don't want to fall back into the old patterns. That's why I don't want you to come here anymore, George. Whatever our marriage was, it's over now, and that's the way it should be." She did not want to get angry with him, but if he continued to try to wear her down, as he had when they were married, she would have to, in order to defend herself from his demands and assumptions. She did not relish having a confrontation here in her office, but she was afraid that if she did not convince George at last, he would become more of an embarrassment than he already was.

"I respect your attitude, Jen, but you still aren't seeing things very clearly. We were *good* together." He looked so sincere when he said it that Jennifer did not know whether to laugh or scream.

"It may seem that way to you now, but that was not your opinion at the time." She started to get up. "I'm sorry, George . . ."—No, I'm not, she thought—"but I can't spare the time right now."

"Another brush-off, is that it? You think I don't know you're afraid to be alone with me? And the reason? You haven't been able to get me out of your system. Well, it's no different for me. Let's give it a chance, Jen." He reached out as if to take her hand, and Jennifer snatched it out of range.

"Stop it, George. I mean it. Stop it!" In spite of all her good intentions, her voice had risen. "It isn't possible, don't you understand that?"

George was about to protest when there was the most perfunctory of knocks at the door and Ross strode into the reception office. George looked shocked, and then his eyes narrowed.

"I don't mean to burst in on you like this, Jennifer," Ross said, as if he barely saw George, "but you are late, and I have to get started for Napa pretty soon if I'm going to get those errands done."

Jennifer picked up her cue admirably. "Oh, Ross, I'm very sorry. I would have had the material for you on time, but, as you see, I have a visitor and . . ."

Ross turned toward George. "I think we've met before, haven't we? I'm Ross Benedetto of the Benedetto Vinyards. You're George . . . is it Howard?"

"Yes," George responded, taking Ross's proffered hand with an expression of distaste. "Jen and I were having a private conversation. . . ."

"That's why I hesitated to interrupt," Ross said with such affability that George was nonplussed. "But since you're in the restaurant business, I thought you'd understand. I think you'll excuse us. There are a few things Jennifer and I have to discuss. It's urgent." He held out his hand to George again, and when George did not take his hand, he looked at him steadily. "Mister Howard, I know that you and Jennifer were married once, but you aren't anymore. You're imposing on her kindness and good manners, and that isn't very much to your credit. If you want to court her again, find a way that doesn't detract from her business." He motioned to Jennifer. "Come on, Jennifer. Get that material for me, will you, please?"

Jennifer was torn between relief at Ross's intervention and annoyance at his high-handedness. She did her best to look crisply professional as she came out from behind her desk. "All right. And then we can verify the wine order for November."

"Good." He nodded toward George and held the door for Jennifer. "Mister Howard, I don't think it would be worth your while to wait."

George turned toward Ross as if he had not heard him correctly. "What are you saying?" he demanded.

"You know," Ross answered coolly, and went out the door.

"I can't tell you how pleased I was to see you," Jennifer confided as soon as they were a little distance away from the office. "I thought I'd never get rid of him."

"Glad to be of service," Ross said, and opened the door to the terrace that ran around the main floor of the hotel. "It looks as if there's another storm blowing in."

The cold wind caught her hair and whipped it about her face. "What was that nonsense you were talking? I couldn't make any sense of it."

"I hope George couldn't, either. That was the whole point of it. That, and to warn him off." He put his arm around her shoulder. "Have you notified the winners of the elephant contest, Jennifer?"

"The telegram went out today, and as soon as the Duttons acknowledge we'll set their reservations for the week between Christmas and New Year's. Eric and Elvira Bush will be here then, too, and we'll get a private concert out of it, which is good." She frowned.

"Something the matter?" Ross asked at once.

"In a way," she answered evasively. "Not to do with this, precisely, but more about Eric Bush." She did not want to discuss Drew's private life with Ross, not when it concerned so public a person as Eric Bush. "It's cold, isn't it?" She was wearing a soft cashmere sweater over woolen slacks, but it was not enough to ward off the sharp bite of the wind or to provide her much protection from the damp chill of the afternoon.

Ross nodded. "I wanted to give George a chance to leave before we went back into the building, but if you'd rather . . . " He motioned toward the door.

"You're probably right," Jennifer admitted. "Okay, let's take the back stairs down and go to the hotsprings for ten minutes or so. Knowing George, he's going to stop for a drink and a sandwich before he leaves."

With a resigned gesture, Ross consented. "The hotsprings it is. How is that going, by the way?" He let Jennifer precede him down the spiral stairs to the ground level.

"Not very well. Wilbur phoned yesterday to tell me that none of the variance applications have been approved, and that includes mine." She shook her head. "If I were paranoid, I'd start to feel that someone was out to make things as difficult for me as possible. But it doesn't make much sense that they'd go to all the bother to revise the codes only to keep me from opening my hotsprings for my guests." She folded her arms, but this did not do a great deal to keep her warmer. "It affects too many other people, for one thing. Now if there were a plot to put *all* old hotels into hot water, that might be different, but that makes less sense than ever."

They reached the door to the elaborate spa building and Jennifer pulled out her keys. "We can go in, if you like. It's warm inside, even if the smell isn't the sweetest in the world."

"Fine with me," Ross said, looking back toward the white bulk of the main hotel building. He had the uneasy sensation that they were being watched, and worried that George might have kept them under observation.

Inside, the walls were dingy and the air was musty and faintly sulphuric. The large main room was warm from the hotsprings that kept the four large pools filled all year around. Jennifer turned on the lights. "Sorry that it isn't very interesting at the moment, but we can go over to the bay window and sit. If you don't mind."

"What's this sudden concern about me? If you wanted to go out for a dip in the trout pond, I'd be happy to keep you company, though I might think it wasn't the best notion you ever had." He took her hands and pulled her close to him. "I like being alone with you, Jennifer."

"I'm happy for that, today of all days. What brought you

here, anyway? Are you really on your way to Napa?" She was chagrined as she asked, fearing that she was keeping him from his own work.

"I'm here to get you away from George," Ross said frankly, not wanting to lie to her for any reason.

"To get me away from George? How did you know he was here?" Jennifer could not keep the edge of irritation out of her voice. "What's going on?"

"I had a call from one of your staff who's worried about you. I was informed that George was back, and I said I'd come over." He knew she was angered by this and sought to calm her. "Don't blame your . . . friend for interfering. There's a lot of affection for you here, and your employees don't like to see you taken advantage of. George isn't exactly secretive about his visits, and he's been telling some of your people that he'll be taking over soon. I'm not making that up, Jennifer."

"Drew," Jennifer said with certainty. "It was Drew, wasn't it?" When Ross remained silent, she nodded. "Of course it was Drew. He knows George, and remembers the old days at the Savoia. Oh, God, I wish he hadn't . . ." She felt her ire evaporate to be replaced with a mild depression. "Thank you for coming. I suppose I should thank Drew, too, but . . ."

Ross looked directly at Jennifer. "I don't like him hanging around, Jennifer, and that's not only because I love you. I don't like that man. He hurt you before, and he may well hurt you again." He wanted to take her in his arms as an affirmation of his protection, but resisted the impulse, thinking that Jennifer would see it as coercion.

"I don't intend to let that happen," she said primly. "He's got to learn that he has no claim on me anymore."

"But do you think he will? I wish you would talk to Drew and find out what George has been saying." He did not add that Drew had called him two days before to say he feared that George would try to wear Jennifer down, as he had done in the days of their marriage and partnership. "Jennifer, don't underestimate George. If Drew says that he thinks he has a claim on you, then you can believe that it's true. Drew loves you and knows George, and probably sees him more clearly than you do."

"It could be," she said in a neutral voice. "But . . ." She stopped. "I don't like being watched, and it sounds as if you're all watching me. I know it's meant well, and I don't want to be ungrateful, but don't you understand that I don't want to be protected and hemmed in? Hell, Ross, I want our relationship to be private, and if this is going on, we might as well make love on one of the dining room tables." She turned her hands up in frustration. "I would prefer that George not come here, but if every time he comes here he's greeted by the palace guard, you can be certain he's going to assume he's making progress, and it will simply take longer to get him to keep away permanently." She reached up impulsively and put her hands on Ross's shoulders. "I'm very pleased that you want to look after me. I don't need the guard service, but I'm happy that you want to give me your protection."

Ross felt several conflicting emotions as he embraced Jennifer. He was exasperated at her for not taking George more seriously, he was proud of her courage and independence, he was worried on her behalf, he was also accepting the full impact of being in love with her, and the recognition of his feelings was not entirely welcome. It had been easier when he had not acknowledged the depth of his involvement with her. He might have been able, however reluctantly, to turn away from her, but that was no longer possible. Whatever came of it, he was bound to her with ties that he could no longer deny. As their lips met, his arms tightened fiercely around her, and he made a sound in his throat halfway between a chuckle and a groan.

When at last they broke apart, Jennifer laughed a little uncertainly. "You're . . ."

"I'm what?" he asked when she did not go on.

"You're different. What is it?" She had no words for what she had sensed in him, but the intensity of his touch had startled her.

"Nothing bad, Jennifer." He ruffled her hair. "Nothing to worry about."

"That makes me more apprehensive than ever," she remarked lightly, taking a couple steps away from him.

He took her arm gently and started back toward the door. "We can go down to the kitchens and say hi to Drew. He'll know if George has left yet."

"I wish I could think of a way to tell him that I don't want him to spend so much time worrying about me," Jennifer admitted as she went to the door. "You, too, Ross. I can handle myself. I found it out the hard way, but I do know that I can manage."

Ross was about to give an inoffensive answer, then changed his mind. "I know you can manage, Jennifer. I know that you've come through a lot worse than your troubles now. But I would like to see you do more than just manage or get along. I'd like to see you happy and satisfied and enthusiastic. Oh, I know, once in a while you're all of those things, but I'd like to see you be that way all the time." He stood in the half-open door. "If there's anything I can do that would help you, will you let me know what it is?"

"I'm not in the habit of asking for help," she answered carefully.

"I know that. But try to get into that habit with me, please. Please, Jennifer." He watched her while she considered this, and restrained himself from pressing his argument. Whatever she decided would have to be without insistence from him.

"I'll have to think about it for a while," she said as she closed the door behind them and checked the lock. "I think I could get used to the idea of having help available, and then it might not always be. I have to consider that, Ross. Don't say more right now. It's my risk, not yours." She felt the first spatterings of raindrops on her face. "We'd better hurry, or we'll be soaked."

Ross reached for her hand and together they ran toward the lower rear door, so intent on speed that neither saw the man glaring down at them from the rear window table of the Howdah.

Ted Hatfield cornered Jennifer before the Board of Supervisors meeting. "You can't be serious, Jenny. No, you can't. An offer like mine, with all the costs you're facing, you can't turn it down out of hand. You have to think about it for a while." He looked around the Supervisors' chamber and turned back to Jennifer. "You know they're not going to reconsider your variance, but they will give permits to me for condos. You know that. You'd be set for life. What the hell, I'd be willing to work out points with you if you'd take a little less up front. That would bring you a good income for a long, long time."

Jennifer stood with her arms folded. When she knew she could get a word in, she said, "I've told you before that I'm not interested."

"Besides," Ross said, after listening to the exchange, "I have the land abutting the White Elephant property, and I would oppose giving permits for condos. All that increase of traffic, demands on water and potential pollution is bad for my grapes, and the Benedetto Winery also brings in revenue directly in taxes as well as indirectly in salaries. I think you'd find that the supervisors would listen to me, Ted. And I intend to advise Jennifer to continue to decline your offer."

"You're ganging up on me," Ted said lightly, but with a sulky turn to his mouth. "I can't get either of you to hear sense."

"Wine is sense in the Napa Valley, Ted, and you'd better remember that," Ross said, wishing that Ted had chosen some time other than this evening to accost Jennifer.

"That's one of the attractions of the place," Ted said, hardly missing a beat as he got back into his pitch. "The vineyards, the countryside, the richness of it all. That's what makes people so anxious to live here, and you will admit that condos are better than endless sprawling subdivisions. I don't blame the supervisors for being wary of subdivisions, but condos are something else. They're more sensible, and if I guarantee to use geothermal and solar power for most of the heating and cooling, they'll be more than willing to consider my application."

"You have to have the land first," Jennifer reminded him icily, "and you do not have mine. That goes for Mr. Bronson and the power company, and you, too, Ross." She moved away from both men and found a seat in the second row near the center aisle.

Ross joined her there a few moments later. "Sorry you had to go through that song and dance again."

"So am I," Jennifer said. She put her hand up to her temple. "I didn't need this."

"I'll remind you just this once that my offer to lease is still on, and that it would be doing me as much a favor as it would you. If you decide that's acceptable, I'll call Henry, but not until you tell me to." He saw her flinch at his words, and it distressed him. "I don't want you to feel you have to do anything, but I do want you to know you don't have to consider Ted's offer, or any other, if you don't want to."

"Thanks," she said tonelessly. "I have to think about it."

The first two supervisors had come into the room and taken their seats at the long table at the front of the room.

"If there's anything I can do . . ." Ross murmured.

"I know. Ask. I won't know until I get the estimates on the hotsprings building approved by Henry. If he doesn't accept them, then I'll have to do something, or delay the new cottages, and that would not be very wise, since we've already got reservations for them for next summer." She opened her purse and took out a number of neatly-typed sheets, folded in half. "There are a few questions I hope they'll get around to tonight. I have some figures that might make a difference, but I don't know."

Wilbur Cory came in and waved a bit self-consciously to Jennifer and Ross. "Good you folks could make it."

Ross nodded for them both and gave his attention to the front of the room.

"This meeting will be called to order in three more minutes. You might tell those guys talking out in the hall," said the oldest member of the Board.

"I will call you if I have to," Jennifer said reluctantly to Ross, and then opened her folded papers and started to read over the material one last time, so that she would be prepared to speak.

"You make it sound like a terrible thing to do," Ross said, feeling a bit sad.

"Don't be silly," she said absently, and wholly without conviction.

∽ November ∽

The blustery storm had deterred only the most timid from Helene's victory celebration. The parking lots at the White Elephant were full, and more than half the rooms were booked for the night. Drew had done the best he could on short notice, and had turned out four kinds of fondue as well as two large glazed fish and a very hot lamb curry with more than a dozen condiments.

"To our new state senator," Helene's partner, Jeff Templeton, said from the bandstand when the band took its first break. The toast was enthusiastically echoed by the guests while Helene herself made her way to the bandstand and accepted Jeff's assistance in climbing up the narrow, steep stairs.

"To all my constituents who made it possible. I'm going to do everything I can to justify your faith in me." She raised her glass and drank the champagne with a theatrical toss of her head.

"Not too bad for November," Muriel said to Jennifer from their post by the door.

"Not too bad, period," Jennifer agreed. "We're not doing too badly. What are you doing here, by the way?" she added as she glanced at her watch. "You're supposed to be home doing bride-things. Aren't you?"

"You needed extra help tonight. Ivy's had to go home; she's got some kind of bug, and I don't think you want her giving it to the rest of the staff." Muriel looked over at the buffet. "Sheridan is coming here later. Do you think Drew'll have anything left for us?"

"He will have if you ask him to set it aside for you. He's very good about that," Jennifer reminded her. "Who's covering for Ivy?"

Muriel studiously avoided direct eye contact with Jennifer. "I think Ben will do it, if he's asked. He's assisted at the front desk before, and after midnight I don't think we're going to have very many people registering, do you?"

"Depends on how many people decide they don't want to drive home tonight," Jennifer said rather darkly. "What's been going on around here? I feel as if I'm completely out of touch."

"That's because you've had your hands full with this. Be grateful that your staff is competent enough to cover minor emergencies." Muriel laughed nervously. "Jennifer, don't let this bother you, but I think you ought to know that George was here this afternoon. I told him you weren't in, and he made it pretty clear he didn't believe me. He said he'd be back tomorrow evening to talk to you. If you want to be out, I'm sure you can arrange it." She raised her brows and glanced to the end of the buffet where Ross and Drew were in deep conversation.

"Maybe," Jennifer said, then swore. "Damn George, anyway! Why can't he simply leave well enough alone?"

"He's determined to get back with you," Muriel said. "It looks that way to me, and Sheridan agrees. You better not see him."

"I'll think it over," Jennifer said with a sigh.

The band started up again and Helene and Greg Lennard took to the floor in solitary grandeur while flashbulbs erupted like artillery fire. The band played more loudly and a few other couples ventured onto the floor.

"You've done a great job," Ross said quietly in Jennifer's ear.

She turned, startled. She had been so engrossed in watching Helene and Greg that she had not noticed his approach. "It was a challenge," she said, raising her voice as the drummer began to show off.

"Everyone is pleased." He rested his hand on her shoulder. "You want to dance?"

"I'd better not. But thanks for the offer. I mean it." She frowned; she did not like turning him down, and felt her own disappointment as much as his.

"Can I have a raincheck?" he asked, unperturbed.

"For when? It's raining now." Though it wasn't entirely wise, she moved a little closer to him and slipped her arm around his waist.

"What about the next party?" he asked. "The one on the fifteenth? Sheridan's and Muriel's? Or have you forgotten that one?"

"Hardly. I feel guilty about letting Muriel work with her wedding coming up so soon." She tried to find some good reason to refuse, knowing that it was proper to do so.

"Don't try to convince me you're not going to dance at Muriel's wedding, because I don't believe it. She'd be insulted, and you don't want that. If you think it's too conspicuous to dance just with me, Drew will ask you, and so will Sheridan. You can't refuse your righthand man and the groom, can you?" He was teasing her, and they both knew it.

"I can't refuse, can I?" she asked as lightly as possible. "All right. Next week we can dance together and I won't say no because I own the place." She did not want to move away from him, but she knew it was best to do so. "Next week it is," she said, to soften her departure.

"And I'll want a few minutes of your time before I leave tonight," he added, making no other attempt to detain her. "You've got your hands full tonight."

"I sure do," she agreed before approaching Larry Bronson of the power company. "I had your letter, Mr. Bronson, and I can't say that my position has changed. I'll provide you with a letter to that effect, and I hope you'll discontinue your requests."

"Don't call us, we'll call you, eh, Ms. Wystan?" Larry Bronson asked. "Well, I have my job to do, and my bosses want me to make every effort to . . ."

"They don't like you to badger people, do they?" Jennifer asked sweetly. "Your letters really are intrusive, and I would very much prefer they not continue. I'm going to mention that in my reply, as well."

Larry Bronson grinned nervously. "It's business, Ms. Wystan."

"I agree. That's why I intend to ask your bosses to back

off." She did not know how pretty she looked standing there, tall and coltishly slim in a suit of slate-blue velvet. She thought of herself as neat and efficient, not stunning, and was surprised at the intensity of the reaction she provoked in Larry as well as Ross. "Do I make myself clear?"

"Completely," Larry said weakly.

"I'm pleased to hear it," she said, her manner softening slightly. "It's good that we understand one another at last."

There was a sudden blare from the bandstand and so Larry was saved the trouble of making a polite response. He used it as an excuse to turn away and was soon deep in conversation with Helene's new secretary.

Jennifer was not fooled by Larry's action, but decided not to point this out. She began to walk around the periphery of the crowd, listening occasionally to conversation, greeting many of the guests with her usual cordial manner.

"You do that very well," David Howell said to her when she came up to him.

"Thank you," she said. She had not talked to the reporter for some weeks and was a little surprised to see him at the celebration.

"The *Dispatch* is taking credit for Helene's election, of course. That shouldn't surprise you." He was a bit tipsy, but aside from a slight jauntiness he usually lacked, there was no difference in his behavior.

"I suppose not." Jennifer did not want to admit that she had paid very little attention to the political contest, and almost none to the press coverage of it.

He took a deep pull on his drink. "I read about the results of the name-the-elephant contest. You handled that like a seasoned pro."

"I *am* a seasoned pro," Jennifer said quietly.

"No, no, you're not. You're a gifted pro, but you aren't old enough to be seasoned. I know you'll be all of twenty-nine late next month; no one is a seasoned pro at twenty-nine. In a decade, maybe, but not until then." His tie was not quite properly knotted and he fumbled with it. "I'd take this damned thing off if Morton weren't here."

"In another half-hour, no one should notice your tie," Jennifer said without any malice. "Wait a bit, Mr. Howell, and you'll be fine."

"Thanks," he said dryly. "Say, what's this rumor I hear about you selling this place to developers for condos?"

Jennifer blinked in surprise. "Selling the Elephant?" she asked incredulously.

"That's one of the things I've heard." He sounded a bit apologetic, but there was professional curiosity in his manner, as well.

"Well, it's one rumor you can discount entirely. In fact, I'd consider it a favor if you would. The White Elephant is not going to be sold to anyone in the forseeable future. I'm already making arrangements to bring the hotsprings up to code, and I wouldn't be spending that kind of money if I were going to sell the place. I intend to be here for a good long time, Mr. Howell." Jennifer saw that there were a few late arrivals, and knew that she ought to excuse herself and be sure that the newcomers were greeted and properly taken care of. "If you hear such a rumor again, will you let me know about it?"

"If I remember," David answered. "I'm going to get another scotch."

"Good." As Jennifer turned away from him to cross the Grand Ballroom, she was nagged by what the reporter had told her. Someone thought that she was going to sell the White Elephant to a developer. That meant that someone wanted it believed this was happening. Ted Hatfield? As brash and opportunistic as the man was, she doubted that he would spread such a rumor before he had some way to back it up. If not Ted, then who? There was no one who stood to gain from such a rumor but Ted. Jennifer was puzzled but she put the matter out of her mind as she went forward to meet some newcomers.

"But I've already had my vacation," Muriel protested when Jennifer called her two days later and told her to take the next ten days off.

"Then call it a wedding present. You can send me a thank-you note next month." Jennifer signaled to Dean to stay where he was for the moment. "Come out to lunch tomorrow and we'll finish the reception plans, and you can get yourself some rest as well as getting your packing done."

"Are you sure you can handle things with me gone?" Muriel asked, not able to keep the satisfaction from her voice.

"Yes. We'll get by for ten days, it being the slow season," Jennifer teased. "Just so long as you're back in time for organizing Thanksgiving, everything will be fine."

Muriel still hesitated. "Wouldn't it be better if I worked half-days? That way if there's any difficulty . . ."

Jennifer cut in on her. "If anything difficult comes up, I'll call you, how's that?"

Muriel gave in. "That's great. Thanks. I *can* use the extra time. There *is* a lot to get done and . . ." She stopped rather abruptly. "And the party?"

"We'll talk about it tomorrow. Drew's doing something with crab for us. Be here at twelve-thirty and we'll go over the plans and make sure it's all settled. If you have any changes you want in the plans, we'll settle that tomorrow, and then we should be clear for the fifteenth."

"I hope that storm they're predicting doesn't blow in until it's over." Muriel sighed a bit. "Sheridan's been telling all his patients not to have any emergencies on the fourteenth or fifteenth."

"I hope they don't," Jennifer said sincerely but humorously.

"Me, too. I can see that marrying a doctor has its disadvantages." She paused and went on more quietly, "Thanks, Jennifer. I don't think any of this would have happened without you. The job, meeting Sheridan, everything."

Jennifer felt strangely embarrassed by Muriel's gratitude. "In a place like this, you would have run into each other eventually. And I don't think you would have ignored each other, even if you'd needed his help with a sore throat."

"That's kind of you to say," Muriel told her, and then added, "I won't keep you. See you twelve-thirty tomorrow."

"Fine. Goodbye." She hung up and looked at Dean. "Well?"

"The Duttons will be here for the holidays and the Bush concert will get a lot of attention, especially at that time of year, when there's so little to compete with it." He looked at the note. "They have a twelve-year-old son and they want to bring him. I don't know how you want to handle that."

"Include him, by all means. Assign them to the . . . Jack London Suite. That's got two bedrooms, and a sitting room. They'll probably prefer that arrangement. Now, if I can only think of some way to keep a twelve-year-old boy amused between Christmas and New Year's. If the weather is pretty good, there's the trout pond. But he can't spend every waking hour fishing." She leaned back in her chair. "I'll have to give this some thought. Thanks for warning me."

"We've had three more reservations for Thanksgiving, by

the way. Another fourteen and the hotel proper will be full. A few of them have specifically requested cottages, and that will free up a few interior rooms."

"That's great, Dean. I'm going to see Drew so that we can finish up all the Thanksgiving orders. It looks as if the dining room will be full; we're doing two seatings that evening, one at four and one at eight. Try to get the families with children to take the earlier seating, will you?" She got up. "You're doing a very good job, Dean. I appreciate it."

Dean smiled. "Thanks," he said. "Oh, your ex-husband called to say he'll be up to have dinner with you." This was reported in so neutral a tone that Jennifer knew George had been more than usually high-handed with Dean.

"It's unfortunate that I have a previous engagement, isn't it?" she said. "If he'd taken the trouble to ask me, I would have told him that and spared him the long drive, and all for nothing." She went to the door and followed Dean out of the room. "I'll leave a note to that effect. It might make things easier for you."

"I don't mind telling him you won't be here," Dean said, as he put the reservations book back on the front desk.

"He's not always very polite," Jennifer said, then added, "Send him down to Drew. That will spare us both the trouble of dealing with him."

"Where are you going to be? In case he asks . . ." Dean inquired.

"Out." Jennifer started down the stairs, hoping as she went that Ross or Muriel would not mind having an unexpected guest tonight.

"It's nice to see you looking so pretty," Sheridan Robb said to Jennifer halfway through his and Muriel's reception. "You don't make the most of your face and figure, most of the time."

Jennifer stared at him, a bit startled by what he said. "I'm usually on business when I come to functions at my own hotel."

"Muriel and I often talk about that," Sheridan said, unperturbed. "Those neat suits and sleek dresses are all very well, but they're nowhere near as fetching as that red thing you've got on."

"It's cranberry," Jennifer corrected him.

"Whatever it is, it's flattering. The lines are soft and velvet does beautiful things for you." He looked across the room at

Muriel who was deep in conversation with the Hasslunds. "I'm a very lucky man."

"Yes, you are," Jennifer agreed with alacrity, relieved to change the subject.

"We're both very grateful to you, Jennifer." Sheridan kissed her cheek and strolled away toward his new wife.

"I tend to agree with him," Ross said quietly from somewhere behind her left shoulder.

"You were eavesdropping," Jennifer accused him.

"True enough, but can you blame me?" He came around in front of her, very elegant in a dark suit, pearl-gray shirt and maroon silk tie. "I've been thinking the same thing for months, but didn't know how to tell you."

Jennifer put her hands on her hips. "Is this some kind of conspiracy? Do Jennifer Wystan over?"

"Nothing like that," Ross said, taking her hand in his.

"This isn't the most private place in the world," she reminded him, fearing that there would be those who would notice his attentions.

"That's fine. It's time people got used to the idea that we keep company. I like that phrase, don't you? Kind of old-fashioned, but friendly." He started onto the dance floor. "Remember you promised. I intend to claim my waltz."

Jennifer looked at the four musicians and realized that they were getting ready to play again. She knew that it was not entirely proper for her to dance, but she no longer cared about propriety. If she danced with Ross, Sheridan would be pleased, and so would Muriel. It was their party, she reminded herself, and smiled happily as Ross's arm went around her. The waltz was an arrangement of the *Blue Danube*, and until they began the smooth, circling steps, she had forgotten how much fun it was to swirl the length of the room to the rapid, overdone music. The turning and speed seemed to shut out everything but Ross and the music, and she recalled that when the waltz had come into fashion more than a hundred and fifty years before, it had been considered scandalous.

"You do this well," Ross said as they went into a reverse turn.

"So do you." She was feeling a bit breathless, but not because of the dance.

"My mother insisted I take ballroom dancing when I was a kid. I hated it. Then." They spun down the hall and swung around the end of the ballroom. "You busy next Saturday?" Ross asked when they had caught their breath.

"In the evening," Jennifer said.

"What about noon? We can get together for lunch." He would have liked more than that, but he did not want to put pressure on her now that she was so comfortable with him. "Or Sunday. I'm free after four."

"Sunday's better." They broke apart as the music ended and both applauded politely.

"Muriel's radiant," Ross said as he walked off the floor with Jennifer. "And Sheridan's so pleased with himself, he's going to pop all the buttons on his shirt."

"Must be love," Jennifer said lightly, and then realized she was blushing.

"It's great," Ross said, wanting to keep her near him, but knowing she would not permit it. "I'll meet you back at the buffet in half an hour."

Jennifer, to her shock, realized she had wanted him to try to persuade her to remain with him a bit longer. She would have refused, but it would have been refreshing to have him ask. . . . She chided herself for this attitude and nodded. "Half an hour. Thanks for the dance."

"Let's do it again sometime," Ross said, and watched her as she went to the bandstand to have a word with the musicians. He liked looking at her, at the leggy, unconsciously graceful way she moved, at her elegant carriage. He caught her eyes. The pleased but slightly uncomfortable expression he read there made him turn away, and he discovered that Drew was standing nearby.

"She looks great tonight, doesn't she?" Drew asked.

"Terrific." Ross grinned at the chef. "You've done quite a job tonight."

"I have, haven't I?" Drew agreed. "It's a pleasure to do this for Muriel. I like her."

"So do I." Ross regarded the other man. "Has George been around?"

"Yes, but Jenny hasn't. George is not pleased. I get the feeling that he's far from giving up. I've mentioned it to Jenny, but she doesn't believe me. I hope that you do." He looked steadily at Ross.

"I do. I've met the man twice now. Both times, I thought he'd like to be rid of me. Permanently. Do you expect him back?"

"Naturally. And I'll call you when he arrives." Drew pursed his lips. "How about the wines for Thanksgiving? Is all that arranged?"

"I have your order and the cases will be delivered two days before. Is that satisfactory?" Ross was not quite sure why Drew had changed the subject so abruptly, but knew enough to follow his lead.

"Sounds fine." He looked away from Ross and gave a broad, practiced smile to another couple standing near the buffet tables. "Good to see you again. Is there anything I can get you?"

As always, Ross was impressed with Drew's acuity and discretion, and he took advantage of the moment to move away. Then he caught sight of Sheridan coming toward him, and smiled happily at his friend. In all the years he had known the physician, he had never seen him so truly cheerful. Ross's concerns for Jennifer were set aside for a little while as he offered his congratulations for the fourth time to his friend.

The storm was violent; wind poured through the hills like an enormous, endless, invisible tidal wave, alternately crooning and howling as it battered away at trees, vines, houses, automobiles or any other thing not flush with the ground. Rain sluiced out of the skies and poured down the hills into the gullies until they ran like torrential creeks and the creeks gushed and rolled like rapid rivers. According to the weatherman, most of northern California would look forward to three more days of the same thing, and the second of those three days was Thanksgiving.

"We've got a meatlocker full of dead birds!" Drew said dramatically when the lights flickered for the second time. "God, no. I can't have this going on!" He turned toward Jennifer, who was huddled in the largest of his chairs.

"We've got the generator," Jennifer reminded him. "If the power lines go down, we'll switch over. There's fuel enough to get us through the weekend, and then we can order more. Relax. I want to make sure we're set for Thursday."

"Better have one of the groundsmen stand by with the generator," Drew said brusquely. "I don't think the power lines are going to be with us a lot longer. Damn!" He glared at the fading lamp on the Japanese occasional table by the door. "We're gonna need the generator, Jenny-boss."

"I'm afraid so." She sighed and got out of the chair,

tugging at the waistband of her tweed slacks. "I should have these taken in."

"You mean you should gain a couple of pounds. You're much too skinny, girl, and you know it. Thin may be beautiful, but bony isn't. You're as thin as your bones will let you be and all you're getting is drawn." He folded his arms.

"You're probably right," Jennifer said, making no objection to this lecture because she knew it was true. At her five feet, seven inches, she was a reasonable size ten, and felt most comfortable at around one hundred twenty-five pounds. At the moment, she was just over one hundred ten pounds, and she knew her energy was lower than it ought to be.

"Come on, let's go hunt up the groundsmen and have them start up the generator," Drew offered. "Then I'll make us something sinful like cream of crab soup, and we can have an orgy in the kitchen."

"Sounds good," Jennifer conceded, and started toward the door of the sitting room. "I hope that this goes well. I hate being out in that rain."

Jennifer pulled off her jacket as she stepped back inside the hotel, then made her way up the stairs. Her hair was bedraggled and half-soaked. As soon as she finished taking care of the bar and office, she decided that she would have to go up and tidy up, perhaps change.

"It's a slow afternoon, Ms. Wystan, and no doubt of it," Hugo said as he leaned over the bar. The lights flickered and Hugo looked up at her questioningly.

She pulled up one of the stools. "We're switching onto the generator in a little while."

"Oh, great," Hugo said, sincerely. "Probably a good idea. This storm, I tell you . . ."

"It's supposed to keep up through Friday," Jennifer interrupted. "I don't know what they're expecting on the weekend."

"Probably another storm front," Hugo said philosophically. "That's the way it is: the same thing over and over."

"That's the way the hotel business is, certainly," Jennifer said. "Do you have a little coffee? I could use a cup."

"Sure," Hugo said, reaching for a heavy mug and the percolator at the same time.

By the time Jennifer got up to her quarters, her hair was half-dry. She was no longer chilly, but she could feel the onset of caffeine jitters, and decided that she would have to take Drew up on his offer of soup. She peeled off her sweater, and was just reaching for a heavy woolen shirt when the lights flickered again. She stopped what she was doing and waited while the lights winked and then burned steadily. "It's the generator cutting in," she said to the walls, and went back to changing. She was into her dry clothes and about to go out the door when the lights quavered again. She went out, leaving the room sunk in the gloomy dusk of a rainy afternoon.

A few seconds later, the phone on her desk rang. Jennifer hurried to answer it. "I know," she said before the caller could speak. "What's gone wrong with the generator?"

"I don't know." Dean was flustered, and he cleared his throat three times before he was able to continue. "We're in the dark down here and we need lights . . ."

"The gaslights work," Jennifer said at once. "Drew knows how to work them. When we first moved in, until the new wiring was approved, we used the gaslights all the time." She glanced at the brackets on her office wall and thought that she ought to check them out, just to be sure they were working properly. This was not the time to have any more malfunctions.

"All right. I'll do that." He sounded lamentably grateful for these simple suggestions.

"There's a bracket right over the registration desk. Start with that. Hugo can find the ones in the Howdah, and there are extra candles he can light. I'll be down in a minute." As Jennifer hung up, she was already thinking of the various measures that were open to her, and she felt her annoyance recede for the moment. There was too much to do.

By ten o'clock, everything was under control, save one matter. The guests regarded the whole thing as an adventure and were delighted to make their way along the corridors with candles and kerosene lamps to stay in rooms lit by gas brackets rather than electric lights. One of the guests went so far as to suggest that they make it a feature of the hotel so that everyone could enjoy the experience. Jennifer had laughed weakly and made no other comment. The one thing that bothered her was the loss of electricity to the kitchen. When

Hugo guaranteed that he had enough ice on tap to last the rest of the evening, Jennifer went downstairs to Drew.

"What can be done?" the chef demanded dramatically as he pulled open the cold locker doors and gestured at the turkeys hanging there. "We can't keep this place cold enough to keep the turkeys good. It might be okay, but you don't want your diners coming down with intestinal distress because the meat went off. There's too much of a risk. Get that generator back on! I won't be responsible for more than another eight hours." He slammed the door closed for emphasis.

"I've got phone calls out to the power company and to the emergency repair station, and both of them have us on their lists . . . very long lists, too, by the way," Jennifer said wearily. "There's a power failure at the County Hospital that comes first, and then the one at the airport, and *then* they get around to the likes of us." She folded her arms and looked around the gaslit kitchen. "It's very romantic, of course, but I don't think I'd want to have to live this way, do you?"

"Jenny, don't be sarcastic," Drew said, sinking down on his workstool. "I wish I could think of something that would make a difference, but I can't. I know in my bones we aren't going to get the generator fixed until morning, and that means we'll have a bunch of useless fowl in the locker. I've thought about moving them over to the freezer, but I don't think it would make that much difference, and besides, there are all those finger-sandwiches in there, to say nothing of the stuffing fixings. It's bad enough having the turkeys go bad, but losing the pearl onions and sausage and giblet puree . . . it would be a *disaster.*"

"This isn't exactly minor as things stand," Jennifer murmured. "I'm going to make a few more calls. It could be that Chaney's will have someone willing to come out for double the usual rate. We might get it fixed that way." She didn't think it was very probable, but she had to exhaust every possibility. "And you," she added to Drew, "had better get on the phone and round us up some more turkeys."

"At least the meat's in the freezer," he said, trying to reassure himself. "Thank heaven I didn't put the beef in with the fowl."

"Start phoning," Jennifer told him firmly as she started toward the door. "Now."

"Yes, sir, Jenny-boss. Right away." He gave her a mock salute, and reached for the phone.

"How do we stand?" Muriel asked when she arrived at seven-thirty the next morning, and went on without pausing, "You look as if you'd been up all night."

"I had some sleep, about three or so," Jennifer admitted. "I haven't been able to get the generator fixed, Drew can't find replacement turkeys and there's no more ice in the bar. Other than that, everything's fine. We're pushing omelettes for lunch and trying to get a line from the power company. But so far, nothing." She leaned back a bit and put one hand to her eyes. "I'm too tired to think straight, and there's so much to do."

Muriel grinned at her. "Why don't you leave it to me? Get yourself a few hours' sleep and I'll get on the phones. If there's a real need for it, I'll waken you, but otherwise I don't expect you back here until around one. Is that a deal?"

"All right." Jennifer sighed.

"That's a dead give-away of how exhausted you are," Muriel told her as she went toward the door. "Most of the time, you would have flatly refused."

"True enough," Jennifer said, and went out of the office.

When she returned, it was quarter to one, and she was much more refreshed. She had slept and showered, and looked neat and composed. Her hair was tied back neatly and the suit she wore was wine-colored wool with a black cowl-necked sweater. She came into the office and nodded to Muriel, who was finishing up a sandwich. "How goes it?"

"Well, Chaney's sent someone out to have a look at the generator about an hour ago. No word yet, but they're working on it. The power company says that they'll have the lines up by late tonight. The weather is interfering with getting the lines back in service. The weather report is unchanged. We're trying to find turkeys, and Drew has a recommendation from an old friend of his in the city who says that he can set something up for him, but it means driving down to Turlock to pick the birds up."

"In *this* weather?" Jennifer protested. "I . . . it's pouring out, and Turlock is quite a distance." She did not want to make the drive herself, but knew that it was her responsibility to do so. "I hope I've got enough gas in the Datsun."

"Drew said he'd take care of it," Muriel remarked.

"And who's going to do the dinners?" Jennifer asked. "At the moment, I can spare me more than I can spare him. Turlock. Damn."

"Better than no turkeys," Muriel said. "Do you want Ben to go with you?"

"They might not like me taking him out of school, but . . . " She reached for the phone. "He's supposed to be out here at three-thirty in any case, so we might as well wait until then, and make whatever arrangements are necessary."

As Jennifer began to dial, Muriel made a last suggestion, "There are a couple of vans over at Benedetto, and you know Ross would provide you a driver."

"I've got my own van, thanks," Jennifer answered.

"And someone to ride shotgun?" Muriel asked, and was waved into silence as Jennifer said, "Hello, this is Ms. Wystan at the White Elephant. Can you give me a progress report on the power lines in this area?"

Muriel sighed, and decided not to tell Jennifer that she had taken it upon herself to call Ross and tell him what was going on at the White Elephant.

By the time Jennifer was off the telephone, Drew had come up to the office, flushed and annoyed, and smelling of the most marvelous scents. He had his hands on his hips and he glared at Jennifer. "I got the call. We can have the turkeys, but we'll have to pay through the nose for them. And we can only get a dozen of them."

"A dozen?" Jennifer asked in dismay. "But that's not nearly enough. . . ."

"It's better than nothing, and I can do something toward finding pork. I can do standing crown roasts of pork. It isn't ideal, but it will make it possible to feed the entire gang that shows up." He sat down and after a nod to Muriel, regarded Jennifer. "Well, what do you think, boss?"

"I think it's terrible, but what else is there?" She put her hand to her forehead. "Okay. As soon as Ben gets here, I'll start for Turlock. Expect me back at . . . let's see, around midnight, if there are no delays. Ben's going to have to get permission from his parents to do this." She looked down at the outfit she was wearing and thought she had better change to something much less elegant and a bit warmer. "I wish there were more than just twelve turkeys. While I'm gone, will you try to round up a few more?"

"Just go out with a lasso and rope a few?" Drew inquired.

"Any turkey running around loose out there should fear for its hide." He flung his arms open. "What do you think I've *been* doing?" Muriel shook her head. "You'd both better get to work then." She paused, "Jennifer, see about Ben riding with you, will you? I don't feel right about you going on that long drive by yourself, not in this weather."

Although Jennifer shared her misgivings, she laughed shortly. "Don't be worried, Muriel. I've done stranger things than this."

Muriel's mouth was unusually thin, but she held her peace while Drew gave a melodramatic sigh.

"Jenny, I don't like it, either, and you can be damned sure that we're not the only ones who feel that way. I mention no names, I cast no aspersions, I do nothing more than hint. *But* I think you're not being very wise. And that's the last you will hear from me on the subject, because I know how unreasonably stubborn you can be."

"Stop it," Jennifer said, between amusement and annoyance. "We're not in a position to worry about such minor matters. What we have to have is turkeys, and turkeys we will get." She looked at the wall clock. "I'd better get the rest of my jobs done then, because there won't be much time for them. How's the gas holding up?"

"Well enough," Drew said. "I don't know how it will be for all the cooking, but I've already sent in a call for more gas to be delivered and they said they'd give it priority. After that, it's a question of getting the food made. Johnny's working on the yams with cardamom and vanilla in butter, and Carol is taking care of the things for salads. We'll be ready to serve dinner tonight at the usual hour and then we'll all have to work like hell." He got out of the chair and bowed to the two women. "Good luck with your end of it, ladies. I must get back to the proverbial hot stove."

Jennifer watched Drew go, then started out into the lobby, going toward the stairs and a brief conference with Caroline in the housekeeper's office.

Behind her, Muriel hesitated, and then picked up the phone and dialed. "Mr. Benedetto, please," she said, and waited while the phone receptionist connected her. "Ross? This is Muriel Wr . . . Robb again. Jennifer's driving down to Turlock this evening to pick up a dozen turkeys, but that's all Drew's been able to find."

"Turlock?" Ross asked. "It'll take hours." His first concern was for Jennifer, and it was with difficulty he bit back the impulse to ask what precautions she had taken. "A dozen turkeys? Is that all?"

"It seems to be. Look, I feel awkward about calling you, but you've told me that if there was anything Jennifer needed, I ought to let you know." Muriel was toying with the pencil beside the phone and now she began to doodle with it.

"I appreciate your position, Muriel," Ross said at once. "If you think you shouldn't do this, I'll understand, but I want you to know that I think it's important to Jennifer that she have help right now—am I right?"

"Yes," Muriel admitted. "More than you know." She looked at her doodle and could make no sense of it at all. "We'll have those dozen turkeys, and we need them, but I don't know where Drew's going to find the rest, not at this late date. And the Board of Health would close us down if we took a chance on any of the turkeys hanging up in the locker. It's been too long since they were at a controlled temperature."

"What do you want from me?" Ross asked.

"Well, you said that your uncle had some frozen birds. . . ." Muriel began a bit defensively.

"Yes. But not turkeys. He's got geese and ducks." He paused, thinking over the problem of getting them. "They're frozen."

"How many do you think we could buy?" Muriel asked at once.

"Nary a one," Ross answered cheerfully. "But I can get some of them for you, and bring them over." He considered a bit. "Do you think Drew would cooperate?"

"For fowl, I think he'd sacrifice anything he doesn't need for cooking right now," Muriel answered. "It's pretty bad."

Ross made a sympathetic noise. "Tell you what, Muriel. I'm going to call my uncle right now and find out what I can get from him. I'll get back to you after that. He lives near Ukiah, so it'll take me a little while to get the birds, but if he's agreeable, I'll go at once, okay?"

"Don't ask me," Muriel said with a trace of humor. "I'm not making the offer, you are."

"Well, you clear it with Drew, and I'll give you a call in about half an hour. And see if you can talk Jennifer into taking someone with her." He did not wait for the comments, but made a brief goodbye and hung up. He thought a second

or two before he dialed again, trying to come up with the best
way to approach his Uncle Nicolo.

"Tell him I'll kiss his feet," Drew said enthusiastically when
Muriel relayed Ross's message. "I'm not fussy anymore, God
knows. I'd stuff an emu if I could find one."

"Good. If he says it's on, I'll let you know." Muriel wished
she could see Drew, to know how much mischief was
operating in him, but she did the best she could, and judged
by the tone of his voice that he was not in the mood for
pranks. "It might be better not to mention this to Jennifer just
yet. We can let her know we're getting birds, but she's a bit
touchy about taking things from Ross and . . ."

"Say no more," Drew declared. "I know precisely whereof
you speak. And don't feel bad about it, Muriel," he added
with gentle insight. "Where Jenny's concerned, I've learned a
bit over the years. Believe it or not, I can be both tactful and
discreet. If you want me to keep this to myself, I will. But I'd
better tell you that I think it would be a mistake not to tell
Jennifer what Ross had done. After he does it, of course. I
ain't giving up those birds to misplaced pride, you can bet on
it."

Muriel was guardedly optimistic. "I'll get back to you as
soon as I can. Where's Jennifer, by the way?"

"Out with Chaney's men working on the generator, of
course, and then . . ." He would have said more, but there
was the sound of something dropping to the floor and a loud
curse, and he said, "Let me know," and hung up.

Ten minutes later, Ross called back. "I've talked to Uncle
Nick and he's willing to let me have fifteen geese and a dozen
large ducklings. Ask Drew if that's okay, and if it is, don't
give me a call. If there's a problem, I'll want to hear about it
in twenty minutes. If you don't call, I'll leave for Ukiah at
once. It's about five hours, round trip, so figure I'll deliver the
birds by eight at the latest. I'm going to keep the birds
properly wrapped but not on ice, and they should be thawing
by the time I bring them to the hotel. Is that tolerable?" He
had already decided that he would get the birds, but he knew
he had to provide an out if Drew required it.

"I don't think he'll turn you down, Ross," Muriel said,
chuckling. "He was making jokes about poaching a while
ago, and he didn't mean a way of cooking." She looked about
anxiously, as if she expected to be overheard. "Ross, don't let

anything Jennifer says just now worry you too much. She's under a lot of pressure."

"Not surprising. I would have thought she'd be having screaming fits by now, but it doesn't seem that way." He checked his watch. "Call Drew for me, will you, and call me back only if he objects."

"I will," she promised, and rang off quickly, then buzzed the kitchen.

"Now what?" Drew demanded, sounding more than annoyed.

"How would you like fifteen geese and a dozen large ducklings?" Muriel inquired.

"Is this academic or serious?" Drew responded at once. "Because if it's not serious, you're in trouble, Mrs. Robb, I promise."

"It's serious," Muriel answered. "Ross Benedetto has an uncle who's willing to let us have the geese and ducklings. They're frozen, but that's better than nothing." Muriel was not quite sure how the temperamental chef would respond.

"Glory hallelujah!" Drew exclaimed. "Really? You're not kidding, are you? Muriel, don't joke about a thing like this."

"I'm not joking. Ross said he'd go get them for us, if you wouldn't mind."

"Wouldn't mind? You mean *this* is what you were talking about before? I thought it was a couple of turkeys, not geese and ducklings. Thank God fasting! We're not going to blow it, after all."

"That means you accept his kind offer?" Muriel asked unnecessarily.

"Don't be a simpleton, Muriel, it isn't your style," was Drew's caustic comment. "Fine. Great. Wonderful. I would no more turn down those birds than slit my throat with my roast-carver."

"Good. He'll have them here by around eight."

"Have there been any cancellations of reservations for tomorrow?" Drew asked breathlessly, then shouted, "Not there, you idiot!"

"Not so far," Muriel said. "But we'll probably have some no-shows."

"But we can't plan ahead for those," he lamented. "Johnny, don't . . . " With that, the connection was broken, and Muriel decided to leave the kitchen alone until much later that afternoon.

Jennifer came back to the office half an hour later. "There's something wrong with the generator. Chaney's man found that one of the parts is . . ."

"Broken?" Muriel finished for her.

"Not just that. It might have been tampered with. He's offered to take it back to Chaney's and examine it more closely. He said it could have been done any time between now and the last time the generator was used, and that was more than a year ago. So I don't even know where to start." She dropped into the chair. "I'm going to change and then get ready to go to Turlock. I've arranged for a soup and sandwich now, and Drew's insisted on making me a thermos of his dark-roast coffee. It'll keep me up all night, but I have a notion that's not a bad idea." She looked over at Muriel. "How's it going here?"

"Not too badly. The Flood Control District says that we're not in any danger in this area and that if this should change, we'll be notified in plenty of time. He did say that the last time there was any real flooding around here was more than seventy years ago, which means it doesn't happen all that often." She did her best to make this sound as optimistic as possible, but Jennifer was not enthusiastic.

"I just hope they've taken precautions between then and now." She touched her hair and found it was wet. "Muriel, I don't know what else can go wrong, but there's a nagging suspicion in the back of my mind that if I'm not careful, I'll find out."

"Don't think that way. It's not productive and it's not like you." Muriel looked at the notepad beside her. "One of the waiters has flu. He called in, and Sheridan confirmed it."

"See what I mean?" Jennifer asked.

"There's also a replacement already. You remember Tommy Franklin, don't you, from the work-study program? He said he'll fill in. So we're covered so far. That's good news."

"I just hope we'll have a meal to serve. Any progress on that? Or shouldn't I ask?" She was already getting to her feet.

"Yes. It looks like we're getting some geese and ducks. We'll be okay. Drew's pleased with the arrangements so far." Muriel flushed a bit because she could not bring herself to tell Jennifer about Ross's generosity.

"I hope so. I'd better change. If there are calls while I'm still here, I'll take them on my line." She moved her shoulders experimentally, feeling the tension in them and anticipating the long drive with dread. "I'll give you a call myself when I start back from Turlock. If I can talk the man out of any more turkeys, tell Drew I'll bring them."

"Good," Muriel said at once. "We'll manage, Jennifer."

"I hope you're right," she responded dubiously, and left the office, thinking as she walked that the gaslights were lovely but she hated the sight of them.

By eleven o'clock, Jennifer was so tired that she was not entirely certain she could continue driving. Her shoulders ached and her eyes were sore from the rain and glare. She took a degree of satisfaction in bringing back not twelve but sixteen turkeys. With grim determination, she stayed on the road.

It was twenty minutes to one when she finally parked at the back of the hotel. The rain had slackened a bit, but there was still a great deal of wetness in the air and the wind was undiminished. Jennifer stood by the van, her head throbbing from the sound of the engine and overwhelmed by the comparative silence. She steadied herself on the side of the vehicle and looked up to the muted lights in the Howdah. In spite of the power loss, there were a number of people sitting at the windowside tables. She hoped that the bar receipts were good, because the turkeys had been ruinously expensive. She walked unsteadily toward the loading door and leaned on the buzzer.

"You're back!" Sheridan Robb said as he pulled the door open.

"Yep," Jennifer said, so tired that she forgot to be surprised to see him. "There are sixteen turkeys in the van. Someone will have to bring them in."

"You bet," he said. "Johnny and I will take care of that while you get a bite to eat. Drew fixed eggs Benedict about half an hour ago, and I know he saved enough for you. Come on, Jennifer. There's work to be done."

"I know," she said as she stepped into the shelter of the lower hall. "I want to get changed, though. These slacks are starting to feel like used saddle blankets." She fingered her down jacket. "How are things going?"

"Quite well. The ducks are all stuffed and the geese are almost thawed enough for stuffing. We've been having a private party with Drew, getting these birds ready. It's a lot different from working on patients—the birds don't complain." He chuckled at this rather weak witticism and shook his head. "We're all a little . . ."

"Punchy?" Jennifer supplied.

"Giddy, maybe. We've been working in the kitchen for the last six hours and it's catching up with us. Go get changed, and by the time you're down from your room we'll have the turkeys ready to go." He waved Jennifer toward the stairs and signaled to Johnny as he came around the bend in the hall. "Turkey delivery, Johnny."

"Great," Johnny said, pausing long enough to grin at Jennifer before going off with Sheridan.

Sheridan was as good as his word, and by the time Jennifer had changed, the turkeys were laid out in the kitchen and there was a plate of eggs Benedict set out at the far end of the main preparation table.

"Oh, God," Jennifer said as she came into the kitchen. "Are *all* of you helping with Thanksgiving?"

Muriel and Sheridan started to speak, but Ross cut them short. "Naturally. What else did you expect, given the problem?"

Jennifer shook her head. "Muriel. You should be off honeymooning, or whatever you planned to do. I don't know what Ross is doing here, and Sheridan might have an emergency to take care of . . . ." She suddenly realized how ungrateful she sounded. "I didn't mean it that way . . . ." she said in conscience-stricken tones. "I'm so worn out, and I don't want the rest of you to . . ."

Ross cut her short. "Say thank you and eat your eggs, or Drew will be insulted."

"I will," Drew agreed. "These are good birds. They didn't cheat you on quality, but they're pirates."

"They had us over a barrel," Jennifer said as she sat down to eat. "This smells so good. I can't tell you how hungry I am. That drive . . ."

"I wish you'd taken someone with you," Ross said, in spite of all his good intentions not to sound over-protective. "On a night like this, all sorts of things could go wrong."

"And then there'd be two people wasting hours at the side of the road instead of one," Jennifer said as she cut through the ham and English muffin eagerly. The kitchen was redolent with herbs, spices and wine, but the first tangy taste of the hollandaise sauce was like ambrosia.

Ross held back his rejoinder. He did not want Jennifer to know all the things he had been fearing when he thought of her on the road this stormy night. He had, in the last four hours, pictured her in accidents of every sort, trapped by rising water at the edge of the San Joaquin Delta, falling asleep at the wheel and driving off . . . He smiled at her, not knowing how much of his emotions showed in his eyes, and was a bit startled when she blushed. "How'd it go?" he asked as he rubbed garlic butter on the inside cavity of one of the turkeys.

"Not bad. It was slow coming back. There were two sections of the road where it was narrowed down to one or two lanes, and we just crept." She went back to eating, then asked something that had nagged her while she was changing clothes. "What are you doing here?"

"Helping." He finished with one turkey and went on to another. Muriel had warned him that she had not told Jennifer who was providing the ducks and geese, and he was not certain how to broach the matter. He had a half-formulated plan when Drew made it unnecessary.

"He's being too modest, boss. You might say he's looking after his own interests since he was the one who bailed us out. How're the eggs Benedict?"

"The eggs Benedict are fine," Jennifer said, a bit too precisely. "What do you mean, bailed us out?" Although she asked it of Drew, she was looking at Ross.

"He got us the geese and ducks. One of his uncles had them, and he . . . You didn't know about it?" He looked from Jennifer to Ross. "Uh-oh. Something seems amiss here."

"So it does," Jennifer said firmly, resisting the urge to burst into tears. "What . . . ?"

Ross had given himself a few seconds to improvise. "I got them from my Uncle Nicolo. When I offered to try to help out, Muriel said you needed fowl. It took a while to reach Uncle Nick and to find out if he would be willing to part with any of the game in his locker. You were gone by the time I left for his place," he assured her.

"Was that what you were talking about when you said there was a line on some ducks and geese?" Jennifer asked Muriel.

"Yes. Ross had offered, but . . . " She glanced at her husband as if looking for help.

"You mean you talked your uncle out of some of his own

game?'' Jennifer demanded of Ross, trying to ignore the pleasure she felt at this. It was unprofessional, she reminded herself sternly.

"Not exactly. He's always said I was welcome to some, since he lives alone now and doesn't eat that much of it. He's given away tons of fowl over the years, and he's said that he wants it to go to someone who appreciates it. I figured you'd appreciate it.'' He did his best to offer her a jaunty smile, but the apprehension never left his china-green eyes. "I've told Drew that Uncle Nick is coming to dinner. Right now he's over at the house drinking port with Aunt Rosa. They're brother and sister and they don't see enough of each other.''

Jennifer did not allow herself to be sidetracked. "That's the least we can do for him, it seems to me. We should offer to put him up here for a month. But why did you go to all this trouble?''

"Jennifer," Ross said seriously, "I did it because you needed help and this was something I could do. You don't owe me a damned thing. This was my idea from start to finish. You didn't know about it until now, so you can't take the responsibility for it, and that's that. It's a gift.''

"Yes. It's a gift," Drew repeated. "And while you're bickering, no work is getting done. Jenny, finish eating and give us a hand. We have fifteen more turkeys to stuff before any of us can go anywhere. Ross, when you've finished doing the cavities, get the syringe and inject that wine-and-herb stuff, there, under the skin. Lots of little bits is better than one or two big blobs. When they're stuffed and trussed, the skin should be buttered. Back to work, all of you.'' He bent down near Jennifer and said quietly in her ear, "I know you're worn out, Jenny, and it's been a bitch of a week, but don't make it any harder than it has to be. Okay?''

The bit of ham Jennifer was swallowing suddenly felt the size and texture of a large pebble. She was able to nod, thinking that she had gone well beyond the bounds of good manners now. Then she pushed these unhappy thoughts aside, and turned her attention to the matter at hand.

"There's even one duck left over," Drew announced with glee the morning after Thanksgiving. "I'm going to turn it into the soup du jour. That'll use up some of the veggies we have left over, too. Let me recommend the soup. In fact, I think I'll do one of those soup-and-salad specials for lunch. That will simplify things in the kitchen." He grinned at

Jennifer. "We came out of this a great deal better than we should have."

"Thanks to Ross," Jennifer said quietly. She was still tired, and had the first heavy dullness of the onset of a cold.

"To everyone." Drew made an expansive gesture and nodded toward Muriel's desk. "Thank Muriel and Sheridan, too. They spent *hours* in the kitchen for no reason more than we needed the extra hands. Speaking of Sheridan, I think you'd better go see him this afternoon. You look like you're getting one of those head things."

"It's the season for it." Jennifer reached for her phone. "I'll give him a call after I talk to the men at Chaney's. I still want that generator fixed. Is that good enough for you, Drew?"

"It isn't me who's coming down with a cold," he said, and started toward the door.

Jennifer started to dial. "The power company should have us hooked up by this afternoon, or so they said when they called earlier. Thank goodness, the storm is supposed to clear up by tonight." She looked at the receiver. "Oh, yes. Hello. This is Ms. Wystan at the White Elephant. You had men out here working on my generator and . . . yes, I'll hold on."

Drew waved at Jennifer and went to the door. "Talk to you later, boss," he called to her and then was gone.

"Ms. Wystan, this is Pete Chaney," said a new voice. "Say, we've been going over the parts my men brought in, and we all agree that they've been tampered with, and quite recently, probably the last few months. Pardon me for saying it, but you'd better get a little tighter security out there."

"How do you mean?" Jennifer asked, feeling suddenly cold.

"Well, Ms. Wystan, whoever did this wanted to cause trouble. It wasn't like the generator was just busted, the way it usually happens, and it wasn't done by an amateur. The generator looked all right and ran all right at first. That means that the person or persons who did it weren't interested in wrecking the generator, they were interested in having it stop when in use. I'll inform your insurance company and the cops, if you like, but I think you'd better call them, too."

Jennifer put a hand to her head. "All right. Yes. I'll call them. Now?"

"That would probably be best," Chaney said. "If there's someone going around doing this, there are other people who ought to look at their generators. We haven't had any reports of this kind of failure, but maybe the other repair services have. You owe it to yourself, Ms. Wystan. And your neighbors."

"All right. Thank you, Mr. Chaney," she said, wishing she could sink through the floor. "I'll come by your shop later this afternoon, if that's all right."

"Any time after two," he said, and said goodbye.

Jennifer buzzed the front desk. "Ivy? I've got to go into Calistoga this afternoon. I need to talk to the groundsmen at noon. Will you let them know about it? And I'd better call San Francisco, too."

Ivy waited for a break and said, "There's a Mr. Hatfield here to see you. He says it's important."

"Not him!" Jennifer declared, thinking that all that was lacking to make the day completely discouraging was another surprise visit from George. "I can't talk to him now, Ivy. There's too much going on. You can tell him that I haven't changed my mind, and I very much doubt I will."

"He's pretty insistent," Ivy said in a doubtful tone.

"He's always insistent," Jennifer told her. "I haven't got time for him. That's that. I'm going to be talking to Henry Fisher and then my insurance company. After that, I suppose I'll have to make an appointment to talk with the police."

"The police?" Ivy repeated in disbelief while she made a helpless shrug in the direction of Ted Hatfield, as if to let him know she was doing her best.

"Someone tampered with the generator," Jennifer explained. She was about to break the connection, then added, "Ivy, will you tell Mr. Hatfield that my hands are too full at the moment to fence with him." She rang off and began to dial Henry Fisher in San Francisco.

"She's busy, Mr. Hatfield," Ivy told Ted. "I'm sorry."

Ted's color was a little heightened. "You tell her that I'll be back. And tell her that Bronson has got orders to push for those hotsprings. If she thinks the Board of Supervisors doesn't listen to the power company, she's crazy. Tell her that, too." He turned abruptly and stalked off across the lobby.

Wilbury Cory looked over the sheets Jennifer handed him. "I'll do what I can, Mrs. Wystan, and that's a promise. I think we ought to accept it, but the way things are, I can't tell you how the Board will go. By the time we have the meeting tonight, I'll be conversant with your figures, and that will help." He smiled at her. "Ben tells me you had a bit of trouble out there over the weekend."

Jennifer gave him a wide, false smile. "Oh, it's fine now. There was some . . . malicious mischief, and with the power lines being down, we were back to gaslight for a couple of days. Everything's fine now, and we're arranging for some checks on the damage to our equipment." It was a reasonable summary of what had happened, one that would be acceptable to the public.

"Damned shame. I hope your Thanksgiving went well," he added as an afterthought.

"It turned out well, yes," she answered. "And yours?"

"Great. Trudy always fixes more than twice the number a person could eat, and I'm gonna hate turkey sandwiches by the end of this week, but it was real nice, having the family around and all." He stood up. "I won't keep you, but I would count it a pleasure if you'd come in a little early tonight. Just in case I have any questions. You see, the thing is, I want to tell you what we're up against. I won't know until later." He held out his hand.

Jennifer took it. "Thank you, Mr. Cory. I'll see you at . . . seven?"

"Seven would be fine. Don't you worry. We'll get you your clearances."

Jennifer smiled, but the sinking feeling inside her did not go away.

∾ December ∽

"This is Icewine," Ross said, holding the glass out to Jennifer. "I think you'll like it. It's got a very strong taste." He lifted his own glass in silent toast to her.

The potent scent of grapes filled her head as she brought the crystal glass to her lips. The wine was slightly chilled but it was hot as brandy on her tongue, and the bouquet was so intense that she was afraid she'd get high on the smell of it. She breathed in over the wine and had to force herself not to cough; as she exhaled, her head seemed to buzz. "It's remarkable," she said when she could speak again.

"There isn't much of it made here. It's more a German thing than French, and it's quite costly to produce, so the price for the wine itself is high. But I decided to take a chance on it about five years ago, and it's my not-so-humble opinion that it paid off." He took another small sip and put the bottle back on the buffet and sank down on the cushion beside her. "You know, Jennifer, that color really becomes you." He touched the softly-rolled neck of her pale plum sweater.

"Thanks." She permitted herself another taste of the Icewine and blinked at the penetrating flavor. "Why is this so strong?"

"It's made from late grapes—they're almost raisins. The

pressing is a very slow process, but what you end up with, if you do it right, is this." He held the glass out so that the firelight danced through the wine. "I think it's delicious, but I like wine and grapes."

"So do I," she reminded him with false indignation.

"Yes, you do, and you have a feel for it, but you didn't grow up with it the way I did, and learn to love it about the time you learned to talk. My father taught me, as his father taught him. Not many businesses are like that anymore. Benedetto hasn't changed a lot in the last five generations." He touched her cheek with the back of his hand, stroking gently. "I'm glad you came over, Jennifer. I've missed having you here, these last two weeks."

"I've been digging out from under Thanksgiving," she said. The Board of Health had required they bury the turkeys which had spoiled, and it had struck Jennifer as completely bizzare to have to go to such lengths for them. But she did not want to get into disputes with the county authorities, not now when things were balanced again.

"You managed that beautifully, you know. A lot of women —hell, a lot of *men*—would have fallen apart." He braced himself on one elbow and reached out for her.

Jennifer resisted a little. "Falling apart doesn't do any good," she said quietly. "There was a mess to be cleaned up."

"And you cleaned it up," Ross agreed at once.

"Thanks," she said, and recklessly finished the wine. "But if you're handing out medals, keep a couple for yourself. Without your ducks and geese, to say nothing . . ."

"Uncle Nick's ducks and geese," he corrected her mildly.

"Whoever they were, we couldn't have managed without them, and then all those hours you helped in the kitchen. They ought to let you into the union." She rested her head against his shoulder. "Sometimes I get almost frightened, I have such good friends and they mean so much to me."

"I'm not just your good friend," Ross said in a low voice.

Jennifer turned her head to kiss him lightly, and tasted Icewine on his lips. "I wasn't saying you were," she whispered, thinking his kiss was more intoxicating than Icewine could ever hope to be.

"Good." He touched her, first over her clothing, then under, the softness of cashmere on the back of his hands, the silk of her skin on his fingers and palms.

They made love without haste, letting each new sensation have its full due. She discovered that he was ticklish at the tops of his thighs and that he almost purred when she kissed the inner bend of his elbow. He had her writhing with pleasure as he licked first her nipples, then her navel, then the hidden, seashell-moist recess of her femininity. Their joining was languorous and smooth, filled with quiet passion that grew with each touch, each thrust, each subtle movement and shift, until it glowed like a furnace melting steel.

Jennifer leaned back on the pillow and smiled, satisfaction glowing within her. "Oh, how I love you," she murmured as she kissed Ross's shoulder, tasting the tang of his sweat.

"Your sentiments are returned," he told her. "I'm giddy with you. I feel as if I should do handsprings, but I'm probably too weak right now."

"Poor thing," she crooned to him.

He rolled onto his side and grinned at her. "I haven't made love in the living room before. It must be the fire."

"You've had fires before," she pointed out.

"If it's not the fire, it must be the company." His tone was tender and playful, but there was something more profound in his china-green eyes that was at once startling and welcome to Jennifer.

"The fire hasn't been necessary," Jennifer pointed out, matching his banter with her own.

"Then it must be you." His voice deepened, and he abandoned his teasing manner. "Jennifer, Jennifer, why did it take so long to find you? Why didn't you seek me out before now?" He pulled her close to him and held her with such fierceness that she was concerned for him. She had not realized until that moment that his emotions were as powerfully involved as her own. She had no answer for him but the one she gave with her body and her love.

"Another slice of French toast?" Aunt Rosa asked Jennifer the following morning as she and Ross had breakfast together.

"I shouldn't," Jennifer began, then shrugged. "Sure, I'd love one. And some of those wonderful berry compotes you made. That boysenberry and strawberry combination is just superb." She could not help but think of Drew's reaction to such foods. He would be delirious with pleasure and envy.

"Are you going to the supervisors' hearing tomorrow night?" Ross asked as he refilled his coffee cup.

"I have to. If they don't decide on that variance, then we'll have to close for three weeks while we have a complete reinspection, and then, if they decide that we're not within the new codes, we'll have to stay closed until it's approved or we're sufficiently reconstructed to satisfy them. I can't afford to have the place closed for three weeks, let alone all the additional construction costs." She had not discussed this with him very much—she preferred to leave such matters aside and lose herself in the joys of their love.

"You don't think they're really going to require that, do you?" Ross asked.

"Why not?" Jennifer countered, her chin rising a fraction.

"You're a business. You've gone to a great deal of trouble already to make your hotel safe and authentic at the same time. You employ a lot of people, and if you're forced to lay any of them off, that means a financial crunch that would have an impact on the community. You've shown that you're willing to meet reasonable demands, and if they ask anything of you at all, you'll be able to negotiate the terms with them so that you're not over a barrel." He poured homemade syrup over his French toast and waited for her to speak.

"I wish I were as confident as you are, that's all I can say." She looked at Aunt Rosa and gave an awkward smile. "Hardly good breakfast conversation."

"Ross tackles all the big things in the morning," Aunt Rosa answered, clearly a bit annoyed with her nephew. "You'll have plenty of chance to go over these things later, Ross."

"Well, we can't ignore business, can we? Jennifer's got the kind of work that takes up almost all her waking hours. And so have I. You can't have us and not have business, can you?" His smile was not quite smug, but he certainly felt pleased with how neatly he explained matters.

"It's true," Jennifer admitted as she drank her orange juice. "But, Ross, if you were in my position right now, don't you think you'd be worried? It's not as if I've been here five generations, or even five years. I'm still an unknown quantity so far as a lot of the county goes, and you can't blame the supervisors for sticking to their original position. They've got to apply the new codes throughout the area with real equality, or they mean nothing. You know that as well as I do."

"But, Jennifer," Ross said cheerfully, "you've done the most thorough job of anyone around here. You haven't tried to put anything over on the supervisors and they know it. You're in a very strong position, and I wish you'd believe it."

"But I don't think it *is* that strong, Ross," Jennifer said with a bit more emphasis. "More than ever, the supervisors are going to have to stand firm on their decisions, and that means that I'm going to be a test case for them, I know it." She leaned forward, bracing her elbows on the table.

"You're kidding yourself. I don't blame you for being a little worried, but you're making a mountain out of a molehill. . . ."

"For heaven's sake, Ross," Aunt Rosa told him as she came back into the breakfast room with a platter of sausages.

Neither Ross nor Jennifer had noticed she had gone to get the rest of their breakfast, and they were surprised by her outburst now that she had returned.

"Aunt Rosa . . ." Ross began.

"Pass the sausages to Jennifer and have some yourself. And I'm warning you, no more business until the table is cleared."

"She means it," Ross said to Jennifer, and kept to the weather and holiday plans until Aunt Rosa removed the plates, platters and silverware and retired to the kitchen.

"About the supervisors . . ." Ross said once the door was safely closed.

"Ross, please . . ." Jennifer said, feeling suddenly tired.

"I simply want you to know that I think you'll be okay. I don't want you to over-react to the threat of closure. They're always saying that, just to be sure their regulations are noticed. It gives them more room for negotiation, but it doesn't mean that they shut down profitable businesses." He looked at her with genuine concern. "You're letting yourself get worked up over nothing."

Jennifer gave him a long, critical look, which gradually turned to a frown. "If it were your winery they were discussing, would you still feel that way? It's easy to tell me that I'm being an hysterical female—and it sounds damn like that's what you're saying, Ross—but it just could be that I'm in as much of a bind as I think I am. And your dismissal of it doesn't help a bit."

"I didn't mean to dismiss your worries, I just want you to examine them a little more rationally." He paused and tried to think of the best way to go on. "If you let yourself be panicked, you'll make mistakes that won't help you solve the problem. You're usually the most level-headed hotelier in this part of the world, and you're acting like a kid afraid of a Latin exam."

Jennifer's frown turned to a glare. She had a terrible suspicion that he was at least partially right, but she refused to admit it now. "I don't think I'm panicking. I'm trying to anticipate the difficulties before they all drop in my lap and give me a *real* reason to panic. This way, I hope to have a few contingency plans around so that it won't be too awful when . . ."

"See? You're talking as if it were an already-established fact that you will have to close, at least for a while. After that, you plan to get things organized again. That's no kind of attitude for you to have, Jennifer. You're too capable for this." He was seriously concerned for her, but did not know what would be the best way to tell her. He knew by the set of her jaw that he was making a mess of it. "Why don't we both take the day off and go down to the city and do something frivolous?" He knew at once that the suggestion was a mistake.

"I don't think so," Jennifer said sweetly. "I have a few incapable, irrational chores to do before appearing before the supervisors. And I do think I ought to be prepared. If you want to spend the day in San Francisco, that's your privilege, but I have too many responsibilities to take care of." She got up from the table and called out, "It was a wonderful breakfast, Rosa! Thanks! Sorry I can't stay longer." With that, she flashed an unhappy smile at Ross, and turned abruptly away from him. "I'll let myself out."

Ross had risen and reached out to detain her, but she escaped him, going quickly toward the hall. He started after her, but was stopped by his aunt.

"Right now you'll only make it worse," she said sympathetically as the front door slammed.

"She really is scared," Ross said, trouble in his eyes. "It's ridiculous for her to be scared. There's no reason for it." He spoke as if he wanted to convince Aunt Rosa of his position.

"You don't have to have a reason to be scared, Ross. Don't you remember how terrified you were of exposed tree roots when you were a boy? You refused to go near the oaks because you were afraid that the roots would reach out of the ground and grab you. It took you more than three years to be able to walk under an oak tree without screaming. I'd say that Jennifer has a much more sensible reason to be frightened than you had, and she's doing her best to prepare for the worst. It's her way of dealing with it so that it doesn't get hold of her, the way the tree roots. . . ."

"But I was trying to show her she was being . . ." Ross started to protest, but Aunt Rosa went on.

"We're going to get hold of you, young man. You don't do

her a service by belittling her fears." She put her hands on her hips and stared up at him.

"I wasn't belittling them," he said, a shade too defensively.

"What do you call it, then?" Aunt Rosa asked, and did not press him to reply.

"Damn!" Ross muttered as he heard Jennifer's Datsun cough in the frosty morning.

"Some guys from the sheriff's office were out this morning," Drew said to Jennifer a week later, when she came in from another unrewarding hour in Wilbur Cory's office. "They're completing the report on the generator breakdown. One of them asked about other accidents around the place that might have been the result of malicious mischief. I told them about the fire at the cottage and the solvent all over the linen, and they said they'd check it out." He shrugged. "I don't see what they can do. Those things happened months ago."

"How long ago did they leave?" Jennifer asked when Drew paused for breath.

"Less than an hour. They had a long talk with Muriel and asked Caroline a bunch of questions and they said they'd be talking to some of the others on the staff. I gave them Hugo's home phone number in case they don't catch him here." He looked at the large box Jennifer carried and gave her an arch smile. "Did you buy something devastating, boss?"

"I hope so," Jennifer said with a trace of a laugh. "I've had doubts all the way home, because it cost so much. I haven't spent this kind of money for a dress . . . ever."

"Lord have mercy!" Drew exclaimed, grinning with delight. "It must be ravishing! Let me see it, Jenny." He held out his hand for the package, but Jennifer hesitated.

"It's nothing like any of my other clothes. . . ." she began as a kind of apology.

"Good! High time you tried something new." He continued to hold his hand out and she at last relinquished the package. "Very classy," he said as he looked at the name on the box. "I thought they charged admission just to breathe their rarefied air." He slipped the restraining ribbon off the box and folded it open, then turned back the lace-patterned tissue. "Ve-ry nice!"

"Do you really like it?" Jennifer asked, all her doubts about the dress coming back full force.

"What color do you call that? Tawny plum?" He lifted the

dress from the package and whistled slowly. "It's gorgeous, Jenny." He held it up to her and regarded her critically. "That's a very interesting neckline."

"You don't think it's too low, do you?" That had worried her more than anything else.

"Empire"—he pronounced it *ahm-peer*—"gowns are supposed to have low, scooped necklines. It's perfect. How many yards of fabric are there in the skirt?" He lifted the soft fold and weighed it. "That's very good silk crepe, and not too nubby or shiny. It's very elegant. Make sure you've got all your panache with you when you wear it."

"But do you think it might be a bit too much? I loved it when I tried it on, but you know that not everyone thinks women in my position should dress so . . . conspicuously." She looked longingly at the dress, thinking that if she did not wear it for their holiday concert she might never wear it at all, since there were few social occasions that called for such a formal long dress.

"Eric will be flattered that you take so much trouble for him. He likes grand occasions, and so does Elvira. If no one else here looks right, at least you will." He handed the dress back to her.

"Sounds as if you plan to wear tails," Jennifer said, a bit uneasily.

"No, just my tux." He paused, then said, "George is up at the Howdah again, getting smashed. I told Hugo to keep an eye on him, and not mention when you come in."

"Thanks. I've had about all I can take today, and George would be one thing too many. Wilbur Cory's doing his best, but a couple of the supervisors, he tells me, are adamant." She finished putting the dress back in the box. "When is Eric getting here?"

"Next week. He and Elvira will be up for a few days before the concert, and then she's going back to the city. She has a whole series of tests to go through at the medical center. She's very philosophical about it, but her doctor always wants to try for some improvement. She thinks it's been too long since the accident and that there isn't enough left of the muscles and nerves to permit any real improvement, but it could be that she can manage a little better than she does." He flushed. "She's not bitter about it anymore, but she said that the first two or three years afterward were pretty awful."

Jennifer tried to think of something to say, but in the face of such an enormous personal tragedy, she could think of no polite phrase that conveyed her feeling for Elvira Bush. "I'm looking forward to seeing her again," was what she settled on.

"Good. So am I." Drew folded his arms. "Why don't you take that luscious thing up to your closet and then find out what Muriel's been up to? She said that we're getting quite a few holiday reservations. That's encouraging. Also there's something about a playground?"

"Oh, good. I've been trying to get a few bids on a good-sized playground for kids. We need it, if we're continuing to have families here." She tucked her package under her arm. "Wilbur wants to see me next week again, after Henry talks with him. Henry's coming up for it. God, what a mess."

"Don't worry about it. Worry about how we're going to get enough fresh vegetables for that feast we're giving. I want to do that vegetable salad, but so far I haven't found any place I can get decent fresh squash." He sighed heavily. "Squash. What a thing to be worried about."

"All right, all right, all right. I get your message." Jennifer laughed and ran out of the room, feeling less apprehensive than she had been, and was so distracted that she did not see George weave out of the Howdah toward her.

"Jen! Hey, Jen!" he called unsteadily, his voice levels changing radically from syllable to syllable.

Jennifer stopped cold. "George."

He wagged a finger at her. "Trying to sneak in without talking to me? Eh? Not very nice of you, Jen, but you're not very nice, are you? Always trying to get away with this and that. This and that." He came a few steps closer to her and she backed away. "There's no cause to do that, Jen, no cause at all. You like those kinds of games, but they're not my style. I don't want to make you think that you have to run away from me. I mean, we're adults, aren't we? Aren't we?"

"Whatever you say, George," Jennifer said in a flat voice. "If you'll excuse me . . ."

He caught her arm. "Hey, not so fast. Not so fast. I have to talk to you. I came a long way to talk to you, and you're not going to go running off until you hear me out." His tone had turned quite belligerent, and he was leaning closer to her, his face reddened from drink and choler.

"George . . ." Jennifer began, and saw out of the corner of her eye that Dean had lifted the receiver behind his counter.

"Don't you take that high-handed attitude with me. We're married!"

"We *were* married. We're not now." She tried to push past him, thinking that the last thing she needed was a scene in the middle of her own lobby.

"Oh, come off it. You're not going to tell me that you don't still think you're married to me, do you?" He made an exaggerated and deliberately derisive gesture, then planted his hands on his hips, like some mocking figure out of the commedia dell'arte.

"I haven't thought that for some time, George, but you've convinced yourself otherwise. Now if you will let me go, I'll get back to my work." She took a step away from him, and was almost knocked off her feet as he lurched after her, grabbing for her.

"You're a real tough cookie, aren't you, Jen? Aren't you?" He tried to put his arm around her, but she pushed him away.

"That is enough!" she said, her blue eyes turning hot with anger. "I will not have you mauling me and embarrassing me! Now take your things, pay your bill, and *get out!*"

"Not until we've reached an understanding," he told her much more soberly.

"We reached that over a year ago. Leave." She saw two of the regular patrons of the bar and restaurant by the door, one of them shaking his head, but clearly unwilling to get involved in the conflict. Not only would they see her harassed, Jennifer thought with dismay, but they might very well tell the story for the amusement of their cronies, and she would find herself the subject of the worst kind of gossip.

"Leave!" he repeated, jeering. "You're becoming as Victorian as this hotel! Next you'll learn to simper." He laughed at his own humor, and then an expression of disgust crossed his face as he looked over Jennifer's shoulder. "Well, well, if it isn't the Fairy Princess."

"Pu-lease!" Drew said at his campiest. "Fairy Godmother."

Jennifer took a deep breath. "Let's call this off right now. George, go home and don't come back. Drew, let's not make more of a circus of this than it's already become."

"Sure, boss," Drew said with a cooperative smirk. "I just want to be certain that my former employer—who, by the way, still owes me nine hundred forty-two dollars and thirty-seven cents in retirement benefits—settles his account with us, since he won't be coming back."

"Now wait a minute. . . ." George objected.

"George," Jennifer said quietly, "if you do anything more

—*anything*—I will call the police and obtain a court order to keep you away from here. Do you understand me?"

George's expression changed again, and now he looked like a sulky boy. "God, I don't know why I let you get away with this," he mumbled, but started toward the Howdah.

"I'll keep an eye on him, Jenny," Drew said softly. "Go up and fix your hair or polish your nose or whatever it is you do to calm down."

"Thanks. I will." Jennifer turned toward the registration desk. "And thanks to you too, Dean. I appreciate your calling up the reinforcements."

"Glad to do it," Dean answered.

Jennifer was able to smile at both men, and it was only when she reached her room that she gave way to sudden trembling which made her feel numbingly cold.

Wilbur Cory sounded unexpectedly tired to Jennifer when she took his call the week before Christmas. "Is something the matter, Wilbur?" she asked, concerned for him.

"Yeah, I'm afraid something is the matter," he answered heavily. "I shouldn't be making this call, really, but I think you and a couple of others are owed an explanation."

"An explanation?" Jennifer repeated, looking blindly at the printer's proofs of the concert program on the desk in front of her.

"I'm afraid so."

"Dear God," Jennifer said, fearing that there had been a misfortune or tragedy in Wilbur's family. "Is there anything I can do? You've been helpful to me, and if you need anything . . ."

"No. It's not that kind of thing," Wilbur corrected her, then cleared his throat. "We've been having a bit of an investigation here. We've been quiet about it because we didn't want to create any more problems than we already had. It's not easy to tell you about this, Mrs. Wystan. I wish I didn't have to, and that's the truth."

"But what is it?" Jennifer prompted him.

"Look, you know those regulations we've had brought into the zoning, and how there's been all that resistance to the variances you've applied for? Well, you aren't the only hotel owner filing for them, but you know what it's been like getting them." He cleared his throat again, and Jennifer had to restrain herself from screaming at him. "Well, this is related in a way. It's important that you know that, because it means that there won't be any action, one way or the other, on your application, or the other ones. It's very unfortunate this had to happen, but it . . ."

"What *has* happened, Wilbur?" Jennifer asked, as puzzled as she was out of patience.

"It's a bad thing. We're all shocked. Well, not shocked. There was the investigation. We knew something was going on, but we all hoped—you know how you do—that there was another answer." He coughed once.

"Tell me, Wilbur, please." Jennifer set the proofs aside and pulled one of her notebooks closer. She wanted to be sure she understood anything Wilbur told her so that she could explain the difficulties to Henry Fisher.

"There's been . . . irregularity on the Board," Wilbur announced.

"Irregularity?" Jennifer asked.

"Favors. You know. Bribes." He coughed again. "Three of them have had their hands in the wrong pots. We're all . . . upset."

"Oh, Wilbur, I'm sorry," Jennifer said with total sincerity. She could feel Wilbur's distress through the phone. "You must be so . . . disappointed."

"Yeah. That's the truth. I never thought that there'd be this . . . disgrace." His voice caught, and Jennifer realized that he was perilously near tears. "I went along with the investigation because I was sure, so sure, that there was nothing to it, that a few people had just opened their mouths a bit too wide at cocktail parties, or gone to the wrong gym for handball. But I've seen the report, and it's nothing so innocent. There are records of money and trips and other things, and it's all pretty damning. Helene's going to be so angry when she finds out."

"Helene? Is she involved?" Jennifer asked, alarmed at this. Her feelings toward Helene were always mixed, but she would not have thought that the new state senator was the sort of woman to compromise her position so foolishly.

"Not directly, no, but her campaign manager is, and not always on her side." He cleared his throat nervously once more. "It's not the worst we found, not by a long shot. So those of you whose variances were being blocked, we're giving you all three months before we consider your applications again, and in the meantime, any evidence of trying to come up to code will count in your favor."

"But why block the variances?" Jennifer wondered aloud.

"So property could be condemned or sold. Land's at a premium in the Napa Valley, for grapes and recreation and homes. There's a bigger demand than the supply, that's certain, and there are some out there who don't mind playing dirty to get the acres they want."

"Acres?" Jennifer questioned weakly.

"It looks like Larry Bronson's in on it, but he's not the only one. We have to file our complaints this week, but I didn't want you to read about it in the paper or get it secondhand and inaccurate. You better tell your lawyer about this, and make sure he understands what the Board's position is now. We'll have to have a special election in a couple of months. It's a rotten business, every bit of it." He hesitated. "There's nothing certain about Larry's acting on orders, by the way. His bosses said that he did it on his own, and they're as mad about it as we are. Even if it's not true, we're not going to be able to show any different. The others might have covered themselves a little better, but our investigators don't think so. We'll find out about it, and when we do, you'll be informed. There were certain target areas, and you're in one."

"It's too bad, Wilbur," Jennifer said, scribbling a series of terse notes she could read—she hoped—to Henry before too much time passed.

"It is. Time was when no one would have let this happen, but these days, when everyone thinks that men in office are crooks, it's not as hard to be dishonest. It makes me sick. These are men who accepted the public trust, and are supposed to serve the interests of their constituency. Instead, they're out lining their pockets with other people's money." His indignation was as genuine as his shame, and Jennifer found herself liking the man better than she ever had before.

"Well, that's all I called about," he said after a short silence. "You talk to your lawyer and listen to whatever he tells you. I'll expect to hear from him in the next few days. You tell him to write to me personally. We've got so much going on here that if he doesn't, it'll take weeks to get around to it, and with Christmas so near, it's even worse."

"Thank you, Wilbur. I know how difficult this must be for you." Jennifer looked at the clock and thought that there was a very good chance that Henry would be back from lunch.

"Well, I didn't make the mess, but it's on my floor, nevertheless. It's kind of you not to hold this against me," he said wearily. "I'll talk to you later, Mrs. Wystan."

Jennifer said goodbye, and after she had hung up, she

glanced over her notes to be sure she could make them out, then dialed Henry Fisher's number in San Francisco.

"The concert will take an hour and forty minutes, with one intermission, then there will be an hour break for the buffet downstairs, and then there will be dancing until two. With a little luck we'll have most of the place cleared out by three, since tomorrow *is* Christmas," Jennifer said to Muriel. "If we're ready at seven, that should be about right."

Jennifer looked at the boxes containing the programs. "Ben and three of the kids from the work-study program will do the ushering for us tonight, and that will make it much easier."

"I'm a little surprised that so many of them are willing to work on Christmas Eve," Muriel said as she looked over the list of names.

"Well, Daryl's a musician, John's in need of money, and Dick is on the high school paper, so he'll be covering it for academic credit." Jennifer chuckled.

"Speaking of the school paper, is anyone else going to cover this event?" Muriel asked.

"Well, someone's coming from the Napa paper and there's a reporter from Sonoma. I've set aside a couple comps for them."

"Good. Thanks. I want to be sure that we're ready to do this evening on time, and with a minimum of fuss," Muriel said. "How's Mr. Bush feeling?" she continued.

"He says he feels fine. Elvira told me that he's always a little withdrawn before a concert, but that as soon as it's over he brightens up and makes jokes. I saw him play once, at Davies Hall, and I was very impressed. It wasn't just the playing, it was the way he was."

"Yes," Muriel agreed. "He's like Frederick the Great, or one of those musican kings permitting his loyal courtiers to hear him perform."

Jennifer laughed. "That's a little extreme, but I know what you're saying." She picked up the files she needed and went off toward the lobby, calling a cheery greeting to Dean as she passed him.

There was a tall Christmas tree in the outer lobby, decorated with all the old ornaments Uncle Samuel had so lovingly collected for more than forty years. It was a very traditional tree, with candycanes and popcorn and cranberry strands looping about the branches. Only the winking lights made a concession to the present; the rest of the holiday rigs were contemporary with the building. Jennifer had spent the better part of two days getting the eleven-foot Douglas fir properly decorated, and had endured the teasing remarks of her staff. Now, she noticed, they all took a great deal of pride in it.

"Oh, there you are," she heard Elvira Bush's voice behind her, and turned toward the woman in the wheelchair.

"How are your pre-concert nerves, Elvira?" Jennifer asked as Elvira rolled up to her.

"I haven't had any in decades; but, then, I don't perform. Eric is going through his usual routine. He's had a long, hot bath and is reading a murder mystery. He simply devours those books, and I haven't any idea why it must be a murder mystery." She nodded toward the entrance to the Howdah. "May I buy you a drink, or don't hotel owners permit such things?"

"Of course you may," Jennifer said at once, thinking that she could spare twenty minutes from her schedule for someone who had gone to so much trouble for the White Elephant.

"Very good. I won't keep you too long, you know. I'm sure you have a great deal to do before you're ready to start this evening." The canny expression in Elvira's eyes revealed more than her good manners. "You've been wonderful to us these last few days."

"I have? What about you? We couldn't be having this concert without Eric, and when I think of what he usually gets for a concert, I can't tell you how I feel." Jennifer had been a bit bothered by the pianist's generosity, especially since she had stumbled upon the relationship of Eric and Drew.

"It's been a pleasure for him, I assure you. He doesn't have many opportunities to relax, and you've provided him an excellent one, as well as the chance to play a few pieces he doesn't often have the opportunity to perform." They had reached the Howdah and Jennifer had chosen a table near the window toward the end of the bar, where Elvira would not be required to negotiate the narrow space between tables and chairs.

"Would a little champagne be appropriate?" Jennifer asked. "It *is* supposed to be a festive day."

"Champagne is always appropriate," Elvira answered at once, and positioned her chair while Jennifer gave their order to the cocktail waitress. As soon as the half-bottle arrived, Elvira gave the label a critical glance. "Benedetto. That's quite good. But you're neighbors, aren't you?"

"Yes," Jennifer answered rather curtly. She did not like to

be reminded that she had seen Ross only twice, and then briefly, since that disastrous breakfast. She had so far resisted the urge to call him and tell him what Wilbur had told her, but she had been hoping he would learn of the discoveries and tell her that she had not been such a fool, after all. She could not find any way to conquer her pride enough to call him.

"It's very good. I remember liking those wines for many years." She smiled at the waitress as their glasses were filled, then lifted hers in toast. "To a very joyous holiday and a prosperous New Year," she said, and sipped. When she put her glass down, she spoke in a lower voice. "I wanted to have the chance to talk to you alone for a little time, and it hasn't been possible, you've been so busy. But I thought perhaps I should tell you that I would count it as a personal favor if you could permit Drew time off in January. We've invited him to go with us on Eric's tour, but he's said that he can't leave you with only his assistants to watch after him." She stared down into her glass. "You see, there is a fairly good chance that I won't be able to make the tour this time, since my physician is determined to embark on some more tests and treatment. Eric wants me to do it, and for that reason, I will. But he really shouldn't travel alone—he's dreadful when he's on tour by himself. Drew will look after him certainly as well as I do—actually, a good deal better."

Jennifer hesitated, not knowing what to say. "Drew is more than welcome to vacation time, and January will be the slowest month since we've opened. Not many people want to come to the wine country in the freezing rain."

"How diplomatic you are," Elvira said with an amused twinkle in her tired eyes. "You ask none of the obvious questions. I assume you know about Eric and Drew. Poor Drew, you know, is convinced he's concealed the relationship from you and everyone else but me. I won't disabuse him of that, if you don't."

"I hadn't planned to say anything," Jennifer said.

"Just as well," Elvira responded. "I would appreciate it if you'd encourage Drew to go. Eric does need him, and I wouldn't worry if Drew were with him." She had more champagne. "Don't think that I'm being the martyr wife, because I'm not. Eric has stayed with me through a great deal, and I love him with all my heart. I've never doubted his love for me. And I've never doubted his love for Drew. It isn't just sex, if that's what you're thinking. If it were, the relationship would not survive the long periods of separation.

Drew has an ability to understand Eric's . . . pain. I don't think anyone else ever has, including me."

Jennifer had no idea what she should say, so she nodded and tried to look sympathetic and detached, the way she remembered her college psychologist did.

"I would count it as a personal favor if you'd go along with the plans, Jennifer," Elvira said after a brief hesitation.

"If Drew asks for the time, he can have it, but I don't think I can force him to take a vacation," Jennifer answered carefully.

"Knowing Drew, that wouldn't work, anyway." She put her hand over Jennifer's "Thank you. This means a great deal to me."

"You're welcome," Jennifer answered automatically, without knowing precisely why.

"Everything looks lovely," Jennifer said to Caroline when she had taken a last look around the Grand Ballroom before the doors were thrown open for the concert. "Including you."

Caroline was dressed in a velvet jacket and tartan skirt with a ruffled blouse, an outfit considerably more formal and attractive than her usual navy-blue garb. Surprised by the compliment, she blushed and began to stammer her thanks when the door opened.

"What is it, Ben?" Jennifer asked the young man who stood there, looking awkward in what was clearly his best suit.

"Nothing much, Ms. Wystan. I went out on rounds before I changed and I noticed that there was a light on in cottage sixteen. I didn't know anyone was staying there, but I thought I'd better mention it, just in case." He made an awkward adjustment of his tie and shrugged. "I don't want to alarm you or anything."

"Thank you, Ben. I'm sure it's all right. Sometimes the groundsmen inspect the empty cottages to be sure there's nothing wrong. I'll check with them shortly." She hoped that the apprehension she felt was baseless, one more phantom to be dismissed and laughed over.

"Do you need me yet, or is there time for a cup of coffee?" Ben asked.

"Have your coffee, then report back here. Where are the other ushers, do you know?"

"They're all here, Ms. Wystan. Should I go to the kitchen?" He saw Jennifer's nod and bolted from the room.

"Kids," Caroline said with understanding good humor. "What about that light? Do you think it means anything?"

"I don't know," Jennifer answered. "I doubt it. But I think Steve's on duty tonight, and I'll give him a call, just in case."

"It'll put your mind at rest," Caroline said placidly, and then changed the subject to the matter of seating, and Jennifer got so caught up in the excitement of the concert that it was not until the music was over and the audience was trickling down to the buffet that the matter occurred to her again.

"Something the matter?" Aunt Rosa asked Jennifer as she stopped on the stairs.

"No," was her slightly distracted answer. "I just remembered something I forgot to do. Damn!" Steve, she knew, was gone. "It's probably not important, but . . ."

Aunt Rosa grinned at her. "I know you. You won't be easy until you get it done. Well, no one will notice if you're gone a few minutes. From what I can tell, everyone's so excited and hungry that they'll be eating and talking for the next hour. Run along and do your chore." She looked away, then added, "I ought to apologize for my idiot of a nephew not being here, but it's not my place to say anything. *He's* the one who ought to be talking to you, not me."

Jennifer gave a fragmentary response, thinking that it was indeed Ross who ought to apologize. She had been saddened by his absence at the concert, since she knew he had been looking forward to it. It was painful to think that what they had had might really be over, but she knew that was a possibility, unwelcome though it was. She had been doing her best not to think about it since that morning at Ross's. "Excuse me," she said to one of the guests as she went toward the stairs leading down to the kitchen.

Johnny Chang waved to her. "How's it going?"

"The concert was wonderful and the audience loved it." She nodded to the two kitchen assistants. "They're all hungry now."

"We'll handle them," Johnny said, then asked, "Anything the matter?"

"Not really. Ben said something about a light being on in one of the cottages and I forgot to have it checked out. . . ." Jennifer felt strangely lax in this confession. She, of all people, should not have overlooked her work.

"Probably Steve. He went on rounds this afternoon. I was

outside a little earlier and everything was dark." Johnny put the finishing touches on one of three St. Honoré's cakes, then asked as he inspected the glacéed fruits, "Want me to check it out?"

"You've got your hands full," Jennifer said. "I'll step outside and . . ."

"It's pretty cold out there," Johnny cautioned her. "I'll be free in half an hour or so."

Jennifer almost acquiesced, then decided that she ought to look after her own interests more responsibly. "No. I'll take care of it."

"Then take my peacoat. It's hanging up over there." He pointed toward the half-dozen lockers which were available to the kitchen staff. "Otherwise, you're gonna freeze your little . . ."

"I can guess," Jennifer said dryly, and took the heavy wool jacket. As she tugged it on, she felt slightly amused—a navy jacket over a designer gown. What all well-dressed hoteliers wear for late-night inspection. She let herself out the back and looked around, her eyes unused to the dark. There was lightspill from above, but aside from the guard lights marking the pathways, she could see no other brightness. "It's probably nothing," she said aloud, as if to convince herself. Then she shook her head and started toward the path leading to cabin sixteen.

The darkness enveloped her like a cloak, and the icy chill ate into her more deeply than she had thought possible. The wind rushed through the trees as if hurrying away on an important errand. Jennifer heard the tap of her high heels on the stepping-stones like the sound of a distant summons. She tried to tell herself that the eeriness she felt was the hour and the time of year, the weather and the aftermath of excitement. It was foolish to think that there could be any real danger at this deserted—and dark—cottage at her own resort hotel. This reassurance failed abysmally to comfort her. She had not remembered to bring the key, but this did not stop her, for she knew where the groundsmen hid their passkeys, and it was the task of little more than two minutes to find one. As she told herself the whole thing was silly, she let herself into the parlor side of the cottage.

There was that faint, musty smell that haunts all unoccupied buildings, and a sharper tang of disinfectant. Jennifer felt along the wall for the light switch, and when she turned it on, was already giving a sigh of relief when she caught movement from the bedroom door and George's voice said,

"Hello, Jen. Glad you could make it."

Ross stared at the flickering image on the television screen, and realized that he had no idea what he was watching. He had turned the set on shortly after Aunt Rosa had left for the concert, and had remained in front of it for the better part of two hours. He tried to recognize the figures and decided that it must be some sort of special for the holidays. He rubbed his jaw and tugged at his lower lip, his abstracted stare returning. What was Jennifer wearing tonight? He tried to make light of the thought and turn his mind back to the television set, but nothing could distract him from her image once he called it into his mind. He got up restlessly and poured himself a generous amount of sherry, which he drank too quickly. How was she wearing her hair? He paced down the room and switched the set off impatiently. "The trouble with you," he said aloud to himself, "is that you are too damn pig-headed for your own good." Ever since Wilbur Cory had called him three days before and told him about the investigation of the supervisors, he had been nagged by the realization that Jennifer had had very real reason to be afraid. He had mocked her fears, and now was both contrite and ashamed that he had ignored her and dismissed her worry. Jennifer, Jennifer, Jennifer, he thought, savoring her name. She would be beautiful tonight, he knew it, and she would manage all the guests with a practiced ease that would make many hostesses irate. He wished now that he would be able to see it.

Impulsively, Ross started down the hall. It would not take long to get to the White Elephant. He would ride over and surprise her, have a taste of that fabulous banquet Drew was putting together. If he saddled Nicodemus, he could be there in less than twenty minutes, if he took the back road to the White Elephant. He could tell her that he'd been a perfect ass, a complete boor, anything so that she would not shut herself away from him; and he damned her for not coming to him first.

The slacks and sweater he wore were not truly proper dress for the concert and ball being held tonight, but he decided that it would not be that crucial. He pulled his best tweed jacket out of the hall closet and grabbed a muffler as he decided that his dark dress Wellingtons were good enough footwear and warm enough for the ride.

Nicodemus was restive at being taken out of his stall at this unusual hour, but after a few preliminary objections and a disdainful toss of his head, he allowed himself to be bridled and saddled. When Ross led him out of the stable and swung up into the saddle, Nicodemus sidled nervously until Ross had the reins firmly in hand and had clapped his heels lightly to the gelding's sides.

As he rode along the familiar, dark trail, Ross admitted to himself that the reason for riding over instead of taking the second car was that he would be able to come and go largely unnoticed. Should Jennifer not wish to see him, he would be able to leave without attracting a great deal of attention. He gave a rueful grimace as he recognized this about himself. He was willing to swallow his pride, but not with half the county for an audience. He shifted in the saddle and, in response to this, Nicodemus broke into a trot.

"I told you to leave here," Jennifer said with a calm she was far from feeling. Her hands were clammy and her spine was cold as icewater. In a moment, she was afraid her teeth would chatter.

"And I did. But I came back." He did not come much closer to her, but he gave her that wide, possessive grin that she remembered with dread from the days of their marriage. "We've got to settle a few things, Jen."

"We've settled them, George. They were settled when we divorced." She was breathing too fast and the words came out in childish haste. She thought of all the times George had made her feel this way, and the anger that filled her drove the worst of her weakness away. "You have ten minutes to get out of here." She made an abrupt turn on her heel and started toward the door, trying not to run.

George grabbed her and jerked her back toward him. "You're not going anywhere. *You* were the one who started this with those notes, and you're going to finish it up."

"I never sent you any notes. Now let go of me."

" 'Now let go of me,' " he mimicked her cruelly. "That wasn't the way you sounded in those notes. On your own stationery and everything. What's the matter? You turned into a tease or something?"

By now, Jennifer was possessed by a sick dread. She knew

George in these moods and she would be fortunate if all he did was abuse her verbally. "I never wrote to you. I want nothing to do with you. Now let me go and get out of here, before I call the cops."

"You're going to cry rape, are you?" George laughed.

"I'm going to accuse you of breaking and entering, of harassment and threat of assault, unspecified." She tugged her arm away from him and started to flee the room. She reached the door and had it half open when a shoulder slammed into her back and the door closed with a sudden, loud finality.

Ross rode toward the glittering bulk of the White Elephant, his mind occupied with forming the phrases he would say. He attempted one and then another, discarding each in turn as completely unsatisfactory. It was beginning to frustrate him as he let himself through the gate and onto White Elephant land. There had to be a way to tell her that he had not meant to treat her badly, that he had intended to allay her fears, not to dismiss them. He was getting closer to the hotel; the first of the guest cottages were in sight, and there was the distant sound of conversation and partying from the hotel, like the drone of bees. He drew Nicodemus in while he began one last desperate attempt to find the right words to say, and was distracted almost at once by a single bang, like the crack of a rifle. Ross rose in the stirrups and held Nicodemus steady as the bay danced on stiffened legs. Was it more trouble? he asked himself, and decided at once it was not. He was about to continue on to the hotel itself, when he decided to investigate. It was probably nothing, he insisted inwardly, and just as quickly reminded himself that he had chided Jennifer for apprehensions that had seemed baseless and now were revealed as rooted in graft and corruption.

The fourth cottage down the row had lights on in the rear windows. Ross pulled Nicodemus to a halt at the door. He dismounted, then almost faltered, thinking how embarrassing it might be to interrupt Jennifer's guests if they wished to be private. Then he heard a piece of furniture overturn and a sharp oath, and he moved swiftly, rapping the door with his knuckles with the air of authority.

"Who the hell is that?" George demanded as he tried to pin a desperately-struggling Jennifer to the wall.

"I don't know," Jennifer shot back at him as she tried to

bring her knee up to his groin. She kept telling herself that this could not be happening. Not after everything she had been through already.

"We have a report of a disturbance," said a voice from the other side of the door.

Jennifer recognized it at once, and for the first time since she entered the cottage, she felt courage rise in her. "Ross!" she cried out. "*Ross!*"

"Shut up!" George ordered her, slapping her twice very hard.

"Ross!" Jennifer repeated as she strove to break away from George. He caught her around the waist and they fell to the floor in a heap, Jennifer's senses wobbling at the stunning impact. George reached to restrain her and the long, flowing skirt of her gown ripped. Heedless of the damage, Jennifer squirmed in the attempt to escape from George, determined now to get out of danger.

At the sound of Jennifer's scream, every hesitation left Ross. He reached for the door handle and was surprised to find it would open. His surprise turned to rage when he caught sight of Jennifer.

She lay on the floor, her skirt in tatters, her hair undone, two red marks on her face where George had struck her. She was being held by George, who was astride her, trying to pummel her shoulders. She looked up with so much emotion in her eyes that Ross could not contain himself.

"Get off her, Howard!" Ross said in a tone of voice that was as strange to him as anyone else in the room.

George did not do that, but he froze. "Get out of here."

"Do as I told you." Ross did not speak loudly, but with such icy command that this time George reluctantly obeyed him.

"Move away from her," Ross said to George. "Don't do anything that would make it worse."

Jennifer wanted nothing so much as to fall into a deep, long sleep, one that would end with the realization that this had been nothing more than a nightmare. But she could not bear to grovel before George, not even in a nightmare, and so she pushed herself onto her knees and then reeled to her feet. She was afraid that she might vomit.

Drew stuck his head in the kitchen door. "You seen Jenny around?" he asked of the three people there.

"Earlier," Johnny said while the coffee grinder whirred behind him. "She borrowed my peacoat."

"Why?" Drew was baffled.

"Said she had to check something outside. Said there was a light on in one of the cottages." He turned off the coffee grinder and began to pour the grounds into a fluted white filter.

"A light on in the cottages? There's no one out there," Drew said. "How long ago was that?"

"I don't know. Fifteen minutes, maybe. I haven't been keeping track." Johnny was reaching for one of the two gallon-sized teakettles.

"But she isn't back yet?" Drew persisted.

"My peacoat's still gone," Johnny answered laconically. "Maybe there was something to it. Vandals or something." He did not sound worried, and it was apparent that he did not believe that such a thing could be possible.

"Or something," Drew said harshly, and went out the door where he almost collided with Eric.

"You're troubled," the pianist said at once.

"I can't find Jenny. Apparently, she went outside about a quarter of an hour ago. I don't think she's come back in." His brow furrowed with worry. "It's probably nothing, but . . ."

"But you would prefer to check it out for yourself." Eric nodded. "You must, of course. Would you like me to ask Dr. Robb to assist you? I would be quite discreet."

"No," Drew said, and at once changed his mind. "It might be better if you did. Thanks, Eric." He smiled with abiding affection, then sprinted off down the hall toward the loading door while Eric turned and started back toward the stairs to the upper floors.

Ross launched himself at George, his hands reaching for the other man's throat.

The pain that shot through Jennifer when she stood was blinding, and she toppled into one of the two occasional tables in the cabin parlor, overturning it and smashing the lamp. The room fell into darkness.

There was a scuffle, a sound of blows and a cry of protest, and someone's leg slammed into Jennifer's side. Ross swore loudly, and then there was the sound of two well-placed blows.

Jennifer had pulled herself to the wall and now sat with her back braced, staring into the darkness, searching for the dimly-perceived shapes of the combatants as if she could will them into visibility by the intensity of her gaze. Breathing hurt, and when she tried to get to her feet, her mind clouded and she fell back, whimpering. What was happening? she wondered. She had been so overjoyed when Ross had arrived, but now she feared the outcome of the fight going on so close to her. What if Ross were hurt? What if George killed him? Her throat tightened.

Then she heard Nicodemus whicker, and rapid, regular footsteps, and Drew's voice. "Jenny? Boss? Where are you?" He was not calling loudly, but with great clarity.

"Here," she said, but could hardly make a sound.

One of the two combatants blundered into a chair and there was a grunt and a yelp at once.

Jennifer forced herself to swallow, and with more effort than she had ever made, she raised her cracked voice enough to be heard. "Sixteen!"

Drew's steps came nearer at once, and there was an oath of surprise as he encountered Nicodemus outside. Then he stepped through the door and the beam of his flashlight went around the room. "Good God," he said, stunned at what he saw.

The fight broke off as the light struck the two men.

"Oh, Drew," Jennifer muttered as she had a brief glimpse of his quick strides across the room. She was so deeply relieved that she was hardly startled when she saw the flashlight he carried rise and then descend sharply.

"Thanks," Ross mumbled, looking up at the dapper chef.

"A pleasure, believe me," Drew answered. "Whom have I hit? George?"

"Yeah." Ross moved the unconscious man aside and lumbered to his feet, one hand to his brow where there was a large, bruised cut that had bloodied most of the right side of his face. "Damn."

"It's a double pleasure then. I've wanted to hit him for years." Drew shone the light around the room, and this time he picked up Jennifer in its beam. He gasped. "Jenny!" As fast as he moved toward her, Ross moved faster; tactfully, Drew held back, though he was horrified at what he saw.

Jennifer's face was livid now, and one eye was starting to swell. There was a cut over her lip and a scrape on her collarbone where the peacoat had come open in her fall. Her hair was wholly disordered, her makeup was ruined. She was the most beautiful thing Ross had ever seen. "I'll be okay," she said as Ross dropped on his knees beside her. Then she saw the blood on his face as Drew's light played over them, and she burst into tears.

"Hey, hey," Ross said as he gathered her gingerly into his arms. "It's all right. It's all right. Jennifer, love, don't cry. It's all right."

Drew went to examine George, smiling with satisfaction as he noticed the lump near his hairline. It was small enough revenge, but he enjoyed it.

When Sheridan arrived a few minutes later, he found Drew tending a groggy George, and Jennifer, in a delayed reaction, on the edge of hysterics.

"Don't let anyone know what happened," Jennifer insisted between crying bouts. "I'm sorry. I don't mean to act like this. I'm sorry." She began to weep again.

"Not at the moment, no," Sheridan soothed, "That's for later. Right now, you'd better let me have a look at you."

"Howard kicked her," Ross said tightly.

"No doubt." Sheridan gently but firmly extricated Jennifer from Ross's arms. "You can have her back in a little bit."

"He should be . . ." Ross began, but Sheridan cut him short.

"You've already had a go at it from the look of you. Be satisfied with that unless you want to do Jennifer a disservice." Sheridan looked around impatiently as he bent over Jennifer. "Isn't there any light in the place?"

Belatedly, Drew searched and found the switch for the indirect lighting over the hearth. "Better?"

"Yes, thanks." Sheridan had learned over the years to conceal his reactions behind his energetic bedside manner, but the sight of Jennifer thinned his mouth to a single, tense line, and his face grew hard. "I won't take long, Jennifer. I want to get an ambulance for you—you, too, Ross—and take some x-rays."

"An ambulance?" Jennifer asked incredulously. "But the guests . . ."

"Tell them to come around the back, without sirens," Ross suggested, and suddenly had to sit down as his shock caught up with him. "Do they take doubles?" he asked weakly.

"If it's necessary," Sheridan said, then glanced up at Drew. "Call them, will you? Give them instructions, and then think of a good reason for Jennifer to be gone from her own Christmas party."

"I'll take care of it," Drew assured him, and started toward the door. "And you take care of her." He smiled fleetingly at Ross. "Take care of both of them."

Ross watched as Sheridan conducted his cursory, delicate examination, and when the doctor rocked back on his heels, he smiled down at her. "God, I love you so much, Jennifer."

As she started to cry again, Jennifer asked, "Why don't you ever say so, if you do?"

"From now on I will," he promised her. "Often. I should have before."

Sheridan rather prudently said nothing, and after a silence while he inspected the bruises on Jennifer's face, she looked up at Ross.

"I did try to fight him. I kicked, and I think I was able to bite him once. I did try, Ross."

"I know, love, I know." He reached out to touch her, but Sheridan brushed his hand away.

"Not yet. I need about five minutes more." He felt her scalp, a slightly vacant expression on his face, so intent was his concentration. "Doesn't feel like anything worse than a goose egg or two, but I'm going to need pictures of it, just in case."

"You see," she went on urgently to Ross when Sheridan let her talk, "it was so sudden."

"What did George do to you, Jennifer?" the doctor asked.

"He attacked me. He wanted to . . ." Jennifer stopped, unable to continue. She had got her tears somewhat under control, but her breathing was not quite steady. Pain was part of the problem, but not all.

"Did you argue?" Sheridan asked with a quick, warning look at Ross.

"I told George to get out and tried to leave myself when he wouldn't," Jennifer said in a small voice, pleased that she could say this so calmly, and knew it was because it still seemed so unreal to her. "But he tackled me and pushed me against the wall, and then to the floor."

Ross, who was growing steadily more restive with each question, interrupted the doctor. "Why this cross-examination, Sheridan?"

"Because these are the kinds of questions the police are going to ask her, and they're going to be far more skeptical than I am. There's only her word against her ex-husband's. . . ." Sheridan replied patiently.

He moved aside to allow Ross to hold her again. "Be careful with her. I think she's got a couple of broken ribs."

He saw the alarm in Ross's face and hurried on. "Not badly broken. We'll have to tape them up, but it's not that serious."

"A broken bone is serious," Ross said belligerently as he got onto the floor and wrapped his arms around Jennifer once more.

"That's so good," she whispered as she leaned her head against his shoulder.

"Yes," Ross agreed, joyously content despite his throbbing headache.

"This man has a concussion, if either of you are interested," Sheridan announced from the other side of the room where he was starting to check out George.

Apparently, neither of them were. Jennifer snuggled as close to Ross as her hurts would allow, and waited in the haven of his arms for the ambulance to arrive.

❧ January ❧

"When's Henry getting here?" Muriel asked Jennifer on the day before Drew was scheduled to leave on a two-week vacation.

"Tomorrow afternoon. Are you going to be ready for him?" Jennifer asked. "All that work to do the taxes!" She was more troubled by it than she would have been if she were fully recovered. As it was, her immobility caused by the tape protecting her ribs made her feel helpless and incapable. "I wish it was all taken care of."

"So do I," Muriel said. "But this is the last installment, and then we can go into the final figures for the year. It hasn't been too bad, you know."

"You've said so," Jennifer said cautiously. "We've had all those extra expenses."

"Be grateful for them," Muriel advised her. "You've got good documentation on all of them, and they're all reasonable."

"And we have got our variance," she added, thinking of the evening the night before last when Wilbur Cory had made the public announcement of the results of the investigation and presented Jennifer and three other local landowners with

294

their variances. "We can get the hotsprings open at last, and then the stable can go in."

Muriel chuckled. "As soon as I make sure we can afford it. Henry might want to advise you on it, too."

"Henry will be cautious because he always is," Jennifer said, dismissing the subject. "I'll want to get some plans in the works as soon as possible. We might as well let the Board of Supervisors have a crack at them while they're in a cooperative mood."

"Good luck with it," Muriel said, getting up from her desk. "You ready? Drew's lunch is about to begin."

"Good Lord, is it that late?" Jennifer asked. "I haven't got half the work done I ought to." She got awkwardly to her feet, finding the heavy tape around her waist and chest more irritating than usual. She had been told yesterday that her reaction was a good one because it meant that she was healing, but at the moment it seemed to her that she was more on the road to frustration than recovery.

"There's plenty of time for that," Muriel said, seeing the aggravation in Jennifer's eyes. "The bruises are almost gone and Sheridan says you're doing very well."

"It's easy for him, no disrespect to your husband," Jennifer remarked ungraciously. "I am getting so *bored*."

Muriel had reached the door before Jennifer and held it open for her. "You've been saying that you wanted a little rest." There was just enough teasing in this that Jennifer took it in good part.

"Sure, but I didn't mean this way. I think Drew's handling things better—ten days in Europe, two in New York and two in San Francisco. Now, *that's* more what I had in mind." She waved to Dean as she closed the office door. "One of these days, perhaps."

"Why not start planning it?" Muriel suggested.

The lobby was a touch chillier than usual; a rare powdering of snow had whitened the rolling Napa hills, and the wind off it was bitingly cold. Though the furnaces in the White Elephant worked with all their creaky vigor, they could not dispel the frosty presence of the wind entirely.

"You know, Muriel," Jennifer said as she buttoned her cardigan sweater up over the lambswool turtleneck she wore, "it might be worthwhile to investigate hooking the hotsprings up to the heating system again. They'd had that sort of arrangement back when the place was first open, but discontinued it after 1906, when it was damaged in the quake. So long as we've got that heat sitting out there, we ought to make use of it."

Muriel agreed at once. "How expensive would it be?"

"I haven't got any figures, but I think it's worth finding out." They had reached the smaller of the function rooms near the restaurant.

The room had been decorated with streamers and a few of the Christmas decorations that had not yet been stored away for next year. Three long tables were laid out for the staff, and behind a row of chafing dishes, Drew busied himself in combining the liqueurs for crêpe suzettes.

"Jenny!" he cried out as she came in.

"What are you doing back there?" she inquired. "You're supposed to be the guest of honor."

"But I *love* making crêpes," he protested, "and I won't be able to for days and days. Besides, I want to have the fun of a high-calorie orgy before heading off for fourteen sybaritic days and nights in glorious, decadent Europe."

"I hope you'll enjoy every minute of it," Jennifer said to him, and leaned across the table to kiss his cheek. "Have a wonderful time, Drew. I can't thank you enough for all you've . . ."

"God, don't remind me," he said, turning her compliment aside. "Just remember that you're the boss, Jenny, and no one does that better than you." He blinked quickly once, then said more brightly, "I expect you to be out of that tape when I get back. I don't want any more excuses about not eating." He then indicated the two wide, shallow copper crêpe pans before him. "And you've got to make an exception today. This is special, and one indulgence isn't going to ruin you for life."

Jennifer grinned at him. "I'll eat anything you put in front of me, Drew. For the next twenty minutes."

"What a challenge!" He winked at Muriel. "But I won't take advantage of it, this time." He motioned them away so that he could continue his preparations.

"Sheridan told me that Drew handled everything like a pro on Christmas Eve," Muriel said as they took their places at a deuce by the window.

"Yes, that's what Caroline said, too. I can't get over how efficient he can be. I knew he had it in him, from all those years at . . . the Savoia." Just saying the name of the restaurant was difficult, and brought back all the shock and humiliation afresh. "But I didn't know he'd do so well in a pinch. No one thought anything was wrong, only that there'd been some minor problem with a break-in and I had to accompany the police to file the complaint. No one saw the ambulance or . . ." She had not been able to talk about that night until the last two days, and she still approached the matter cautiously, with care and circumspection.

"He pulled me and Caroline aside, and gave us an abbreviated version of what happened. He didn't mention that anyone had been . . . hurt, but he did say that George Howard was the instigator of the problem, and that we shouldn't mention his name, but to deny all knowledge of the identities of the vandals. It was so smooth; no one got too worried, though Mrs. Hasslund offered to drive down to the police station and pick you up later. Caroline simply said that it would probably be quite late and Drew had already made arrangements for you."

"It's good to know that everyone does so well in an emergency." She looked up as the orangey scent of Grand Marnier wafted through the room. "That smells so wonderful."

"Indulge yourself," Muriel recommended. "You've earned a few goodies."

Jennifer's smile was wan. "I suppose so. Poor George." She saw that Muriel was about to object indignantly. "No, I mean it. I'm furious with him, and I don't think I'll ever forgive him for what he did, but he's so . . . sad. He was in a panic because his partners are going to take the restaurant out of his hands entirely. He can stay on as host, but that's a sop they're throwing to him. I'm not surprised, knowing him as I do, that he decided that . . . he was entitled to something from me." Her face was faintly flushed and there was a single, angry line between her brows, but she was able to speak calmly. "He's . . . He needs help, a lot of professional help. I know he honestly believes he's a great businessman. He probably believes that I was being petulant and capricious when I divorced him, and really wanted him back." She stared down at the ecru tablecloth and shook her head slowly. "I don't know. One minute, I hope they throw the book at him, but then I think about a trial, and having to talk about Christmas Eve again, and go through it all one more time and . . . it makes me sick. So, then, I hope they'll put him through a psychiatric exam and find out he has to be put away for a while, and I won't have to face him, or have a couple of lawyers pull everything I say to bits and . . ." She stopped abruptly.

"I know," Muriel said with quick sympathy. "And this is a small community. That kind of thing is . . ." She turned up her hands and shrugged. "You know that Sheridan would support you, and Ross, but there are those who spend a great deal of time sniffing out any taint of scandal, and . . ."

"Yes," Jennifer said. "I don't know what else I can do but try to keep this as quiet as I can. I don't want George to get away with it, and I suppose I'll have to do something, but the more private the better." She bit her lower lip.

"I still can't believe George acted entirely on his own. I can believe that members of the Board of Supervisors were taking bribes. I don't like it much, but it's conceivable. But I can't seriously believe that one of the supervisors paid someone to intimidate anyone in the Valley. Why? It doesn't make sense. I've had more than a week to think about it, lying around all taped up, and I couldn't figure out why any of them would. One of the companies paying bribes, maybe. That adds up a little more. But which one? They still don't know where some of the bribes were coming from, and they have to do a lot more investigating before any more indictments are brought. So where does that leave us? Where does it leave me?" Her voice had become a little louder, and she forced herself to keep it low as she asked her questions.

"I don't know," Muriel answered honestly. "But at least you're protected."

"Protected! Between the police and Ross, I'm surprised they haven't put guardposts at the gate. I wish they wouldn't be quite so obvious. If I were trying to frighten anyone, I'd stay well away while all the show was going on, then, when the fuss had died down, I'd go back and really do something awful. I'm afraid some of those people think exactly the same way." She paused and looked at the approaching waiter.

"The first crêpe, courtesy of the chef, *madame*," he said with his most formal good manners as he placed the plate before Jennifer. Then he turned to Muriel. "The second crêpe will be presented as soon as it's ready."

"Thank you," Muriel said, trying to match the waiter in dignity, and ruining it with a snort of laughter.

The waiter paid this no heed. "Very good. Shall I bring the coffee now?"

"Tea for me," Jennifer said, remembering how jittery coffee had made her recently. "What about you, Muriel?"

"I'll have the coffee if it's that dark French roast," she said promptly, and was rewarded with a profound nod.

"Are you frightened, Jennifer?" Muriel asked after a moment of hesitation.

"Yes." She could not meet the older woman's eyes. "I'm very frightened. I used to think that once I got away from George, I wouldn't need to be living in fear all the time, and then I found out that nothing had changed. At least with George, I knew what I was up against." She made an odd, apologetic gesture and put her hands to her face while she brought her surge of emotion under control.

"What can I do?" It was a senseless question, and Muriel knew it, but could not keep from asking. Otherwise, she would feel helpless, which was almost as bad as feeling frightened.

"Nothing, really. Listen to me when I get silly like this. Let me know if there's any kind of trouble around the place. Oh, I don't know." Her eyes snapped with impatience. "Let's eat these crêpes," she said in another tone as the waiter returned with the second plate. "Otherwise, Drew will come over and brain us with a spatula."

Muriel accepted this. "Good idea."

The crêpes were tissue-thin and sweet without being sugary. By the time they were finished, Jennifer was discussing the replacement chef who would run the kitchen in Drew's absence, and would not be brought back again to the matter of her safety.

By the end of the week, Jennifer told Sheridan that if he did not do something about the tape around her, she would cut it off herself and take her chances. "I haven't had a proper bath in three weeks, ever since you put this blasted thing on me. I itch under it and every time I move I feel as if I'm wearing one of those kinky corsets."

"If you're well enough to complain, you're mending quite well," Sheridan said without distress. "But you ought to stay taped another week at the least."

"Torture," Jennifer announced. "I can't stand it."

Sheridan regarded her steadily, then said, "All right, Jennifer, I tell you what. I'll put a little less restrictive wrapping on you while you're here, and you can have a shower or a bath between tapings. That's the best deal I can offer."

Jennifer gave an extravagant sigh. "If that's the best you can do, I suppose I'll have to take it."

"Good for you," Sheridan declared, and pointed at the little dressing room at the side of the examination table. "In you go, and take off everything but the tape. I'll have Mrs. Curry get either the shower or the bath ready. But before you do that, I want to check you over. Most of the bruises are gone and the cuts are pretty well healed, but it doesn't change my caution one iota. In you go."

Jennifer did as she was told, and when she emerged in the open-down-the-back garment provided, she shook her head with despair. "No wonder you never make passes at patients. No one in the world can look good in one of these things."

"Reverse psychology," Sheridan said blithely. "You get so disgusted at how you look that you forget to feel ill."

"Is that how it works," Jennifer said as she got back on the table. "All right. Do your worst."

By the time Sheridan had finished the examination, Jennifer had ordered a bath and was beginning to feel a bit more at ease.

"Well, there's nothing to worry about with the rest of you. I'm glad we took those photographs of the damage George did as soon as we got you into the ambulance. You're looking much too healthy and happy now for the District Attorney to make a case out of you. The ribs are still pretty good persuasion, but the way juries are, I wouldn't want to have to convince anyone that you were badly injured." He closed up the white, shapeless garment and looked long and measuringly at Jennifer. "Have you been sleeping well, Jennifer?"

"Pretty well," she answered in a guarded tone.

"Nightmares?"

"I wouldn't go that far. A few bad dreams." She was on the defensive now.

"What has Ross said?" Sheridan asked.

"He hasn't . . . We haven't slept together since . . . I'm taped up and, I guess, jumpy." She could not meet his gaze now, and her voice faded away.

"I see." Sheridan considered her, then drew up the folding chair from the wall and sat down. "Jennifer, I don't want you to think I'm interfering, or that I'm trying to force you into anything you dislike, but don't you think it might be easier if you . . .?"

"Used sex as a cure-all?" she asked quietly.

"No. I wasn't thinking of sex. If that's what you want, it will be available, I don't worry about that. Actually, I was thinking about love. It seems to me that having a little extra love right now might make things easier. You know, an evening cuddle and some gentle hugs. Don't you want something like that?"

Jennifer's eyes filled with tears, and she looked away, shamed by them. "I . . . don't know, really."

"I think you do," Sheridan countered sympathetically. "And I think you need affection."

"I get affection," she told him.

"Yes, and I know your friends care about you, and you about them, but that's not the same thing, is it? Ross won't make unacceptable demands of you if you ask him for help. I'm not sure you appreciate how much he loves you. Give him a chance to show you, won't you?"

"Are you pleading his case?" Jennifer asked, feeling suspicious in spite of herself.

"I guess I am," Sheridan said. "I hadn't intended to, but you're not happy, and from what I can tell, you're withdrawing into yourself. That's understandable, but it isn't very constructive, for you or for Ross. Think about it, Jennifer. There's nothing wrong with needing love. We all do."

"You make it sound so . . ." She could not find the right word.

"Clinical?" he suggested helpfully. "That's the way my job is." He got up. "I think you're afraid to admit your need. Not your love or your desires or your affection or your need. You don't want to become dependent. In a certain sense, you're dependent on food and water, but you don't resent it. The dependency doesn't . . ."

"It's not the same thing," she interrupted.

"It's all nourishment, Jennifer. And you might not need Ross, but he most definitely needs you." He nodded at her. "Now, how about that bath?"

Aunt Rosa made no comment as she opened the door to Jennifer, but there was a softening at the corners of her eyes that indicated her pleasure.

"Where's Ross?" Jennifer asked, knowing it was rude, but afraid that if she let herself get caught up in pleasantries she might not have the courage to approach Ross again.

"I'll take you to him. He's in the back parlor." She led the way down the hall, saying little, but filled with relief that increased as she walked. At the door to the back parlor, she motioned Jennifer to keep still, although she had said nothing. "He's watching T.V. I'll leave you two alone." With that, she pulled back one of the sliding doors, then went quietly away, toward the kitchen.

Ross was sitting in a recliner chair, his eyes directed at the television screen about fifteen feet away, but obviously paying no attention to the latest story on *Sixty Minutes*. He was casually dressed in faded jeans, a heavy sweater over a faded tartan shirt. The cut over his right eye had almost healed, but there was still an angry, raspberry-colored seam above the arch of his brow. He did not turn when he heard the door slide open, but said rather tersely, "Who was at the door?"

Jennifer took a cautious step into the room. "I was."

"Jennifer?" Ross said in disbelief. He turned slowly, as if afraid he would be disappointed. When he saw her, dressed very much as he was, a muffler around her neck and heavy boots on her feet, he nearly stumbled as he got out of his recliner to reach her. "God, I've missed you! How are you?" He opened his arms to her, but did not close them until she had stepped forward to embrace him.

"Better. Fine, now." She sighed with contentment. "I wish you'd come to me."

"I've called every day," he protested as he tangled one hand in her dark hair.

"It's not the same thing," she said, then kissed him tentatively.

"In the hospital, you said . . ." He could still recall the distress in her eyes when one of the orderlies had nonchalantly cut away the shreds of her gown and tossed the peacoat to the paramedic. Both men had been harshly reprimanded later by Sheridan, but it did not erase the callousness of their behavior. Ross had promised himself then that he would not impose on Jennifer. The days since had been a trial to him, but he felt her acceptance of him in the way she held him.

"That was different," she murmured.

"Good." He started to tighten his arms, and then remembered her taped ribs. "Am I hurting you?"

"A little," she admitted, though she did not want him to let go of her.

"I don't want to hurt you," he said, with so much feeling that Jennifer thought she might weep.

"You won't," she said, and then they fell silent, having other things to do than talk.

The crowd wasn't bad for the 20th of January, Jennifer thought as she watched the guests file toward the Grand Ballroom. Forty-two people for a birthday party, a cold buffet, five cases of champagne, a three-piece band and the additional bar tab, made for a fairly profitable weekend. Her mind was not entirely on the function, since she would soon have to appear before the Board of Supervisors and try to explain her proposed expansions for the White Elephant. She had had a long conference with Henry Fisher and had been assured that the trust fund would stand a little more depletion now that she was into her second year at the hotel.

"Penny for your thoughts," Ross said as he came and stood beside her.

"Business," she said lightly, leaning against him as he put his arm around her shoulder.

"Are you going to be all tied up in business when we're married?" he asked with a chuckle.

"Not all, but some." She looked across the dance floor to the host for the evening. "He looks good for fifty, doesn't he? She's forty-four, I've heard."

"Don't change the subject," Ross said. "How much time are you planning to devote to business?"

"The usual amount," she answered without thinking.

"With you, that's twenty-four hours a day. Can't we negotiate for a little better division of labor?" He looked aghast, but his chuckle dispelled any real worry he might have created.

"Well, we can talk about it."

"Fine." He hugged her briefly. "How soon can you get away from here?"

"A couple of hours," she said, thinking it over.

"Okay, two hours it is. I'll meet you upstairs and we can have supper. In the meantime, I suppose I ought to dance with Marcia Peersmyere for the sake of the neighborhood."

"If you dance with me, we might shock the world," Jennifer said, with a faint touch of jealousy which surprised her.

"I'd rather dance with you," he said quickly.

"Me, too," she said, and moved away from him before she could be caught up in the enchantment of his company.

Ten minutes later, she went down to the kitchen to make

her habitual check. "Hello, Johnny. How's everything going?"

"Real well, boss. We've got everything ready and set to go." He indicated the platters, bowls and dishes. "We're setting up the ice tables right now, and then the whole thing will go up in the elevators."

"That's fine," Jennifer said automatically. She was about to leave when she noticed an acrid smell. "By the way, what got burned?"

"Burned? For a cold buffet?" Johnny laughed.

"Then what's the smoky smell?" Jennifer wondered aloud. "If you didn't . . ."

Johnny paused in his work. "Say, there *is* smoke. . . ."

Jennifer reached for the phone on the wall and pressed the emergency number. "Johnny, please go upstairs and . . . Yes, hello. This is Jennifer Wystan at the White Elephant. We've got something burning here and we need help. Right away. There is a private party in progress, about forty-five people plus staff. There are thirty-eight guests registered in the hotel. We will begin evacuation at once." She paused as she heard the first, discreet beep of the smoke detector. "Whatever is burning is in the north wing. The ground floor alarm has sounded. We'll take the guests out through the function room near the dining room and onto the south terrace. We have the winter windows up on the porch there, so they will be protected unless the place begins to burn badly. I'm relying on you to keep that from happening." Jennifer felt that peculiar calm come over her, the coolness that had so often seen her through emergencies. She hung up and turned to Johnny. "Get the groundsmen and the kitchen staff and take them out to cottage number two. Use the phone there to stay in contact with the Fire Department."

"Okay," Johnny said, looking a bit worried now that he had smelled the smoke for himself. "What if . . .?"

"Don't start that, or you won't get things done. Right now you have to get people out of here. Don't stop for heroics. That's how you can get killed." She looked around the kitchen. "Better alert the housekeeping staff, too. Tell them to use cottage number three. Open up eleven and twelve. We will have to put guests in them." With that, she started away toward the stairs and heard the smoke detector on the second floor of the north wing begin to beep.

"What's wrong?" Ross asked as soon as he saw Jennifer's face.

"There's something burning in the north wing. We'll have to take these people out of here, through the room next to the dining room and onto the terrace. We have registered guests who have to leave, too." She took a deep, shuddering breath. "What's happening here? I thought it was all over, and now this."

"Don't be . . ." He stopped. What could he say that would comfort her now? "I'll start people moving," he volunteered. "I'll take care of this, you take care of the guests. How's that?"

"Thanks," she said rather weakly, then straightened up and turned away toward the stairs. Outside, she picked up the house phone and buzzed the front desk. "Start evacuation," she said to Ivy when she answered. "Avoid the north wing. Get everyone out of the Howdah and into cottage twelve. There's a portable bar in there, and Hugo can do as he thinks best about serving. Take the records files out of the office if they're in the brown file, otherwise lock and leave them. They're fireproof, and so is the safe. Don't let anyone leave until the fire equipment gets here."

"All right, Ms. Wystan," Ivy said faintly. "I don't know . . ."

"Think of that later," Jennifer told her, and put down the receiver. Behind her in the ballroom, she heard the band break off and Ross's voice begin:

"Excuse me, ladies and gentlemen, but there's been a minor emergency. Would you please take your wraps and come with me down to the main floor?"

How wonderful it was to be able to depend on him! She did not stay to listen to more, but went up the stairs and to the two big suites that flanked her office. The honeymooning couple in the Champagne Suite might object to the interruption, but she was sure that they would prefer the embarrassment to harm.

By four in the morning, the Fire Department had finished with most of their work, the guests were reshuffled to cottages and rooms in the south wing, those not registered in the hotel were long since departed, the first damage assessment was underway, and most of the hotel staff had gathered in the—luckily undamaged—kitchen, while Johnny made a light supper for them and the firemen.

"At least nine rooms were wrecked," Jennifer was saying. "Another dozen will have to be repainted, carpeted and all the rest because of smoke damage. There's minor smoke damage in another fifteen, including my office and my rooms. There's smoke damage on part of the ceiling of the Grand Ballroom, but not, thank goodness, in the Silverado Suite. We're reasonably sure that the worst is over. The wiring in the rest of the hotel appears to be okay and the firemen haven't found any hot spots for over an hour. The Howdah is in pretty good shape, but the north and east windows will have to be replaced, probably. And that's all I know." It was enough, she thought, as she catalogued the damage in her mind. Repairs would be costly and she was afraid that the insurance company would balk at paying for the work. Now that the worst was over, she was becoming disheartened. Only the presence of her staff kept her from breaking down.

"What caused it?" Ivy asked. She was white around the eyes and mouth, and her wispy hair had come out of its bun and was making a disordered, mouse-colored cloud around her face.

"I don't know, Ivy. Some sort of malfunction." Jennifer picked up the sandwich Johnny had put at her elbow and took a bite of it. She realized with a bit of a shock that she was very hungry.

"What about the rest of the hotel? Is it safe?" Edgar asked.

"I think so. I doubt the firemen would let us back into it if they thought we were in any danger." She looked up at Johnny. "This is delicious."

"Don't let Drew hear you say that," Johnny answered, and was rewarded with a half-hearted laugh from the others.

"He's in Paris or somewhere like that," one of the groundsmen said wistfully.

"Lucky bum," Hugo agreed.

There was a general lull in the conversation while the exhausted people ate the sandwiches and French-fried zucchini set out for them.

"Where did you get this?" Jennifer asked, holding up one of the zucchini strips. "It's January."

"I've found a gardener doing hydroponics. He's doing some vegetables for us." He grinned. "It was Drew's idea."

"Good for him," Jennifer said, wondering what else Drew had been up to.

The kitchen door opened and Ross came in with the county fire chief, a tall, thick-bodied man with a wiry head of badger-gray hair. He looked at the staff, avoiding Jennifer's eyes, then said very quietly, "It was arson."

"Arson?" Jennifer asked, anger making her weak.

"Yes, ma'am. No doubt about it. And a clumsy try at it." He had meaty hands which he braced on his hips as if to increase his stability.

"Clumsy," Jennifer repeated. "How do you figure that? Half the north wing is burned or useless. That doesn't seem very clumsy to me." Her indignation was joined by outbursts from the others.

"Ma'am," Chief Whittacker said firmly, "if that job had been done by a competent arsonist, the whole hotel would have burned, and most of you and the people here with it. You had plenty of time to get out and it took less than two hours to bring it all under control. That's an amateur at work. I know. I've seen what pros can do." He looked around the room, into silent, sober faces. "If any of you can tell us anything, I'd appreciate it. We're going to have to talk to the cops about this, and the more information I can give them, the easier their work, and ours, is going to be."

There was a welter of disclaimers from the people in the room, and the chief took a deep breath.

"Did you find evidence?" Jennifer asked, motioning the others to be quiet once more.

"A rubble-heap worth of it," Chief Whittacker said. "That's another thing that tells me this was an amateur. You happen to know anyone who'd want to burn down your hotel?"

"Not offhand, no," Jennifer said with sharp sarcasm. "On the other hand, it's not the sort of thing someone *would* tell me, is it?"

"Jennifer," Ross said in a low, kind voice. "I know how you feel. . . ."

"Do you?" she shot back, and regretted it at once. "I'm sorry."

"I do know how you feel," he said. "And you know it."

"Yes," she said. It took her the better part of a minute to bring her temper under control. "Chief," she said when she was sure she could speak evenly and rationally, "I've had a rough month. This, coming on top of . . . everything else, leaves me a little staggered. I'm sorry I've been sharp with you. Believe me, if I can think of anything that would help your investigation, I'll let you know at once. And so will anyone else on my staff. Is that agreeable to you?"

"That's all I can ask for. And all of you," he said, addressing the room at large, "don't think that you have to

entertain us. We don't want you to make up incidents because
you think they might get us on the right track, and don't
over-dramatize what you do know so that we can get more
out of it. That doesn't help us at all, and it slows things down.
You tell us what you know, as closely as you can, how it
happened. All right?" He looked over the staff and nodded at
them to seal their pact. "Well, you probably want to get to
sleep, all of you, and I have a bunch of paperwork to do."

"Chief," Hugo said, stopping the man as he was about to
leave. "I'm the bartender here. I been working here since the
place opened last spring. Sometimes I hear things. There's
something that a few of the people were talking about in
November that might have some bearing on this. It's nothing
much, but . . ."

"Go on," the fire chief said.

"There were a couple of developers here, having a drink
after the Chamber of Commerce luncheon. They were worried about being over-extended. Both of them said that they
needed more land to get the loans to build that they needed,
because of the high interest rates. One of them remarked that
they ought to try some of the dirty tricks that Hatfield used. It
might not mean anything, but I know that Hatfield has been
trying to get at this place for months. It's probably nothing,"
he ended lamely, "but I thought I should mention it."

There was a glint in Chief Whittacker's eyes that was gone
almost before it was visible, then he shook his head. "Now
that's the kind of information I was talking about, and told
just right. You're probably making a mountain out of a
molehill, but it might bear looking into." He made a gesture
not unlike a salute, and wandered out the door.

Jennifer looked at Ross, her head cocked to one side.
"Well? Is there anything else, or is that it for surprises
tonight?"

"That's it, I hope. If there's anything more, I pass." He
took one of the sandwiches from the large platter on the
central cutting table. "I've put in calls to the papers so that
this doesn't get made into more than it is. The press have
been told to talk to the Fire Department first, since they're in
charge of the investigation. I also called Helene's home, and
told her."

"Helene? But why?" Jennifer was perplexed by this.

"A crime's been perpetrated against one of her constituents, for one thing, and it might be tied into the investigations
of the supervisors, for another. She's said that she wants to

help the people of this county. Let her do it by keeping an eye on this and making sure that no one gets away with anything." He rested his hand on her shoulder. "Helene will keep things stirred up until they're solved. She's looking for something to put her on the map, and this will."

"You're probably right." It was strange, Jennifer thought, that three months ago hearing Ross mention Helene would have brought all her doubts back to her, and she would have been hurt that he talked about her. Now she was grateful that Helene was interested enough to follow up on her case.

"She'll call you tomorrow, at a reasonable hour. At my home." There was no opposing that tone of voice, or the warmth in his eyes. Jennifer nodded and finished her sandwich.

"We've had a lucky break, that's all," Chief Whittacker said a week later, when he came by the White Elephant for the meal Jennifer had promised him. Drew had been back for two days and had outdone himself in celebration of his trip.

"How do you mean?" Jennifer asked as she watched the wine-steward decant the twelve-year-old Cabernet Sauvignon.

"Well, there was that guy with the burns over at Lake Berryesa who blabbed to the doctor, and that was the start of it." Chief Whittacker did not appreciate the food he was being served, preferring simpler fare, but he knew that gratitude was rare in the world, so he ate without complaint. "We got a call about it and sent one of our investigators over there with a couple of spare sheriff's deputies. The guy gave 'em a long song-and-dance about camping, and then admitted that he had been paid to start the fire here. He's got a record—most of it petty—and he was out of a job, so he agreed to set the fires. There were two of them, by the way. He got paid a thousand bucks for the thing, which isn't all that much, considering the risk. He made a point of telling the cops that he was scared and mad, so he wanted the guy who hired him to get caught more than he wanted to give the cops a bad time. He's agreed to testify, and that's something. He wants to use that to plea-bargain, and it looks pretty good for him on that." Chief Whittacker had some more of the capon—which didn't taste any different from chicken as far as he could tell—and went on. "Bright's been red in the face ever since I told him about this. Seems that the guy has been up to a lot of things around here. He paid some local kids to set fire to your cottage in the summer, and probably paid to have your fish killed. Bright didn't do much of a follow-up on that cottage-burning. If he had, we might not have had to wait so long to catch Hatfield."

"It *was* Hatfield?" Ross asked, speaking for the first time since they had sat down at the table in the bow window.

"Yep. What your bartender told us checked out. Hatfield wanted to borrow some more money so that he could start his next project, but the banks turned him down for lack of collateral. He found out that if he had enough land, they'd give him the money he needed, and so he tried to get some. This place not only has a fair chunk of real estate, it has this resort hotel. If he could have picked this up . . . well, he wouldn't have any trouble financing the purchase, and that would give him the funds to get his shopping center under way, and then he could work on the condominiums he'd been planning. He's in pretty deep on both those deals. From what I can find out, there's three or four million tied up now, and it might be more. Hatfield doesn't always deal on the up-and-up." Whittacker had a taste of the wine and wagged his head in approval. It wasn't much different than any other wine he had tasted, but he knew that something was expected, so he made a show of liking the stuff and said to Jennifer, "That's very good."

"Thank you," Jennifer responded, then waited for him to go on. "You said that there was difficulty with the financing. I don't see how setting fires here would make any difference in his financing."

"He was counting on you to throw in the towel and sell him this land for a song," Whittacker told her. "That way, he'd have all the collateral he needed, and a place to develop when he had the other things under way. Scaring you off was the first step, and you didn't scare all that easy."

Ross's hands tightened on his napkin, but he was able to keep a pleasant expression on his features. "By scare her off, you mean he intended to set fires and do anything else necessary to make her willing to move out. Is that right?"

"That's about it," Chief Whittacker agreed. "He heard about the kind of things the power company had been doing, and thought that it was his style. So he added a few maneuvers of his own and set to work. That's where he got the idea that it was possible to buy the kind of help he needed." He did not know if he ought to tell Jennifer or Ross that the man they had arrested had indicated there had been other plans in the works, plans that would have been more cruel and destructive than anything that had been done so far. He decided to keep silent about such matters, and he contented himself with saying that he had decided that Hatfield was a desperate man and capable of a great deal of harm.

"Why did he think I'd sell the White Elephant?" Jennifer asked, puzzled by that aspect of the matter.

"Why? Because he'd get you when you were down on your luck and scared. He assumed that you'd knuckle under when you ran out of money." Whittacker gave Ross a quick, penetrating look, as if encouraging him to change the subject.

Apparently, Ross didn't get the message. "You mean he was trying to force Jennifer to nickel-and-dime herself right out of business? That doesn't make much sense."

There was no way to answer this comment without going into the other things that had been discovered, and Chief Whittacker had no intention of doing that. "Well, men who are that far out on a limb, you know . . ." He turned his attention to the capon.

"Was he paying bribes to the Board of Supervisors?" Jennifer asked over dessert, in a last attempt to find out why she had been the target for the man's malice.

"Yeah, it looks like it. One of the supervisors at least was getting money from him to block improvements and up-gradings. It would lower the commercial value of the property in the short run, and it was Hatfield's intention to buy up a fair amount of acreage. That was after he dealt with the power company and found out that they were trying to keep several places from making improvements so that they would be off the desirable lists. It's crazy, but that's the way it was."

Jennifer thanked Chief Whittacker before she excused herself and Ross, leaving the older man to enjoy his baba au rhum over ice cream in solitary splendor.

It was raining, steadily, lightly, with little wind. The hills were turning from winter olive-drab to spring green, and there was the scent of earth and growing things in the air, the first promise that the earth would renew itself yet again.

Ross put his arm around Jennifer's shoulder and together they walked around the hotel toward the burned north wing. "What are you going to do about repairs, do you know yet?"

"I still haven't heard from the insurance company," Jennifer said unhappily. "There isn't enough in the trust fund to take care of the repairs, so I don't know where I stand."

"How about letting me repair it? California's a community property state, so I'll have half-interest in this hotel. I might as well look after my investment." He spoke flippantly, but his china-green eyes were hopeful.

"But . . ." Jennifer frowned. "It's apt to be very expensive."

"I'm not worried. In case you were unaware of it, love, I am a very wealthy man. You are marrying a fortune." There was no boasting in this, but the simple statement of fact. Benedetto Wineries and the related businesses were successful and well-established. "You've never bothered to ask, but I might as well tell you that you'll be completely comfortable with me, whether or not the White Elephant turns a profit."

"But I *want* it to turn a profit," Jennifer said, scandalized at the suggestion that she would think otherwise.

"That's fine with me. So what about the wing?" Both of them were getting soaked, but neither seemed to care.

"Sure," she said when she had considered it. "Then we can have our honeymoon in the Champagne Suite and . . ."

"Oh, no," Ross interrupted her. "Nope. You and I will have our honeymoon while the repairs are being made, and we can come back to a hotel ready to go back into full swing. I don't want you leaping up in the middle of the night because there's been a malfunction of the freight elevator or someone's lost the shipment of asparagus. I want you away from here all to myself, where the only grapes we have to deal with are already in bottles and the only hotel staff is employed by someone else." He bent over and kissed her brow.

Jennifer sighed. "I've scheduled work to begin next week," she said uncertainly.

"Good. It takes three days to get a marriage license. Figure another two to plan the thing. How does next Wednesday suit you?" He looked up at the charred beams and blackened wood of the north wing. "How long do you think they'll need to repair that? Two months, maybe?"

"Ross, you can't plan to be gone that long." Jennifer could not keep from laughing, but she maintained a severe demeanor.

"Probably not, but I can dream, can't I? Three weeks is more realistic. But Jennifer, I wish I didn't have to be realistic where you're concerned." He caught her up in his arms and covered her face with kisses.

Her voice was breathless when she was able to stop him. "You can't mean to be married next Wednesday."

"No, I'd like it to be tomorrow, but the law requires three days. You need a day to shop and phone your friends. So Wednesday is the earliest possible day." His mouth was eager on hers, and she made no pretense of resistance.

"Ross," she whispered to him when she could, "I won't give up the White Elephant."

"Nobody asked you to," he answered, his voice deep and husky with awakening passion.

"And I won't turn it over to someone else to run."

"Of course not," he said.

"And I expect you to take an active interest in the place," she went on, giddy with excitement.

"I always protect my investments. Ian will probably insist on advertising the hotel in every major travel magazine in the USA." He didn't want to talk business anymore, but Jennifer had one last item to bring up.

"And I expect to stay over here whenever there are evening functions," she said, waiting for his response.

"Over my dead body," he chuckled as his arms tightened around her. They stood locked close together, oblivious to the burned hulk beside them, and the myriad, gentle kisses of the soft winter rain.